Brian Wilson Aldiss was born in Norfolk in 1925. During the Second World War he served in the British Army in the Far East. He began his professional career as a bookseller in Oxford and then went on to become Literary Editor of the *Oxford Mail*. For many years Brian Aldiss was a film reviewer and a poet. Two outspoken and bestselling novels, *The Hand-Reared Boy* (1970) and *A Soldier Erect* (1971), brought his name to the attention of the general book-buying public, but in the science fiction world his reputation as an imaginative and innovative writer had long been established. *Non-Stop*, his first science fiction novel, was published in 1958 and among his many other books in this genre are *Hothouse* (1962), *The Dark Light Years* (1964), *Greybeard* (1964) and *Report on Probability A* (1968). Also in 1968, Aldiss was voted the United Kingdom's most popular SF writer by the British Science Fiction Association.

Brian Aldiss has also edited a number of anthologies, a picture-book on fantasy illustration (*Science Fiction Art*, 1975) and has written a history of science fiction, *Billion Year Spree* (1973). His most recent novels, published to critical acclaim, are a compelling Gothic odyssey, *Frankenstein Unbound* (1973), a space opera, *The Eighty-Minute Hour* (1974), and *The Malacia Tapestry* (1976).

Outstanding critical acclaim for *The Malacia Tapestry*:

'Just the kind of tour de force we might expect from the author of *The Hand-Reared Boy*'
The Scotsman

'Great fun in rich colours and textures, but there is a thought, erudition and a superb narrative prose to go with the action'
Tribune

'It is as full of variegated, burgeoning life as a Breughel, or a Giles cartoon'
Oxford Times

'Brian Aldiss has written his most imaginative novel yet'
British Book News

Also by Brian W. Aldiss

Fiction

The Bright Fount Diaries
The Primal Urge
The Male Response

The Hand-Reared Boy
A Soldier Erect
Brothers of the Head

Science Fiction

Non-Stop
Hothouse
The Dark Light Years
Greybeard
Earthworks

An Age
Barefoot in the Head
The Eighty-Minute Hour:
    A Space Opera
Enemies of the System

Fantasy

Report on Probability A

Frankenstein Unbound

Stories

Space, Time and Nathaniel
Canopy of Time
Airs of Earth
The Best Science Fiction
    Stories of Brian Aldiss

The Saliva Tree
Intangibles Inc., and Other
    Stories
The Moment of Eclipse
Last Orders

Non-Fiction

Cities and Stones
The Shape of Further Things
Billion Year Spree

Hell's Cartographers
    (with Harry Harrison)
Science Fiction Art
    (Editor)

Anthologies and Series (as Editor)

Best Fantasy Stories
Introducing Science Fiction
The Penguin Science Fiction
    Omnibus
Space Opera

Space Odysseys
Evil Earth
Galactic Empires 1 & 2
Periless Planets

with Harry Harrison

Nebula Award Stories 2
Farewell Fantastic Venus!
The Year's Best Science Fiction
    (annually from 1968)
The Astounding-Analog Reader
    No. 1 & No. 2

Decade 1940s
Decade 1950s
Decade 1960s
The SF Master Series

Brian W. Aldiss

The Malacia
Tapestry

TRIAD PANTHER

Published in 1978 by Triad/Panther Books
Frogmore, St Albans, Herts AL2 2NF
Reprinted 1979

ISBN 0 586 04497 3

Triad Paperbacks Ltd is an imprint of
Chatto, Bodley Head & Jonathan Cape Ltd and
Granada Publishing Ltd

First published in Great Britain by
Jonathan Cape Ltd 1976
Copyright © Southmoor Serendipity 1976

Made and printed in Great Britain by
Richard Clay (The Chaucer Press) Ltd
Bungay, Suffolk
Set in Linotype Plantin

For Margaret

time under prisms
dawn and pollen clouds afloat
presaging changes

you are the glimpsed light
in my smokey existence
frail but enduring

oTiepolo

You sing of the old gods easily
  In the days when you are young,
When love and trust seem not at odds;
But I know there are gods behind the gods,
  Gods that are best unsung.

K. G. St Chentero
(XVI Mil.)

Illustrations

The illustrations to the text are reproduced by kind permission of the British Library Board and the Victoria and Albert Museum (Crown Copyright Victoria and Albert Museum).

Contents

Book One

Mountebanks in an Urban Landscape

Smoke was drifting through my high window, obscuring the light.

Something was added to the usual aromas of Stary Most. Among the flavours of fresh-cut timber, spices, cooking, gutters, and the incense from the corner wizard, Throat Dark, floated the smell of wood-smoke. Perhaps the sawdust-seller had set fire to his load again.

Going to my casement, I looked down into the street, which was more crowded than usual for this hour of day. The gong-fermors and their carts had disappeared, but the Street of the Wood Carvers was jostling with early traffic, including among its habitual denizens a number of porters, beggars, and general hangers-on; they were doing their best either to impede or to further the progress of six burly orientals, all wearing turbans, all accompanied by lizard-boys bearing canopies over them – the latter intended as much to provide distinction as shade, since the summer sun had little force as yet.

The smoke was rising from the sweepings of an ash-merchant, busily burning the street's rubbish. One good noseful of it and I withdrew my head.

The orientals had probably disembarked from a trireme newly arrived. From my attic, between roofs, its furled sails could be glimpsed alongside Satsuma, only a couple of alleys distant.

I pulled on my blue ankle-boots, made from genuine marsh-bags skin; the black pair was in pawn and likely to remain so for a while. Then I went to greet the day.

As I went down the creaking stair, I met my friend de Lambant climbing up to meet me, his head lowered as if compulsively counting the steps. We greeted each other.

'Have you eaten, Perian?'

'Why, I've been up for hours doing nothing else,' I said, as we made our way down. 'A veritable banquet at Truna's, with pigeon pie merely one of the attractions.'

'Have you eaten, Perian?'

'Today not, if you refuse to believe in pigeon pie. And you?'

3

'I found a muffin lying idle on a baker's tray as I made my way here.'

'There's a ship in. Shall we have a look at it on our way to Kemperer's?'

'If you think it holds any advantage. My horoscope isn't profitable today. There's women in it, but not just yet apparently. Saturn is proving difficult, while all the entrails are against me.'

'I'm too hard-up even to get my amulet blessed by Throat Dark.'

'It's marvellous not to be troubled by money.'

We strolled along in good humour. His doublet, I thought, was not a shade of green to be greatly excited about; it made him look too much the player. Yet Guy de Lambant was a handsome fellow enough. He had a dark, quick eye and eyebrows as sharp and witty as his tongue could be. He was sturdily built, and walked with quite a swagger when he remembered to do so. As an actor he was effective, it had to be admitted, although he lacked my dedication. His character was all one could wish for in a friend: amusing, idle, vain and dissolute, ready for any mischief. The two of us were always cheerful when together, as many ladies of Malacia would vouch.

'Kemperer might give us a breakfast snack, even if there's no work.'

'That depends on his temper,' de Lambant said. 'And *that* depends on La Singla and how she has been behaving herself.'

To which I made no answer. There was some slight jealousy between us concerning Kemperer's wife. Pozzi Kemperer was the great impresario, one of the best in Malacia. Both de Lambant and I had been in his company for the better part of two years; our present lack of employment was nothing new.

On the quayside, a swarm of men were in action, mostly working bare-chested and barefoot, heaving on ropes, tugging winches, hauling boxes. The trireme was being unloaded. Various onlookers were delighted to inform us that the vessel had come up the River Toi from Six Lagoons, trading from the West. The optimists thought it might carry statuary, the pessimists that it might bring plague.

As we arrived, customs officials in tricorne-hats were marching off the vessel. They would have been searching for forbidden goods, in particular any new thing which might upset the

4

mellow flow of existence in Malacia; although I could only approve their mission, they were a poor, mothy collection, despite their hats and uniforms, one man limping, one half-blind, and a third, judging by appearances, lame, blind and drunk into the bargain.

Guy and I had watched such scenes since we were children. Boats arriving from the East were a better spectacle than those from the West, since they often carried exotic animals and black female slaves. As I was turning away, not unprompted by the rumbling of my stomach, I noted a strange old figure hopping up and down on the deck of the trireme.

His body was cut into pieces by the yards, but in a moment he turned and came down the gang-plank, carrying a box under one arm. He was stooped and white of hair, while something about his dress suggested to me that he was a foreigner – though he was not one of the mariners; indeed, I believed I had seen him about Malacia before. He wore a tattered fur jacket, despite the heat of the day. What took me was the mixture of delight and caution on his whiskery countenance; I tried setting my face in the same expression. He made off smartly into Stary Most and was lost to sight. The city brimmed with crazy characters.

Several carriages were drawn up along the Satsuma. As de Lambant and I made off we were hailed from one of them. The carriage door opened, and there was my sister Katarina, smiling a sweet smile of welcome.

We embraced each other warmly. Her carriage was one of the shabbiest there, the Mantegan arms peeling on the coachwork. She had married into a ruined family; yet she herself was as neat as ever, her long, dark hair pinned severely back, the contours of her face soft.

'You're both looking very idle,' she said.

'That's part nature, part artifice,' said de Lambant. 'Our brains are quite active – or mine is. I can't speak for your poor brother.'

'My stomach's active. What brings you here, Katarina?'

She smiled in a sad fashion and gazed down at the cobblestones.

'Idleness also, you might say. I came to see the captain of the vessel to find out if there was word from Volpato, but he has no letters for me.'

Volpato was her husband – more often absent than present and, when present, generally withdrawn. Both de Lambant and I made consoling noises.

'There will be another ship soon,' I said.

'My soothsayer misled me. So I'm going to the cathedral to pray. Will you join me?'

'Our Maker this morning is Kemperer, sweet sister,' I said. 'And he will make or break us. Go and act as our Minerva. I'll come and visit you at the castle soon.'

I said it lightly meaning to reassure her.

She returned me a concerned look. 'Don't forget, then. I went to see Father last evening and played chess with him.'

'I wonder he had time for chess, burrowing among his old tomes! *A Disquistion on the Convergences* – or is it *Congruities* or *Divergencies*? – for I never seem to remember – *Between the High Religion and the Natural Religion and Mithraism and the Bishop's Nostrils!*'

'Don't make fun of your father, Perian,' Katarina said gently, as she climbed back into her carriage. 'His work is quite important.'

I spread my hands eloquently, tilting my head to one side to show pity and resignation.

'I love the old boy, I know his work is important. I'm just tired of being lectured by him.'

As de Lambant and I walked along the quay in the direction of the Bucintoro, he said, 'Your sister in her dove-grey dress – really quite fetching in a sober way ... I must visit her in her lonely castle one of these fine evenings, though you are disinclined to do so. Her husband similarly, it appears.'

'Keep your filthy thoughts off my sister.' We talked instead about de Lambant's sister, Smarana, whose wedding day, determined by a useful conjunction of constellations, was little more than five weeks away. The thought of three days of family celebration cheered us, not least because the two families involved, the de Lambants and the Orinis, had engaged Kemperer's company to play on the second day. We should have work then, at least.

'We'll perform such a comedy as all will remember ever after. I'm even prepared to fall down the stairs again for the sake of an extra laugh.'

He dug me in the ribs. 'Pray that we eat before that date, or

I can see us treading the boards in the Shadow World. Here's the market – let's run different ways!'

The fruit market stood at the end of the Stary Most district. At this time of morning it was crammed with customers and buzzing with argument, gossip, and wasps the size of thumbs. De Lambant and I slipped among the stalls at a trot, bouncing off customers, swerving round posts, to arrive together at the other end laughing, with a good muster of peaches and apricots between us.

'A day's work in itself,' de Lambant said, as we munched. 'Why bother to go to Kemperer's? He has nothing for us. Let's make for Truna's and drink. Portinari will probably be there.'

'Oh, let's go and see the old boy anyway, show him we're alive and thin for want of parts.'

He struck me in the chest. 'I don't want for parts. Speak for yourself.'

'I certainly wouldn't want to speak for what is doubtless unspeakable. How the women put up with those disgusting parts of yours is beyond credit.'

At the corner of a certain scrivener's stair stood an ancient magician called All-People. All-People stood at the scrivener's stair whenever the omens were propitious, and had done so since the days when I was taken to market on piggy-back. His face was as caprine as that of the billy goat tethered to the post beside him, his eyes as yellow, his chin as hairy. On his iron altar a dried snake burned, the elements sprinkled on it giving off that typical whiff of the Natural Religion which my priest, Mandaro, referred to contemptuously as 'the stench of Malacia'.

Standing in the shade of the scrivener's porch consulting All-People was a stooped man in a fur jacket. Something in his stance, or the emphatic way he clutched a box under his arm, caught my attention. He looked as if he was about to make off faster than his legs could carry him. Always watching for gestures to copy, I recognized him immediately as the man who had come smartly off the trireme.

Several people stood about waiting to consult All-People. As we were passing them, the magician threw something into the hot ash of his altar, so that it momentarily burnt bright yellow. My attention caught by the flame, I was trapped also

7

by All-People's amber gaze. He raised an arm and beckoned me with a finger, red and twisted as an entrail.

I nudged de Lambant. 'He wants you.'

He nudged me harder. 'It's you, young hero. Forward for your fate!'

As I stepped towards the altar, its pungent perfumes caught me in the throat, so that I coughed and scarcely heard All-People's single declaration to me: 'If you stand still enough, you can act effectively.'

'Thanks, sire,' I said, and turned after de Lambant, who was already hurrying on. I had not a denario to give, though advice carries a high value in Malacia.

'Guy, what do you think that means, if anything, "Stand still, act effectively"? Typical warning against change, I suppose. How I do hate both religions.'

He bit deeply into his peach, letting it slobber luxuriously down his chin, and said in an affected scholarly voice, 'Highly typical of the misoneism of our age, my dear de Chirolo – one of the perils of living in a gerontocracy, to my mind ... No, you turnip, you know well what the old goat's on about. He's a better critic of the drama than you suspect, and hopes by his advice to cure you of your habit of prancing about the stage stealing the limelight.'

We were falling into a scuffle when my sleeve was clutched. I turned, ready for pickpockets, and there stood the old man with the fur jacket and the box. He was panting, his mouth open, so that I had a view of his broken teeth and chops; yet his general expression was alert and helped by blue eyes, which is a colour rarely met with in Malacia.

'Forgive me, gentlemen, for the intrusion. You are young Perian de Chirolo, I believe?'

He spoke with an accent of some sort. I admitted my identity and presumed that he had possibly derived some enjoyment from my performances.

'I'm not, young sir, a giant one for performances, although it occurs I have myself written a play, which—'

'In that case, sir, whatever your name is, I can be of no help. I'm a player, not an impresario, so—'

'Excuse me, I was not about to ask for favours but to offer one.' He pulled the jacket about him with dignity, cuddling his box for greater comfort. 'My name, young sir, is called Otto

8

Bengtsohn. I am not from Malacia but from Tolkhorm at the north, from which particular adversities what afflict the poor and make their lives a curse have drove me since some years. My belief is that only the poor will help the poor. Accordingly, I wish for to offer you work, if you are free.'

'Work? What kind of work?'

His expression became very severe; he was suddenly a different man. He regarded me as if he believed himself to have made a mistake.

'*Your* kind of work, of course. Playing.' His lips came together as if stitched. 'If you are free, I offer you work with my zahnoscope.'

Looking down on him, I formulated the resolve, not for the first time, never to become old.

'Have you work also for my good friend here, Guy de Lambant, almost as famous, almost as young, almost as poor, almost as skilful as I, old Bengtsohn from Tolkhorm?'

And de Lambant asked, 'Do the poor help only one poor or two poor?'

To him the old man said, 'I can afford only one poor for my modest design. All-People, as well as my personal astrologer, indicated that the one should be Master Perian de Chirolo, according to the presentiments.'

I asked what on earth his zahnoscope was. Was it a theatre?

'I have no theatre, Master.' His voice became confidential. Picking at one of my buttons for security, he edged his way between de Lambant and me. 'I do not wish talking in the street. I have enemies and the State has eyes. Come at my miserable place and see for yourself what thing I am offering. It is something more than of the moment passing, that I will say. I stay not far from here, on the other side of St Marco's, into a court off Exhibition Street, at the Sign of the Dark Eye. Come and see, conform to the forecasts.'

A gilded berlin, lumbering too close, gave me the chance to move away from him without forfeiting my button.

'Go back to your dark eye and your dark court, my venerable friend. We have other business, nothing to do with you or the stars.'

He stood there with his box gripped firmly under his arm, his mouth stitched again, his face blank. No disappointment or anger. Just a disconcerting look as if he had me summed in a

9

neat ledger kept in his head. He was indifferent to the people who jostled past him, going this way and that.

'You ought to see what he has to offer. Never miss a chance for advancement, de Chirolo,' said de Lambant, as we went on our way. 'He's bedraggled enough to be a wealthy miser. Perhaps he came away from Tolkhorm with the city treasure.'

I imitated the old man's Northern accent. ' "I have enemies and the State has eyes . . ." He's probably a Progressive or something equally shady. I'm a fair judge of character, Guy. Take it from me that that old eccentric has nothing to offer except a certain scarcity value.'

'You could be right.'

'I've never heard you concede that before.'

He spat a peach-stone into the gutter. 'I'm a pretty fair judge of character too, and my judgment is that Pozzi Kemperer will offer us nothing but the point of his buckskin boots if we manifest our faces at his house this morning. I'll keep to my original intention and go to Truna's. Portinari should be there, if his father spares him. And Caylus, if the bulls have spared him. I grow increasingly friendly with Caylus, bless me. Come with me.'

'You agreed to come to Kemperer's.'

He pulled an impudent face. 'Now I *dis*agree. I know you only want to see Kemperer's little wife. She favours you more than me, being a myopic little hussy. We'll see each other at Truna's this evening probably.'

'What has Caylus to offer so suddenly?' Caylus Nortolini was a lordly young man with numerous sword-wounds and maidenheads to his credit; his scornful airs were not to everyone's taste.

Assuming a cringing air, holding out one paw like a beggar, de Lambant said, 'Caylus is always in funds and generous with them. He likes to impress, and I'm very impressionable . . .' The paw turned to a claw and the voice altered. 'My impression is that his sister, Bedalar, is extremely beautiful and generous. I met her with Caylus at the Arena, where the appearance of the lady inflamed my heart and much else besides.'

Then he was off, assuming what was intended for a lecherous gait.

He cut through the cloisters of the Visitors' Palace while I made for the Fragrant Quarter, where our worthy impresario lived. Here, throughout the palmier centuries of Byzantium, spice ships had sailed in to the end of the Vamonal Canal and off-loaded their aromatic goods into tall warehouses. The trade was less brisk nowadays, and several warehouses had been converted into dwelling-houses. The street was quiet. Two flighted people swooped overhead playing flutes.

A faint aroma of cardamom and cloves lingered in the air like memory as I presented myself at Pozzi Kemperer's court-yard gate. There was always some difficulty about gaining entrance. I was admitted past snarling dogs, broken carriages, and bits of statuary. In a cage in almost permanent shadow sat Albert, a melancholy ape-sloth brought long ago from the New World. Albert had once been a favoured household pet but was sentenced to this shady exile – so the players said – on the day that, surprising Pozzi naked in the arms of a Junoesque prima donna, he had sunk his teeth into his master's buttocks in irrepressible expression of animal envy. Now he ate with the dogs. The titbits of the table were gone for ever. Kemperer was not a forgiving man. Nor were his buttocks quick to heal.

My timing was faultless. Coffee still steamed on the breakfast table. The chairs had been pushed back and Kemperer and his wife were through the curtains on the far side of the room, taking a snatch of rehearsal. For a moment I stood in the gloom, while their figures were outlined sharply by sun shining through tall windows at the other end of the apartment – a light that in its clarity matched La Singla's beautiful voice.

Neither saw me, so preoccupied were they. She was in another world, his eyes were on her. As I moved towards them I gathered from the table thin slices of cheese and smoked ham where they lay curled on patterned plates, cradling them into a still-warm bread roll garnered from its nest in a wicker basket. I tucked this snack inside my shirt for safety.

La Singla began to expand her voice. She looked every inch a queen, she was a queen, as Kemperer conducted with prompt book in hand. He was a thin man, often gawky in his move-ments, yet in rapport with his wife so graceful and involved that it would be difficult to determine which inspired the other.

Now her regal mouth cried of damnation. She was dressed still in deshabillé, with flimsy slippers on her feet and her golden hair trailing about her neck, knotted carelessly with a white ribbon. Good and ample though her figure was, it held something of the stockiness of the generations of Malacian peasants from which she had sprung (at least according to one account of her origins). Yet it also radiated majesty as she ranted to a dying lover on a battlefield long ago.

' "Oh, I will be revenged for your lost life, Padraic, never fear! Far worse than enemies, friends it was who brought your downfall. This is not war but treachery, and I will root it out – for am I not come of a great line of warriors, of generals, admirals, high-mettled princes? My remotest forebears lived in the old stone towns of Sasqui-Halaa, and from them rode out to vanquish those half-human armies of Shain and Thraist, a million years ago—" '

'No, my thrush. "A *million* years ago ..." '

'That's what I said. "A *million years* ago, from out—" '

'No, no, my dear, confound it, listen: "a *mill-i-on* years ago ...", or else you break the rhythm.' He offered her some yellow teeth which achieved at one glint both wolfishness and supplication.

' "A *million* years ago, from out the tepid prehistoric jungles swarming. So shall the armies of my hate—" '

She noticed me by the curtain and became La Singla again. The transformation was sudden. Her face broadened as she smiled in sheer good nature. Maria, La Singla, was about my age. She had good teeth, good eyes, and a good brow; but it was her good nature I most loved. Kemperer, furious at the interruption, snarled at me.

'How dare you sneak into a gentleman's house, you puppy, without being announced? Why is my privacy always invaded by rogues, relations, and renegade mummers? I've but to call one of my men—'

'Darling Pozzi-wozzy,' remonstrated La Singla.

'Hold your tongue, you minx, or you'll get a cudgelling too!' Such abrupt turns of mood caused us to fear him and ape him behind his back.

'How could I not be drawn in at the sound of that divine tragedy of Padraic and Heda?' I asked, assuming the role of diplomat.

'There's no work for you today, as you well know. You flounce in here—'

'I don't flounce. You mistake me for Gersaint.'

12

'You sneak in here—'

'Maestro, allow me to hear more of the Padraic tragedy. I never weary of it.'

'I weary of you. My little thrush Maria is to give a recitation before the joust at the Festival of the Buglewing, that's all. I merely coax her, coax, as fox coaxes fowl, to smooth the ragged edges of her diction.'

'I'd never dare to make an appearance without your coaxing, my good spouse,' piped the fox's wife, coming so near the fox that she could peep over his dandruffy shoulder at me.

Mollified, he tickled her chin.

'Well, well, well, I must powder my wig and get down to the jousting field to see that our box is properly constructed. Do it yourself or it'll never get done ... Attention to detail, the mark of a man of genius ... True artist never spurns the practical ... Reality the common clay of fantasy ... "A *million* years ago, from the tepid prehistoric jungles swarming ..." A bold line, if not mouthed to death.'

As he chattered in a way I knew well, Kemperer was whisking about the room with La Singla and a manservant in pursuit, preparing to venture out. I took the opportunity to pull my provisions from their hiding-place and have a bite.

When he had his wig in place and the servant was helping him struggle into his coat, Kemperer glanced suspiciously at me and said, 'You understand what I say, de Chirolo? You shall play Albrizzi at the de Lambant-Orini marriage ceremonies, but, while Byzantium is in such a bad way, engagements are few and far between, so it's no good your hanging about my doors hoping for favours.'

'Then I'll stay and coax La Singla in her part as Heda,' I said, taking up his prompt book where it lay open on a sofa.

He flew into a tiny rage, snatching the book from me. 'You'll coax her in none of her parts. Show her impeccable respect and that's enough. You young nincompoops, think yourselves bucks, trying to spoil the peace of mind of my dear wife! You'll come with me. I'm not leaving you loose in my house.'

Drawing myself up, I said, 'I shall be happy to accompany you, Maestro, since to be seen walking with you can but increase my reputation – provided I understand correctly that you cast no slur on my unsullied regard for La Singla, the great actress of our day.'

Mollified, but still given to the odd mutter, he seized my arm before I could take elaborate farewells of his wife, and led me across the courtyard – glancing neither right nor left, not even to take in Albert, who set up a forlorn chattering at the sight of his master.

When the gate closed behind us, and we stood in the street, I asked him which way he was going.

'Which way are *you* going, de Chirolo?' He always had a suspicious nature.

I pointed hopefully north towards St Braggart's, thinking that he would have to turn south to get to the Arena, where the jousts were held in time of festival.

'I go the other way,' he said, 'and so must deprive myself of your company. What a loss, dear, dear! Remember now – nothing happening until Albrizzi, unless I have you sent for. Don't hang about. And don't imagine I like an idle season any more than you do, but in the summer the grand families go away to the country. Besides, there's a confounded Ottoman army marching about somewhere near Malacia, and that's always bad for theatre. *Anything's* bad for the theatre.'

'I look forward to our next meeting,' I said.

We bowed to each other.

He stood where he was, feet planted firm on the ground, arms folded, watching me walk to the corner and turn it. As I turned, I glanced back to see him still observing me. He waved a mocking farewell, dismissing me with every bone in his skeletal wrist. Once round the corner, I hid behind the pillars of the first doorway I came to, and there I waited, peeping out to see what happened. As I expected, Kemperer appeared round the corner himself. Looking foxy, he scanned the street. When he had made sure it was clear, he muttered to himself and disappeared again.

Giving him time to get well away, I retraced my steps, to present myself once more at his gate. I rang the bell, and was soon admitted into the sunny presence of La Singla.

Since I left her a few minutes before, she had thrown a robe of blue silk over her flowing night garments, but could not be said to be any more dressed than before. Her hair still lay on her shoulders, golden. Ribbons fluttered about her person as she moved.

She sat at the table, daintily holding a coffee cup to her lips.

'Remember, I must show you my impeccable respect,' I told her.

'And much else besides, I expect,' she murmured, glancing down at the white cloth on the table, thus giving me the advantage of her long lashes.

Bounding forward, I knelt beside her chair and kissed her hand. She bade me rise. I crushed her to me, until I felt the cushioning of her generous breasts doing its worst against a mixture of ham, cheese and bread.

'Dammit, my tunic!' I cried, and snatched the mess from its hiding-place.

She burst into the prettiest and best-rehearsed laughter you ever heard.

'You must remove your shirt, dear Perry. Come into my boudoir.'

As we trotted into her fragrant room, I said, laughing in high humour, 'You see how famished a poor actor can be that he sneaks food from the table of the woman he admires most in the world! You discover ham in my tunic – what may not be concealed in my breeches ...?'

'Whatever is there, it shall not take me by surprise.' Matching action to words, she put her hands behind her back and started to tug at the laces which held her dress.

In another moment, the two of us were one, rolling in delight, naked upon her unmade couch. Her kisses were hot and thirsty, her body gloriously solid, while she had, as the orientals say, a little moon-shaped fishpool, into which I launched my barque until the waters grew altogether too delightfully stormy for sense. After which, rapturously shipwrecked, we lay about in the bed and I gazed upon her soft and verdant shores.

'... "the torrid prehistoric jungles swarming ..."' I misquoted.

She kissed me juicily until my barque ran up its sail again. As I reached for her, she wagged a finger at me in slow admonition.

'The secret of any happiness is never to have sufficient. Neither the rich nor the revolutionaries recognize that profound truth. We have enjoyed enough for both of us, provided the future promises more. My husband can't be trusted to stay away for any length of time. He is insanely suspicious, poor dear, and takes me for a perfect harlot.'

'So you are perfect,' I declared, reaching for the scrumptious mounds of her breasts, but she was away and slipping into her shift.

'Perfect, maybe, but not a harlot. In truth, Perian – though you'd never comprehend this, for you are a creature of your lusts – I am far more affectionate than promiscuous.'

'You're lovely as you are.'

When we were dressed, she gave me a glass of melon juice and a delicious cut of cold quitain. As I was eating, I asked her, 'Do you know someone called Bengtsohn? – an old man with blue eyes, a foreigner, who says he has enemies everywhere. He comes from Tolkhorm, and has written a play.'

She was getting restless. 'Pozzi has used him to paint scenery. He was a good worker but I think he's a Progressive.'

'He offered me work with his zahnoscope. What's a zahnoscope?'

'How you do talk! Pray eat up and permit me to let you out of the side door, or Pozzi will come back and fall into such a frenzy of jealousy that we shall have no peace for weeks on end.'

'I wanted to talk to you ...'

'I know what you wanted.' I picked up my drumstick and made off obediently. There was no fault in this fine girl, and I was anxious to please her. Her main interests were bed and the play which, I supposed, was the reason she was always so sweet-tempered. It seemed no more than just that Kemperer should pay tax in kind on such a precious possession.

In the street, my elation began to wear almost as thin as my clothes. I had nothing, and was at a loss. My father was no support; I could not sponge off my sister. I could go to a tavern but, without a single denario to my name, could hardly expect my friends to welcome me with open purse. Most of them were in similar straits, except Caylus.

For want of better amusement I followed various citizens, studying their walks and expressions, until I reached St Marco's Square. The usual morning market-stalls were set up, with the usual crowds of country men and women in attendance, their horses and mules tethered along the shaded side of Mount Street.

About the edges of the great square, clustering particularly under the colonnade of the Old Customs House, were booths

16

for less serious-minded personages and children, where one might view two-headed calves, dioramas of ancient time, animated human skeletons, oriental jugglers, live ancestral animals, snake-charmers from Baghdad, fortune-tellers, marionettes, gaudy magic-lantern shows, and performing shaggy-tusks no bigger than dogs.

How I had hung about those enchanted booths with my sister Katarina as a child. The magic-lantern shows, with their panoramas of shipwreck, noble life and majestic scenery, had been our especial delight. Here they still were, unchanged.

What was unusual about this day was that it was the first Thursday of the month, the day set since time immemorial for the Malacian Supreme Council to meet. Not that the affairs of those greypates concerned me, but older people took an interest. I heard them murmuring about the Council as I walked among them.

Bishop Gondale IX blessed the Council in public, but the deliberations of the Council were held in secret. The results of those deliberations were never announced; one could only deduce what had happened by observing who disappeared into the capacious dungeons of Fetter Place, there to be strangled by capable hands, or who was beheaded in the public gaze between the great bronze statues of Desport's slobbergobs in St Marco, by the cathedral, or who reappeared as piecemeal chunks about various quarters of the city, or who was found with his mouth nibbled away by pike in the whirlpools of the River Toi. If the Council saw fit to despatch them, then they were troublemakers, and I for one was glad to know that everything worked so well for the contentment of our citizens. The immemorial duty of the Supreme Council was to protect Malacia from change.

I found a hair in my mouth. Removing it from between my teeth, I saw it was golden and curly. Ah, the Supreme Council could drown all its citizens in the canal, if so be I might get near enough to La Singla to pasture on that same little mountain.

The traders at their stalls were discreet, knowing well the system of informers which helped maintain the peace of Malacia, but I gathered from a couple of them that the Council might be discussing Hoytola's hydrogenous balloon, to decide whether or not it could be approved. Nobody understood the principle of this novel machine, but some magical property in that phrase, 'Hoytola's hydrogenous balloon', had given it a certain lifting power in the taverns at least. The reality had yet to be seen; it was the Council which had ultimate say on such possibilities.

One of the traders, a tallowy man with blue jowls and the same innocent look as the dead geese in his basket, said, 'I reckon the balloon should be allowed to fly. Then we'll be the equal of the flighted men, won't we?'

'All that's interesting happens on the ground,' I said. 'Heroes, husbands, heretics – leave the air to sun and spirits.'

I knew nothing of Hoytola. The sending up of small hot-air balloons had been a child's pursuit in Malacia for ages. I remembered my father ponderously explaining how a whole fleet of hot-air balloons tied together might transport an army to surprise the Ottoman enemy. He had had a pamphlet printed concerning it. Then a captain in the Militia had called on him and dissuaded him from taking further interest in current affairs.

It was enough that there were flighted people not greatly different from us, except for wings. They talked our language, married, died of the plague, much as we. Three of them soared above the square as I strolled through it, to settle by their cote at the top of St Marco's campanile, traditional eyrie of these traditional sentinels of Malacia.

I was hailed several times by stall-keepers as I went by. They had been groundlings when I performed here or there, and still cherished my performances. What a thousand shames that I should have arrived at the highest pitch of my art to find no chance to exhibit it to those who would appreciate it.

As I scowled to myself, a figure close by said, 'Why, Master de Chirolo, you look to bear the cares of the old wooden world on your shoulders!'

Sidling up to me was the gaunt figure of Piebald Pete, so known because of the tufts of black hair which survived on his head among the white. He was the fantoccini man; the large, striped frame stood behind him, its red-plush curtains drawn together.

'I haven't a care in the world, Pete. I was merely acting out a drama in my head, as your marionettes act it out in their box. How's the world treating you?'

I should not have asked him. He spread wide his hands in des-

18

pair and raised his black-and-white eyebrows in accusation to heaven. 'You see what I'm reduced to – playing in the streets to urchins, *me*, me who once was invited into the greatest houses of the state. My dancing figures were always in demand – and my little Turk who walked the tightrope and chopped off a princess's head. The ladies liked that. And all carved out of rosewood with eyes and mouths that moved. The best fantoccini figures in the land.'

'I remember your Turk. What's changed?'

'Fashion. Taste. That's a change the Supreme Council can't prevent, any more than they can prevent night turning into day. Only a year back I had a man to carry the frame, and a good man he was. Now I must hump the frame everywhere myself.'

'Times have been easier.'

'We used to do great business with evening soirées. That's all but gone now. I've had the honour of appearing at the Renardo Palace more than once, before the young duke, and before foreign emissaries in the Blue Hall of the Palace of the Bishops Elect – very proper, and no seduction scenes there, though they applauded the Execution and insisted on an encore. I've been paid in ten or more currencies. But the demand's dropped away now, truly, and I shall go somewhere else where the fantoccini art is still appreciated.'

'Byzantium?'

'No, Byzantium's a dust-heap now, they say, the streets are paved with the bones of old fantoccini men – and of course the Ottoman at the gate, as ever. I'll go to Tuscady, or far Igara where they say there's gold and style and enthusiasm. Why not come with me? It could be the ideal place for out-of-work actors.'

'All too busy, Pete. I've only just come from Kemperer's – you know how he makes you sweat – and now I must hurry to see Master Bengtsohn, who beseeches something from me.'

Piebald Pete dropped one of his eyebrows by several centimetres, lowered his voice by about the same amount, and said, 'If I was you, Master Perian, I'd stay clear of Otto Bengtsohn, who's a troublemaker, as you may well know.'

I could not help laughing at his expression. 'I swear I am innocent!'

'None of us is innocent if someone thinks us guilty. Poor

men should be grateful for what they get from the rich, and not go abusing them or plotting their destruction.'

'You're saying that Bengtsohn—'

'I'm not saying anything, am I?' Looking round, he raised his voice again as if he hoped the whole bubbling market would hear it. 'What I'm saying is that we owe a lot to the rich of the state, us poor ones. They could do without us, but we could hardly do without them, could we?'

The subject plainly made Pete and everyone nearby uncomfortable; I moved on. Perhaps I would visit Bengtsohn.

As I walked down a side-alley towards Exhibition Street, I recalled that Piebald Pete had performed in my father's house on one occasion, long ago. My mother had been alive then, and my sister Katarina and I little children.

The show had enchanted us. Afterwards, when the magic frame was folded and gone, my father had said, 'There you have observed the Traditional in operation. Your delight was because the fantoccini man did not deviate from comedic forms laid down many generations earlier. In the same way, the happiness of all who live in our little utopian state of Malacia depends on preserving the laws which the founders laid down long, long ago.'

I slipped through a muddy by-lane, where a few market-stalls straggled on, becoming poorer as they led away from the central magnet of St Marco, towards the sign of the Dark Eye. At the entrance to the court stood the Leather-Teeth Tavern, its doors choked with red-faced countrymen, drinking with a variety of noise, enjoyment, and facial expression. Fringing the drinkers were whores, wives, donkeys, and children, who were being serenaded by a man with a hurdy-gurdy. His mistress went round the crowd with a cap, sporting on a lead a red-scaled chick-snake which waltzed on its hind legs like a dancing dog.

Beside the tavern, stalls of fresh herrings had been set up. I tucked my coat-tails under my armpits to get by. Beyond, a couple of bumpkins were urinating and vomiting turn and turn about against a wall. The overhanging storeys of the buildings and their sweeping eaves made the court dark but, as I got towards the back of it, I came on Otto Bengtsohn washing his hands at a pump, still clad in his mangy fur jacket.

His arms were pale, hairless, corded with veins; ugly but useful things. He splashed his face, then wiped his hands on his jacket as he turned to examine me. Beyond him, lolling in a doorway, were two young fellows who also gave me an inspection.

'So you altered your mind to come after all! What a cheek you gave, also! Well, you're only once young.'

'I happened to be passing this way.'

He nodded. 'All-People was right.' He stood contemplating me, rubbing his hands up and down his jacket until I grew uncomfortable.

'What's this zahnoscope of yours?'

'Business later, my young friend. First, I must have something for to eat, if you don't mind. I'm on the way to the Leather-Teeth, and perhaps you'll join me for some bite.'

'It would be a pleasure.' There was merit in the old man after all. 'I am feeling peckish.'

'Even the poor have to eat. Those of us what are going to change the world must keep ourselves fed up ... We aren't supposed to think about change in Malacia, are we? Still, we'll see ...' He grinned at me in a sly way. He pointed up at the leather-toothed ancestral depicted on the tavern sign, its segmented wings outspread. 'You have to have jaws like that creature to eat here. Do you mind visiting our slum, de Chirolo?'

We pushed into the tavern.

There, Bengtsohn was known and respected. In short order, a grimy girl placed soup, bread and meat balls with chillies and a pitcher of ale before us, and we set to, ignoring the jostling bodies at our elbows. I ate heartily.

Sighing after a while, and resigning myself to his pouring me more ale, I said, 'It's good to feel the stomach full at midday for a change.' There I checked myself. 'Why should I say "for a change"? Everyone today seems to have been talking about change – it must be because the Council's meeting.'

'Well, talk, yes, but talk's nothing – foam off from the sea. Malacia never changes, hasn't done for thousands of years, never will. Even the conversations about change don't change.'

'Aren't you introducing change with your – zahnoscope?'

He dropped his fork, waved his hands, shssh'd me, leant forward, shook his head all at the same time, so that I found my face peppered with half-chomped meat ball. 'Remember that whereas talking about change is proper and fit, anyone who

21

makes bold as to implement change IN THIS DEAR OLD STABLE CITY OF OURS' (said loud for effect as he groped with his fork) 'is liable to finish up in the Toi with his throat cut to shreds ...'

Silence while we ate. Then he said, in a tone of voice suggesting that the statement might be of particular interest to any eaves droppers in the vicinity, 'I work in the field of art, that's all what interests me. Happily, art is a central interest of this dear city, like religion. Art's safe. Not a better place in the world for to pursue art, though heaven knows it don't pay all that much, even here. But of course I don't complain of that. How I'll go through next winter with a greedy wife ... Come on, mop down your platter with the crust and let's get back at the workshop. Work's the thing, if it earns fair pay.'

Back through the court we went, and into the workshop, which was a dim and dirty place, cluttered with all manner of objects. Bengtsohn waved his hand in a vaguely descriptive way which took in a number of apprentices at benches, some munching hunks of bread.

'You have a busy place.'

'I don't have it. It isn't of mine. I can be to booted out from here tomorrow, with boss's boots. This is an extensive works, biggest in Malacia. These workshops and glass factories back on the great exhibition gallery. You've been in that, I suppose – the gallery of the Hoytola family, Andrus Hoytola.'

'Hoytola's hydrogenous balloon.'

'That's another matter. I've been here during some years now, ever since I have come from Tolkhorm with my family. There are some worse masters than Hoytola, I'll grant you that. Here's Bonihatch – he's foreign to Malacia too, and a good man.' He made reference to one of the apprentices, who loitered up in shirt-sleeves.

Bonihatch was my age, dark, small and wiry, with untidy blonde whiskers. He nodded, looking suspiciously at my clothes without addressing me.

'A recruit?' he asked Bengtsohn.

'We'll see,' Bengtsohn replied.

After this enigmatic exchange, Bengtsohn, with Bonihatch in surly attendance, showed me some of his work. A small den off the main workshop was stacked with slides for magic lanterns, all categorized on shelves. He pulled slides down at random and I looked at them against a flickering oil lamp.

Many of the scenes were Bengtsohn's work. He was an artist of a rough but effective order. Some of the hand-painted transparencies, especially those depicting scenery, were attractive, the colour and perspective harsh but nevertheless effective. There was an arctic view, with a man in furs driving a sledge over ice; the sledge was pulled by a reindeer, and the whole scene was lit by a sky full of northern lights which reflected off a glacier. As I held it before the lamp, he saw something in my face and said, 'You like it? As a young man, I have gone beyond the Northern Mountains to the ice lands. That's what like it was. A different world.'

'It's good.'

'You know how we make these slide-paintings?'

I indicated the stacks of glass round about, and the long desk where assistants worked with brushes and a row of paint-pots. 'Apart from your genius, Master, there's no puzzle about the production.'

He shook his head. 'You think you see the process but you do not see the system behind the process. Take our topographical line, what is popular perennially. Travellers from far parts will make sketches of the fabulous places they have visited. They return home to Byzantium or Swedish Kiev or Tolkhorm or Tuscady or some other great centre, where their sketches are etched and sold, either as books or separately. Our factory then buys the books and artists are converting the pictures to slides. Only the slides live, because light itself puts the finishing touches to the painting, if you follow me.'

'I follow you. I too am proud to call myself an artist, though I work in movement rather than light.'

'Light is everything.'

He led me through a choked passage where great sheets of tin stood on either side, to another shop. There, amid stink and smoke, men in aprons were making the magic lanterns which formed part of the Hoytola enterprise. Some lanterns were cheap and flimsy, others masterpieces of manufacture, with high fluted chimneys and mahogany panels bound in brass.

Eventually, Bengtsohn led me back to the paint shop, where we watched a girl of no more than fifteen copy a view from an etching on to a glass.

'The view is being transferred to the slide,' announced Bengtsohn. 'Pretty, perhaps, but not *accurate*. How could we transfer the view to the glass with accuracy? Well, now, I have developed a perfectly effective way so to do.' He dropped his voice so that the girl – who never looked up from her work – should not catch his words. 'The new method employs the zahnoscope.'

Bonihatch spoke for the first time. 'It's revolutionary,' was all he said.

Gripping me by the muscle of my upper arm, Bengtsohn took me through into another room, poky and enclosed, where the window was framed by heavy curtains. A support rather like a music-stand stood at one end of the room with a lamp burning above it and a water globe next to it. In the centre of the room was something which resembled a cumbrous Turkish cannon. Constructed almost entirely of mahogany and bound in richly chased brass, its barrel comprised five square sections, each smaller than the next and tapering towards the muzzle. It was mounted on a solid base which terminated in four brass wheels.

'It's a cannon?' I asked.

'It could cause a breach in the walls of everyone's complacency – but no, it is my zahnoscope merely, so-called after a German monk what invented the design.'

He tapped the muzzle. 'There's a lens here, to trap rays from the light. That's the secret! A special large lens such as Malacia's glass workers do not produce. I received it from ship only this morning – it has just been fitted. You saw me with it when All-People summoned you.'

He tapped the breech. 'There's a mirror in here. That's the secret too! Now I shall show how it works.'

Taking a coloured topographical view from a shelf, he propped it on the music-stand, turned up the wick of the lamp, and adjusted the water globe between stand and lamp so that the beams of the lamp focused brightly on the view. Then he drew the curtains across the window. The room was lit only by the oil lamp. Bengtsohn motioned me to a chair by the breech.

It was as if I sat at a desk. The flat top of the desk was glass. And there, perfectly reproduced on the glass, was the topographical view, bright in all its original colour!

'It's beautiful, Master! Here you can have a perfect magic-lantern show.'

'This is a tool, not a toy. We place the glass of our slides over the viewer and can adjust the barrel – what adjusts the *focal length* of the lenses – until we have the exact size of picture necessary for the slide, no matter what the dimensions from the original etching. We can then simply paint over the image with accuracy.'

I clapped my hands. 'You are more than an artist! – You are an actor! Like me, you take the poor shadowy thing of real life and magnify it and add brighter colours to delight your audience ... But what do you want me here for? I can't handle a paint-brush.'

He stood pulling his lower lip and squinting at me.

'People come in two kinds. Either they're too clever or too foolish to be trusted. I can't reason out which group you're in.'

'I'm to be trusted. Everyone trusts Perian de Chirolo – ask Kemperer, for whom you once worked, who knows me minutely. His wife will also say a good word for me.'

He brushed my speech aside, stood gazing into the distance in very much a pose I have used for Blind Kedgoree.

'Well, I need a young man not too ill set-up, there's no denying that ... The older you get, the more difficult things become ...'

At last he turned back to me. 'Very well, I shall take you in my confidence, young man; but I warn that what I tell you must not be repeated with nobody, not with your dearest friend, no, not even with your sweetest sweetheart. Come, we'll walk in the exhibition gallery while I will explain my invention and my intention ...'

He drew back the curtains, turned down the lamp, and led me back to the workshops. We climbed some steps, went through a door, and were in another world where disorder was forgotten. We had entered the elegantly appointed gallery itself, the walls of which were lined with thousands of glass slides, aligned on racks for easy viewing. The slides could be hired for varying amounts, depending upon quality and subject. There were long sets of twenty or thirty slides which told in pictures heroic stories of old, as well as vivid portrayals of brigandage or disaster, which were most popular. Well-dressed people were walking about and gazing at the pictures; Bengtsohn kept his voice down.

'Despite this place stinks of privilege, it preserves a part of the cultural thought of Malacia as well as Count Renardo's state museum. Andrus Hoytola exploits cheap labour, no use to deny that – a class enemy if there was one – yet he is not a merchant just but also an artist and a man of foresight. However, to my invention . . .'

There was a secretiveness about him which did not suit my open nature. He manoeuvred me into a corner, saying he would lecture me upon matters not generally understood.

'It has long been known through the learned alchemists that there are certain salts what have an empathy with or aversion against the light, so that some say they are fallen from the sun or the moon. I have developed here a process whereby a judicious mixture of silver iodine will secure on a slide of glass an image of whatever is placed before the zahnoscope. A second process involving oils of lavender and heated mercury fixes the image permanently on the glass. This is painting without hands, my dear de Chirolo . . .'

When he beamed at me, he looked years younger.

'Why tell me your secret?'

He shook his head. 'It's not mine but Nature's. All what wish can share it. You do not realize the oppressiveness of the state what we live in—'

'I love my native city.'

'I what am a foreigner should not criticize? Nevertheless, any such scientific processes what I describe are suppressed . . . Justice is denied – and beauty.'

He snatched from one of the exhibition racks a slide which he urged me to hold up to the light. It was a volcanic eruption. I stared through a volcano in full spate, with streams of lava furrowing its snow-clad slopes – to see one of the most beautiful faces I had ever come across, a face with a high-bridged nose, two dark-golden eyes, a mouth that was flashing a brilliant smile – though not in my direction – and a delicate head of cultivated unruly hair, jet-black and tied with a length of blue ribbon at the back.

Even as this face materialized through the volcanic eruption, it turned into profile and then went into eclipse, with only the tresses and ribbons at the back of the head available to my view. Even that was thrilling enough; but never had I seen a profile so adorable, or so originally designed, with the entire physiognomy depending from that patrician nose, without the nose being too large even by one delicious millimetre.

Lowering Mount Vesuvius slightly, I regarded the body to which this fabulous head was such an exquisite adjunct. Though I beheld it only from behind, I saw that the waist was slender, the hips generous, and the buttocks altogether matchless enough to put the snowy slopes of any volcano to shame. The whole enchanting figure was sheathed in a long, crisp dress of apricot-coloured silk which swept to the floor. My aesthetic senses, roused by the proportions of the face, were overtaken by my carnal ones and I resolved to approach this beauty at whatever cost.

All the while, Bengtsohn was talking in his cranky way, mistaking the subject of my absorption, '... this beautiful view was never touched by human hands ...'

'Glad I am to hear you say it.'

'The exciting effect of fire and snow in conjunction ...'

'Oh, yes, and that conjunction ...'

'Yet this is but an imitation of an imitation ...'

'No, that I can't believe! This is the real thing at last.'

'You flatter me, but the zahnoscope can be made to capture the real thing, to go straight to life rather than art ...'

I put the slide down. The vision was preparing to leave the gallery; I might never see her again and my happiness would never be complete.

'You must excuse me, Maestro – I do have more preference for life than for art, just as you do. You must manage your affairs and I mine—'

Seeing I was making to go, he grasped my arm.

'Listen, please, young man. I'm offering you work and money. All-People can't be mistaken. You have not work or money. I want to do a new thing with the zahnoscope. I want to mercurize – that's how I call it – I want to mercurize a whole story on slides, using real actors, not just paintings. It will be a dazzling new success, it will be revolutionary – and you can take prominently part in it. Now, come into the workshop and let me explain properly all.'

'I've just seen a friend – who's the fair creature at the far end of the gallery?'

He answered sharply. 'That's Armida Hoytola, daughter of the gallery-owner, a difficult, flighty girl. She's a parasite, a class enemy. Don't waste your time—'

'A thousand thanks for the meal, but I cannot work for you. All-People looked at the wrong constellation. There is other work more fitting ...'

I bowed to him and left. He drew himself up, folding his arms over his ancient coat, with the funniest expression on his face.

At the far end of the gallery, beyond the counter, was a doorway into a coffee lounge. My fair creature was making her way through it with a friend. No chaperons that I could see. The friend was about the same age as – Armida? – Armida! – and striking too in her own way, a plump girl with chestnut ringlets. On an ordinary day she would certainly have attracted one's attention; her only fault was to be caught with the divine Armida. They made a pretty pair as they moved into the lounge, although I had eyes for only one of them.

Pausing in the doorway, I wondered whether to appear tragic or cheerful; the poverty of my clothes decided me on the latter course.

The two of them were settling at a nearby table. As Armida sat back, our eyes met. Streams of animal magnetism poured across the room. On impulse, holding her gaze, I went forward, seized one of the empty chairs at her table, and said, 'Ladies' – but I addressed myself only to her – 'I see in your faces such human warmth that I venture uninvited to thrust my company upon you. I desperately need counsel and, since we are total strangers to each other, you can give me impartial advice at a time when my whole life is in crisis.'

There was hauteur in their manner directly I started speaking. As they looked at each other, I saw that the companion with the brown hair was quite a beauty, by no means as elegantly slender as Armida, but with a chubbiness that had its own undeniable attractions. Whatever passed between them I know not; I only know that when they looked back towards me, the ice had slightly melted.

'Perhaps your crisis will allow you time to drink chocolate with us,' Armida said in a voice freighted with light musics.

Gratefully, I sat down. 'Five minutes only ... Then urgent business must take me elsewhere. You were enjoying the exhibition?'

'It's tolerably familiar to us,' said Armida, waving a dismissive hand. 'What is your crisis, sir? You have us agog, as I expect you intend.'

'We all confront crises in our lives . . .' But that would not do. 'My father,' I said, thinking quickly, 'he's a stern man. He is forcing me to decide my future career. I have to tell him by the week's end whether I will enter the Army or the High Religion.'

'I'm sure your heart's pure enough for the Church,' said Armida, smiling with enough warmth to cook an egg. 'Is it not brave enough for the Army?'

'My dilemma is that I wish as a good son to please my father, but I want to become something more fulfilling than a monk or a grenadier.'

Two pretty heads went to one side as they gazed upon me. My head was turned completely.

'Why not,' said the brown-haired one, 'become a player? It's a terribly varied career which gives pleasure to many.'

My hopes rose within me, so much so that I reached forward and seized her hand where it lay on the table. 'How kind of you to suggest it!'

Armida said, 'Pooh, not a player! They're poor and the stories they play out are dull . . . It's the lowest form of animal life! There's no advancement in it.'

The effect of this speech from those lips was enough to cool my blood by several degrees, down almost to frost level. Matters were only saved by Armida's leaning forward and adding, confidingly, 'Bedalar's latest fancy is a player – he's handsome, grant you that – so she thinks nothing male is of any use unless it basks before the limelights every evening at seven.'

Bedalar put out a pretty tongue at her friend. 'You're only jealous!'

Armida showed her an even prettier tongue back. I could have watched such rivalry all evening, while thinking how cordially I would receive that nimble little tongue into my own cheek. So involved were my senses that only later did Bedalar's name register on me; I had heard it before that day.

Armida's air of imparting a confidence had soothed me, but there was a chill in the conversation, as the two girls gazed at each other and I gazed moodily at them.

Fortunately, chocolate arrived in a silver pot, and we occupied ourselves with drinking.

Setting down her cup, Bedalar announced that she must leave.

'We all know whom you're going to meet, so don't be coy,' said Armida. Turning to me as her friend left, she said, 'The new-found player. He's out of work, so they can enjoy a rendezvous at any old time that Bedalar's chaperon is out of sight. I have a friend of high connection – one must not say whom – who is involved with his duty today, and many other days as well.'

I thought this was more unkindness and said, 'Perhaps you wish me to leave ...'

'You may go or stay as you like. I didn't invite you to sit down.'

It was no good sulking before this little minx. 'I came voluntarily, yes; I now find myself unable to leave voluntarily. I am already under such a spell as it would take a dozen gentlemen of connection, drunk or sober' – I thought I'd strike there – 'to disperse.'

She half-pouted, half-laughed.

'How silly I shall look on the street with you running behind my carriage. And you even sillier, following rather like a carriage dog.'

'I make it a rule never to run behind carriages. Let's walk together instead. Come, we will walk in Trundles Park and see who laughs at us.'

I rose and offered my arm. She got up – and what a movement that was! La Singla could not have managed it better – and said with exquisite seriousness, 'And I'm supposed to pay for the chocolate consumed by all and sundry?'

'Is this not your father's establishment? Do you insult them by trying to offer them money?'

'You know who I am ... I don't frequent many strata of Malacian society, so I have no notion who you are.'

When I told her my name, I noted that it was unfamiliar to her, although in view of her poor opinion of players that was possibly as well.

I offered my arm again. She rested four gloved fingers upon its upper surface and said, 'You may escort me to my carriage.'

'We are going to walk in the park.'

'You are presumptuous if you believe I will do anything of the sort. I could not at all afford to be seen in the park with you.'

We stood looking at each other. Close to she was startling. Hers was a face which beauty made formidable; yet there was about her mouth a kind of wistfulness which seemed to contradict the hauteur.

'May I see you tomorrow, then, in whatever circumstances you prefer?'

She adjusted her hair and the ribbons in her hair, and put on a bonnet which an assistant brought. A smile grew about her lips.

'You'll be involved in battles or canticles tomorrow, won't you?'

'Swords and holy vows alike mean nothing to me where you're concerned. You are so beautiful, Miss Hoytola, I've never seen anyone like you.'

'You are certainly a forward young fellow – though I don't necessarily hold that against you. But I begin a special commission – not work of any kind, naturally – tomorrow, and so shall not be at liberty.'

We moved towards the door, which a lackey opened, bowing low and hiding a glint of envy in his eye. We emerged into the mid-day street, almost empty as siesta took over Malacia.

'What sort of commission, Miss Hoytola?'

A frown, barely rumpling the exquisite brow. 'That's no concern of yours. It happens to be something to please the whim of my parents, who fancy they cannot have enough portraits of me, doting things. So I am to pose a little for a mad foreigner in our employ, one Otto Bengtsohn. He's something of an artist in his fashion.'

Although I had lingered to the best of my ability, we were at her equipage. The carriage shone like a crown with sun and polish. A highly groomed mare waited between the shafts. The powdered driver was opening a door for Armida. She was lifting her apricot skirts, preparing to climb in and be whisked away.

'We must part here, sir. It was pleasant making your acquaintance.'

'We shall meet again, I feel sure.'

She smiled.

The door was closed, the driver mounted behind. The whip was cracked, she waved, they were off. Stand still to act effectively; it had no application here.

As I turned, the gallery was closing for siesta, the blinds were being drawn down. I walked slowly away.

Of course I could not be in love.

Strolling down the street I ran over our brief conversation in my mind. I was far too poor for her, for Armida Hoytola. Yet she had been interested. Her friend could be Bedalar, Caylus Nortolini's sister, whom de Lambant had mentioned. If Bedalar deigned to look at a player, then her friend might also find it fashionable. Unbidden, a picture came to my mind of my marrying Armida and walking secure in the sort of society I knew I would enjoy ...

The vision passed, and I was left with her words about the commission with Bengtsohn. There lay my opportunity!

At once I turned down the expansive Exhibition Road and into the narrow alleys behind, until I found myself again in the gloom of the Court of the Dark Eye.

A group of men, all dingily dressed, stood in the darkest recesses of the court; there were women among them, old and young. They turned guiltily as I entered. One of them came forward, carrying a stout stick; it was the apprentice I had met, Bonihatch.

'What do you want?'

'I need to speak to Bengtsohn.'

'We're busy. There's a meeting, can't you see? Shove off, as you did before.'

But Bengtsohn moved up behind him, saying mildly, 'It's siesta and we talk of pigeon racing, de Chirolo. What do you wish from me? You left me abruptly enough.'

I gave him a bow. 'My apologies for that discourtesy. I had a mission.'

'Thus it seemed.'

'I am interested in the work you offered me, if you would be kind enough to tell me what exactly you require.'

'Come back this evening. I have business now. I will then talk with you.'

I looked at Bonihatch, who stood ready with his stick.

'I may have become a monk by evening, but I'll see what I can manage.'

Love, what a power it is! Nothing but love could have induced me to enter that dreary court three times in one day – and what dedication I showed, for the lady had revealed herself to be uncertain-tempered, vain, and I know not what else besides. Also irresistible.

How wise one feels to be a fool of love!

'Even a fool can do this job,' Bengtsohn said. 'Is why All-People indicated an actor, I suppose.'

By night, moving behind smoky lanterns in intermittent shadow, Bengtsohn looked almost sinister, his sunken eyes sometimes hiding, sometimes glittering, in their sockets. His long fingers were talon-like as he wove his explanation.

'I told how I have discovered the method to mercurize real views through the zahnoscope, so that they have become implanted on glass slides. My ambition is to tell a story by such methods. People I need, actors. A simple story to begin. Big acorns from little oaks grow. I will mercurize the actors against real or painted settings. The product will be of an extraordinary originality and cause certain consequences. You shall be one from the four characters in the simple drama. The scenes of the drama will be emblazoned on glass far more faithfully than what artist could ever depict. This will be the real image, painted by light – light, that great natural force what is free for all, rich and poor alike.'

Keen to make him look a little less inspired, I said, 'It will only be like a stage play with the action stopped, and paralysis suddenly overtaking everyone.'

'You players are so ephemeral, your actions sketched in the air and then gone, the whole thing forgotten when the final curtain will come down. But when you are mercurized through the zahnoscope, why, then your actions become imperishable, your drama continuous. I will not mind wagering that the drama what you will enact for me will still be viewed by connoisseurs after you yourself will have grown old and died, young Perian!'

At that, I had to laugh. He was cutting an absurd figure, stroking an old japanned magic lantern with fluted chimney as he spoke, as if he expected a genie to emerge.

'And what is this great drama you wish me to perform? Are we to put Sophocles or Seneca on glass?'

He came closer. Then he took a turn away. Then he returned, and clutched my hands in his. Then he dropped my hands and raised his to the sky.

'Perian, my life is beset with difficulties and hedged by enemies. Let there be trust between us, as well as business also.'

'You told me when we met that you had enemies and the State had eyes.' The proposition was somehow more reasonable here in the stuffy darkness of his workshop than it had appeared in the sunlit street.

'We must each trust each. We are both in a same situation – namely we don't have no security in the world. I am old and have a wife for to support, you are young and free but, believe me, the gods – and society, more important – are against us both. That is a political situation. I have two passions, art and justice. As I grow more old, justice becomes more important- er. I hate to see the poor grinded down by the rich, hate it.'

'That's a natural law. I intend to be rich one day.'

He scratched his head and sighed. 'Then we will defer justice for a day later and instead talk about art. Is that more to your taste?'

'Tell me about your drama.'

He sighed again, staring about the untidy workshop, shaking his head. 'Young men care so little.'

'You have no business saying that. Why do the old always hold the young in contempt? I'm a fine actor, as you can discover if you enquire, and my art is my life. My life is my art. Tell me about this drama of yours, I ask you, if you want my help.'

'My dear young man ... Well, let's keep to art if you wish it! I have a love for all the arts, *all* the arts, including the drama, though I am always too much poor to pursue them. For the first mercurized production, I have written a contribution to drama, entitled *Prince Mendicula: or, The Joyous Tragedy of the Prince and Patricia and General Gerald and Jemima.*'

'A striking title. What is a Joyous Tragedy exactly?'

'Well, Doleful Comedy, if you will – minor details aren't too clear in my mind yet – clear, but not too clear ... I have some troubles with *detail*. Indeed, for simplification on to glass, I plan a drama *without* detail ...'

'Am I to be Prince Mendicula?'

He beamed, showing his shortage of teeth. 'You, my dear boy, you have insufficient years for to be Prince Mendicula. You shall play the dashing General Gerald.' And he began to unravel the beauties of a plot which would enrich, if not indeed terminate, world drama. I paid what heed I could. As he talked with increasing rapidity, he took me to a lumber room and showed me some props for his drama. They were very poor, the clothes almost threadbare.

My interest in Bengtsohn's affairs was generated by the understanding that they would involve the divine Armida Hoytola. I began to see that there might also be profit for my career here; Bengtsohn was supported by a powerful patron, the Hoytola family, and, if the novelty of his mercurized melodrama were to catch popular fancy, it would be advantageous to have my name associated with it.

I broke in on the old man's account and said, 'Will you not let me play the Prince?'

He drummed the fingers of his left hand upon his stringy cheek. 'Gerald is more suitable for you. You might make a good general. You are not venerable enough for Mendicula.'

'But I can make up my face with beard and black teeth and a patch and what-you-will. Whom have you marked out for this princely part?'

He chewed his lip and said, 'You understand this is a – what's the word? – yes, unproved venture. We all take a chance from it. I cannot afford to pay for more than one real player, and that is yourself. Your looks and modest reputation will help. Whereas to play the Prince I rely on one of the boys in the workshop, the not ill-favoured man called Bonihatch.'

'Bonihatch? With the yellow whiskers? What acting experience has he? He's just an apprentice!'

'For a mercurized play, little acting is required. Bonihatch is a good man, what I depend on. I must have Bonihatch, that's my decision.'

'Well. The others? Princess Patricia?'

'For the Lady Jemima, with whom the prince is captivated, I will hire a seamstress who lives in this court, by name Letitia Zlatorog. She will be happy to work for a pittance. Her family has a sad history what exemplifies injustices. Her uncle is a friend of mine, a friend of poverty. A pretty girl, too, with quite an air about her, is little Letitia.'

'And what blazing bundle of talent and beauty is destined for the role of Princess Patricia?'

He gave me another mouth-numbing smile.

'Oh, I thought you had discovered that. The success of our

enterprise, alas, depends heavily on my employer. So we are exploited. To satisfy his whim – and not from other reasons – the role of the Princess Patricia will be played by Armida Hoytola. It is a consolation that she is not ugly.'

'Armida as Patricia ... Well, you know that my art is all to me. It comes as a surprise to learn that Armida, whom I scarcely know, is also to act in your drama. Even so, I will work with you for the sake of this marvellous new form of drama you have perfected.'

'Arrive here punctually at eight of the morning and that will suit me. There'll be time enough for speeches then. And let's keep secret the enterprise for a while. No boasting, if you can withstand it.'

It is a curious fact about old people that, like Bengtsohn, they do not necessarily soften if you speak them fair. It is almost as if they suspect you of being insincere. This trait manifests itself in my father. Whereas you can always get round friends of your own age.

But Bengtsohn was civil when I appeared next morning, cutting me a slice of solid bread-and-blood pudding for breakfast; he even paid me half a florin in advance for my work, from his own pocket. I helped him, his wife, and Bonihatch load up a cart with the things he needed, including the zahnoscope, a tent, several flats, and some costumes, before the others arrived. As we worked a true seigneur rolled up, the great Andrus Hoytola himself stepping down from his carriage.

Andrus Hoytola was a well-built, dignified man, lethargic of movement, with a large, calm face like a pale sea. He wore a flowered silk banyan over pantaloons that buckled at the knees. He had white silk stockings and his feet were thrust into slippers. His hair was done in a short stumpy queue tied with grey velvet ribbon. He looked slowly about him.

I gave him a bow. Bengtsohn made a salute and said, 'We are getting forward with our matters, sir.'

'One would expect so.' He helped himself to a pinch of snuff from a silver box and strolled across to regard the zahnoscope. I had hoped for an introduction; none was forthcoming. My consolation was the sight of his daughter Armida, who alighted from the other side of the carriage.

Her reserve was perhaps to be accounted for by the presence

of her father. She evinced no surprise and little interest that
I was engaged to act with her in the drama of *Prince Mendicula*;
her attention was rather on her dress. Like her father, she
was fashionably garbed, wearing a plain *decolleté* open robe
of ice blue with long, tight sleeves which ended in time to display her neat wrists. When she walked, her skirts revealed a
hint of ankle. A fragrance of patchouli hung about her. And
what a beauty she was! Features that tended towards the por-
cine in her father were genuinely inspiring in Armida, especially
when they lit as she said smilingly, 'I see that the walls
of neither monastery nor barracks have closed about you
yet.'

'A blessed reprieve.'

The cart was loaded and harnessed to a pair of mules, black
of visage, long of ear, and inclined to foam at the mouth. We
climbed on or walked behind, while the Hoytolas returned to
their carriage. Bonihatch explained that we were heading for
the Chabrizzi Palace beyond the Toi, where our play would be
enacted.

The Palace of the Chabrizzis was set in a striking position at
no great distance from Mantegan, where Katarina passed the
days of her married life. The Palace was built under a last
outcrop of the tawny Prilipit Mountains, to stare loftily across
the city.

Within its gates we rolled to a stop in a weed-grown courtyard. Two urchins played by an elaborate fountain. Windows
confronted us on all sides, straight-faced. To one side, cliffs
loomed above the rooftops.

Everything was unloaded and placed on the flagstones.
Armida climbed from her carriage. Her father merely sat back
in his seat and suddenly, at a whim, drove away without speaking further to anyone.

Bonihatch made a face at Bengtsohn.

'Looks as if the Council didn't make up their mind regarding
the hydrogenous balloon.'

'Or maybe the zahnoscope either,' said Bengtsohn grimly.

'I'd prefer you not to discuss my father's business,' Armida
said. 'Let's get on.'

Later, the mule-cart was driven off. While a primitive outdoor stage was being set up, Armida talked to a timid girl in
work clothes. I went over to speak with them and discovered

that this was Letitia Zlatorog, the little seamstress engaged to play Lady Jemima.

It would be difficult to imagine anyone less fit for the role, although she was pretty enough in an insipid way. She was pale, her hands were red, and she had no mannerisms. She appeared all too conscious of the honour of meeting a player from the great Kemperer's company. I took care to appear rather grand; nevertheless, when Armida's attention was elsewhere, I slipped an arm about her waist to set her at ease.

Even more strongly than before, I felt that I, as the one professional member of this ludicrous cast, was entitled to play the Prince, and so be married to Armida. I knew how the simulated passions of the stage often translated by sympathetic magic into genuine passions off stage; to think of the cocky apprentice Bonihatch embracing Armida was not to be borne.

Having failed to convince Bengtsohn on this point, I took Bonihatch himself aside, intimating as tactfully as I could that as mine was the name which would win audiences, mine should be the right to play the title role of Mendicula.

'Think of this as a co-operative enterprise,' he said, 'in which all work as one, not for profit or fame, but for the common good. Or is such an ideal too much for your imagination?'

'I see no disgrace in fame as a spur! You talk more like a Progressive than a player.'

He looked at me levelly. 'I am a Progressive. I don't wish to make an enemy of you, de Chirolo. Indeed, we'd all be glad to have your co-operation. But let's have none of your fancy airs and graces round here.'

'Take care how you speak to me. I imagine a good thrashing would impress you.'

'I said I didn't want to make an enemy of you—'

'Now now, young gentlemen,' said Bengtsohn, bustling up. 'No quarrels as we inscribe a new page in the massive volume from Malacia's history. Give me your hand to setting up this ruin.'

He had some flats representing a destroyed town. Bonihatch and other apprentices went to his aid. I tucked my arms under my cloak and made myself look tolerably moody, remarking to Armida, 'This is a melancholy old place. What has become of the Chabrizzis? Did they all kill themselves in a fit of spite, or have they gone to look for the Lost Tribes?'

38

'Poor Chabrizzis, they squandered several fortunes in the service of the Nemanijas and Constantinople. One branch of the family turned to Mithraism. Of the remainder, one of them – my great grandfather – married into the Hoytolas, though for a noble to marry a merchant's daughter was generally condemned. They both died of the plague within a twelvemonth, leaving a little son. So their history may be reckoned, as you say, a melancholy one. All the same, I love this old palace and played here often as a small girl.'

'That news makes it sound immediately more friendly.'

One part of the inner courtyard was bathed in sun. Here Bengtsohn's paraphernalia was set up. In rooms nearby we disguised ourselves in his scruffy costumes, except for Armida, who wisely insisted on retaining her own dress.

'Capital!' cried Bengtsohn, clapping his hands as each of us emerged into the sunlight.

He began to pose us, moving us about like chairs. Bonihatch, absurd in Prince Mendicula's tinsel crown, stood to one side, gesturing to the nearest wall and the flat of the sacked city. Feeling hardly less silly with cork sword and general's tricorne made of paper, I stood behind him, while Armida in a small tinsel crown was placed close beside me.

When he had us as he wanted, Bengtsohn aimed the zahnoscope at us, adjusting its barrel and flinging a velvet cover over the glass panel at the rear.

'Stand still, all of you!' he cried. 'Not a movement, not one movement, for five minutes, or all will be spoilt.'

Then he ran round to the front of his machine and removed a cover from the lens. We stood there until I grew tired.

'When do we begin to act?' I asked.

The old man swore and replaced the lens-cover, shaking his hands before his face in wrath.

'I tell you just to stand still without even a movement for five minutes, and you begin immediately to talk!' he cried. 'While the sun is bright, we must make so many pictures as we can, but each image takes five minutes for to form on the prepared slide. For the image to be crisp, you must be still – as quiet as rats. Don't you understand?'

'You never told me that item in your secret recipe,' I said angrily. Armida and the others were looking at me in disapproval. 'We shall be here all day, standing like statues for five minutes at a time. That's got nothing to do with acting, the secret of which lies in mobility.'

'You do not act, you stand like dead statues. Thus for several days. That is why you are having so well paid. We have fifty slides to make to contain the whole drama of the Prince. Now, prepare yourself again. This time neither a word nor a twitch, de Chirolo.'

I said, 'But you begin before we have learned or even read our parts. What is the story? What sort of a drama is this?'

'Don't be silly, dear,' Armida said. 'We do not speak. We supply only the images, in a series of tableaux. When the slide-drama is eventually shown to audiences, Otto will recite what is happening, to bring out the beauty of the tableaux. Can't you understand the principles of a mercurized play?'

Titters from Bonihatch and Letitia.

I froze, and again Bengtsohn went through his mysteries with the machine. There we all stood like waxworks, while he counted the time on a large hour-glass. It is no easy matter standing still for five minutes, particularly in the open air, where idleness alone induces a tendency to sneeze.

At the end of the first five minutes, I was already preparing to make my excuses and abandon this exercise, despite the proximity of Armida. But Bengtsohn seemed so pleased, scuttling his first slide away into a dark baize-lined box, that I had not the heart to upset him. All the same, I was happy that my friends de Lambant and Portinari could not see our antics.

'Famous, famous!' quoth Bengtsohn. 'Now we will perform an indoor scene, where the Prince leaves his lovely princess in General Gerald's care.'

As I made to move into the palace, the old man caught my arm.

'I should have explained to you as I have to the others, for to make our matters crystal-clear. Owing to the present limitations of the zahnoscope, what needs plenty of light to achieve its miracles, we have to mercurize even the indoor scenes outside.'

A sofa was drawn up, a curtain pulled behind us. 'Indoors' was parodied. This scene was more to my taste. Bonihatch made a noble gesture, arms spread wide, while I as Gerald bowed and clutched Armida's hand. Five minutes of that was easily borne, as I felt the little living thing sweat gently in my grasp.

In reminding me of all the other treasures of hers which might fall into my grasp, it was enough to make me stand rigid.

The five minutes up, Bengtsohn clapped his hands and fiddled with another slide.

'The next scene will also be indoors, what is situated at a country tavern. We shall see Prince Mendicula meeting with Jemima. Letitia, if you will step forward please, and look a little haughty. Not at him but rather above or *through* him, yes, through him, to indicate that you are of good birth ... I hope the zahnoscope does not become too hot, or the salts will fail.'

All was ready. Bonihatch and Letitia assumed rigid poses, becoming their idea of the noble prince and the Lady Jemima. With a few tawdry props behind them and the sun shining overhead, history would be made. Bengtsohn looked raptly at the velvet cover over his slide, as if the secret of the universe lay there. Time stood still. Armida and I, waiting on one side and watching the tableau, found ourselves also transfixed. The minutes took longer to pass than when we ourselves stood before the zahnoscope.

Eventually the sand lay in the lower half of Bengtsohn's hour-glass, and he called for the pose to be broken. We all came alive again.

Patting his dark box grimly as he tucked the third slide into it, he said, 'These I will mercurize in the workshop this evening. If they develop well, then we again proceed tomorrow. If luck is not on our back, then we re-enact the same scenes. So, to do another while the light is good. Meanwhile, to keep occupied your minds while we work, I shall recite to you the story of our drama, just as I shall recite before audiences ... provided anything so novel is allowed for to be shown to Malacian audiences ...'

The morning passed in little-five minute loaves of time as Otto Bengtsohn unfolded his preposterous tale of Prince Mendicula, while his characters confronted the sunshine with tinsel crowns and cork swords.

Prince Mendicula: or, The Joyous Tragedy of the Prince and Patricia, as Intertwined with the Fates of His General Gerald and the Lady Jemima (announced Bengtsohn, blowing a fake fanfare through pursed lips in order to convey an impression of grandeur commensurate with the occasion). A co-operative production by the Bengtsohn Players, mercurized by Otto Bengtsohn of Tolkhorm, under the grand patronage of Andrus Hoytola, to whom our humble efforts are unworthily dedicated with all gratitude and undue prostrations, and so on and so on, to the limits of the capacity …

The great and handsome Prince Mendicula, what you here see in the full glory of his youth, power, and privilege, has just conquered the city of Gorica, what lies in ruins for all to see and sorrow over in the background.

Mendicula has been aided by his general, the noble, powerful, and privileged Gerald, who is almost as personable as his prince. As you see.

General Gerald has become the close friend and adviser of his prince, what has encouraged Gerald in every way and made him a favourite in preference over many other estimable courtiers. Here you see the two of them inspecting the ruined city. The conquered city, that is to say; conquest is a princely habit. With them Mendicula's wife is, the beautiful Princess Patricia. You observe with what delight she views the vanquished of Gorica, whose hearts go out to her.

Here you see her telling her husband, the Prince, how enchanted she is by his prowess in war. He clutches her hands. So consumed by love of her is he that the prince bestows the city – without consulting the feelings of the inhabitants, of course – upon her for a gift, what makes the first three years of their happy life married.

The general expresses content with this arrangement. Here he announces that from henceforth he will abstain from warlike action – as generals enjoy to do after battles – thinking what they may get their heads shot off next time. He declares that he will hang up his arms to marry a charming lady of Gorica what he has just met. They will settle in Gorica – or Patriciagrad, as the unfortunate city will shortly be ceremoniously rechristened, once the corpses are cleared from off the streets.

Amid general enthusiasm, Prince Mendicula leaves his wife Patricia in Gerald's care and goes for a tour of his new territory – you see it in the background – to meet alike nobility and peasants, but chiefly nobility, of course. At a certain country

42

inn by a lake, Mendicula decides to rest for the night. We see him entering – observe tankards arranged by the window – and here he meets the enchanting mystery woman, Lady Jemima, what claims to be the daughter from the landlord, though the prince cannot believe this. In fact, he believes that anyone so pleasing cannot spring from such low society. As you may notice, the little Lady Jemima is as dark of hair and complexion as the Princess Patricia is fair. Well, we get the ladies' hair colour correct, we hope.

She spurns his advances, gracefully but inflammably with what looks like a slap of the face. The prince orders local wine and becomes hopelessly inebriated in the course of the evening. Fortunately he is anonymous, so that nobody notices nothing remarkable in his insobriety.

This is early dawn, as you can see, shining bright. Prince Mendicula, whose head feels so thick as that of any low serf, wakes to repent of his folly and have a conscience attack as he recalls his neglected wife Patricia back in Gorica. We witness his agony – the clenched fists, the look to heaven – as he becomes afraid that Patricia might have been unfaithful to him, yielding during the night to the advances of the General Gerald. He rides furiously back to Gorica, a prey to remorse and jealousy.

Arriving early at the Gorica Palace, his spurs clattering over the marble corridors – well, matting, as you can see – the prince finds both Patricia, his beloved, and his general are slumbering vituously in their different compartments in different parts of the building. How sweet she looks asleep, those lovely pink cheeks – she is always well fed, our princess! Mendicula awakens her with a kiss and pours out his love.

At this point in Bengtsohn's story, I thought to myself, Well, it is all very splendid for Bonihatch that he plays the prince! He enjoys most of the excitement and both of the women! This is what I get for acting with a pack of Progressives. Now I understand why the State suppresses them. Sooner or later, Bonihatch is going to linger a whole petrified five minutes – which in the circumstances rates considerably longer than eternity – with his lips upon Armida's lips, as the slumbering Patricia. He'll be more than mercurized, the low churl! I should have played the prince!

And what impression will I make on my audience as the stupid General Gerald, lying guilelessly abed, eyes closed and moustaches rolled in a white handkerchief. This fustian does me no favour.

Even as Prince Mendicula embraces Patricia and pours out his affectionate declarations (continued Bengtsohn, moving us about for the next tableau as if we were dummies) she can smell that he has been drinking away the night. Instinctively, the sensitive girl a trifle draws away from him.

Examine, if you will, the psychology in his countenance! For how does he respond to this slight withdrawal of hers? Why, a tiny seedling from doubt blooms in his mind. Perhaps the withdrawal implies that she after all did lie with the general. Much pleasure of the intimate sort may be had in two hours without spending all night about it, particularly if you are of the passionate disposition what he knows Patricia to be, because she lives off the best meats and fruits, unlike the poor.

Ah, this next picture! 'Trust vanquishing Doubt!' No more soon does dark mistrust spring in the prince's mind up than he suppresses it with scorn. He believes it to be a reflection of his own guiltiness and unworthy totally of him – also of her what he loves and honours. (Here we shall move the zahnoscope so that we see only Mendicula's noble face in the appropriate slide ...)

Abolishing all base doubts like apples from an orange tree, Prince Mendicula from this moment holds Patricia and his soldier-hero more highly than ever in his self-esteem. More, he encourages them to be friends, to share confidences, and to enjoy generally each other's company without fear of restraint on his account. Witness the three of them, arms about each, people of noble birth behaving nobly, eh?

Contentedly, Mendicula steps back and engages himself in administering the realm, allowing General Gerald to escort Patricia to balls, to the opera, and other idle occasions. Far from showing to her husband gratitude for his trust, Patricia is slightly cool towards him, as he notes with sorrow, hand on brow. Again, far from blaming her, he still blames himself for having chased Jemima.

So he is forced into a position where thoughts of Jemima

pursue him. Although she repelled his advances, he knows she liked his company. We'll have some music here. One day, he rides back through the forest to see her. To the prince's delight, Jemima still resides at the inn. He discovers her polishing one of the tankards. They fervently talk for hours. He presses her for a kiss, which she warmly bestows. Although she permits no liberties further, her company is so animated that Prince Mendicula sits all night up talking to her. As you observe, the Lady Jemima also plays the lute and sings well.

Night passes too soon. When dawn filters across the lake, which of course is outside, the Prince once more remembers the realities of his life. Embracing Jemima and thanking her courteously, he tears away himself from her to saddle his horse and ride furiously back to Gorica. Or possibly he will have to run furiously, since Bonihatch and I cannot find no horse what will stand motionless in a galloping position for five minutes in a time.

Back to the city, he bursts into Patricia's room. He has dismounted first, by the way, if he has a horse. If not, then not. Her bed lies unemployed. The prince then runs to General Gerald's apartments. The general's bed is empty also. In anguish, he rushes through the entire building, to come upon them both in the garden of roses.

Sharply, he dismisses his general, what goes out looking so angry as you can observe, and questions sharply his wife about her actions. She becomes as cold as a snowman, explaining how it happened merely that both she and Gerald rose early and met in the garden by accident. This is after all a day of festival, when many people rise early. Here we see some of them, having risen. She says he has no right to question her.

Trouble-sore and saddle-sore, the prince sinks to a bench. She says nothing. He faintly asks her if she and Gerald kiss like lovers. At this, she becomes more angry, evades his question, and demands to know where he has been all night; word has reached her ear – you see how beautiful it is – that what he has somewhere a woman outside the city. The prince replies that no woman means anything in his life except her to what he is wedded to. Patricia scorns this remark, saying that she has observed how he is continually interested in women. We see them stand backs to backs in a picture of frustration and good breeding.

This difficult position is resolved by the return of General Gerald in his military hat. He has put on a good face and a new tunic to announce that on the morrow he will bring his betrothed to Gorica to meet the prince. Patricia walks away with her bunch of roses. Or perhaps just one rose, to save expense.

Once again, Mendicula summons up all his upbringing and dismisses suspicions to the wall. He shakes warmly hands in the eternal emblem of friendship with Gerald, proclaiming what a good friend he is and commending Gerald for his attention to Patricia at a period when their marriage goes through a difficult tunnel. He would do anything to make Patricia happy. Gerald says he would also. They agree.

In a little formal speech, so typical of a military man, Gerald thanks the prince for his indulgence, praising his enlightened attitude and jealousy lack. As we see, they on the shoulder slap each other and Prince Mendicula then admits, man to man, that there is another lady for what he feels attraction, and begs Gerald to continue undeterred his kindnesses to Patricia.

That is rather a long conversation. Perhaps we shall enliven it for the performance with views of sportive nymphs and shepherdesses, or something refined.

So now good relations appear to be restored between the prince and his lovely wife. They amiably ride together on a hunt for ancestral animals in a nobleman's park. The bag will provide food for the nuptials forthcoming of General Gerald. Towards the end of this golden afternoon, when they are by a lake – that flat will serve twice – a messenger arrives from Gorica with a message for Mendicula. As we observe, he tears it opened. It comes from the Lady Jemima, announcing her arrival in the city and craving a mere hour from his time in order to him bid farewell.

In this scene, note the high colour of the participants. Mendicula tells Patricia that urgent matters of state require attention, so he must leave for a while. She is suspicious. She becomes angry and accuses him of assignations. He in turn angers. He begs her to practise toleration, just as he tolerates her fondness with General Gerald. She replies that that relationship has to do nothing with their marriage. He cannot understand this remark, but keeps quiet wisely and rides from the park in high dudgeon. Or perhaps he *strides* from the park. Or we possibly may procure a stuffed horse what will hold still.

Prince Mendicula goes to the palace to change into state regalia and slip into a crown. There he is met by a deputation from the defeated city councillors. They have honest faces but gloomy ones. They try to prevail upon him to issue an immediate proclamation curtailing activities of his soldiery. These soldieries have been laying waste the countryside and, more importantly, looting, pillaging and raping, and – where rape is inapplicable – seducing in the streets of Gorica in a thoroughly traditional military manner. Mendicula admits the tradition is obnoxious and agrees that a proclamation shall be made through his general. This is the messenger being despatched to Gerald, asking him to curb the natural inclination of soldiers, possibly by shooting a few. We shall not show actual scenes of rapine. These things are best left in the imagination.

This important meeting takes a while, so that the prince is some hours late by the time he arrives to the noble house at what Jemima is lodging.

Here a servant admits Mendicula to Jemima's room, and the prince is seen standing aghast at the sight of her alone and weeping in a lace handkerchief. In response to his agonized enquiries, she says there is one what she loves; it was for his sake that she rebuffed the prince's advances, and not because she intended disrespect to the royal line. Now she has learned that this lover of hers has been faithless, consorting with another woman even as he prepared their marriage ceremony, a splendid affair to last three days and no spared expense, which we shall not have fortunately to show. Jemima's tears fall like the outlet of a fountain. She wets her lute.

The prince is so much moved that he falls on one knee. Or maybe two. Putting his arms about her, he endeavours to comfort. One thing leads to another thing; in particularly, condolence leads to prurience. They go together to the bed, lying in rapture in one another's arms as if it was habitual to their mutual comfort and amusement. The slides here will be optional, depending on the company. We will not try Letitia's modesty too far, since she is not a real actress. It's a challenge.

More pictures. Dawn, if not exhaustion, brings a change from mood. Jemima awakes from a nap and sits up with a look of total repentance for expression. Here comes her wedding day and she faces it a soiled woman – although she freely admits that she is less soiled than if she would have laid with a commoner. Nevertheless, royalty is no substitute for chastity. She declares that she must kill herself.

Assuming the royal breeches, Mendicula attempts to dissuade. He also has a high code of honour but she is exceeding.

Petulantly, she cries that he has placed her into a situation where she would prefer to die. She is no landlord's daughter. She also has some good blood. The poor must live with all their disgraces about them; she must not. He has her utterly undone, while the man what is to be her husband has spent the night undoubtedly with his paramour.

Mendicula is struck by the coincidence that this will be her wedding day and that also of his close friend, the General. He pronounces Gerald's name. Jemima gives a cry and reveals that he is none otherwise than her betrothed.

Together they cling. She weeps afresh. The prince feels heavily that he has dishonoured her and his friendship, but he can clear at least half of her double disgrace.

Ringingly, he proclaims that he can deaden the unworthy suspicions what she entertains for General Gerald. For Gerald's supposed paramour is none otherwise than his spotless own wife, Princess Patricia. He explains how he has heard from Patricia's own fair mouth that nothing untoward passes between her and Gerald. They have his secure trust, and only since a previous few hours she assured that her fondness for Gerald will not harm their marriage in every way.

Jemima is so cheered that she dresses behind a screen. But the happy night what she and the prince have just passed cannot be blotted so easily out. She bursts forth, crying dramatically with a slight tearing of the hair how she feels herself doubly guilty of misconduct if Gerald is the honourable man what Mendicula just described. Mendicula protests that she is too scrupulous. He and she will forthwith part, despite the fondness what they hold towards each other; he will never more seek out her. Anything between them is now ended, and it will have been as if their joyous one night never will have existed.

Moreover, he will bestow on his general a title, together with another city what they will overrun, where Gerald can live in content with Jemima, so that the parties need never to be exposed against temptation again. Amid music, we see them laugh and cry and embrace each other for the last very time, that doleful phrase in love's book.

Returned at the Gorica palace, Prince Mendicula goes to the princess's compartments, full still of goodwill. There is Patricia with her toilet. He passionately declares to her that never again will he vex by looking at other women; he has found his true centre and implores of her forgiveness.

Great his consternation is when Patricia greets this announcement with coolness, turning away as if she heeds scarcely what he says. Shaken, he repeats that he is aware all too much at having neglected her, but that the neglect will end, has already ended. She is his true love.

In a cold voice, perhaps moving to the window, Patricia declares that everything he says is a confession merely that he has a secret lover, as she just suspected and he has denied. She supposes that Mendicula has quarrelled now with the hussy and needs to come back creeping to her. He protests with spirit everywhere. Angry by the way his magnanimity is received as if it is old clothes, he admits with ill-timed honesty that he has been interested in another lady, but that he now has put her for ever away.

Patricia becomes at this even more remote and haughty. She enquires if he makes all this fuss because of herself and Gerald.

The prince does not understand her meaning. He repeats that he relinquishes the other lady and her friendship because simply it is causing pain both to her and Patricia, what he cannot bear to hurt. He ascribes Patricia's continued coolness to her suspicions making her unhappy; now she has no further need for coolness or unhappiness.

Once more on his knees, the prince admits freely her right to have disapproved and asks forgiveness for hurts done; the matter is entirely between the two of them and has no concern for Gerald, what has stood by them nobly all along. Why does she introduce his name at this juncture?

We'll need powder for you here, Miss Armida. Patricia becomes pale of cheek. She turns away from her husband. Her hands shake as she tugs at the curtain. She says in a distant voice that he may repent as much as he likes but it has come too late. She does not intend to discontinue her affair with Gerald – she is enjoying it too much.

At these words, the prince clutches his heart. With dry throat, he forces himself to ask – are she and Gerald then lovers?

'Of course we are! What else do you think we shall have been doing?'

Mendicula falls back, ashen of face, unable to speak, looking silly.

She turns on him. 'You have your affair, I have mine.'

He can only shake his head.

'And you knew Gerald and I were lovers,' she cries, very haughty.

'No, no, I trusted you both.'

'You knew and you encouraged. The other day only you spoke with him privily and commended him, commended him for what he was doing. You told him at his face that he was good for me. That happens to be true! He took your meaning and praised your enlightened attitude. Why, you told him even you had a woman – oh, yes, he informed what you said! And you told me that you tolerated our fondness. You knew what was happening.'

'If you believed really that you were not deceiving me, then why did you so falter from revealing the truth to me now?'

She merely rages at him and throws a hairbrush or something.

All the prince's ideals fall like rags from his eyes. He does not even then beat her or berate. Instead, he tries to explain that when he found them both innocent of vice after the first night he spent away from Gorica, he accepted the virtue in them both, thinking them honourable people who could hold their lusts in check for the greater interests of friendship and policy. From then on, he quelled unworthy doubts what arose and trusted them to sustain a proper friendship. That he had encouraged, and he did not deny. She needed a good friend in a strange city and, since Gerald was *his* sworn friend, owing him many debts of favour, he banished entirely any suspicions of dishonour as dishonouring them. Was his code of behaviour so unworldly? What sort of man would he be if, as she pretended, he had acted as pander to his own wife with a friend as gigolo?

To these questions, she had no answer. Hers is the way of scorn.

'I thought your behaviour generous and wise. So Gerald did. We honoured you then.'

'In bed you honoured me?'

'Now I merely scorn you. So he will.'

Far from being penitent, she is unmoved alike by his anger or his misery. She says that she and Gerald simply amused themselves. She has no intention of now relinquishing Gerald, when they are enjoying both the affair.

'I tried to be all in all to you. Why are you so cold and hard now?'

'You were never enough frivolous for my taste.'

'But he ... he ... has someone else ...'

'He can have many women, so long as I am one of them ...'

'Patricia, my love, do not degrade yourself! He has debased you ...'

Something of that sort. The prince is gentle in his despair, but at that moment, General Gerald himself enters the room, very light and airy – as you do so well, de Chirolo.

In rage, the prince charges him with vile deception in seducing the wife from a man he has called his closest friend, and in betraying totally the trust laid upon him. Gerald uneasily laughs. He adopts a superior attitude and says that the prince has been trifling also. The two wrongs make a right: it is after all the way of the world, and Mendicula would do best to keep quiet. He suspects that if Patricia cares to investigate the matter, she shall discover that the prince has seduced several of her maid-servants.

'You smooth villain, you lie to save your face!'

Gerald takes Patricia's arm. She clings to him.

'Besides, admit, my spoilt prince, you encouraged me. By keeping Patricia happy, I merely was trying to improve your highness's marriage.'

This is more than the prince can tolerate.

'You will make a fool of me no longer!' he cries, drawing his sword. Gerald draws also. They fight. Patricia looks on, pale and unmoving. Well, of course unmoving on the slide.

After many a desperate parry, Gerald draws back, his sword arm pinked. He trips on a rug, sprawling against the princess's bed. He is open utterly to a mortal wound.

As Mendicula hesitates, an army messenger hurries in and announces that the Lady Jemima has been found dead in her room by a maid, dressed in full bridal array. A note by her head declares that she felt herself too much dishonoured to marry such a man of honour as the General Gerald.

At this news, it is the prince who falls back in grief. Seizing his chance, Gerald snatches up his sword and runs it through Mendicula's side. With a last glance at Patricia, the prince dies upon her bed.

Sad fanfares herald the end of our drama of the Prince Mendicula.

Promptly at siesta hour, the Hoytola carriage arrived at the Chabrizzi Palace, with Armida's chaperon, Yolaria, sitting rigid inside. Armida made her farewells and was whisked away.

Next day, the same procedure was followed. I was not to see as much of her as I had hoped. Bengtsohn was secretive about the mercurization and would let nobody view the results. But all appeared to be well because we continued to work slowly through the tableaux. With Armida, it seemed as if mercurization had not taken place between us. I wondered how I could change matters. Accordingly, I walked through the thick afternoon heat to speak to All-People. De Lambant came with me for support.

All-People stood stooped in his whiskery nook by the bottom of the scrivener's stair. His antiquity, his frailty, made it appear that his stiff raiment supported him. His goat was tethered nearby; bluebottles investigated its beard. Neither man nor animal moved. Slow smoke trailed off the iron altar and slipped round the corner about its own business. Because of the hour, nobody was waiting to consult him.

I put down a few paras, all I could spare from the money Bengtsohn had paid me.

'You were correct in what you said, All-People.'

'I see the truth is worth little.'

'Alas, so am I. You said, "If you stand still enough, you will act effectively". You referred to old Otto Bengtsohn's zahnoscope, didn't you? Why was I chosen?'

He threw a crumb of powder on his ashes. They gleamed dully. The stench of Malacia was in my nostrils.

'The Earth lies in an everlasting penumbra some mistake for light. The Powers of Darkness created all. One shadow merges with another.'

'There is a girl, All-People, also involved in Bengtsohn's

53

affairs. How can I make sure that my shadow crosses hers?'

'I am not the one who blesses your amulet. Go ask of him.'

'I will consult Seemly Moleskin, of course. But you already have a hand in my affairs. I am ambitious and hope you can encourage me more.'

He closed his eyes, lids falling like wrinkled lips, as if to end the session. 'The Lord of Darkness has his brand on every one of us. To please him, you must gratify your senses until the carriage shatters.'

I stood looking at him, but the long yellow face had closed itself off from my ken. I shuffled, the goat shook its head, nothing else happened.

Going over to de Lambant, who stood at a respectful distance, as the custom was – to overhear someone else's predication was fatally to entangle your own lifelines – I said, 'Why does the Natural Religion always rouse fear and confusion? Why do I never understand what the magicians tell me?'

'Because it's all old-fashioned rubbish,' said de Lambant. 'I haven't had my amulet blessed in weeks and am I any the worse for it? You're taking this girl too seriously. Let's get Portinari and have a drink.'

'All-People said something about my body being shattered. My carriage, a carriage. It sometimes crosses my mind that life's more complex than you think. I'll go and see Mandaro.'

Guy shook his head. 'My dear de Chirolo, priests are worse than wizards, Stay away from them. Come, it's hot. Let's tip Portinari out of bed and have a drink and a chat with him.'

'You go. I'll come along later.'

We parted. I told myself that it was absurd to have a heavy heart when my purse was so light. The priest would do me no good. The company of my friends would be a lot more cheerful. I turned. De Lambant was not yet out of sight. Giving him a call, I ran to join him, and we headed together for Portinari's house.

On the third day of our enactment of the tragedy of *Prince Mendicula*, the mighty zahnoscope was trained upon us when a great clatter started in the courtyard and Bengtsohn bid us wait.

The Chabrizzis were leaving for their summer vacation in the Vukoban Mountains. In other years, Armida told me, they holidayed in a fertile valley in the Prilipits to the south of Malacia where they owned estates; but this year there were reports of Turkish armies moving in that area. As usual, Malacia was encompassed by enemies.

Soon we were surrounded by a congregation of coaches, carriages and waggons piled with luggage and musical instruments, horses, dogs, pet snaphances, cattle and poultry, not to mention adult and infant Chabrizzis, together with their friends and servants. It was all too much for our tableau. Bengtsohn's wife, Floria, tried to dispel the crowd, but it was not to be dispelled until it was ready. Our impresario dismissed us and walked away grumpily with his dark box under his arm.

We were interrupted in the scene where I as the dishonourable General Gerald was taking Princess Patricia to grand balls (represented by one other dancing couple) and similar splendid occasions (represented by a painting of a marble staircase). Such enforced intimacy served to ripen the relationship between Armida and me, not only because we were the two left outside a Bengtsohn-Bonihatch comradeship which extended to most of the rest of the workshop, but because she had taken a dislike to Mendicula, whose bonithatchian sidewhiskers tickled her unendurably for minutes on end as well as – so Armida said – smelling of stale custard.

She took me to one side. 'The Chabrizzis will leave the palace almost empty, with only a few servants to deter robbers,' she said. 'They'll all be gone in another five minutes. Fancy, I haven't entered the old place for years – there was some coldness between our families. Now's my chance to explore those nooks and crannies I recall so well before Yolaria arrives with the carriage.'

'Don't get lost – or found!'

She slipped her hand into mine. 'Oh, I dare not go alone. You see how grotesque the palace is, standing under that looming rock. Besides, it is haunted by an ancient wizard with flaming eye-sockets.'

'I'll come too. Shall we take a bucket of water in case we meet the eye-sockets?'

'Slip round the side so that nobody will notice us. Come on, it'll be fun!' She turned her face up, smiling in excitement.

I followed her round to a side door and we plunged together into the gloom of the palace. The clatter of the courtyard was lost. In a way, it was like being trapped inside the zahnoscope, with long vistas of light and shade contrived by window and tapestry and wall and corridor. What a place for an assignation! It was up to me to rehearse General Gerald's role as thoroughly as possible, and I followed Armida's ice-blue robe with despatch.

I mentioned that the palace was set under an outcrop of rock. At this point, the Prilipit Mountains had deposited a last great chunk of limestone, some hundred metres high, upon the landscape. The ingenious Chabrizzis, for reasons of defence, had built their home under and into the face of this mass of rock, upsetting the symmetry of composition intended by their architect.

The interior of the building was confusing. The men who built the place had been so baffled by topography that they had in some instances left a curve of staircase incomplete, or caused a passageway to double back upon itself in despair, or left a potentially grand chamber unshaped, its rear wall broken rock.

Armida, a small venturesome girl again, pulled me through the labyrinth, in and out of compartments, up or down large and little flights of stairs, through small doors that yielded enormous prospects, and a banqueting hall that led into a cupboard. Through tall windows, we saw the vacationing party move slowly out of the main gates and down the hill.

When we were exploring an upper floor, Armida led me outside to a ledge of rock otherwise inaccessible, situated several metres above ground level. The ledge was used as a small park in which the Chabrizzis traditionally kept a few tame ancestral animals. Now only three old siderowels were left. In bygone times, these squat beasts had been employed for battle, chained together in rows with lighted fuses on their tails, to throw disorder among the enemy.

The three remaining siderowels were lumbering about, grunting; their sharp side-armour had been filed blunt, to protect them as well as their keepers from harm. Armida ran to fondle one, and it ate leaves from her hand. Initials had been carved on segments of its shell; we found one initial with a date over two hundred years old. These were among the last siderowels in Malacia. All the ancestral animals were dying out.

Inside the palace again, we crept at last to a little chapel, where the richly carved pews of the Chabrizzi faced towards an altar accommodated in a wall of limestone rock. The rock shone with moisture; a trickle of water ran down it with a permanent tinkle of sound which deepened the mystery of the chamber. Ferns grew in the rock, sacrificial candles burning nearby. There was a grand solemn painting of the Gods of Dark and Light, one horned, one benevolently bearded, with Minerva and her owl between them.

We went to the chapel window. It was set against rock. A continual splash of water rained down the panes, dripping from the limestone. From this narrow view we could observe Mantegan in the distance, where my sister and her negligent husband lived. Looking down we gazed into a servants' court. A thin ray of sun struck down into the shadows of that dank area, picking out two figures. I clutched Armida's arm in its tight sleeve and directed her gaze to the couple.

A man and a woman stood close in the court. Both were young, though the man was a slip of a youth and the woman fairly buxom, in apron and mob cap. We could see her face as she smiled up at him, squinting in the sunlight. His face could not be seen from our angle. He bent towards her, kissing her, and she offered no resistance; he placed one hand on her ample breast, while his other hand stole up under her skirt and apron. The familiar actions were embalmed by the sun's rays.

'Naughty idle servants!' Armida said, looking at me half-mischievously and half-defiantly. 'Why are servants always so wanton?'

I kissed her then, and played with the ribbons in her hair, letting my other hand steal under her skirt, much as the servant had done.

Armida immediately broke away, slapping my hand. I saw she was laughing and reached out for her. She moved away and I went in pursuit. Whenever I got too close, she would slap my wrist – except once when I caught her and we started kissing affectionately, with her lips gradually parting and my tongue creeping through her teeth; but then again, when matters were becoming warm elsewhere, she went skipping round the chapel.

At first it was fun. Then I thought her childish.

Tiring of the game, I sank down on one of the quilted stalls and let her sport. Above the altar were two curved folds in the rock, gleaming with moisture, which met in a V where water trickled and flashed, and a fern sent out a spray of fronds.

Now an imp had got into my lady. She was unlike her usual restrained self. She removed her clothes as she pranced, humming a tune at the same time. With a remote expression on her face, she cast away her white stockings, moving her arms and legs as if performing to a select audience – I mean, an even more select one than I provided. Very soon she peeled out of her dress. I paid close attention, only half-believing that this was intended for my benefit. One by one her undergarments came away, the bodice last of all, and there was Armida of the Hoytolas, dancing naked for a poor player, just beyond that player's reach.

Although her body was on the slender side, nothing about Armida was less than perfectly formed. Her breasts bounced so beautifully, and her taut buttocks, to a rhythm of their own. The hair at the base of her small stomach was as dark and vibrant as that on her head. My eyes stood out like her nipples at this marvellous entertainment. What a peach of a girl! And what did she intend? I prayed that it might be the same as I did.

Finally she stopped before me, still out of reach, holding her hands before her private parts in belated modesty. Her garments were strewn all over the floor.

'I danced here like this once before, long, long ago,' she said in a meditative voice, 'and have always longed to do so again – free of my family, free of myself. How I wish I were a wild creature!'

'We are in a shrine to female beauty. If you turn about, you will see what I mean upon the wall.'

This I said ponderously, pointing at the V in the limestone wall and slowly rising from my seat as she turned to look.

'The rock has delineated the fairest parts of a spectral female. The fern grows where it does out of modesty, do you see what I mean, Armida?'

By which time I placed an arm round her neck from behind, pointing with my free hand until, as I nibbled her ear, that hand was allowed to drop and circumnavigate her swelling hip, where it found its way along a curve of her V and nestled among the foliage growing there. By which time, she had turned about in my arms and our mouths were together. With the other hand now relieved of its duties about her neck, I tore off my own clothes.

Soon I kicked away my boots and breeches, and we were lying together without encumbrance on the wide prayer-bench of the Chabrizzi, who had certainly never had a better altar to worship at than the one I now clasped.

Armida's last restraints were shed with her clothes – or so it appeared at first, for she seized with delight on what I had to offer and pressed her lips upon it, babbling to it as if it were a dolly, until I feared it would babble in its turn. And yet – even then, she would not allow what I desired. That was reserved for the man she married, she said, or she would have no value in the marriage market; such was the law of her family.

With that I had to rest content – and became content enough for the interdiction entailed the use of pleasant ingenuities to which many lovers have become accustomed in our land. The world was lost, transmuted, in her delicious embraces. We enchanted each other until the sun faded from the rocks outside and the siderowels bellowed for their evening gruel. We dozed awhile. We went downstairs languidly, hand in hand through the bewildering passages, into a conflict of shadows. There were no ghosts, only changes in the air as we moved, vapours, and patches of chill or warmth or damp, to which our skins felt unusually sensitive.

Out in the front courtyard Armida's coach was waiting. With a last amorous glance at me she ran forward, leaving me to wait in the gloom of the porch until I heard the rattle of the coach's wheels die on the cobbles.

At that hour, my friends would be drinking in one of the inns of Stary Most. My mood was elevated; I felt no inclination to share my happiness. Instead, I walked through the city as evening thickened, determined to call on my priest of the High Religion, shaven-pate Mandaro.

Mandaro lived in a room with another priest, in one of the surviving quarters of the palace of Malacia's founders. This edifice was the original Malacia. It had once been – and even in decrepitude still was – an enormous pile, almost a city in its own right. Most of it was dismantled, its stones, its gargoyles, its component parts pilfered to form later buildings, including the cisterns under the city and the foundations of St Marco's itself. Of the surviving palace, not one of the original rooms remained to serve its original function in its original shape. The shifts of the poor hung from balconies where once the scarcely human ladies of Desport, our founder, had basked in the sun.

The denizens of the present, scratching a living for themselves, filled with noises the warren through which I moved. The atmosphere still whispered its linkage with the blind past.

Working my way into this slum, I climbed to the third floor and pushed Mandaro's wooden door open. It was never locked. Mandaro was there as usual in the evening, talking to a man who rose and left with downcast eyes as I entered. The room had been partitioned down the middle, for the privacy of callers as much as for the priests; I had never seen the priest who lived in the other half of the chamber, although I had heard his deep melancholy voice raised in a chant.

Mandaro was on his balcony. He beckoned to me and I joined him. From a tiny cupboard he brought out a tiny spoonful of jam on a tiny plate, together with a glass of water, the traditional welcome of priests of the High Religion. I ate the jam slowly and drank down the yellowy water without complaint.

'Something troubles you. Otherwise you would not have come.'

'Don't reproach me, father.'

'I didn't. I spoke a fact with which you reproached yourself. I can see that it is a pleasing trouble.'

He smiled. Mandaro was a man of early middle-age, well-built if thin. He looked hard, as if he were made of wood; something in the sharp planes of his face suggested he had been roughly carved. He grew a beard to compensate for his shaved head. The brown whiskers had a curl of grey in them, the sight of which reassured me; somehow it made him look less holy. His eyes were sharp, of an impenetrable brown rather like de Lambant's and he directed them at you all the while.

I glanced away over his crumbling balcony, where night was closing in. The Satsuma lay below us, fitfully lighted, with its wharves and ships. Then came the Toi; a restaurant-boat floated down it, accompanied by sounds of music and a smell of cooking oil. On the far bank stood groves of ash jostling a line of ancient buildings. Beyond them, darkly, were vineyards and farther still, the Vukobans, visible as little more than a jagged line cut from pale night sky. The evening star shone. A chick-snake barked towards the Bucintoro. Singing drifted up, punctuated by laughter and voices from nearby rooms.

'Something troubles me, and it is partly pleasing,' I said. 'But I feel myself as never before caught on the fringes of a web of circumstance. Those circumstances offer me advancement and a beautiful girl; they also involve me – well, with people I do not trust as I trust my friends. According to All-People there are dark things in the future. I shall gratify my senses until my carriage shatters.'

'The wizards and magicians always offer dark things. You know that.'

'I don't believe him. Priests threaten dark things. What's the difference?'

'You don't want a lecture on the differences between the Natural and the Higher Religions. They are opposed but allied, as evening mingles with dawn in our blood. They agree that the world was created by Satan, or the Powers of Darkness; they agree that God, or the Power of Light, is an intruder in this universe; the fundamental difference is that adherents of the Natural Religion believe that humanity should side with Satan, since God can never win; whereas we of the Higher Religion believe that God can triumph in the great battle, provided that human beings fight on his side rather than Satan's.

'This night seems peaceful, but fires burn under the earth . . .'

He was away, his imagination warmed by the drama he saw being surreptitiously enacted all about. I had heard and admired him on this theme before. While the performance was one I enjoyed, I hoped for more personal advice. Without wishing to be impolite, I could not appear one of the vacant faithful, swayed by eloquence as if I had none of my own: I remained gazing at the dark, flowing Toi. Like all priests, Mandaro could squeeze a message from a pebble, and incorporated my inactivity into his talk.

'You see how peaceful night looks, how calm the river. Beauty itself is Satan's most powerful illusion. How beautiful Malacia is – how often I think so as I walk its streets – yet it suffers under our ancestral curse. Everything is in conflict. Which is why we must endure two complementary but conflicting religions.'

'But this girl, father—'

'Beware of all things fair, my son, whether a girl or a friend. What looks to be fair may be foul under the surface. The Devil needs his traps. You should regard also your own behaviour, lest it seem fair to you but is really an excuse for foulness.' And so on.

As I left him I reflected that he might as well have burnt a serpent on an altar as counsel me the way he did. I found my way down through the intestines of the ancient palace, until I was free of its whispering. The flavours of the river came to me, and the thought of Armida. I walked slowly back to the Street of the Wood Carvers; it was delicious to believe that Mandaro was right, and that Fate was keeping a goat-like eye on me.

The days passed. I neglected my friends and grew to understand Armida's circumstances better.

Like all young ladies of her rank she was well guarded, and never officially allowed in the presence of men without Yolaria, her prune-faced chaperon. Fortunately, this rule was relaxed in the case of the Chabrizzi Palace, since the Chabrizzis were relations of the Hoytolas.

There was also a simple administrative difficulty which worked to our advantage. Armida had been promised a light town carriage of her own as a present for her eighteenth birthday just past; owing to a fire at the coach-builder's, the carriage had not yet been delivered. Meanwhile, Yolaria enjoyed riding about town in the family coach, and we were able to turn her late arrivals at Chabrizzi to our pleasant advantage on more than one occasion.

Armida was surrounded by regulations. She was not allowed to read lewd authors like du Close, Bysshe Byron, or Les Amis. Before she could act in front of the zahnoscope, she had had a long lecture from her parents about consorting with the lower orders. She had little talent for acting – even acting of the limited kind required by the zahnoscope – but to escape from the confinement of her family was tonic enough.

Otto Bengtsohn and his wife were supposed to act as chaperons to their employer's precious daughter on these occasions. Their indifference to such a task rendered it easy for us to slip away into the shadowy aisles of the Chabrizzi. There I came to know Armida Hoytola, her desires and frustrations. I was lucky to receive what I did receive; and, despite her fits of haughtiness, I found myself caught by a desire that was new to me. I longed to marry her.

She was telling me about their great country estate, Juracia, where some of the great old ancestral animals still roamed, when I realized that I would overcome all obstacles in our path to make her my wife – if she would have me.

Malacia was acknowledged throughout the civilized world to be a near-utopia. Yet it had it laws, each law designed to preserve its perfections. One such law was that nobody should marry a person of a different station in life *until the necessity for it had been proved*. The hard-headed and anonymous oldsters of the Council would certainly not admit love as a necessity, though they had been known to admit pregnancy on occasions. I, a common player despite some good connections, could not expect to marry Armida Hoytola, a rich merchant's only daughter with far better connections.

Either I must take up more dignified work or ... I must become an absolute dazzling success in my own chosen line, so that even the Council could not gainsay my rise through individual merit to the heights.

My art was my life; I had to shine on the boards. Which was difficult at a time when the arts in general were depressed and even an impresario like Kemperer was obliged to close down his troupe.

The mercurized play of *Prince Mendicula* began to assume almost as much importance to me as to Bengtsohn. I pinned many hopes upon it. By the time this state of affairs became apparent to me, I was secretly betrothed to Armida.

It happened on a day when the zahnoscope was busy capturing scenes between the Prince and the Lady Jemima. While Bonihatch and Letitia were undertaking to petrify time, Armida and I escaped, and I escorted her, swathed in a veil, to Stary Most and the Street of the Wood Carvers. For the first time, she stood in my little nook in the rooftops lending it her fragrance. There she commented on all she saw with a mixture of admiration and derision characteristic of her.

'You are so poor, Perian! Either a barracks or a monastery would have seemed luxury compared to this garret.' She could not resist reminding me of my pretence that I had been about to join the Army or the Church.

'If I enlisted in either of those boring bodies, it would be from necessity. I'm here from choice. I love my attic. It's romantic – a fit place from which to start a brilliant career. Take a look and a sniff from the back window.'

My tiny rear window, deep sunk into the crumbling wall, looked out over one of the furniture workshops, from which a rich odour of camphor wood, brought by a four-master all the way from Cathay, drifted upwards. As she tipped herself forward to peer down, Armida showed me her beautiful ankles. I was immediately upon her. She responded to my kisses. She let her clothes be torn from her, and soon we were celebrating our private version of love. Then it was she agreed that we should be secretly engaged to marry, as we lay on my narrow truckle bed, moist body to moist body.

'Oh, how happy you make me, Armida! At least I must tell my good fortune to de Lambant. His sister is to be married soon. You must meet them – he's a true friend and almost as witty and handsome as I.'

'He couldn't be, I'm certain of that. Supposing I fell in love with him instead.'

'The mere thought is torture! But you have better sense than to prefer him. I am going to be famous.'

'Perry, you are as over-confident as Prince Mendicula himself!'

'Let's leave that farrago out of our conversation. Of course I hope that Bengtsohn will be successful, and that the play will do well for us, but after all as a story it is such rubbish – banal rubbish, too.'

'Banal?' She looked quizzingly down her pretty nose at me. 'I love stories about princes and princesses. How can such things be banal? And Princess Patricia is so marvellously proud when she is found out ... I have a good opinion of the piece. So does my father.'

'My father would be very scornful. The situation is as old as the hills. Man and best friend, best friend seduces friend's wife; the deception is discovered, they fall out and become enemies. Blood is shed. Why, that sort of thing could have been written a million years ago.'

'Yet Otto has set out the old story in a novel way, and draws a sound moral from it. Besides, I like the setting in the captured city.'

I laughed and squeezed her.

'Nonsense, Armida, there's no moral in the piece. Mendicula

is a dupe, Patricia unkind, Gerald a false friend, Jemima just a pawn. Perhaps that represents Bengtsohn's view of the nobility, but it makes for a poor tale. My great hope is that the astonishing technique of mercurization will carry the charade through to success – aided, of course, by the outstanding handsomeness of fifty per cent of the players.'

She smiled. 'You mean the fifty per cent lying here on this bed?'

'All glorious hundred per cent of it!'

'While you are playing with these figures – and with *my* figure too, if you don't mind – may I refresh your memory on one point? Otto's venture will come to naught if my father does not settle his dispute with the Supreme Council. Father is very ambitious, and so is feared. If he falls, then so fall all who depend on him, including his daughter.'

'You refer to that business of the hydrogenous balloon? Balloons have sailed from Malacia before, for sport and to scare the Turk. I don't understand what all the fuss is about. Nothing is going to be changed if the balloon does go up.'

'The Council think differently. But if popular opinion is too much against them, then they may yield. Alternatively, they may strike against my father – which is why he now seeks powerful friends.'

I rolled on to my back and gazed up at the patches on the ceiling.

'It sounds as if your father would be best advised to forget about his balloon.'

'Father intends that the balloon should ascend; it would be an achievement. Unfortunately, the Council intends that it should not. That is a serious situation. As common usage comes between us, so it can come between my father and his life. You know what happens to those who defy the Council for too long.'

What I saw in my mind's eye was not a corpse in the sewers but its daughter sharing my little bare garret.

'I would defy anything for you, Armida, including all the fates in opposition. Marry me, I beg you, and watch me excel myself.'

She would have to have a dozen horoscopes read before she could consent to that; but she did agree to a secret betrothal, and to the same sort of bond that existed between General Gerald and the fair Princess Patricia, our absurd alter egos.

Scents of sandalwood, camphor and pine mingled with patchouli and the precious aromas of Armida's body as we forthwith celebrated our intentions.

A Balloon over the Bucintoro

When you take a stroll through our city along the banks of the River Toi, and especially along the elegant Bucintoro, where pavements are of gold, you can look north and regard verdant expanses of countryside stretching into the Vokoban Mountains, which are themselves, at least on their southern slopes, green and well-flavoured.

When from any other vantage point in Malacia you gaze towards the country, you see nothing so enticing. True, there is the long, dusty road to Byzantium, while to the south-east lies the Vamonal Canal, tree-fringed for most of its course; but in general the vistas consist of undulating plain – ochre, sullen, primitive; all those things against which the idea of Malacia is most opposed. To the west lie the no less uninviting Prilipit Mountains, where the terrain is distorted and uncouth.

Among the folds of the Prilipits, even as Armida and I were luxuriously plighting our troth, gathered an Ottoman army intent upon laying waste Malacia.

There was a general alarm and a mustering of arms. Not a citizen but feared for his well-being, his wife, or something he held dear. But such armies had gathered beyond our fortifications before, had been defeated, and had retired in disarray.

The Council and the generals did what they deemed necessary. They paraded our own forces, they polished our cannonballs, they set the blue and black flag of Malacia flying from every battlement, they drew a barrage across the rivers, they increased the price of fish and flour in the markets.

While these high strategies were in process, groups of citizens climbed to vantage points in the city – up rickety staircases to belfries – to espy the gaudy tents of the foe; but most of us saw it as our duty to continue living as usual, whilst paying more for loaves and sprats.

Some there were, of course, who fled the city, going by barge to Vamonal or by foot or litter to Byzantium. Others bolted themselves in houses or cellars. For myself, I feared nothing; Armida had cast a spell over my life.

All know what it is to be in love. When I opened my casement window and the breeze wafted down from a meadow outside the city, that breeze might have touched *her* cheek on its way to me; when I trod the street, the ground beneath my feet led somewhere to *her*, was trodden by her feet; when I glanced up and happened to see a bird flying in the sky, it might be that *she* saw it at the same instant, so that our gazes interlocked. Whenever I touched an object, it reminded me of touching *her*; when I ate, the action made me recall that *she* ate; when I spoke to anyone, I recalled what it felt like to speak to *her*; when I kept silent, it put me in mind of *her* lips, unspeaking. The world became a conspiracy of *her*.

In the circumstances, the Ottomans could not weigh down my heart or my considerations by a denario's worth.

One evening, when a Turkish spy was caught in the main square and had his neck extended by a good half-metre before Fetter Place, I went with de Lambant to visit Otto Bengtsohn and enquire how the mercurization was progressing. Such was his secretiveness that, as yet, he had shown nobody his results.

'How appropriate that you should be immortalized on glass,' said de Lambant. 'You are such a transparent character, my friend.'

I had paid for the wine that evening. 'Then we must see that you are posted to posterity on skin and flint,' I said.

We went in through the court by the sign of the Dark Eye and into the workshop, where Bonihatch and other assistants were still at work, or bowed over their painting desks pretending to work. Slapping the erstwhile Prince Mendicula on his back, I led the way into the gallery which at this hour was closed to the public.

Catching in the air a fragrance of patchouli, I spied the fair Armida in the distance, carrying an oil lamp which lit her features from below, suffusing them with a magical luminosity as if she were composed of nothing more substantial than cloud. What a pleasant surprise to see her – I had imagined her incarcerated at home as usual. Here was my chance to introduce her to Guy.

With her were her father, wrapped severely in a double-breasted tail-coat, Otto Bengtsohn in a cringing attitude and his old fur, Armida's and Guy's friend Bedalar, wrapped in a gold pelisse which matched her ringlets; and a man of quite different ilk from the rest of the party, whose aspect was so singular that it was on him rather than on the ladies that my gaze fastened as I approached the group unnoticed.

'... circumspect conduct which may nevertheless be of service to the realm, if only for an interim period,' this individual was saying, in such a manner as to make Armida look grave and her father to take snuff. The speaker was tall and thin, yet not only thin but decidedly paunchy, while his face, to match this paradoxical effect, appeared gaunt and dark with a puffy pallor to it. His frock-coat was black, very capacious, and frightening, as if it held coils of rope in its pockets. His skull was capped by a grey club wig on which was a black bicorne-hat sporting the blue and black rosette of the Supreme Council. He was a man accustomed to seeing people quail before him; he even had a person to quail behind him, a twisted lackey with lips like raw steaks who kept to the shadows of the gallery.

The member of the Supreme Council turned his gaze on me to such effect that not only did I stop but found myself moving slightly in reverse.

'We will repair to your office without further interruption, Hoytola,' he said, in a voice that came from somewhere beyond the reach of oil lamps.

The party turned their backs on me and moved away. I made no attempt to go farther. His saturnine voice reminded me that on the whole I preferred nice people to nasty people. Armida, bless her, found a chance to flit back and touch my wrist. The lamp and its shadows made of her face a world with sunshine and cloud. She said, 'We're having a meeting, I'll see you tomorrow. Take care of Bedalar.'

With that she vanished, following the party through a green baize door up the dim stair which led to Master Hoytola's apartments and offices. Only Bedalar stayed, holding a candle and looking sheepish at being excluded from the party.

We stood gazing at each other from a distance.

'Well, that's that,' she said.

'Yes. Is there some trouble?'

She inspected her candle and then said, 'I don't know what's happening, do I?'

'What's that man doing here?'

'Business with Armida's father. He's only just arrived.'

'I wouldn't want to do business with him,' Guy said firmly.

69

We went back into the workshop, which was better lit and had less of a feel of ropes in black pockets about it.

Bonihatch and the other apprentices were skipping about with greater animation than they showed when Bengtsohn was there, trying to amuse a pallid waif of about nine years old. The waif, faintly smiling, was a girl who stood holding the hand of our seamstress, Letitia Zlatorog, alias the Lady Jemima. Letitia was looking much less the Lady Jemima tonight in her severe drab dress and worn slippers, although she smiled a smile which, by the glow on Bonihatch's face, had kindled something of a fire in his heart. The waif's thin face was like a candle-flame against Letitia's.

I greeted them, tickling the waif under the chin, despite a suspicion about its cleanliness.

'Letitia has just brought me down a beautiful shirt,' Bonihatch said, coming over to me in a friendly way. 'I can act with you now, Perian! Though Otto provided some bits of costume, I've had to find my own shirt, and had nothing adequate for a prince to wear until now. Now, I could be a king, so overprivileged shall I feel in Letitia's handiwork.'

'Or the queen even better than the king, for that matter, for 'tis very fancy,' I said, handling the new garment.

'Come, say you admire it, Perian,' Letitia urged, coming over. 'It is my uncle's very best pattern, and I stitched every stitch myself.'

'It's better than anything you've got to wear, I'll be bound, for all your airs,' one of the other apprentices, Solly, jeered, pulling a face at me.

Certainly it was an admirable shirt, made of thin cotton, pleated at the waist, with an elaborate, frilled open neck in a style that might seem florid on the street but would certainly answer in all manner of theatricals. The stitches were finely done and an embroidered posy ornamented the right cuff.

I laughed and put an arm about Letitia. 'It *is* a noble shirt, your uncle's pattern rivals anyone's, and it *is* better than anything I have – that I freely confess. You're a clever girl, Letitia, and I'll take you all to the Leather-Teeth Tavern for drinks to celebrate.'

'We apprentices can't leave the shop till Otto comes back,' Bonihatch said promptly.

'Then I'll take Letitia alone. And of course de Lambant and

Bedalar when they're done whispering together in the corner.'

'I mustn't come – I must get back to my stitching,' said Letitia, looking anguishedly towards Bonihatch. 'My sister and I have been away too long. The others will miss us.'

At this the waif by her side set up a wail for food. Letitia squatted by her, took her in her arms, and promised a refreshing glass of tea as soon as they were home. The waif was Letitia's small sister, Rosa. While this domestic scene was in progress, I turned back to Bonihatch, who was now folding up the shirt in a restrained manner, and asked him how much the garment cost, or whether (not knowing their relationship) Letitia had given it to him as a present.

'Not at all like that,' he said in a low voice, giving me a curious look. 'Letitia's family, the Zlatorogs, are the poorest of the poor. I paid the market price – although I'm proud to say that my friends and fellow-apprentices weighed in from the goodness of their hearts and helped me with the cost.'

He told me what he had paid. I whistled to show that I was impressed by his extravagance although the shirt was something of a bargain; even so, it was more than I could command at present.

Letitia and Rosa were now making their farewells. They collected up the sheet of paper the shirt had been wrapped in and smiled at one and all. The seamstress got a kiss and a squeeze from Bonihatch, while the other apprentices gallantly kissed her fingers. De Lambant had managed to disappear with Bedalar; I did not imagine that I would see them again. As Letitia and the child went to the door of the court, I moved in beside them.

At that moment, Bengtsohn appeared from the direction of the gallery. He looked shaken, and went to sit on a chair. When the apprentices went crowding about him, my chance came to speak to Letitia.

'Your little sister is hungry, Letitia – she looks as if she last ate on Halberd-head Day. Let me buy you a glass of wine and her a pastry at the Leather-Teeth, then you can slip home.'

While I was speaking, I urged her into the court. She was protesting and the child began to snivel. There was no lighting in the court except for what filtered through the odd window, in particular the side window of the tavern, above the frosted portion of which I could see men at the time-honoured pastime

71

of pouring liquor down their throats. Catching hold of the waif's hand, I said, 'Come, child, and I'll buy you a pastry straight away.'

I pulled her into the tavern, but Letitia would not follow. She waited by the door, looking vexed. Vexed myself, I bought Rosa a bun stuffed with plums and spice, told her to stay by the counter, and hurried to Letitia's side.

She was a thin girl, as always rather mousey, but by no means formless, even in the worn grey dress. Despite the pallor of her face, Letitia had her beauty. She had been enclosed in her trade too long for anything positive to emerge, yet her eyes were large, while something about her mouth and cheekbones enticingly suggested foreign blood.

'Miss Letitia, you look so pretty standing there. Never wait at an entrance, that's my motto. Come in and drink and part with a mite of conversation to pay me for the wine. We have never talked together.'

'You have more time to talk than I. My uncle needs me to work and we are always busy, day and night.'

'That I am not busy at present is no reflection on my talents – about which agreement it fairly universal.'

'I meant to imply no insult – merely that I work hard and must return home now. I ask you not to detain me.'

'Stay for as long as it takes to swallow a spiced bun! No? Very well, then, I may perhaps be allowed to accompany you to your door.'

Rosa, anchored to the bun but impermanent at her post, had joined us. Since she had no free hand, Letitia took her by the shoulder and steered her into the darkness of the court. Following, I moved to her side.

'We need not be together merely when the zahnoscope is trained on us, Letitia. It has no magical powers. Let's meet one evening when you are free to enjoy yourself.'

'And when you are free from Armida Hoytola? Very rightly you have no eyes for me when she is about.'

'You should at least get to know me well enough to have the right to be jealous.'

'Jealousy – that's a very expensive luxury, above my station.'

We came to a door in the smelly recesses of the court, where it was so black that I held Letitia's arm for guidance. She brought out a key and unlocked the door, which she opened to

72

reveal a bare, well-worn staircase, lit by a stub of candle guttering in its socket.

'We have to part here, Perian. Rosa and I thank you for your kindness in buying her the bun, which we hope will not spoil her appetite for supper.'

'Let me come up with you, if I may. I like hearing you talk, and believe you have more to say, if you feel so inclined.'

'I'm sorry, my uncle will require me to help with the work. We have two dozen damask table-cloths to be hemmed before morning.'

'Then I'll speak to your uncle as well, for you'll surely need company. Don't look so scared, girl – I have no intention of running off with your table-cloths – shirts are much more in my line.'

'Oh, I knew there was something you wanted . . .' But by dint of trundling Rosa before me as if she were a new kind of battering-ram, I was moving up the stairs; Letitia had no option but to lock the door on the inside, snatch up the thumb of candle, and hasten after me.

'Please understand, Perian, we are very poor people—'

'Don't be ashamed, don't be ashamed, I haven't the price of a new plume myself.'

'I'm not ashamed of being poor, Master Perian. It's the people who make us poor should be ashamed of that. My family works hard to make ends meet, and that's less of a disgrace than idleness. I am just afraid that you may have no stomach for our meagre way of life.'

'Truth is, I find other people's poverty easier to bear than my own.'

Meagreness was indeed the keynote of the chamber into which we were emerging. As our heads rose above the level of the stairwell, a bone-bare space, most of it in gloom, came into view. The first item that caught my eye was a stretch of naked rafter overhead, with the underside of the tiles showing, and mortar bulging between tiles like fungus. On this uneven surface, like fishy shapes cast over the barred sand of a lagoon, were huge, moving shadows, projected by some people gathered round a table. This table, with its attendant seating – boxes did service for chairs – formed almost the sole furniture of the room.

Four people sat at it. Their faces were turned towards the lamp in the centre of the table; their backs were in permanent eclipse. They bent over the table as if at prayer.

A stale, sickly smell, permeating the room, made me pause. Letitia, leading Rosa, pushed past me to offer explanations to a grey-haired man who half-rose at the table, his face questioning. The others spared me only a hasty glance over one shoulder before continuing work.

Moving further into the room, I saw a round window at one end and perceived from the general disposition of the space that it had been a hay loft. Now it contained the robust old man with grey hair, with whom Letitia was conversing, a frail woman dressed in black, a girl of about Letitia's age and appearance, and a boy of about fifteen years whose dull bovine glance betrayed the mental defective. Near the stair were some scruffy mattresses laid together on the floor. A line of ragged washing hung nearby. The only beautiful thing in the room was the damask, spread on the table and forming a focus for the family's activity.

The old man, propping himself upright with the aid of a stick, made a speech of welcome. For all his years, he had a good, red countryman's face, in contrast with the pallid countenances round him – and in contrast with the scant curls on his head, two of which stuck up like white horns on either side of his brow. He said, 'You're very welcome here, sir, though this is not the place to which I would welcome a gentleman of your standing.'

'No, no, don't say that, please. I'm glad to know where my friend Letita lives. I can see you do indeed work hard, Letitia.'

'She's fine at her craft, sir,' said the old man. 'You must excuse me that an affliction in the legs prevents me rising. But we are all as cheerful as we are poor in this house, if that is not too grand a word for our loft, and we try to be grateful for our mercies.'

'Your skill is certainly a mercy, sir, for I saw the fine shirt you made for Bonihatch.'

'Although we make light of our troubles, our skills are exploited. If the Ottomans don't slay us all, I'm bound to make many more such shirts before I'm done for, thank you for saying what you do. But we Zlatorogs are too poor, I fancy, to provide the Turks with a target.' Here he glanced speculatively at Letitia, as if realizing that there were qualities other than wealth which might attract a marauding Ottoman.

74

He then proceeded to introduce me to the rest of the company: the dim boy and the girl, who were Letitia's brother and sister; and the woman in black, who was Letitia's mother. She was toothless, but she spoke to me with a grace that had clearly shaped Letitia's upbringing.

'We were mountain farmers, sir, from the Triglav area,' she said. 'My husband was drowned in the spring floods when I was giving birth to this dear child here—' pointing to the dull boy. 'My brother Joze, who is a good man, and never complains of the pains in his legs, has looked after us ever since. At least we do make a living, and things are better in Malacia than in our own country.'

As she spoke, she worked on the white damask, her pallid fingers ceaseless above the cloth, every stitch as correct as a spider's strand.

'Of course, I'd rather be out in the fields with the cows and the beehives and the hay,' said Letitia's uncle, taking up the tale. 'But since my misfortune I've learned to stitch as beautifully as a lady, and now that we have connections in the courts, why, we do pretty well.'

'And those court connections rob and cheat us at every turn, for all they're supposed to be so religious,' Letitia said.

'That's the way of life, my dear,' said her uncle, turning to me to add, 'She's rebellious, you see, like all the young.'

'Master de Chirolo isn't rebellious,' Letitia said fiercely.

'As I say, we do pretty well,' continued the uncle. 'This next winter, we should be able to afford a little stove in here, to burn under the table, and that'll keep us cosy all day and every day, provided we manage about the fuel.'

His hands were big and broad and scarred; they showed dark against the faultless white of the table-cloths. Like his widowed sister's, Joze's hands moved surely as he talked, spinning a web to keep the family lives together. Noticing where my gaze rested, he said, 'I don't consider it unmanly to do this – if it brings food to our mouths, why, then, it's man's work, isn't it? I can make almost any garment now. All it needs is to be shown once – and Letitia's the same, aren't you, love? Dress or frock coats, paletots, monkey jackets, fishing coats, benjamins, beavers, shooting coats, parade uniforms – we turn them all out without argument, if it brings in money. Our garments imitate only the best.' He gave me an ingratiating smile.

'You are an artist, sir, in your way,' I said, since a compliment was required.

Letitia had seated herself and resumed work as soon as we came in, settling little Rosa beside her. While Rosa sucked her thumb, Letitia kept her gaze on her swift-moving fingers. Now she raised her head to give me a bold look.

'No, we are not artists as you understand, Perian. We are sweated labour. We sit here from nine in the morning till nine every night, all days of the week, if the work's available, for a pittance.'

'Except when you are playing Jemima in Bengtsohn's play.'

'That grand romance earns me more in a day than would the making of a sturdy shooting coat which might last a nobleman ten years.'

'We hope to see Letitia's performance on the slides, young sir, when Otto's finished his work,' her mother said, deflecting her daughter's complaints. 'I'm sure her acting's capital.'

'Oh, capital,' I said, 'since it consists merely of standing still. And none of us ever muffs our lines, since there are no lines to muff.'

'Still, it's a beautiful, romantic story,' said Letitia. 'It makes me cheerful just to think of it.'

'She's told us the whole story several times over, while we work,' said the mother.

'We all keep very cheery here,' the uncle said, breaking a small silence, 'and when we have made enough money we shall go back to Triglav and regain health and happiness and live like free Zlatorogs on the mountains again. Even with my affliction I can get work with a brother of mine who has a smithy.'

Whereupon he began to hum a song from a well-loved opera of Cosin's:

> Oh there are mountain-sides where I may stray
> Where flashing stream makes roundelay
> Where every trail
> Invites you, 'Come away, away'.

They all began to take up this refrain, even Rosa, who had gulped down the remains of her bun and was now, like the rest, lavishing attention on the damask, over which her hands scrambled like little crabs.

Edging my way round the table, I said at Letitia's left ear, 'I see you don't care much for conversation with me, so I will make my way home. Do me the kindness, pray, to see me as far as your downstairs door.'

A glance passed between her and her mother, who nodded without interrupting the song. Letitia arose, collected the thumb-nail of candle, and awaited me at the top of the stairs. Bidding farewell to the others, I took her arm and went down with her.

'This work's no good for you, Letty,' I said softly. 'You should leave your family and find some interesting job that will pay better.'

'How can I leave my own family? Trust you to say something like that! You're downright selfish, just as Bonny said you were.'

'I bought Rosa a bun, didn't I? Don't be on the offensive all the time, or you'll get nowhere – your uncle Joze evidently understands that simple principle.'

'Never mind him. I won't fawn as he does, if that's what you're hoping. Let me tell you, I'm a Progressive, same as Otto and his wife, and I'm proud of it.'

I held her arm. 'Don't be a silly girl. That'll only bring you trouble, as if you haven't trouble enough. You'd help your family more by getting a better job and contributing to their income.'

'They depend on me and I on them. I'm proud of that solidarity. Truth is, I'd be ashamed to leave them.'

'Do you all sleep together on the floor?'

She hesitated, looking away to hide her face in the shadows. 'There's no other place to sleep, as you've seen ... A friend promises to bring a proper bed one day.'

Slipping an arm about her waist, I said, 'Let me offer you a bed. No, come, I'm serious, Letitia. I'm not the selfish pig you think. You're a pretty spirited girl and deserve better than this. You shall have my bed and I will happily roll up on the floor in my rug. Don't protest! Call goodnight to your uncle and come away with me.'

She struggled but I held her tight until her candle dripped its wax down my jacket.

'You would exploit my situation, too! I know what you're after. I've seen the looks you give Armida – yes, and the way you sneak away with the little bitch, don't you worry, Master de Chirolo!'

'I won't have you say a word against Armida. That's just jealousy speaking. Leave her out of this. I'm making you a proper invitation.'

'Well, then, you shan't have from me what you get so easily from her, and that's my proper answer!'

Rubbing my nose in her hair – which proved none too sweet-smelling – I said, 'Now, enough of that. I only offered you a comfortable bed. A little pleasure would be good for you – any-one can see that you aren't properly appreciated here, except as a work-hand. We could have much more fun together, hurting nobody. Come, don't be shy, really I won't hurt you. Besides, dear Letty, you aren't a virgin, are you?'

She twisted her head away from me, turning it into the darkness again.

'Let me go.'

'Come with me, just tonight. You shall sleep in bed alone, that I promise. You're no virgin, are you?'

Still looking away, blushing, she said, 'Only rich girls like Armida can afford the luxury of virtue. Isn't that it?'

'So it's a luxury, is it? Well, you're obviously not used to luxuries. Most girls I know think it a penance.'

She pulled herself away from me. 'Go home, Perian. Find someone else – I'm sure it's easy for you. I must work for a few more hours yet.'

'I only tried to do you a favour – I don't imagine you enjoy sleeping on the same mattress as your mother and your crippled uncle, however cheerful they may be. Not to mention the kids. But I want to ask you a favour, then perhaps you'll feel better.'

While I was talking, I was working closer to her again, won-dering if a hand slipped up her skirt might not be more effec-tive than reasoning.

'What do you want?'

'Letitia, I've seen how deft your fingers are. Make me a splen-did shirt for my General Gerald, like the one you made for Bonihatch but a little grander ...'

She pushed my hand away. 'Bonny told you the price of those shirts. We'll gladly make you one up if we are paid.'

'Paid! By the holy bones, Letitia! Am I not your friend? Did I offer to charge you for my bed? Can't you just give a friend a shirt? You know I'm pretty well as poor as you, so don't be mercenary.'

'. . . It isn't possible . . .'

'Nothing's possible with you, it seems. Save your miserable wick – I'm off.'

And with ruffled feelings I made her unlock the door and escaped into the dark court.

With the Turkish emergency, more people than usual were about in the streets. I passed several files of pikemen on the march, and a line of cavalry; but I spoke to nobody, and soon climbed the stairs to my lonely billet in the Street of the Wood Carvers.

The next day was a Friday, when I was due to pay a weekly visit to Seemly Moleskin, the family astrologer. Before I dressed, and as I was giving my amulet its daily polish, the Ottomans outside the city began a bombardment.

I heard a cannon-ball crash somewhere not far distant; later, when I was on the streets, people I spoke to said that the damage was negligible, and the barrage soon stopped.

It may have been that they were aiming for a ship newly arrived up the river, which brought a detachment of heavy cavalry to the aid of Malacia. This was a gesture from the Duke of Tuscady, an ally of Bishop Gondale IX. I went by the Satsuma to see the horses being off-loaded, and the cavalrymen talking to their mounts as to old friends.

There was no denying that the previous evening had brought me little success. I had scarcely spoken to Armida, de Lambant and Bedalar had disappeared, Letitia had proved unexpectedly difficult – not that I really cared about her – and I had not got a glance at Bengtsohn's slides. There was every reason to hope that Seemly Moleskin might have something exciting in prospect.

The old man sat as usual at the mid-point of the Maltese Steps, a tied boy sporting among the skins and bronze globes near his raised chair. I greeted him politely, thinking how ashen he looked in sunlight, as if he had been carried here from a century underground.

Pulling his long animal upper-lip, the astrologer nodded, at which his owl also nodded without opening its eyes.

'Are there cheerful tidings for me this week, sire?' I asked, presenting my contribution to his coffers.

'The constellations and signatures are in unfavourable conjunction. Against the heat of Saturn must be set the icefields of idleness. Even those who run free amid the fields of green are also walkers down a slow and narrow alley. For you, buskins are now so thick-soled you no longer tread the everyday ground, so that what you imagine is your territory may be quickly occupied by another.'

'Do you speak, sire, of my work, my play, or my love?'

'I speak in universals, so that what does not specify is specific to each. You hold nothing tight and fall when you believe you fly. Nor can you wear a general's shirt without also being a prince.'

'I wanted to play the prince, if it's Bengtsohn's play you mean.'

'So you shall play the prince, but the occasions that wheel overhead suggest a salutary turn, less regal than legal. Unless you strive to understand Satan better, the rewards of your play may seem a bitter harvest.'

Thus he went on for some while, occasionally burning little scrolls of sweet-smelling paper. Seemly Moleskin was eloquent this week; I took no great pleasure from his current drift. After listening for a while, I ventured to ask him another direct question.

'Sire, I have made a secret engagement to be married. I'm speaking now of my life and not of something I'm playing. Can you say if the lady and I will make a happy match?'

'Though you may think yourself the most flexible of men, yet you are held frozen in an attitude which will undo you. You think you grasp what you grasp; you believe you touch what you touch; but the smoke rises from a dead fire. Fruit smells fresh even as the cucumbers lie rotting by the roadside; the dust you see drifting at the crossroads will not tell you how many men have passed there; and among your friends lies the cruellest deceit which poses as no deceit.'

'Should I mistrust Armida, then?'

'Lie on a bed of thistles if you need to watch zealously all night, yet you may know you will be badly pricked after this omen appears in the sky above Malacia; a black horse with silver hooves.'

Pondering on these riddles, I said, 'Sir Seemly, you have only ash for my spirit today. Is there really trouble coming for me if I see a horse in the sky? A black horse with silver hooves?'

He scratched the great wart on his left cheek, from which blossomed forth a cataract of yellow hairs, curling in every direction like snakes on a miniature Medusa's head.

'First comes the black horse, aslant in the clouds; then your troubles at ground level.'

'I'll try to avoid looking up, then.'

'I'd advise you to look *out*!' he said sharply. He had counselled my mother in her lifetime and my grandmother before that; the mysteries he dealt in had bound the daily lives of Malacia together for millennia. I wished I had saved my pence for a bite of food. Saluting, I left him, though a pungent flavour of goat lingered about me for some while.

The presence of hundreds of Turks outside the city was not enough to interrupt the drama of Prince Mendicula and his unfaithful princess. Still trailing a whiff of goat, I entered the grand gates of the Chabrizzi and prepared to stand once more before the zahnoscope.

Armida had already arrived, looking as fresh as ever in a gown I had not seen before, with a broad sash and buffon over it. Bedalar was with her and conversing amiably with them both was de Lambant. We greeted one another warmly.

'We have a pair of winners here,' Guy said, when the girls were addressing themselves to the subject of clothes.

'*And* undeserved. I had hoped to introduce you to Armida.'

'I thought I'd waited long enough. You're a little pensive this morning?'

'Have you seen any black horses galloping over the rooftops?'

Letitia soon joined the group, giving me an aslant look.

I walked over to less glamorous company, which consisted of Bonihatch, who was practising incorrect lunges with a wooden sword, the bent figure of Otto Bengtsohn, Solly, and another assistant, a lumbering man-boy called Rhino. We were due to play the scene where General Gerald is closeted with Jemima and takes her into a wood; Bengtsohn was supervising the arrangement of necessary properties.

Seeing me, the old man told the others to continue with the work while he took me to one side.

'Am I to inspect the finished slides at last?'

'Pray do not persist about that, what might be a sore point with some.'

'What, then?'

'Are you feeling today courageous, Perian?'

'Like the general, I am always brave.'

'Good. Though bravery isn't a matter always of cutting some figures, you understand, or of playing even a role. It is something what you have to *be*. There are dangers all about, all the time. We may finish in the Toi with our throats yet cut, even if the Ottoman don't slaughter us.'

'You asked me a question and I answered straight. Why then a straight sermon?'

'Not a sermon, think nothing about it. Thinking is dangerous in Malacia. In three days' time there will come the Feast of the Buglewing – then the populace will cease to think and become drunken. But the people what hold power in Malacia, they never cease like machines to think, day or night, feast or fast.'

'Who was the sinister man in the gallery last night, with the black frock coat?'

He directed an upwards gaze at me which filtered through his straggling eyebrows. 'Better for you not to know. Keep him off from your mind.'

'I know he is of the Supreme Council. I cared little for the look of him. Is he part of the reason why you will not show us the mercurization?'

'Better you should not know. Let's speak of other things.' He cleared his throat. 'Listen and take not offence, what I don't intend. The Zlatorogs are mine friends. I know a thousand things from them to your one, so have a care there. Do not fool with Letitia, or her uncle Joze and I will see you regret.'

'Fool with her? What do you mean, fool with her? Is feeding her sister and trying to order a shirt from her improper? Or any business of yours? Or her uncle's? Because I do your wretched play for you, it does not mean you order my life for me.'

'Lives are for ordering. I tell you I know a thousand things from the Zlatorogs to your one. I have spoke on that subject and that is all what I will say.'

'You've already said too much.'

He nodded and continued, 'The other message what I have for you is of more high import. It comes from my mighty and rich master. Andrus Hoytola requires for you to present yourself at him to his mansion in the siesta hour. It is there, and

82

not here before my zahnoscope, that some tax may be put on your courage.'

'If he wants me, I shall be there. Have you been telling tales to him?'

His manner changed, becoming confidential, as it had on the occasion when he first showed me the zahnoscope.

'Listen, I was young once, before I was kicked out of Tolkhorm for my revolutionary views. I know better than to tell tales in that quarter, rest assured. I take care how I tread in Malacia.'

'That black Council coat last evening convinced me there were serious things loose in the world, never fear. What did that man want in Hoytola's gallery?'

In a hurried voice, he said, 'This is not your concern, I have said. That man is the Devil. All I say is, having the Turks at our back door has improved the standing of my master on more than one count, what the Turks alarm the Council. So you get a summons. A little action is wanted.

'Inertia has been always the most chief of Malacia's weapons, whether in peace whether war. Inertia it is what has helped it somehow to survive throughout two thousand millennia from history.'

Bonihatch had arrived, rolling down his sleeves and grinning. He butted in, in his impulsive way, to say, 'Yes, and the Council will rely on inertia again in this new Turkish crisis, if they can, Otto. The plague is on their side – not for the first time in history. Now that the Dog Star falls to bed with the sun, the plague gets in its stride again.'

'There have been ten burials at St Braggart's this week so far, from the plague alone,' I said. 'But that isn't going to protect us from the Ottomans.'

Bonihatch looked knowing. 'Ah, but think how much faster the visitation will move among the ranks of Suleiman's sons, camped with foul water out among the foothills.'

'Is right,' agreed Otto. 'It's just an old women's tale that the Turk don't catch plague. They rot of it just like what we do. Besides, there's word what our enemy are not Ottomans proper, but the followers from the Bosnian king, Stefan Tvrtko. Their faith is Bogumilism. They'll fall easy to the plague.'

Bonihatch dismissed this with a shake of his whiskers and said, 'Our stinking Council hope to sit and wait for death to do their work – in which time we could be invaded as strongly by the plague as by Tvrtko. A plea was sent to Igara and Saville and Vamonal for supporting armies, but in every case nothing has returned except excuses penned on richest vellum. So much for the rotten, corrupt system!'

'Only Tuscady has sent some troops – the rest know how low is our exchequer,' I said.

'We should let the Turk in, to lay waste Malacia – then we could start again clean,' said Bonihatch, savagely.

'No, no, Bonny. That medicine is worse than what is the ailment. Turks must be defeated, then revolution comes from within.'

'So what's to be done? I gather you have some ideas,' I said to him.

Again the transfixing eye peered from under the cliff of brow.

'Ideas enough wicked to please the Council. In particular, the young Duke Renardo supports them. You shall see, you shall see. Go to Hoytola this siesta time.' He altered his tone, and added, 'Change. That's what's needed in Malacia, change from within.' His voice sank still lower. 'Progress.'

I knew students at the university who professed Progressivism because it suited the cut of their clothes; but the word sounded odd from this ageing Northerner, as it had from Letitia on the previous evening.

'Well, Otto, let's get the sofa arranged and the zahnoscope set up.'

When the zahnoscope had done its work for the day, Armida offered to drive me to her father. Bedalar and Guy were off to see Caylus train for the bull-fight, so Armida and I were alone together; proudly, she escorted me to one of the Chabrizzi stables, where her birthday present stood – a neat little post-chaise, with her mare, Betsy, complaisant between the shafts.

At last I had admired and envied it enough and Armida took the reins. The carriage sprang along on its two fragile wheels. Its body was daintily turned, its panels shone like silk, its gilded woodwork glittered in the sun. I coveted it a great deal, desiring a masculine version for myself which I could drive at breakneck speed and astonish my friends. In this charming vehicle we bowled along, Armida and I.

'What does your father want with me?'

'That he must explain. The Turks have something to do with it.'

I fell silent. I already knew what Otto had told me, that the Turkish force was commanded by Stefan Tvrtko the Bosnian; his name was being bandied about town. It was said that he was immense, swart, ferocious, that he was no better than a brigand who had thrown in his lot with the Ottomans for gain. It was said that his kingdom was no greater than a valley in the Balkan mountains, and that he had strangled his son Sebastian. What bearing such a villain had on a man of quality like Andrus Hoytola was a matter as yet for speculation.

The Hoytola mansion stood beyond the Fragrant Quarter and the Avenue of the Armourers, in a secluded street not far from the Vamonal Canal. We drove past it and on to the racecourse, where we found the head of the Hoytola family in the stables, supervising the care of his Arabs. A boy took Betsy's head, and Armida and I walked over to him.

The first piece of information Hoytola vouchsafed me was that he owned eighty horses, a good proportion of them Arab stallions, and most of them kept on the Hoytola country estate, Juracia.

Andrus Hoytola wore a supercilious look, rather like one of his thoroughbreds. He was countrified this morning, in a mustard sporting-coat, breeches and gaiters, after the Northern manner. Breaking off a discussion regarding dressage with his grooms, he turned and addressed me formally.

'The annual Feast of the Buglewing commences in three days. One has to prepare one's thoroughbreds in proper time, in order to make the best display.'

I could think of nothing to say to that; nor did Hoytola appear to expect a reply. After a pause, he addressed me again.

'One hears that you are progressing favourably in the Prince Mendicula play, de Chirolo. Excellent. One anticipates that it will be an interesting thing. Bengtsohn desired originally to apply the story to present-day low life, but that would never do, not even in his native Tolkhorm where manners are more barbarous than here. Set a few millennia ago, among people of proper standing, the story acquires dignity, one judges.'

His words had a dry quality, as if his mouth had developed a prejudice against saliva.

'It would tell against my career to act in a story of low life,' I said. 'Although the silly innocent trust which Mendicula is representing as having in his wife Patricia might be more credible if it were told of a grocer rather than of a prince.'

He put his thumbs in his waistcoat pocket. 'How droll you are! Nobody wants plays about *grocers*. The creatures would get above themselves, for one thing. No audience could conceivably care whether or no a *grocer's* wife was faithful to him.'

The conversation appeared about to expire from difficulty. I glanced at Armida, but she was no help, for she was looking at the horses and rubbing their long noses.

I said to her father, as easily as I could, 'I must admit that the Mendicula tragi-comedy strikes me as absurd. I'm sure Pozzi Kemperer would agree.'

'In what way absurd?'

'Perian thinks the story banal, Papa,' Armida said, flashing me a glance I could not interpret. 'He says it might as well have been written a million years ago.'

'An interesting remark. Surely one's interest in the play is precisely that it might have been written a million years ago. Some things are eternal and must be eternally re-expressed. Those desperate straits of love, which Bengtsohn effectively conveys, appeal to us because they apply as much today as yesterday.'

'I see that,' said I, feebly. 'But there's no moral in the play. The characters are stupid. Mendicula is a fool to be so trusting, the General a scoundrel to cheat his friend, Patricia not much better than a – hm – a loose woman, for all her royal blood, and Jemima is indecisive. I like to have at least one character with a resounding morality.'

'One might judge that the morality lies in the whole rather than the parts,' said Hoytola.

'It certainly doesn't lie in my part.'

There was a small silence. Then Hoytola spoke again, more animatedly.

'One is pleased to see that you are an independently minded young man. My daughter has suggested to one that you might be interested in undertaking a small adventure. One perceives that she has not misjudged.'

The horses as well as the humans were observing me now. There was a strong smell of straw in the stables which made

86

my nose twitch; my instinct told me that it would be undignified to sneeze before Armida's father.

'What sort of small adventure have you in mind?'

'A small adventure that would assist the Hoytolas, that would benefit Malacia, that would confer glory on you.'

It sounded like a large small adventure. When he told me what it was, it sounded even larger. But the eyes of Armida were upon me, no less than the ruminative eyes of the Arabs. I said I would do what he asked, in as bold a voice as the occasion would allow.

On the morn appointed for my small adventure, I was bustling about early, in imitation of the bustle in the streets. This was the first day of one of Malacia's most ancient festival weeks, the Feast of the Buglewing, consecrated both to immemorial victories and the mystical relationship between mankind and the creatures of the air.

That relationship bore heavily on my mind; I was about to become a creature of the air: I kept recalling old Seemly Moleskin's warning about a black horse with silver shoes in the sky. I made my movements vigorous, to dispel gloom.

Perching on the edge of my chair, I penned notes to my father and my sister, Katarina. Writing with great flourishes, I besought them to come from their separate retreats and witness my hour of glory, since it might be my last. I summoned a boy from below, paying him two denarios to deliver the messages expeditiously.

I tried an air on my guitar, I attempted a poem and a farewell message to the world. Then I dashed down the street to Mandaro for his blessing.

In Stary Most, elements of the grand parade were already assembling. The old grey and terracotta walls echoed to cries of men, boys and animals. Two shaggy mangonels were there, standing patiently like all elephants, as their faces were painted white and their long, curving tusks adorned. But the great barbaric sight was at the east end, under the tower of the Stary Dom, for there the civic herd of tyrant-greaves was marshalled. These furious beasts, the kings of all ancestral animals, were herded by their traditional herdsmen, satyrs, who had brought the carnivores in from their stockades on the Six Lagoons road.

Oh, the sight of those primitive beings, half-man, half-goat, trotting round their enormous charges! I was impelled to press among the rabble of small boys and tradespeople who gathered to see the horned herdsmen manoeuvre the tyrant-greaves into line. There were four of the monsters, standing six metres high, their scales dappled yellow and green – or more yellow and grey, for these were old beasts. Their tails were secured in great loops over their backs with chains passed round their necks. Each beast was muzzled, with an iron cage over its predatory mouth. They were subdued enough – only satyrs could handle them – but their enormous bird-feet shuffled on the cobbles as if they longed to dash into the crowd and wreak disaster. Tyrants and devil-jaws can scarcely be cowed. They are never tamed. On holy days, they are essential to the ceremony.

Mandaro gave me absolution. 'There is unity in all things, and duality,' he said. 'We live physically in a fine city; we also live in a forest of dark beliefs. This day, you are granted an occasion to rise above them both.'

'Will you be watching me, father?'

'Indeed. And now I'm going to watch the satyrs and tyrants. Like you, I find the barbarous sight moving. We admit them to the city on ceremonial occasions and no others. That is fitting.'

No sooner had I returned to my room than a knock came at the door. There stood Armida, her whey-faced old chaperon behind her. I got the door between the two of them and poured kisses on Armida's lips, but she wriggled from me and withdrew.

'A carriage is awaiting us outside, Perian. I see you're ready.' Her mood was rather severe – or certainly not plushy enough to greet a hero with.

'I didn't notice any carriage down there.'

'Not in the alleyway, in Stary Most.'

'I'm feeling all the better for seeing you. I confess to a slight attack of nerves. Can we shut your woman outside and stoke each other's fires a little?'

'We must hurry down to the Bucintoro.' All this said in a whisper.

'I'm doing all this for your sake, Armida, as you know.'

'Don't try to blackmail me.'

I grasped her again, slipping a hand down the front of her dress until it encompassed the greater part of one elegant breast. 'Armida, how is it that out of all the young bucks in this throng-
88

ing city, from its grooms to its princes, your illustrious father chose me for this singular and dangerous honour?'

'You want a chance to rise in the world. If we are ever to marry – but there is also the question of your behaviour – then you must distinguish yourself, as we agreed.'

'I see. You put my name to him. That was what I wanted to know.'

She looked at me challengingly as we went through the door, where I bowed to Yolaria waiting on the landing.

'I thought your seriousness should be put to the test, Perian,' Armida said. 'You know that in general I am forbidden to leave the house after dark, unless it is to go to some occasion, so that my evenings are spent playing the virginals or reading Plutarch and Martyn Tupper aloud to my younger sister. I have recently had an account of how you spend your evenings, hanging about low taverns and attempting unsuccessfully the seduction of sewing-women ...'

She was leading the way down the winding stair, Yolaria behind her, then I. I cried out in rage, 'Who has been telling you these tales?'

Without turning her head, Armida replied, 'Letitia Zlatorog. A reliable witness in the circumstances, one might think ...'

I flew into a rage, believing attack the only safe retreat.

'That little creature! How jealous she must be to try and create mischief between us! All I did was attempt to purchase a shirt from her, as Bonihatch has done, and she cooks up a story of seduction! Why, she's so plain! Do I fall about in jealousy when you as Patricia loll in Bonihatch's sordid Mendiculan arms – though I have to watch you enjoying it for minutes at a stretch?'

'I told you I hate him. I hate his whiskers. I hate his odour of oil and acids and custard. I think him plain. But you think Letitia so plain that you must slip your hand up her skirt and invite her to your bed, your bed which I thought sacred to us! How dare you?'

All this passed over and through the bobbing head of Armida's chaperon, which increased my anger and sense of injustice.

'So! Out of spite, you set up this challenge which would show me as a coward if I did not accept – whereupon your father could send me packing ... You have a horrid scheming mind, Armida. You know that little seamstress means nothing to me.

89

She simply intends to make mischief between us.'

'It's you who have made the mischief.'

In fine high tempers, we made our way to the carriage – not Armida's personal one but a little town coupé, with a seat behind for the driver. Biting our tongues – being unable to bite each other's – we permitted the doors to be closed and the horse to be shaken into action. Yolaria sat imperviously between us, presenting an old yellow cheek to us both.

As we rolled out of the ancient square, we came into a concourse of traffic arriving both from the North Gate and from St Marco's. Our progress was slow, and slower for the silence between us. I was so angry that she should think I cared anything for Letitia.

Outside the coupé, the faces of young and old alike were predominantly cheerful. The Buglewing marked the legendary battle of our remotest ancestors, countless millions of years ago, when the forces of the someone-or-other defeated the forces of someone-else in continent-wide battle; consequently, it was a time to be cheerful.

Even with the Ottomans almost within hailing distance, festivities went forward. The guilds were arriving in strength, with rich processions from the Guildhall, bearing the banners and emblems of their trades. And the religious orders were also present, with many representations of Satan, God and Minerva among their banners; they moved in solemn ranks, preceded by trumpeters, carrying torches, jewelled reliquaries and swinging censers which perfumed the air as they went.

In the midst of these holy men in their grey, black and brown gowns was a burst of colour, white, crimson and gold, where the Bishop Elect of Malacia, Gondale IX, was borne along on a canopied throne set on a platform carried shoulder-high by monks. Gondale was thin and so silvered by age as to be almost transparent; he swathed himself in white for purity and encased the white in a magnificent crimson gown which spilled down from the throne to the platform and from the platform almost to the ground. As he progressed, the holy old man scattered silver coin to the crowd with one translucent hand. The coin bore images of Dark on one side and Light on the other.

Following the Bishop's procession were the ancestral animals of his zoo. The crowd roared its pleasure at the sight as if it too were an animal. First came the bird after which the festival was named, chained to the gauntlet of the Buglewing Keeper. It perched drowsily on his raised fist, its brilliant plumage unfluttered, its toothed beak on its breast. By its side a flautist played soothing buglewing music.

Close behind the bird came other ancestrals, after which other festivals of the year were named. First, a great old halberd-head – shatterhorn, in popular parlance – with three horns ranked one behind the other on its enormous skull. It plodded majestically, its rider controlling it with gold reins bolted to the nasal horn.

This living engine of war was followed by two other giants of battles past, the shaggy mangonels I had seen being prepared with riders perched high behind their ears; and wattle-tassets, striding with dignity on their massive hind legs and surveying the mob with shrewd eyes.

After came the lesser fry, led, not ridden – such common ancestrals as yellow hauberks, hopping and croaking; yatterhobs; and a team of tree-snaphances or grab-skeeters, to use their vulgar name, their mottled skins gleaming in the sun.

Last plodded an amiable casque-body – Old Trundles to the multitude. The two lethal spikes had been removed from its tail, but its dorsal plates were intact. It was a male, and a fine one, its head raised by the chained pole on which it was led.

These majestic creatures pleased everybody.

Mighty tableaux suitable to the day followed. They rumbled through the streets on heavy wheels, bearing the most beautiful scenes of mythology and pageantry that artists could devise. The glowing dreams of the world were let loose in St Marco's, and the lower classes ran by the floats, cheering and waving, men and women, as if there was nothing to their lives but glowing dreams. Beside them in a slower stream went the streetsellers, turning the natural appetites of festivity to their advantage, offering all manner of drinks and fizzes and juices and fruits and spiced meats and kebabs, hot or cold; as well as cakes, tarts, fudges, halva, pitta, bourek, ices and other sweet concoctions. The air became full of good smells. Holy and wordly things combined in our nostrils as incense mingled with the fragrance of fresh-baked bread and pies.

During the evening we would be treated to more challenging smells, as heretics were burnt at the stake – men who believed in one god only, or who claimed themselves descended from frenetic apes.

Our carriage proceeded with difficulty through this *mêlée*. Armida called an instruction to the driver and we turned into a side street, thus avoiding the main crowds and arriving safely behind the Bucintoro to which we made our way on foot.

What a beautiful sight is the Bucintoro! Great merchants' palaces flank its southern side while gardens and the slow river flank its northern. The palaces are white in marble or golden in our local stone.

On this occasion, as on similar ones, fences had been erected on the northern side, to keep back the crowds of commoners. The parade itself stretched between the elegant new Park Bridge and the quaint old Stary Most Bridge, with its tumbledown freight of houses, and further even than that, its official length being demarcated at one end by the memorial statue of Founder Despot confronting the First Magician and, at the other, by the ancient stonework of the Merchants' Church. Between statue and church, blue-and-black flags flew every pace of the way. On the towers of the palaces perched the flighted people, enjoying the finest views of the ceremony.

Armoured knights on grandly caparisoned steeds paraded here, as well as town companies of halberdiers and pikemen. The military array was enlivened by the silver band of the Militia, resplendent in gaudy ancestral skins. Among this warlike splendour the four captive tyrants had their place. They entered the Bucintoro skittishly, disturbed by the crowds and the blaze of the trumpets, so that their satyrs had difficulty in keeping them in line. Each monster had a satyr astride its shoulders, perched in a saddle. The tyrants' tails curved high over their bodies and over the heads of their riders. The ends of the tails were linked by golden chains to collars about their throats. Those tails were too powerful to be allowed freedom among the crowds. Since I had seen this barbaric company in Stary Most earlier in the morning, the satyrs had garlanded their heads and horns with laurel crowns and their loins with honeysuckle.

Along the quays was more noise where a pipe band played sea shanties. Many ships, foreign as well as Malacian, were at their moorings. A Navidadian schooner, a fine three-master ship with high prow, and two junks, lay alongside our native galliasses and triremes, so well adapted to the navigational hazards of the Middle Sea. These vessels were dressed overall and bore a considerable freight of sailors in their yard-arms.

All this great assembly would later have its eyes, if not its prayers, set on me. The thought made my stomach turn over like a top-heavy barque. Later there would be tournaments, masques, weddings (the Feast of the Buglewing was a propitious time for weddings), burnings, a circus and fireworks, until well into the night. The fountain in Stary Most would spurt red wine as a gesture from the Council to the poor. All that would take place – all and more, for there could hardly be a soul in the multitude now assembling who had not made some special arrangement or assignation as his or her private contribution to the public celebrations. Later, later. First came I, Perian de Chirolo, in one of my most foolish and least coveted roles!

Armida and I were led by halberdiers to the front of one of the merchants' palaces where, on an improvised platform, stood several dignitaries whose faces were as uninviting as their costumes were imposing. (But not that terrible man from the Supreme Council whose appearance was so formidable; I judged that *he* chose not to venture forth in public; night and privacy were part of his equipment.) Among these dignitaries was Andrus Hoytola, who sauntered forward, beckoned me up on to the platform, and gave me a few unsmiling words of reassurance. I glanced round; Armida had gone.

'One has another hour to wait,' Hoytola said, taking snuff. He turned away and resumed his conversation with a man whose face I recognized. It was the Duke of Renardo, a fair and stalwart youth with florid visage. He looked every inch the nobleman, in his gold mail, with roll-up stockings and shoes with platform soles, square-blocked toes and high-buckled tongues. I'd have given the world – or at least the next hour of the world – for his satin breeches with matching loose coat over the mail. His loose coat had vertical pockets; its seams were decorated with elaborate gold ornamentation into which the motif of the House of Renardo was worked. The Zlatorogs had probably stitched that coat in their sweatshop.

The young duke gave me a glance of appraisal and resumed his talk with Hoytola, which I deduced to be worth a ducat a syllable, judging by Hoytola's favourable response to each syllable as it was uttered. It was this same duke who had been mentioned as supporting Hoytola; he was said generally to be enlightened in the interests of the people, even backing them against the wishes of the Council. Or so it was rumoured; when the Council was anonymous, it was difficult to divine its wishes, although, on a time-honoured principle, the assumption that wishes were for the worst generally turned out to be well-founded where anonymity was involved.

From my exposed position on the platform I could watch everything.

The grand concourse was filling rapidly. The Militia made music at the east end before the Merchants' Church. As usual, the groundlings had assembled before the affluent. Pedlars moved about selling toys and pamphlets as well as food. I tried to pick out my father's face in the mob, but it was hopeless. Nor could I see the Mantegan banner, so I did not know if my sister was present – or even if her husband Volpato was back from his latest bout of travel.

Waving hands attracted my attention. There, behind the barricade, stood my friends de Lambant and Portinari, with two girls. It was Bedalar with de Lambant, while de Lambant's sister, Smarana, was escorted by Portinari. When I made them a bow some people applauded, and the tips of my ears went red.

I stood at one end of the platform, which would shortly be the cynosure of all eyes, slightly apart from the stony-faced dignitaries. The rest of the space was occupied by a number of strange objects, the like of which had never to my knowledge been seen in all the long history of Malacia.

Seven wooden frames or towers had been built above the platform. They were filled with gigantic sacks of silk which wobbled and rustled in their cages as if alive. Danger of fire attended these objects; two men with a hose and pump stood by on the platform, occasionally dousing the cages with water, which gave everyone nearby a splash.

The ends of these seven huge sacks trailed down to seven barrels, one large, six smaller, which had in their time contained wine. The barrels stood on end and were being tended by a crew of men, supervised by Bengtsohn and his man-boy, Rhino. The crew regularly poured liquid into the barrels through spouts set in the staves. They also wheeled up barrows containing a gritty substance with which they topped up the barrels.

94

Beyond this activity, at the far end of the platform, was a groom gentling a stallion, a mettlesome black from Hoytola's stud; it bore his colours as well as the flag of Malacia, draped over its hindquarters. It had been specially shod for the occasion with silver horseshoes. I looked speculatively at the horse. It looked speculatively away from me.

On the pavement below the platform stood a long, black carriage covered with black drapes and guarded by two gentlemen dressed in black, even to masks over their faces. As if aware that they struck a sombre note on a cheerful day, they bore a wreath of white flowers above them on a pole.

It was this mournful cortège as much as anything which made me feel that I was attending my execution. When a messenger came to the platform and thrust up a message between the railings in a cleft stick, I snatched it as if it were a pardon. It was a note from my revered father.

I suffer from the colic yet you never visit me. Or it may be the gall-stone. I do not eat. I am busy with my research, so that I have ceased to bother about feeding myself. It is all very interesting. Never trust doctors.

Your letter was welcome, although your hand does not improve. I think you should not ride horses. You were not successful in that line as a boy, no more than in any other line. Meanwhile, I elucidate much that was obscure regarding the diet of Philip of Macedon, or Makedonia. I have no guilders to spare for fancy shirts or other fripperies. Please take care. Why don't you come and visit me? I never go out since the parrot died.

You must not expect me to approve your foolish antics. You will only fall off. I am better today but shall be worse tomorrow, so send my best wishes.

Your devoted
Father

Well, there, I thought, tucking the paper into my tunic pocket. I must go and see the old swine. Assuming I don't fall off.

To quell a certain shaking at the knees, I went over to speak to Bengtsohn, who was working at the barrels. He had removed his old fur jacket, and a rough canvas shirt adhered to his ribs; his minions toiling beside him were stripped to the waist. His manner was eager and excited as he ordered more liquid to be poured into the largest wine-barrel of the seven.

'So, Otto, you are practising the distillation of Hollands in public. Or is this an example of Progress?'

Conspiratorially, he said, 'Do not utter aloud that word. It is that, to be certain, in as prime a case what this ancient city saw ever. The great Fatember himself should be here to paint this historic scene. We've a new weapon of warfare. It will change things, and all poor men are for change.'

He dashed sweat from his brow, looking about to find something to shout at, but apparently everything proceeded according to plan.

'Why are you so contradictory, Otto? You long to change things, you work for progress, yet you write a stale old drama which might have been performed a million years ago.' I had dropped my voice to match his.

Again one of his searching looks. 'Try to learn, try to understand what the world, what to you seems so good, is like really – full with cruel injustices. If your mind is ordinary, your station in life is sufficient, you are then safe, enchanted, when at least youthfulness is with your side. But if you are poor, if you have a mind beyond ordinary – if you *think*! – then you need to change things, then the world with its powerful men roll against you like a spiked wheel.'

'For you the buglewings fly in vain.'

He made a contemptuous gesture. 'There are those – even on this platform – what continue to exploit us, even on days of festivity.'

'If it makes you so unhappy, then stop criticizing.'

Otto wiped his hands on his shirt and replied almost pityingly. 'When a man ceases for to be blind, does he deliberately then blind himself? You have such a cossetted mind – wake up, Perian, see what's happening really! Yes, I work for change and I write the play in old-fashioned style, just to have it at all accepted. My Mendicula play was the intention to be set in present-day among poor folk like the Zlatorogs, not among princes. You know I love not princes.' He gave me a sly grin. 'Then, with its success, I would do another drama of the poor, for exposing more of the truth. But those what own the Arts don't want for to know about the misery of starvation or seeing die your children, as mine own children died long ago once. All this talk about religion and science and art – they also are the toys from the rulers. They never aid the common people.'

'I see it differently. It doesn't affect everyone in that way.'

My placatory remark excited him again.

'Yes, it does. It does, with certainty. One lie in life affects every life. We swim in lies, to the richest, to the poorest. Only the rich benefit by such lies, spawn them as salmons spawn eggs. The lies even affect your cosy life, though you haven't opened yet your eyes to see how it works.'

'You know I live in a garret, that I have little work, that only a week ago I was trying to scrounge a shirt for my back. Don't be so prejudiced against me.'

'No, you want to be a carriage dog – I have eyes! You won't know hardship till you're married and the kids are dying with worms crawling out from their backsides. As for that shirt you mention – let me tell you something what you fail to see. The Zlatorogs and Letitia slave their fingers to their bones for to make meet ends; they can't afford to give away shirts – it's giving away part from their life-bloods. Couldn't you see that?'

'I saw how poor they were. But Letitia is such a mean little hussy. She doesn't like me. Why, I had a little fun with her and she went straight and told Armida all about it.'

He regarded me sadly. 'She is not mean. She does not dislike. It is only that she is poor and her family also poor. That is all. That's the fact. She it a generous soul, finer than young Armida in every way, much disturbed in her heart by love for you. But family miseries distort every factor in her life.'

I gave a brief laugh. 'She loves me, so she tells Armida what I did!'

He hastened over to Rhino and set him to work on a task which involved hauling up another barrow from the pavement. The barrow contained what I took to be ash. When it was safe on the platform, Bengtsohn turned back to me.

'That's iron filings in there. We have to make careful – the danger of fire is every present but we've survived enough well so far. Where were we? Yes, we spoke of little Letty. Couldn't you try to understand her situation? Letitia loves you but knows she can never have; perhaps she told Armida, of whom she is envious naturally, in order to sow the trouble between you.'

'I am not beholden to her for that. Let's drop the subject.'

'I'll tell you something.' He edged nearer, again favouring

me with his best conspiratorial manner, one eye rising from under a hill of brow. 'Do not repeat or I'll hear, and my friends in the city will make trouble for you.

'Observe again the working of poverty, which is more strong than morality. You know Letitia. You have met her uncle Joze – a fine man, though crippled. It is he, with his penned energies, what keeps going that family. He's brave. The mother is a thing broken since her husband's demise. Now, Perian, on account of poverty, that little family, all five from them, sleep together on the floor on some mattresses, one against the another. The uncle, a man of normal inclinations but ever in that loft, he lies against Letitia. What will you say takes place?'

'She wouldn't – her mother—'

'Her mother, for the peace, for their general survival, *insists* the girl will comply to her brother's wishes. And not Letitia only – her sister Rosa also, indiscriminate. Yes. I had it from Joze, the uncle himself, one night when I took with him a drink. What else do you think can happen in the piteous circumstances, forced by exploitation?'

My pallor could be felt, creeping through me.

'It's monstrous, unnatural!' I shook my head. 'And it's illegal.'

'Far from being unnatural, as you call, it is commonplace when you have evil conditions. Poverty is more strong than morality. That's another reason why for the world must submit to progress. Misery must be decreased before everyone will choke to death on it.'

I felt the blood flow back into my face until I blushed.

'That old crippled casque-body! Are you pretending you don't blame him for what he is doing to Letitia? How do you think *she* feels?'

Otto had turned away, as if to terminate our conversation. Now he turned back.

'All I say it that unequal wealth begets unequal misery, and misery begets sin. All of us among the poor are victims alike. You should grow up and see things as they really are before your eyes.'

'You still insult me! Even the rich know that misery and vice go together, and do their best to remedy the situation. But individuals are still individuals, and have individual responsibility for their behaviour, however unfortunate they may be.'

'The individual is not important in the struggle,' he said. This

98

time he did turn away, presenting his old bent back to me as he set Rhino to work.

It was not only poverty that brought misery; wealth brought Armida a lot of unhappiness. Misery was a quality that had to be fended off with spirit, wherever it appeared.

The proud scene restored my peace of mind. The guilds had paraded round the city and were now drawn up in their ranks along the Bucintoro, adding their bright banners and costume to the colours all about. From the merchants' palaces, various personages were emerging to loll on balconies; many of the women were wearing their most gorgeous gowns. They rested their little hands on stone balustrades, clutched posies to ward off the aroma of the crowd, and gazed down – their looks always as some point resting on me.

My fears vanished. I had a role, the most dramatic of my career. I would perform it to the utmost. As for Bengtsohn, of course it was miserable to be poor, but the world was by no means as bad as he claimed. How could anyone with true heart gaze round the Bucintoro without feeling that heart beat faster with delight?

As for Letitia, poverty or no poverty, she was simply a slut. I would prove myself worthy of the fair Armida, so beauteous and so kind – our recent tiff was purely Letitia's fault, and should be smoothed over the next time I had Armida within arm's reach. At that thought, my chest swelled for all the world like the seven silk bags expanding above my head.

Hoytola and the young Duke of Renardo came over. The latter nodded obligingly to me and I bowed. He was taller than I, with the proper arrogance of his class. When he spoke, it was with gentleness.

'You're looking confident, de Chirolo. Congratulations. You have stirred up much envy among my company, who wish for the honour that is yours; but I tell them that the matter is not under my control.' He nodded at Hoytola.

'One is a little old to sail aloft oneself,' said Hoytola, defensively. He asked me if Bengtsohn had explained how everything worked.

'The principle is new on this scale,' he said, tapping the largest barrel with a gold-tipped cane. 'In these barrels we have a mixture of iron filings and water which can be stirred by the turning of yonder handle. Then Bengtsohn and his men pour in the sulphuric acid through the funnels. The resulting chemical mixture causes hydrogenous air to be expelled, lighter than ordinary air. The hydrogenous air extends upwards through this rubber hose and fills the balloon, displacing the heavier ordinary air just as bad drives out good.'

He tapped his chin with the knob of his cane as we stared up at the great sack, which was now well expanded and pressing against its enclosing wooden framework.

'The sack is made of silk, with rubber solution applied to it inside and out to render it air-tight,' Hoytola said. 'The harness dangling underneath will enable you to have some control over the balloon when it floats free. It will be released when one pulls the cord over here, which draws bolts from the framework and causes a whole section to fall away. As with this major balloon, so with the six smaller ones.'

'Very ingenious,' I said. The stallion was now being led along from the other end of the platform and fitted into the harness below the largest balloon, while, from the opposite direction, a priest was approaching with a look only priests can manage – rehearsed, I don't doubt, from their observations of the dead.

Hoytola ventured to clap me once on the shoulder.

'It is all absolutely foolproof, my boy,' he said. 'The balloons have been filling slowly for two days. In case of misadventure, the priest will administer the last rites to you. One wishes you well.'

After the last rites, a choir burst into song and the assembled multitude applauded. The black horse with the silver shoes was harnessed and induced to stand on a small platform before I climbed into the saddle. Bengtsohn came and slapped the small of my back before pulling on the dangling cord Hoytola had mentioned. The bolts snapped back, everyone fell silent. The upper section of the wooden cage opened. The balloon began to rise. Rhino and an assistant hurriedly corked off the barrel and stood back. Rhino saluted. The reins and harness about me tightened, squeaking as it did so. Rhino's monstrous face fell away. I was airborne!

My mount moved restively, but it was so secured that it could not shy or rear; in fact, I was safer on it in the air than I would have been on the ground.

I looked about in rapture. My eyes met those of a fair charmer on one of the balconies. She threw me a posy of pink flowers which missed by a good margin; women are rarely accurate in such matters. I raised my hat in reply and a cheer went up from the crowd. Again I looked down, seeking a glimpse of my friends and my sister. It made me dizzy. I gazed upwards instead.

Hoytola's hydrogenous balloon was swollen like a drunkard's stomach. It was made of silk panels coloured alternately blue and black, Malacia's colours. Stubby wings of papier mâché had been attached, together with a ferocious buglewing's head of the same material, with open beak and gleaming silvered teeth. I could gauge what impression this contrivance made by the great 'Oooh!' which came up from the throats of the crowd as we drifted between the buildings.

The balloon rose steadily. Such breeze as there was came from the east. I adjusted my seat more comfortably and had time to take in the glint of sun along the Toi and the ships nestled there, their decks peppered with upturned faces. On the far bank of the river the vineyards began in endless array, fading into distance. The entire Bucintoro lay beneath me.

We reached the level of its highest towers. From these towers graceful figures detached themselves, swinging towards me with strong pulses of their wings. I waved my hat at them. They waved back.

These guardians of Malacia, the flighted people, were soon fluttering about me – six of them, three men, three women, dressed simply in a sort of loin-cloth apiece. They made no distinction for gender with regard to clothes, so that the women were bare of breast. At all three of the females I gazed appreciatively. They were young and beautifully formed – their kind lose the gift of flight once youth is over, after which they have to walk the earth like the rest of us. They smiled and called, sporting in the air with abandon like otters in a rock-pool.

Hydrogenous exhilaration filled me. What luck, what good fortune was mine! How I longed for Armida to be with me, that my happiness might have banners!

With my pretty friends fluttering about me, fanned by breezes from the strong pulse of their wings, I drifted across the city in a westerly direction.

There lay Stary Most to my right, smudged by smoke from its chimneys, with Satsuma and the river beyond. Below was St Marco's. The balloon sailed between its twin towers, on which more flighted people stood, saluting, laughing, darting into the air. To my left was the prison, and the university with Founder's Hill behind, crowned with the rambling pile of the Palace of the Bishops Elect. Everywhere, pinnacles, spires and hundreds of statues, springing from balconies, pediments and roofs.

We were still rising, the winged ones tugging impatiently at the ropes of the net which contained the balloon. Ahead – beyond a sprawl of slums – I could see the line of palaces and castles which marked Malacia's old line of defence; Chabrizzi, ancient Mantegan, Dio and the magnificent Renardo. Beyond them lay the foothills of the Prilipits, concealing the lines of our Turkish enemy. Towards that enemy the balloon drifted, helped by my winged escort.

If I wished for Armida, I could not help wishing that Bengtsohn was also with me, seeing for himself how wonderful our little world was. Everything delighted from this lofty viewpoint, even the slums, even the tannery and the slaughterhouses hugging the bend of the river. Riding my silver-hoofed mount, I saw our city-state as a whole, working like an open watch. I saw every part depending on every other, ticking away the millennia in a perfectly arranged manner.

Twisting about in the saddle to see everything, I was overwhelmed by high spirits. I gave out a cheer for the city, and the beautiful creatures accompanying me cheered too.

One of the flighted men called to look ahead. As we rose above the palaces and the fortifications that girdled Malacia, we gained a glimpse of alien tents. Soon the camp of Stefan Tvrtko was in full view.

The enemy forces were drawn up on the banks of a stream which the summer heats had sucked to a trickle.

Tvrtko's eastern lines contained the cannon with which he maintained his desultory bombardment of Malacia. Behind the cannon was what looked more like a small town than a military base.

The tents had been formed into streets and squares. The grandest tents were situated in the middle, the most magnificent belonging to Tvrtko himself; a Turkish love of symmetry had placed it in the precise centre of its attendant tents. Trees had been planted round it; they were dying from lack of water. Carrion birds sat in their branches, rising up at our approach overhead.

Behind the camp was a rag-taggle arrangement of shacks and skins. These housed the hangers-on which attach themselves to armies – Arabs, Circassians and other nomads hoping for loot, Serbs, Greeks, Armenians, Jews, all working to extract some profit from war. A great array of horses and camels could also be seen, their picquet lines straggling along the course of the stream.

Out of the tents poured little figures which shaded their eyes to look up at us. I stared down at the king's tent. There was no sign of him, although a group of three richly dressed figures came out to stand and gaze upwards like the rest. We moved near enough to see that two of the trio had great black beards and black moustaches.

To feel hatred for these people was impossible, although I did my best. In miniature they delighted me.

One of the flighted women directed my attention to a patch of land on the other side of the stream. There a number of wooden posts surmounted by turbans had been raised, along with more ordinary headstones. The camp cemetery already had its permanent inhabitants. Mourners in the cemetery looked up at us in startlement and headed for the cover of trees.

Some shots were fired at us from the camp, but it was clear that the bloated buglewing overhead, with a living man and horse riding under it, struck fear into their hearts. The forces of Tvrtko were reminded of what ancient forces they opposed; their superstitious minds would work dreadfully at this omen.

We sailed over the tents, and had satisfaction in seeing numbers of our foe fall to their knees or run for shelter.

When we had made a circuit of the camp, my companions tugged the balloon in the direction of safety, and it began once more to drift back over the city. It was arranged that I should descend into the Bucintoro to the same platform from which I had sailed.

And now we saw the second part of the Malacian plan – that part, I believe, which had been born in the dark, insanitary head of that terrible councillor in the black coat with the capacious pockets who had come by night to the exhibition gallery. The six smaller balloons were sailing in our direction, towards the Turkish lines, each one bearing a dangling man.

These dangling men were naked. They were of a curious colour. Their faces were distorted, their heads sought unnatural positions on their chests. Here was the explanation of the long, black wagon which had stood beside the platform, guarded by two masked gentlemen in black. That wagon had delivered six bodies from the mortuary.

The plague moves fast in summer sun; like a reptile, it needs warmth for greatest energy. And it travels best among besieging armies, where conditions are insanitary. The hosts of Tvrtko had already enjoyed a visitation; but someone in Malacia had devised a way of speeding their enjoyment. These corpses would land among the sable tents and spread their corruption in impartial distribution.

My balloon passed slowly among the dead as they swung from their harnesses. With tousled head and frosted eye, the dead men went to pay a last visit to the enemy and, if possible, accompany him to the dark hinterlands where their ghosts now found sojourn. I knew, as we returned above the bronze domes of St Marco, that the cheers along the waterfront would drown out the distant screams from the foothills.

How exactly it came about I cannot decide, but somehow it was Andrus Hoytola whose name was toasted, who was called hero, on the occasion of the Festival of the Buglewing. He it was who made the speech from the platform while I was hustled away with the horse.

However, he had no knowledge of the extent to which I became the hero of his daughter Armida's heart. Even Bedalar cast nourishing glances upon me. That evening, while the fountain of Stary Most ran with the Bishop's wine, Armida played truant with me. The two of us, with de Lambant, Caylus and other friends, pledged each other to youth and love and friendship, long life to Malacia, and death to all who interfered with the natural and happy order of affairs.

Book Two

A Feast Unearned

We were staggering rather drunkenly through the dark streets of Malacia, de Lambant and I, each carrying our guitars, and occasionally attempting a ballad. Night was wearing thin about its edges. The second day of the Festival of the Buglewing was over; the bird was on its way towards the third, and nothing was left but dawn.

When Armida and Bedalar were confined to their respective family circles, de Lambant and Portinari and I roistered with our friends in the town until our money ran out. Otto's zahnoscope had been put away during the festivities, but word and an honorarium had come from Pozzi Kemperer, by way of one of his uglier servitors, that there would be work for us as soon as autumn approached. Our credit was restored. We were welcome again in Truna's.

Some time during the course of the evening – it had stretched on for ever – we serenaded both Armida and Bedalar under their windows. Slops had been thrown at us at the Hoytola mansion, and a dog set on us at the Nortolini mansion.

So we tottered back through the lanes of Stary Most. We had lost the portly Portinari. We were out of money and mischief, and unwilling to go to bed. We sang, and were also out of voice.

We were crossing a footbridge over the Rosewater, a stinking ditch despite its fragrant name, when Guy exclaimed and looked over the parapet into the swirling water.

'De Chirolo, fancy a swim? There's a body down here, quick!'

I looked into the flood and saw nothing.

'Your reflection.'

'By the bones! He must have sunk again. He went rolling under the parapet. A man without a head.'

'Your reflection.'

'I saw him. Man without a head.'

'Either it's an omen or you're drunk. There's nothing there.' He looked ghastly. A dim lamp lit the bridge. As we stood and stared at each other, making sure our own heads were in place, a cock crowed.

Arches of old warehouses met here in ruinous corners, leaning against each other for support. Forgotten aberrations of architecture rested their ancient cheekbones against one another. In a derelict potter's shop, shapes of unglazed pitchers stared out at the world like blank faces, while furtive animal lives littered the dead doorways with bones and rubbish. It was an appropriate place in which to encounter corpses.

Glancing about, I saw over my shoulder no corpse but the apparition of a beautiful woman. I nudged de Lambant. The woman stood erect and commanding, clear of eye, ample of breast, her golden hair plaited in two plaits which dangled to her nipples. She wore a loose, white gown which hung from one shoulder, leaving a breast naked and covering the rest of her body down to her feet. A helmet was on her head. She carried a burnished shield.

'De Lambant!' My whisper rasped my throat.

The striking creature appeared to shimmer. As I took a step towards her, she rippled like a reflection in water and was gone. Where she had been stood an old man, an ancient husk, upright, skeletal, without a wisp of hair on his head. He bore a staff and stared fixedly beyond us. His eyes blazed.

'The demon drink again,' I said. 'I could have sworn I—'

'Swear not,' cried this aged figure. 'Whoever swears becomes less than the man he was. You will be here only a minute.'

'We aren't even staying that long. We're off home,' de Lambant said, but the old man spoke again, unmoving in the deep penumbra of his arch.

'I come from the far north and I go to the deep south. I pass by the misty windows of your life like a crane in flight, making for the Sahara marshes, and tomorrow shall have left your city.'

'We are out of money, I'm sorry,' I said, feeling bolder now, for the mouthing of such platitudes as his was a habit common among the ancients of Malacia. 'We were hoping you might stand us a drink. Or introduce us to your lovely daughter.'

'You witnessed an illusion, young fellow. Nor was it my daughter who visited you, but Minerva, mother of us all. She holds special meaning for you.'

'What special meaning?'

'She is wisdom. You must be visited by wisdom ...'

'Come on, de Lambant,' I said, for Guy showed every sign of forming himself into an audience of one. 'I've had enough advice recently, and would prefer to run my own life, whichever way the cranes are heading.'

Although I took his arm and tried to move him on, he resisted and went up to the old man.

'What can you tell me about my life, sire? Am I likely to get a good part in the next drama, do you think?'

The old man, still unbending, said, 'You two will both enact roles and hate each other if you do not heed my words and turn to Minerva.'

'Guy, you're playing the ape just by standing here! Let's go and wake Caylus and scrounge a drink off him. This old louse would turn a lifetime to tatters, given the chance.'

Almost by force, I dragged my friend away. The skeletal man neither moved from his place nor even stared to one side as we left.

'The old chap had a dreadful warning to deliver,' Guy protested.

'Old chaps always have dreadful warnings to deliver, like Seemly Moleskin. Don't listen. It's their stock-in-trade. My stock-in-trade is not listening.

> *The serpent on the staff*
> *It only makes me laugh.*
> *The apes that flitter*
> *Queerly, nearly,*
> *Merely*
> *Make me titter too.'*

'How do you manage to be so poxing cheerful at this time of morning? I feel half dead ...'

We were staggering together. I stopped so suddenly that we almost fell in a heap. Stretched out on a low stone balustrade, with one arm dangling down to the pavement, was the figure of a man. It appeared solid, but lax in death.

'A second manifestation!' This time I did believe – and was preparing an attitude of reverence – when I saw that it was none other than Gustavus Portinari, who stirred as he heard our approach. He sat up and peered at us, yawning, picking up his guitar from his side.

'The dawn gives you an unearthly pallor, friends. Mind you aren't mistaken for spectres. I was resting on my way home. Where did you get to? Dodging me again.'

We went along with him, whistling. Portinari's father kept a dairy, together with a room in which one could eat simple dishes, at the west end of Stary Most, where the evening shadows of the old West Gate swung across the street. Behind their quarters was a small yard, where cows and goats were kept, and a lane winding down to the riverside.

Portinari's parents were already up for the day when we reached the dairy. Holiday or no holiday, they had animals to milk. With much grumbling, the old man set a plate of cold meats before each of us, together with a pitcher of milk, while Portinari, when his father's back was turned, managed to filch some spirits. His mother and sister lit a fire and in no time we were fully awake and singing, much to everyone else's disgust. It was good to eat proper breakfast; not to have sung a catch or two would have been a shame. We kept the songs polite, in respect for the hour. Then we started talking about the apparition of Minerva.

'All that stuff we learned at school is about as much good as the hermetic books,' I said, and Portinari agreed with me. De Lambant thought there was something in the old truths.

'No, my pious friend, the old truths, as you call them, must be dead, because the civilizations that nursed them are dead. The Hellenic World sank below the horizon ten millennia ago, if you recall your history.'

'What if so? Minerva was before that and will be long after. Some things are permanent, you know, like your pimples.'

Hearing what we said as he staggered in with a pail of water, Portinari's father joined the debate.

'Aye, the gods and the qualities they administer live as long as there are ages of the earth, young de Chirolo. Let me tell you, the Portinaris didn't come from these parts. We hailed from Toulouisa in the Frankish Kingdom, which is over ten days' ride on horse north of here, across the flat plains of Habsburgia. My grandparents made the journey in a cart, taking the best part of two months on the journey. I remember it well, although I was only a lad of four at the time. Four or five. And—'

'Oh, let's go home and sleep,' I said to de Lambant. 'With something in my stomach, I shall dream well.'

'We might dream of Minerva with nothing on, if we're lucky,' said my friend, rising with me. We shook Portinari's hand, promising to see him again in a few hours. He gave us his wide, amiable smile.

'Bid my father farewell,' he said. Guy pretended to punch him in the stomach and he doubled up in pretended pain.

As we reached the door, the old man said, 'I remember what I was going to tell you. Your mentioning Minerva reminded me. As I say, we Portinaris came from a long way away, virtually from another culture, as you might put it – from a rural area, too, not a city. And we had never heard of the Greek deities. All the same, we knew about the things they stood for. We had our own versions of Minervas and satyrs, the intellectual and spiritual or the luxuriant, and—'

'I'm sure it must have been so, sir. We go now to exercise our luxuriant side in our beckoning beds, thanking you for the kindly meal, much welcome.'

So de Lambant and I bowed ourselves out.

Outside the day was beautiful with the rosy airs of dawn. A single layer of mist, infiltrating from the Toi, hung almost at eye level. A few smudged lights burned in houses along the way, outshone by the flaming clouds overhead. With a swish of wings, cranes flew by at chimney-top height.

I thought of Tvrtko stirring in his sleazy tent, wondering if he recalled me superstitiously in the sky. People said in the market that the plague was gaining in the Ottoman ranks.

'What a morning! It's good to be alive. Let's not sleep now, Perian. We can do that later. Besides, there'll be trouble if I arrive on our doorstep at this hour.'

'Let's go down to the harbour and see the fish catch landed – I haven't watched that for ages. They may have netted a few siege-whales.'

We fell in together, marching down the middle of the street in step. You would not have thought there was a Turk within a thousand miles.

'And then I'll tell you what we'll do. Smarana's wedding day approaches. We'll go and find her a proper present. My father has promised to pay the bill. Not without complaint, but he has promised.'

'He's made of money.'

'A greater proportion's wine.'

'What will you give your sister?'

'After the delights of the fish market, we'll go and see old Bledlore.'

The loft in which Letitia Zlatorog and her family lived was bad enough. Master Bledlore's studio was altogether stranger and more filthy.

His hideaway would have seemed more appropriate to a hermit than a sought-after craftsman, being merely the empty space under the roof of an old godown. The godown had been perverted from its original use of housing Bishop's merchandise to storing fragrant timbers. Most of these timbers, as I saw when we climbed the rickety stairs, had been stored a long while and had so attracted all the woodworms in the vicinity that every inch of the building was stuffed as much with freckles as wood. Such was the activity generated by these freckles that dust hung everywhere, and the sunlight pouring through the windows turned it into golden columns.

Panting as we reached the top of the stairs, we found ourselves on a narrow landing facing a narrow door. Its orange paint was flaking, falling like leaves beneath our feet. The single sullen word BLEDLORE was written on a card pinned to this door; so long had the card been there that the occupants of the freckles had bored through it on their way in and out of the wood beneath.

When de Lambant knocked, a crumbling sound came forth from the panel.

'Wish I'd brought Bedalar,' he said.

'I wish you had.'

'Her taste is good.'

'I'm sure her taste is delicious.'

'You cheeky grab-skeeter, keep your lustful thoughts off Bedalar! She could exercise her taste in what to choose for Smarana. If the old blighter *has* anything to choose from. He's supposed to be the best glass-engraver in Malacia. I'll wager he charges a fortune. We ought to have brought Armida and Bedalar.'

'I wouldn't expose Armida to your corrupting influence. Knock again. The old fool's probably still in bed.'

'Or dead. We'll see the girls at the fair this morning, if they can get away. Armida'll have to put up with my corrupting influence then.'

'Perhaps he's got a woman in there with him. I hope the toxic effect of your personality won't be so powerful outdoors. Anyhow, Armida's totally absorbed in me. Give another knock, if the door'll stand it.'

'I wonder what exactly you two get up to? I'd love to know. By the looks of her, Armida's a proper little stove, when she gets going.'

I kicked him lightly. He laughed and made the wormy panel emit more crumbling noises.

The door opened at last. There stood Master Giovanni Bledlore, dressed in ragged waistcoat and trousers, with a shawl pinned over his shoulders. He had a grey, unshaven cheek and a fierce, bright eye.

He shuffled on to the landing, an ague-ridden figure, closing his door behind him and coughing dryly as he did so.

'You young fellows are a nuisance to an honest craftsman. You disturb the dust, and dust spoils my colours. What do you want, coming up here? I shall have to go back and sit still for a quarter of an hour before the dust settles and I can open up my palettes again. In that time my bones will seize up.'

'Then you should keep cleaner premises, Master Giovanni,' I said. 'Open up some windows – look at all the bluebottles trying to escape!'

De Lambant soothed him by announcing that he had a commission.

'I need you to make me a dozen goblets with local scenes depicted on them, such as you designed for Thiepol of Saville a twelvemonth ago. A different scene on each, all joyous, for a wedding.'

The old man threw up his hands and wagged his beard in de Lambant's face. 'Spare me your needs! Every one of those designs aged me by a lifetime. Nor has Thiepol, for all his airs, yet paid me, confound him. My eyesight's too bad for any more work of that order. My hand shakes too much. My back aches too much. Besides, my wife is ill and I must care for her, poor old woman. My foreman has deserted me and gone to work in Ragusa. No, no, I could not possibly attempt ... Besides, when would you require them by?'

He needed some persuasion. Before de Lambant had signed

his bond on the deal and paid a token in advance, the old crafts-man had to show us the treasures of his workshop. Holding his vessels up to the light, we admired the beautiful miniatures on which this crock of a man worked, their tiny figures incised on glass, glowing with colour, infused with art.

Bledlore's wife appeared at one juncture, clutching a soiled robe up to her throat. She made an odd contrast with the sub-lime beings, the ever-youthful gods, that Bledlore conjured up in his translucent medium.

'Ah, what accomplishment!' de Lambant said afterwards. We had left the warehouse and strolled over Bishops Bridge to the meadows where gipsies and showmen held their festival fair beyond the city. 'You saw that last azure vase with its vignette? No gods, just two children sporting by an ancient hovel, with a hurdy-gurdy man playing in the background? What could be more beautiful in such small compass? Why has no one bought it?'

'It was beautiful. And isn't perfection greater for being so small?'

'Why not? Smallness is greater for being perfect.'

'Otto Bengtsohn would approve that particular scene of low life more than all the gods and goddesses ... Bledlore con-firmed what I have heard rumoured, that he studies everything from life. The broomstick is copied from an actual broomstick in his niece's yard, the hurdy-gurdy belongs to an old musician living over by the flea-market, and no doubt the two urchins are running ragged-assed round the city gates even now.'

We paused by an ash grove, where an aged casque-body worked, drawing up water from the river. The bony plates along its spine had been sawn off. An oriental sat on its back calling softly to it. We strolled on.

'What a decadent age we live in! Giovanni Bledlore is the last of the grand masters, and scarcely recognized except by a few cognoscenti!'

'Such as ourselves, de Lambant!'

'Such as ourselves, de Chirolo! And the odd connoisseur in Saville, who doesn't pay up. People appreciate merit only on a pretentious scale. Write a history of the universe and it will be applauded, however shoddy, however steeped in errors factual or grammatical; yet paint a tiny perfect landscape on your thumb and nobody will cheer.'

'Just as they still fail to cheer our tiny talents.' We laughed, cheering each other.

A pleasant warbling filled the air. A flute-seller was moving towards us, bearing a tray of flutes and playing one of them as he came. We circled him. I snatched an instrument and played a quick echo to his own charming tune, 'When the Quiet Air Hath Waked'.

'Flutes would be no better if they could be heard half-a-dozen valleys off – you're not suggesting that Bledlore should take to monstrous frescoes in his dotage, to get his name better known?' I asked.

'I'm condemning the general taste, not Bledlore's. He has found perfection because he has first found his correct scale. Twenty sequins per glass! – He should demand ten times as much! Not that father won't grouse at twenty, even for Smarana.'

We stopped by the marionette stall to watch both the puppets and their childish audience.

'The real reward of an artist is his ability, not the applause it earns him.'

We ceased being philosophical to watch the play with its little unreflecting spectators. Robber Man came on with red-masked eyes and tried to break into Banker Man's big safe. Banker Man, fat and crafty, caught him at it. Robber Man socked him with his sack. Banker Man pretended geniality, asked to see how much money Robber Man could get into sack. Robber Man, despite warning cries from the children in front, climbed obligingly into safe. Banker Man slammed safe shut, laughed, went for Militia Man. Met Devil-Jaw Man instead. Children roared with merriment, open and honest, as Devil-Jaw Man closed multitudinous teeth round Banker Man's nose. Magician descended, trapped Devil-Jaw Man in golden hoop. During fracas, Banker's Lady, dressed for the kill, entered to take cash from safe. Released and was walloped by Robber Man. And so on. Continuous entertainment.

Two cool girls near us in gowns that hovered between innocence and indecency exchanged comments. She to her: 'Disastrous low-brow hokum! I can't think how we laughed at it last year!'

She to her: 'Hokum maybe, Armida, but brilliant Theatre!'

De Lambant and I had propped ourselves against the stones of a fallen arch to watch the show. He now said loudly to me,

'Be warned by that sweet female exchange, de Chirolo! Enjoyment in youth gives way to carping criticism in old age.'

At this the girls no longer feigned that they had not noticed us; we no longer pretended that we had not recognized them. We hurried to take Armida's and Bedalar's hands. They ran to take ours, with tales of how they had dodged their chaperons in the market and were furious at having to wait so long for us. It was almost a luxury to have them dressing us down, so pretty a contrast did they make.

Bedalar was the more stocky with her generous figure and plumper face. Her eyes were a mysterious grey, her manner in general was more flirtatious than her friend's; a certain amount of fluttering eyelids was accomplished even in ordinary conversation. The effect was pleasing – it certainly pleased de Lambant. By contrast, my Armida was quieter in manner, and held me with a steady gaze from her golden eyes, which seemed almost to blaze in the sunlight. She had the same wonderful configuration of face which never left my mind's eye, the features seeming to arrange themselves about her nose, although it was by no means prominent. In her dark hair she wore a coil of golden metal which allowed the locks to flow free behind.

'What fun to hear a couple of brainless gallants like you discussing the just rewards of merit,' she said.

'We are artists, and not brainless. And you two are our just rewards of merit.'

'It was instructive for you to hear our sage remarks,' added de Lambant.

'I'd rather go to my maid for instruction,' Bedalar said, flightily.

'Your maid could instruct me in any art she wished, if she were half as pretty as you, my darling,' said de Lambant.

I said, 'She could instruct me in nothing, if you two ladies were present to take the lesson. You would find me an ardent pupil.'

There was a burst of applause – not for my wit, of course, but for the marionettes which the little audience cheered heartily.

The play was ended. The Banker's Lady had run off with the Magician, who proved to be a prince in disguise; the Banker had rewarded the Militia Man; the Joker had had his way with Bettini, the Banker's Daughter; and the Devil-Jaw Man had devoured the Robber Man. The puppet-man appeared from his

116

striped box and it was, as I suspected, my friend Piebald Pete. I remembered his squeaky voices from long ago. He nodded to me before running round with his pewter plate to gather as many coins as possible from the fast-disappearing audience. I borrowed a small coin from Armida and dropped it in his plate.

'You do not believe that your reward should be ability or applause alone, Pete.'

He touched his forehead. 'Thanks, Masters. I need a little fuel as well as flattery for my performance. Come back to this same spot this evening, when I do my proper show with the little Turk who walks the tightrope and chops off the princess's head. Then you'll see *real* artistry.'

'And Perian will strive to bring real money, not borrowed,' laughed de Lambant.

We strolled on, de Lambant taking Bedalar's arm and I managing to get between the girls so that I could have hold of them both; to which manoeuvre no one ventured to object. The stalls detained us a long while. It was typical of my golden fortune that I should win a sum of money at a lottery game and put myself in funds again.

As the afternoon wore on the girls talked about going home. De Lambant and I managed to persuade them that during festival time nobody would be likely to notice their absence, most of the population being engaged in sleeping off the excess of the previous night.

'Besides, we still have some talk to talk,' said de Lambant. 'We were saying that this was a decadent age. And then you two beauties sprang into view. Pure coincidence, doubtless.'

'Aren't all ages decadent?' Bedalar asked.

But Armida said, 'This is a creative age. There are some advances on the artistic front, as Bengtsohn's amazing process of mercurization proves. But arts flourish in decadent times. Nobody would claim that the Turks are decadent because they are so warlike. Don't people often say "decadent" when they really mean "peaceful"?'

I could not resist saying, 'But the Turks *are* now decadent. The great days of the Ottoman Empire ended with the death of Suleiman. Since then, a line of weak and vicious Sultans has succeeded him. The armies are corrupt; Tvrtko himself, drawn up outside our gates, does not attack, as a commander in his position unfailingly would have done, a century or more ago.'

'What a military strategist you are!' exclaimed Bedalar – with sincerity rather than sarcasm, for she squeezed my arm.

'Since he's been playing General Gerald, there's been no holding him in that direction,' said Armida.

'Or in any other direction,' said de Lambant.

The girls laughed so prettily – we were ready to laugh at any nonsense – that their bosoms shook like fresh-boiled dumplings.

'I just hope you're not trying to accuse me of inconstancy,' I said.

'There's much to be said in favour of inconstancy, or at least against constancy – which, like a surly porter, drives a lot of useful intelligence from the door,' de Lambant replied.

It was well said; yet I noted that Armida did not exactly smile over-much, as if recalling that I had tried to drive my intelligence through Letitia's door.

We were walking by the little river Vokoban, near an old, ruined windmill which marked the limits of the fair. A flighted woman came by overhead from the direction of the city. Like many of her kind, she wore long ribbons in her hair which trailed out behind her. She was young and naked. The sight of her passing in the sunlight was pleasing. As she fluttered down to alight behind the windmill we heard the beat of her wings.

'They're so free,' Bedalar observed. 'Can't we fly up into the mountains?'

No sooner suggested than arranged. The flighted people kept a basket-work tower on the perimeter of the fair, where one or two persons could be flown short distances in sedans. We all climbed the tower, which creaked like an old courtesan's stays at every step. Emerging at the top, Armida and I climbed into one of the light sedans and de Lambant and Bedalar into another. Four stalwart flighted men heaved us into the air, while another four attended to our friends.

'Oh, Perian, it feels so unsafe! Will they drop us?'

'It's safer than my hydrogenous balloon.' The fliers had harnesses round their shoulders attached to the carriage, as well as good earnest expressions on their red faces. All the same, I had to admit that there were reasons other than affection for the grasp which Armida threw about me. Her grip prevented me from trembling.

Our sedan was born flappingly just above the heads of the

crowd. The afternoon was wearing on. The crowd was thickening, the scene at the stalls becoming more animated, the smell of spitted meats stronger. After dusk would come the gayest time, when the throngs arrived, when flares were lit and masks donned, and Eastern dancers gyrated on scented stages.

The fair fell away behind us, wing-beat by wing-beat. Vineyards lay below, their grapes clustering in the serried bushes. We threaded our way through a grove of slender birches. Ahead lay another stretch of river, gurgling to itself as it churned over rock. Beyond were some last vineyards and the swelling early hills of the Vokobans.

'Let's be set down here,' cried Armida, but de Lambant shouted excitedly from the other carriage, 'No, no, further on! I know a little nest ahead, free from interruptions.'

So amid great flailing of wings, we sailed up slopes bright with camomile to a wide, mossy ledge with a cliff behind. The flighted men set us down on the ledge. They released the sedans, falling on the grass panting and sweating, and fanning themselves with curled wingtips. Soon they rose, collected their pay, and flew off slowly in the direction of the fair.

We stood and watched them go. Guy and I embraced the girls and all four of us capered about in delight at our newly acquired solitude.

My impulse was to pour out my love to Armida, only the occasion was one more for gaiety than solemnity. So I took her hand and we ran laughing to examine our stronghold, cached from the eyes of the world.

Climbing up huge fragments of rock on which all manner of faces and limbs had been carved, we gained a view of the countryside over which we had been lifted.

Malacia depended for its existence on trade and agriculture. Evidence of the latter lay before us in the vineyards, their geometrical rows wheeling towards the river. All that we could see was bathed in the sane light of afternoon. Instinctively, Armida and I clutched each other, feeling ourselves part of fruitful processes.

Our coign of vantage also commanded a distant view of the fair-booths, the Toi, spanned by its bridges, and the city. Malacia's fortifications, towers and grand buildings lay in a haze as if it were more dream than actuality. A glint of gold came from the Bucintoro.

Beyond the town to the right, where the ground rose again, we could even see the foothills that hid Tvrtko's encampment. Once a day Ottoman cannon bombarded the city, but it remained a half-hearted bombardment; ammunition was short. At this hour the enemy showed no sign of life.

Above us and to one side, the rough grey slates of a mountain village showed. We could hardly see it for olive trees and a low wall of stone which ran about its perimeter, up and down ravines. That was Heyst. The people there were dark and strange – we could see one or two of them toiling barefoot among their vines with their man-lizards beside them. In Heyst they spoke their own language and were unfriendly.

Armida and I rejoined our companions. As we disposed ourselves comfortably, Armida said, 'I've been told that some of these mountain people, who came from the wild north in days gone by, are descended from baboons. They are a younger people than we. Consequently – well, this is what my mother's old nurse told me, so it is probably just a story – but it seems that there were already so many gods in the world that the mountain people's gods could not get born. They are still pent within the rocks, here in the Vokobans.'

'That's a typical nurse's story, Armida,' de Lambant said, kindly. 'If northern gods can't get born, then they'll be pent in the rocks up north.'

'It's an allegory,' I said. 'If there are gods that remain unborn, they'll be pent within us, not in mere rocks.'

Armida showed her spirit as she rounded on us both.

'Oh, you're so patronizing, you men! You always think you know best. If a god is pent in rock, could he not conceivably move in it, a thousand kilometres if necessary, underground. As for "*mere* rocks", Professor de Chirolo, what makes you think people are greater than rocks? Mere rocks throw out stranger things than men do, since men themselves were thrown from rocks when the world began.'

'What? What's that?' I asked, laughing. 'We have developed from the family of bipedal ancestral animals' – but she ignored me, rushing on with her talk.

'Only last year – I heard this reliably from a scholar friend of my father's – a new sort of crab was born from the rocks on the coasts of Lystra. It exists now in hundreds for all to see. It climbs trees and signals to its friends with a claw especially enlarged for that purpose.'

De Lambant laughed. 'That's nothing new in the way of crabs. Those fellows have been signalling to their friends and enemies ever since the world began. Much inconclusive communication must have passed between them by now.

'No, my dear Armida, we require a genuinely new kind of crab – a species that will crow like a cockerel, yield milk every Monday of the month, and raise its carapace when requested to reveal pearls and jewels underneath. Or else an enlarged, tame land-crab the size of that boulder but with a better turn of speed, which could be trained to gallop like a military stallion. Think what a line of such animals could do against the Ottoman! Their shells would be painted in warlike colours.'

It was shameful to see how the eyes of the girls twinkled when de Lambant showed off. I was forced to interrupt his monologue.

'That's not enough. Our new crab would have to be amphibious. Then it could swim over rivers, and carry us across the seas to new and undiscovered lands, lands of legend, Leopandis, Lemuria, Mu, Hassh, Tashmana, Atlantis, Dis, and Samarind.'

'And not only across the seas but under them, ploughing across deep and murky bottoms where time solidifies among cities of coral and forests of weed. We could climb inside the crab's carapace and be secure from the waters outside.'

'And under water, the shell would become transparent as crystal, so that we could see the lairs of ancient sea monsters, where they still live out their days, encumbered by age and barnacles while they grow as civilized as men.'

The girls, carried away by fancies no less idiotic than our crabs, joined in the nonsense.

'I'd grow ivy and brilliant creepers all over my crab, until it looked like a fantastic moving garden, and then it would be famous and everyone would know its name, which would be – er—' That was Bedalar.

'My crab would have musical claws that played as it ran along. Such irresistible tunes! All the other crabs – even yours, Bedalar – would be forced to stop what they were doing and scuttle after it.' That was my Armida.

'Girls, girls,' de Lambant scolded, sniggering a little. 'You take up the silly game so violently that you'll batter your brains out on your imaginations!'

Then we all laughed, and sat down together beneath a wide stone plinth let into the rock, on which was written a legend in the Old Language. The girls asked me to read it; with some effort I did so, for my father had taught me the tongue as a boy.

'This stone has a mocking voice,' I said. 'It bears a verse dedicated to a friend who has passed over into the shades. The date shows that it was written to a defunct Phalander some eleven millennia ago, but the subject is a perennial one. It goes something like this ...'

I hesitated, then spoke.

> *'Phalander, your virtues were never too legion:*
> *Your friendship was feigning, your loving mere folly,*
> *Your lies evergreen as the prickle-tongued holly.*
> *Why do we recall you – now snatched to Death's region –*
> *As one who seduced us to thinking life jolly?'*

Armida laughed, hand raised to her pretty mouth. 'It is written by someone high-born because it's so witty.'

'I find it touching,' said Bedalar.

'It doesn't quite make sense. Fortunately verse doesn't rely solely on sense for its impact, any more than love,' said de Lambant.

Laughing exaggeratedly, he jumped up and turned to the plinth. Swinging it open, he drew from behind it a warm and highly spiced dish, ideal for our refreshment, and set it in our midst. Sometimes gods and men see eye to eye; then stomach and heart are in accord. Saffron rice-grains staunched with sultanas and dates and garlic and little fish, their mouths stuffed with chillies, lay piled in invitation. With a whoop, I felt deeper into the warm rock, bringing out a dish of vegetables and red wine in green clay bottles.

'All we need now is a quartet of Master Bledlore's glasses,' I said as I set the bottles down. 'Here's a meal fit for a king, or for Prince Mendicula at least. Well, a snack, let's say, if not a full meal. It certainly seduces me into thinking life is most jolly.'

I dipped my fingers down into the rice.

We lay against one another and ate the welcome food. Below us, a huntsman appeared, walking quietly among small oaks.

Once we caught a glimpse of the yellow hauberk or chick-snake he stalked. We heard neither scuffle nor cry, so presumed that the ancestral escaped its fate.

'This is surely decadent,' de Lambant said, simultaneously taking up the bottle and our earlier topic of conversation. 'A feast unearned. It makes me feel gorgeously corrupt. A sylvan feast unearned. All we need is music. You didn't have the forethought to steal a flute from the flute-seller, did you, de Chirolo?'

'I'm not that decadent.'

'Or that far-sighted.'

'Enough of your unpleasantries.'

It was Bedalar who spoke next, in a dreamy voice.

'Somebody told me that Satan has decided to close the world down, and the magicians have agreed. What would happen wouldn't be unpleasant at all, but just ordinary life going on more and more slowly until it stopped absolutely.'

'Like a clock stopping,' Armida suggested.

'More like a tapestry,' Bedalar said. 'I mean, one day like today, things might run down and never move again, so that we and everything would hang there like a tapestry in the air for ever more.'

'Until the celestial moths got at us,' de Lambant said, giggling.

'That's a decadent idea,' I said. 'The whole notion of the end of everything is decadent.'

Yet I was struck by Bedalar's vision of becoming a tapestry – presumably for the edification of the gods, who could then inspect us without interference. Looking across the countryside to the city, golden in afternoon sun, I felt a suspended quality in the air. Puffs of smoke, round and white, were dispersing slowly over the Prilipits, signifying another bombardment of Malacia; but no sound reached us in our haven; we might ourselves have been gazing at a tapestry spread for our delight as we ate.

'*Things* can't be decadent,' Armida said. 'Decadence is a human quality. Doesn't it mean something like physical or moral decay?'

'I'm not sure what it does mean, but that needn't stop us arguing about it, my love. We've called this a decadent age, although you disagreed, yet there is physical or moral decay at any time, isn't there? Take our friends the Princess Patricia and

General Gerald. They lived in a heroic age of great military achievement. Yet her behaviour was decadent – not just in being unfaithful, which admittedly happens fairly often, but in being impenitent afterwards, making a virtue of what she did, and practising a deceit that she pretended was no deceit.'

'You have her all wrong, Perian. Patricia pretends nothing. She is deceived by your General as greatly as Mendicula is. It is Gerald who plays the deceiver, deceiving even Jemima whom he professes to love.'

'Well, then her behaviour is decadent. We agree on that?'

'Let's agree about the beautiful taste of the fish,' Bedalar said. 'I tire a little of hearing about your Mendicula play.'

'Agreed entirely about both fish and play,' de Lambant said, brushing rice from his hose. 'Let's agree that this is a *comfortable* age, shall we? No major questions struggling for answer, no cold winds howling in from the dim religious north, and not too many headless corpses in the sewers. I was made for this age and it for me.'

'You speak lightly but you are not correct,' Armida said. 'This is what Bedalar and I were talking about indirectly before we stopped to watch the marionettes.

'There are always wars of some kind, even when heads are not literally blown off. And even when not between races and nations, then between households, between classes, between ages – heavens, Guy, between sexes – and between one side of a person's nature and the other. Those wars could almost be said to constitute life.

'As for there being no major questions struggling for answer, that can never be the case as long as living creatures move about the world's stage. Even the marionettes at the fair raised questions in my breast I could not answer.'

'Such as why and how is Piebald Pete such a poor performer,' laughed de Lambant.

'Such as why was I moved by Pete's trumpery dolls. They neither imitate nor parody real people; they are just wooden shapes, worked to amuse us. Yet I was concerned. I cheered first for Banker Man and then for Robber Man. A sort of magic was at work. If so, was the artistry the puppeteer's? Or was it mine, in that my imagination stirred despite myself and part of me became Robber Man and Banker Man?

'Why do I weep over characters in a play or book, who have

no more flesh and blood than the thirty characters of the print-ed language?'

'Enough, enough,' cried de Lambant. 'I spoke foolishly. You speak copiously.' He knelt beside Armida, placing his clasped hands in her lap.

She smiled at his clowning and placed a hand – I thought contemptuously – on his head, while proceeding to demolish his one remaining point.

'As for your absurd idea about no religious winds blowing, don't we go about in a storm of beliefs? What has our talk been but of contrasting beliefs and disbeliefs?'

'It was mere banter, mistress, mere banter! Mercy, I pray.'

'Banter often conceals deep underlying beliefs. My father taught me that.'

Bedalar took my hand and said, 'Although we went to the same academy, Armida is much cleverer than I. Why, I don't think I have any beliefs at all in my head.'

'I liked your speculation about the tapestry. No doubt you have other nice things up there,' I said.

'Oh, but the tapestry idea was put there by someone else.'

We heard music far off, of a spirited and involved kind. It drifted down the mountainside like a herbal scent. We all turned our heads except de Lambant, who was busy making up to Armida.

'Even I, a fool of love, recognize that there are major ques-tions unanswered and probably unanswerable. The nature of Time, for instance. Before we met up with you two angels, my handsome friend here – Perian de Chirolo, no less – and I visited Giovanni Bledlore, the glass-miniaturist.

'Bledlore works obsessively for a pittance, barely supporting himself and his old wife. Why does he do it? My theory is that he feels Time – and Dust, the advance patrol of Time – as well as its rearguard – to be against him. So he builds tiny monu-ments to himself in the only way he knows, much like the coral insect whose anonymous life creates islands. Time makes Master Bledlore secrete Art. What algebraist ever found a harsher formula than that?

'Now – suppose that Bledlore had all the time in the world. Suppose that a magician gave him a magic potion so that he could live for ever. I'll wager that he would not then lift his hands to incise a single goblet! Nobody would know the abilities

125

in him. Time is one of those big questions, hanging at our door like an unsettled bill.'

The music was nearer, coming and going about the mountain-side as intricately as its own measure. Its effect on me was measureless. I jumped up and took Armida's hand.

'Whoever the rogue is playing, he has Time where he wants it,' I said. 'We've eaten and talked. Armida, it may be Devil-Jaw Man himself at the strings, but I must dance with you.'

She rose and came into my arms, that willowy girl, turning her face all golden up to mine, and we began a kind of im-promptu gavotte. Her movements were so light, so taunting and in tune, that a special spring primed my step, powered by more than music. My spirits rose up like smoke.

Bedalar took the dish at our feet and swung it before her, so that a shower of rice, all that we had not bothered to eat, flew over the ledge and down the mountainside. Then she took de Lambant's hand. They also began to dance.

Another moment and the musician himself came in sight. We scarcely heeded him when he rounded the rock. It was as though he was already part of our company. I noticed that he was old, small of stature and stockily built, and that he had a man-lizard accompanying him. He played a hurdy-gurdy; that cardinal fact we knew already.

As long as the music went, so went we. It seemed we could not stop, or had no need of stopping, until the afternoon itself clouded over. It was more than a dance; it was a courtship, as the music told us – as our own closeness, our own movements, our own glances, told us. We finally bowed, laughing and gasp-ing, and the music died.

We took up the bottles of wine and passed one to the musician and his companion. The hurdy-gurdy player was so small and densely built as to appear in his fustian clothes as thick as a city wall. His complexion was swarthy and we saw how aged he was, with eyes sunken and mouth receding, though there were black locks yet on the fringes of his white head. Guy and I recognized him. As it happened, we had seen his likeness that very day.

'Do you not live by the flea-market, O tuneful one?' asked de Lambant.

The musician did not answer. His throat was too busy encompassing as much wine as possible before de Lambant took the bottle back.

'It's undeniable, sir.' His thin, used voice had none of the brilliance of his music – or of the wine. 'I have a shack by the market, if it's all the same to you, sir. Though I've played to courtiers in my time, and made bears dance as nimbly as butter-flies.'

'We saw your living likeness on one of Master Bledlore's glasses.'

The old musician nodded and a smile spread across the ruin of his countenance. The lizard-man behind him jumped up and down, spilling wine into the dust, where it rolled itself into globules.

'Ah, Giovanni Bledlore, the greatest artist of our city. He cares for the downtrodden. Have a look at this, gentlemen.' The old fellow came forward, offering us his musical instrument. It was heart-shaped and a pale yellow. Below the finger-keys, a picture had been painted, a little miniature depicting two child-ren.

The pose of the children was lifelike. They were chasing each other, the boy running after the girl, each with arms out-stretched. They were laughing as they ran. An imitation sun shone.

De Lambant and I recognized the workmanship at once – and the infants.

'Master Bledlore's art! Who else could get so much into so small a compass? And these little scamps – they're the pair we noted on the azure vase in his workshop!'

'As you so rightly say, sirs,' agreed the musician, retrieving his instrument and tucking it lovingly under his arm. 'The very same little scamps, bless their lovely hearts. Giovanni used them for models more than once. Since he could not afford payment, owing to the dereliction of his rich patrons, he did this minia-ture for me to enjoy as I played. These two darlings are my own grandchildren – or *were*, I am forced to say, *were* my own grandchildren, and the apple of my eye moreover, until the accursed east winds of last winter carried them both off to the shades. Yes, a bad day, that ...'

He sighed, and then said, 'They would dance all day to my music if you let them, pretty little sprites. They had few toys. They never quarrelled. But the magicians at Bishops Bridge set a spell on them and they shrivelled up and died when the wind came from Byzantium. Now they are no more. No more.' He began to weep; the lizard-man put a scaly hand on his shoulder. 'There's nothing left of them, only this little picture of Giovanni's here.'

As he cuddled his hurdy-gurdy to one cadaverous cheek, Armida said pertly, 'How fortunate you are to have that consolation. Now we've heard your sad story, you must play us another tune. We can't dance as nimbly to your tears as to your music.'

He shook his head. 'I must continue for Heyst, my lady, and earn a little money by playing at a wedding. In a few weeks it will be winter, however hard you young people dance.'

He saluted and shuffled on. The lizard-man followed, upright and giving us in passing the tight-lipped smile of his kind. As for de Lambant and I, we started kissing and petting our pretty dears before the two travellers were out of sight.

'Poor old man, his music lit us but could not fire him,' said Armida's beautiful lips, close to mine.

I laughed. 'The object of art is not always consolation!' I pulled her dark hair about my face, till our eyes were in a tent.

'I don't know what the object of art is – but then, I don't know what the object of life is. Sometimes I'm scared. Fancy, Perian, those children dead, and yet their images living on after them, painted on wood or engraved on glass!' She sighed. 'The shadow so eclipsing the substance ...'

'Well, art should be enduring, shouldn't it?'

'You might say the same about life.'

'You dare be sad when what you are enduring is only my hand groping up your silken underclothes ... Ah, you delightful creature! Oh, Armida, there's no one like you ...'

'Oh, dearest Perian, when you do that ... If my family ... No art can ever ...'

'Ah, sweet bird, now if only ... yes ...'

'Oh, my lovekin, that's so ...'

There is little merit in reporting a conversation as incoherent as ours became. Of all the arts, none translates into words less readily than the one we pursued. Suffice it to say that I – in the words of a favourite poet – ''twixt solemn and joke, enjoyed the lady'.

Her lips, her legs, opened on a paradise to which I flew. A few

128

metres away, screened by bushes, de Lambant and Bedalar imitated us.

So much for our fluttering selves. As for the meteorological phenomena, the settled weather brought a sunset of ancient armorial gold, under which the whole landscape glowed like a shield before being quenched by night. Scarcely a zephyr stirred, leaving the atmosphere as untroubled as our joy.

With evening, we lay folded together like old flying carpets whose magic has run out, limp and incapable of further transports. De Lambant and I were relaxed upon the bosoms of our still-loving ladies.

We slept in a huddle, with the lamps of the distant fair our nightlights, and kisses for prayers.

Cold pre-dawn stirrings woke us. Heavy twilight still reigned. All was peace. One by one, we sat up and cuddled each other, scarcely speaking. The girls attended to their hair. In one quarter of the sky, the cloud cover opened like a jaw, showing light in its gullet; but the light was as chill as the breeze moving about our shoulders. We stood and looked about. We jumped up and down to see if our blood would move again.

Holding hands, we started down the mountainside. We found a path among the goosefoot, amaranthus and gaudy spikes of broom, and followed it. No movement or illumination showed from the city which lay among its mists. Only by the grey walls of Heyst, dull-gleaming lanterns showed; the peasants were already astir, going to the well or making for their fields, breakfast bread in hand. Birds began to call without breaking the mountain hush as we walked through an oak thicket. There we came on the hunter we had glimpsed the day before, standing silent in buckskin on the path. He had killed his hauberk. It was slung about his shoulders. Its head hung limp on his chest, an early bluebottle already sipping at its moist eye.

We reached the first vineyards and headed for a wooden bridge across the brook. An oaken satyr stood guarding the spot, as well-weathered as an ancient shaggy-tusk. Flowers had been laid freshly in his wormy hand, even this early in the day. The sound of the brook was clear and refreshing.

A grave happiness moved in my breast.

Taking Armida about the waist, I said, 'However early you wake, someone is awake before you. However lightly you sleep, someone sleeps lighter. Whatever your mission, someone goes forth on an earlier one.'

De Lambant took it up, and then the dear girls, improvising, starting to chant and sing their words as we crossed over the creaking slats of the bridge.

'However light your sleep, the day is lighter. However bright your smile, the sun is brighter.' De Lambant.

'However overdue the dawn, no dues delay it ... And what it owes the morn, in dew 'twill pay it.' That was my clever little puss! So the unspoken rules of the game were set: rhymes were required.

'However frail the blossoms that you bring, year after year, they still go blossoming.' Bedalar, her eyelids heavy from the night.

'The water runs below our feet, ever-changing, ever-sweet, the birdlings burble and the brittle beetles beat!' I again.

'However long night breezes last, day overthrows them, though day's overcast.' De Lambant, a little too clever.

'And what a world of never-never lies in that little word, "However" ...' Armida again.

We skirted the closed fair-booths, tawdry in the new light, and moved towards Bishops Bridge. Sentries were posted there, but they let us cross the Toi without a word.

A watery ray of sun, piercing over the leaden stream, lit the huddle of buildings along the waterfront. Its beam was reflected back by one cracked window. I noticed that it was Master Bledlore's casement, tightly closed. He would be dozing yet, obsessed and stuffy, his lungs hardly moving for fear of stirring the dust in his studio. His old wife stifling a cough. His bluebottles starting to buzz.

As we breathed deep of the outside air, an ancient musty odour came to our noses, the stink of something being singed. Armida clutched my arm tighter and Bedalar moved nearer to de Lambant. We were coming up to two magicians, and would have to pass them to enter the old portal of Bishopsgate.

The day favoured them in their cloaks and tall hats, directing one of its bright rays so that they were lit like characters in a painting, dramatically appearing from the bitumen of sleep. On two blocks of stone, fallen from some long-forgotten variant of the city's geometry, the magicians had built a smouldering fire; beside it, they proceeded on their arcana, eyes askance as cats',

faces square and malign. As we went by, I turned my head to observe the serpents burning on their altar. They symbolized, among other things, the male generative power needed in a new day.

They gave off a blue smoke which hung at heart level. None of us said a word. The ceremony was older even than words.

The magicians moved their archaic bodies stiffly, lifted their withered arms in incantation. Beyond the old tower and the first arcades, daylight was still scarce. But we could see merchants moving through shadows. We passed in under the gate, the four of us, where torchlight was.

Woman with Mandoline in Sunlight

Women have to tolerate much which a man of spirit would never endure. Armida was in immediate trouble with her family when she returned home from our night in the mountain. Her chaperon had discovered her absence: her father was waiting for her in the hall.

Yolaria, according to everyone's calculations, was to have been solaced all night by an ambitious gardener's lad called Hautebouy, but the Powers of Darkness were at their intricate work.

Our plans had been upturned by a favouring wind from the Orient. The busy-body wind brought with it a trading ship belonging to the Renardos. This carrack was loaded with exotic trees and plants for the duke's gardens, peach trees, cherry, and asparagus among them. It happened that the old duke had lost a valued gardener to the plague, and Hoytola, eager to further his friendship with the nobility, had sent along two of his gardeners, Hautebouy being one of them, to assist with the disposition of these rare species. The lad was unable to attend his assignation.

So it was that a fair wind from Cathay caused Armida's chaperon to put in an unexpected appearance, and my Armida to fall sufficiently into disgrace to be banished to her father's country estate for the rest of the festival period. She managed to write a note saying that she was being sent to Juracia, which was smuggled to me by Bedalar.

I was scrupulous in thanking Bedalar warmly for this kindness. To my surprise, she kissed me on leaving and said, 'I know that you expect further kindness from me, now that you won't see Armida for a few days. I find you a very presentable fellow, Perian, make no mistake. Seeing you ride into the sky on that black horse quite turned my head.'

'Did it, indeed?' My wits deserted me. Her kisses were of the sort that would annihilate wit entirely. 'I can't imagine a prettier head to turn. But I must warn you that the ride on the black horse is held by my oracle, Seemly Moleskin, to portend unfavourably. So I'm on best behaviour and keeping my amulet polished.'

She hugged me hard, her eyelashes fluttering. 'Guy says you have a terrible reputation. I must warn you that what you are chiefly after is my own possession, and is not for any man who feels inclined to it.'

'I'm not after anything, dear lady.'

But her specific reference to this charming possession, as she called it, threw me into a fit of desire, although I had not thought of it until that moment. Besides, she was at my door, about to go. I told her what I could imagine doing with such a possession – something beyond where I imagined de Lambant had gone. Her response was a flush that seemed to fill her eyes and mouth as well as her cheeks. It haunted me long after she had closed the door and stolen downstairs.

I stood alone in my room, in its dead centre. When I took up the lines of explanation Armida had written, they meant nothing, so formal were they. I dropped the letter to the floor.

Smells of cooking came to my nostrils. Smart sounds of horses' hooves on cobbles reached my ears. Going to the window, I saw a file of Tuscady Heavy Cavalry pass by, looking immensely important. Between the huddled roofs, I caught a glimpse of the fighting tops and furled topsails of a vessel moored along the Satsuma – probably the very vessel which, by its prompt arrival, had freed Yolaria to discover Armida's absence from her bed.

Everything has its place. But what was my place? If a favouring wind from the Orient could affect me in Malacia, what other winds were influencing my fortunes, unbeknownst to me? To become involved with Bedalar would surely provoke a storm in some murky corner of the heavens of which I had never heard.

Seizing up my guitar, setting one foot on my chair, I began to play. I wanted a song that would connect all things, the large with the small, the real with the ideal. All that came was something of Cosin's:

> *Among the graves each winter's day*
> *There echoing sounds the woodman's blade.*
> *You're far away:*
> *The birds sing not, the spring's delayed.*

No, something more was needed. I required company. Pozzi had taken La Singla to Vamonal until the forces of Stefan Tvrtko were vanquished, or I would have gone to talk with her. Instead, I walked in the streets and began thinking again of Bedalar with her lazy eyes.

By a natural association of ideas I came to recall the gardens of the Renardos. If I could not visit Bedalar, I might go to see her brother Caylus, the thought of whom now became more tolerable than previously.

Nothing in Malacia was more gracious than the gardens of the Renardo palace. The grounds represented a unique combination of nature and fancy. Near the great house were formal gardens, laid out in the classical manner, together with mazes and herbal gardens. Beyond these lay arboretums, zoological gardens housing ancestral and wild animals, and many hectares of manicured wilderness. Everywhere flowers abounded, while the whole was decorated with plants collected by agents of the duke from all corners of the known globe. The grounds were further adorned with streams and pleasant pavilions designed in a variety of architectural styles.

Towards one of these pavilions, Caylus Nortolini and I made our way. We followed a path that led among glades of ginkgo and fern and ancient cycads; these glades were the haunt of slobbergobs – qutun-firs, to give them their proper name – the large, shaggy sloths which once abounded near Malacia.

Since the Nortolinis claimed a distant blood-relationship with the dukes of Renardo, Caylus and I were welcome in the grounds of the palace.

Caylus could be amusing when it pleased him. His face was distinguished but well-equipped for sneering, since his chin was small and the tip of his elegant nose slightly overhung his mouth. His chin was camouflaged by a small beard. He had unexpected grey eyes which could be turned on people with destructive effect; today I saw that they were not unlike Bedalar's. His talk was generally of sport, particularly of bull-fighting, or of his amours.

Statues of goddesses and vanished or imaginary animals peered from the foliage about us. Or we came on a live creature chained and lolling in the sunshine. The slobbergobs were not to be seen, but we passed a mandrill imported from Africa, which drew its brows together and squinted at us down its gaudily striped cheeks.

'Since it insists on wearing its fantastic mask at all times,' said Caylus, 'we cannot tell what sort of face lies beneath it, a savage's or a savant's.'

'In such a mask I would visit Africa and be bombarded by parakeets.'

A mating pair of military macaws flew over as I spoke, flashing blue and sea-green and orange as they alighted in a palm tree.

'There may be savage savants. Sometimes I believe our fighting bulls are enormously wise, sometimes simply ferocious … They say that those hunters who have slain the really formidable ancestrals such as the tyrant-greave or the devil-jaw believe at the moment of the kill that they confront beings of infinite wisdom.'

'I'd better go and see my old savant father. He's not far from here. He knows so much, yet he's never stirred from Malacia.' The mandrill shook his silver chain as we moved away.

'To kill a devil-jaw – that must be the ultimate thrill, to bathe in its blood. When devil-jaws mate, since their forearms are so puny, the male wraps his great, scaled tail about the throat of the female to ensure compliance. Sometimes she is strangled in the act.'

'Dying for love may be highly regarded in the animal kingdom, as in the human. I'm duty bound to go and see him. He sent me a letter full of complaints when I made my balloon ascent. He is rather ill.'

'Fathers are generally ill in my experience. Forget the old fool. Did you ever long to kill a devil-jaw, de Chirolo?'

'What I wish is somehow to encompass all things possible in the world. That doesn't include slaying a devil-jaw. By the bones, perhaps I'm more like my father than I imagined. He also seeks to encompass—'

'Spare me your parents. I have my own, you know. Look, we'll lunch with Gersaint – he's bound to get us hopelessly drunk – unless any better sport presents itself.'

'I'd better go to my father first. He becomes upset if I'm drunk.'

'Of course he does. Old men do. It's one reason for getting drunk.'

'You're right, but I'd better go nevertheless. I haven't been to see him for long enough.'

'Think of Gersaint's board, Gersaint's cellar, postpone your decision – preferably for a week or two. With any luck, your old chap may have shuffled off his mortal coil by then. See this pavilion – let's eye some paintings; it's stacked with queer junk. Sporting pictures, too.'

We were never far from the music of water. The old duke's father had employed Malacia's great engineer, Argenteuil, to design fountains, sluices and waterfalls to punctuate the streams within his grounds. To these light noises was added the sound of strings as we reached the marble stairs leading to an art pavilion. This pavilion was built in the Khmer manner with curling eaves.

At the foot of the stairs, four gardeners with a barrow were labouring in the earth, planting a line of exotic trees. One of the four was a willowy lad; I suspected him of being the Hautebouy who had played an accidental role in my affairs.

At the top of the stairs, among bronze monsters from the East, two women stood playing musical instruments, a girl with a mandoline and an older woman with a viol. They were executing a lively forlana, six-in-a-measure, a relic of earlier times whose tune they gaily tossed to one another.

A velvet-clad man in saffron hose leaned against a column, idly listening. His was a heavy, awkward figure. He wore a plumed hat and animal mask, and was tapping his foot to the music. He paid no attention to us as we approached.

One of the women was well in the toils of time, her hair white and her skin flecked with rust marks. Although her hands on the strings were nimble, her wattle hung like a lizard's and the lines of her mouth had begun to collapse.

Her companion was scarcely more than a girl, but well-built for all that, with golden hair piled on her head – though there was artifice in its colour. To her face she had applied rouge and powder which, in the bright sunshine, was the least pleasing thing about her. It made her skin lifeless. She would be one of the duke's courtesans, to judge by her manner and dress. She eyed us challengingly as we came abreast, without ceasing her playing. Her eyes were haughty and cold. She played to the man in the animal mask.

This striking courtesan wore a gown of shimmering white

137

silk, slightly soiled about its hem, from under which one softly-shod foot looked out. About her throat was a lace collar; a low-buttoning, russet jacket adorned her elegant bosom. This was not day attire, even at the court of a duke. I dismissed her for all her beauty, turning instead to the paintings ranged under the low colonnade. Caylus paused to eye her and take in her melody, so I went ahead of him, stepping into cool shade.

All the time the man in the animal mask paid no heed to us.

The dukes of Renardo had collected many exotic objects during their conquests and travels. The most treasured objects adorned the palace, the least adorned the pavilions.

Since our company was to perform the comedy of *Fabio and Albrizzi* at Smarana's wedding, I needed a costume for my part. My hope was that I should find inspiration for one among the duke's pictures.

Contrast had been the foremost quality in the mind of the genius who built the mock-Khmer pavilion, perched on its artificial hill. He had so contrived the perspectives of his columns and courts that one vista looked towards the steps where the women played, and the pastoral scenes beyond them; while the opposed vista took in at once the ruin of an old palace, with ferns sprouting from its crumbling pediments, and the baroque splendours of the ducal residence. With these two contrasting reminders of nature and art, one turned readily to their echoes in the canvases ornamenting the walls.

'Look at all this beauty!' I said. 'The amount of *construction* in the least of these pictures ... How dearly I love art and drama and opera and music, and all those great things which offer amalgams of our living world and the creator's private world! So wonderful it is, even if this is a decadent age ...'

My head was still full of our beautiful time on the mountain near Heyst, of the conversations we had there, as well as the loving. Also, I have to confess, I always tried to impress Caylus a little. He was such a scoundrel, with his chatter of bulls and mating devil-jaws.

'We live in a dualist universe, but the creator's world is a special, privileged version—'

'Oh, don't go *on*, de Chirolo,' Caylus said. 'You'll be bragging next that you read books.'

'I leave that to my father. He writes them. Music and painting and of course the play, all the *edifices* of art—'

'Hush! You'll shit yourself!'

He placed a hand on my shoulder, humming the air plucked out by the mandoline below. He gazed without exertion at the pictures, while obviously thinking of something else.

'A pretty little painted creature with the mandoline, and no mistake ... She'd make sweeter music than comes from wooden instruments. She looked boldly at me. You couldn't help noticing.'

'Who's the fellow hiding behind the wolf-mask? A favourite of Renardo's, I suppose?'

'What's she to him? Deuce take it, a pretty little painted creature, no mistake.'

I was looking at the canvases.

'What do you think of this "Landscape in Arcadia", Caylus? See that perfect little background behind the huntresses ...' I indicated the mythical scene before me, but he scarcely gave it a glance.

'Too misty for my taste! Founder's bones, if I could get her to one side ... my rooms are near. She'd surely need no persuasion, once that fop disappears. A man has a duty to pay his tribute to Venus every day.'

'My duty to my father ...'

'Come, Perian, we'll stroll upstairs, where the older pictures are. Tell me not about your precious father again.'

'I was telling your sister the other day—'

'Let's leave my precious sister out of the account too, if you don't mind.'

The keeper of the pavilion who was lolling on the stairs, feeding titbits to a small pied dog, jumped up and bowed low as we passed. On the upper floor, the paintings were fewer while the views were finer than those below. It was pleasant here and the dance air still reached our ears. But Caylus remained discontented. He loitered at a low casement, looking down.

'Come and see this delineation of an outdoor concert,' I called to him. 'By a forgotten artist. How poignant the stances of the musicians as they earn an hour's attention from the court! And what words could describe that tender colour – though it's faded – and the mistiness so perfectly expressing a dream of youth and happiness ... the freshness of those clouds in the background, the clarity of the foreground with its grouped figures ...'

'Mmmm ... Perhaps I should go down and kick the buttocks of that fellow in the wolf-mask.'

'True to nature, yet more true ... The tableau living still, its creator long since dust ... "One who seduced us to thinking life jolly ..." Only relegated to this pavilion by a damp stain in one corner. Who executed such a sweet design? How long ago, and in what country? The fashions are not of Malacia ... This gallant here, look, Caylus, in the grand green coat ...'

I ceased. I had found the costume I needed. The cut of the grand green coat was unfamiliar yet not unfashionable, stylish yet not too pretentious – and not without humorous exaggeration, as befitted the character of Albrizzi.

The gallant in the canvas wore a white wig. His features were youthful. The coat was tailored of damask with silver buttons. It hung long, shaped in at the waist and then ample, with ample pockets, and terminated just below the knee, to reveal breeches and elegant hose from which ribbons depended. It had wide cuffs and was embellished deeply with silver braid. Beneath the coat could be seen a waistcoat of brocade, decorated with landscapes done in – I surmised – petit-point. A white tie tight to the throat completed the ensemble. That was it! – Albrizzi to the life! I would send Kemperer's tailor to copy it.

'Caylus, my morning's labour bears fruit!' I said. 'There's no calling this fine gentleman back to life to establish who he was, but his costume shall be restored in time for Smarana's festivities.'

Caylus sprawled half out of the window, unheeding. I went and gazed over his shoulder. The two women stood there, still playing their forlana on the sunny stairs; the courtesan with the golden hair was singing.

Something there disquieted me. When I searched for a reason, I realized that the girl's perfume had drifted up. A trace of it had reached me as we passed her. It was the same distinctive patchouli that Armida wore.

The fop with the wolf-mask was making off down the steps. Suddenly I thought I recognized him – the walk mainly, but also the figure. Although costumes and circumstances were opposed, this was the man from the Supreme Court, the sinister black figure who had been in Hoytola's gallery.

I watched as he disappeared into the grove. I could not be sure it was he. Yet just to recall that sinister figure made me uncomfortable.

'She's alone now,' said Caylus. 'Look at her lovely hands!'

Indeed, they were fine; so supple that the fingers became an integral part of the music, as they plucked out notes with a light tortoise-shell plectrum. From where we stood looking down, I could note the unusual design of the plectrum. It had two little horns on one side, as if fashioned in the likeness of a satyr. The touch seemed characteristic of the girl, for whom I felt distaste, I knew not why.

'Perian, I'm going down to her before another rival appears!' said Caylus. He sprawled at the casement regarding me, smiling as he pulled at his little beard. 'I declare I'm out of my mind about her already!' He patted his codpiece to show where he kept his mind.

'Caylus—' I wished to tell him that my feelings warned me the girl was somehow dangerous; yet why should my distrust of her be important to him? And what had I against her, save that she allowed herself in sunlight with a painted face, and smelt like Armida? He misinterpreted my hesitation.

'Don't say it! Let me leave you alone with your art! You're going to visit your father in any case ...'

Still smiling, he turned and commenced down the stairs, thumbs in pockets. As he went, he called over one shoulder, 'I'll be in my rooms for a siesta this afternoon. Come along if you care to, and we'll play some cards – unless I have good fortune at this other game!'

For a while I stood at the top of the stairs and chewed my lip.

Glancing out of the window, I saw the woman with the mandoline turn to watch Caylus approach, although he was concealed from my view. I noted again her brazen glance and her fingers on the plectrum. Then I also went downstairs and out at the opposite door without a backward look.

There were worse things to do than see my father.

Beyond the grounds of the Renardo palace the grand avenue with its acacias petered out in a maze of alleys, through which

I picked my course. At this hour of morning there were few people about, though women could be glimpsed working in the rooms close on either side. From the nearby canalside I heard a barrel-organ; the tune it played, 'This Sweet Perspective', was one familiar to me from childhood.

I came on a wider avenue. Beyond it was the street of the goldsmiths. At the far end my father's house stood behind tall tiled walls.

Beppolo, our old servant, eventually let me in and closed the creaking gates. Doves took wing and clattered away to the streets. Familiar scents surrounded me. I walked through the side courtyard, cool in shadow, noticing how overgrown it had become, and how shaggy were the bushes of laurel on either hand, which had once been so neatly clipped. The stable was deserted; no hounds frisked as in bygone years. Our carriage had long been sold. Those few windows of the house which were not shuttered looked down expressionlessly.

At the other end of the court the green door stood open. I went through it, to be enfolded by the silence of the house. I looked in at what we had called the Garden Room as I passed; the light through the jalousie revealed it only in monochrome, its informal furniture pushed to one side, neglected.

My father would be in his study at this hour – or at any other hour, for that matter. I hesitated before his door, studying the cabalistic signs painted on its panels, listening for sounds from within. I fingered my amulet. Then I tapped and entered.

So recently had I come from the sunlit outside world that I failed to see the figure standing in the shadow of an alcove, poring over a manuscript. He turned slowly and raptly, and I made out the lineaments of my father. Negotiating a way across the lumbered room, I took his hand in my hands.

'It's a long time since you came to see me, my boy. It's so dark in here! Didn't you know I have been unwell with the colic?'

'I had your note, father, and came as soon as I could manage. Did Katarina visit you? Are you better now?'

'If it isn't the colic, it's the stone. If it isn't the stone, it's the spleen, or the ague. You know I am never better. Your sister rarely bothers to come round here. I can eat nothing. At least I am not afflicted by the plague, which I hear gathers strength in the markets. Why don't the Ottomans go away? Malacia has its share of earthly woes, to be sure.'

'Why complain? Plague's always about – it is part of life, just as darkness seems part of yours. Caylus tells me there are reports of the Turks leaving. Let me open a shutter! How can you see to read in this twilight?'

He went before me, spreading his hands to bar my way.

'Whether horse-flesh doesn't spread the plague is a question some scholar should look into. How can I think when the light is hurting my eyes? What does that good-for-nothing Caylus know about military matters? And what's all this about the Turks? Why aren't you working? Idleness spells mischief always.'

'I have worked all morning, Father. And Caylus is well connected.'

'And what have you to show for it? So you came as soon as you could, did you? ... Katie did stick her head in here once – without her fly-by-night husband, naturally. Do you know what I have found out this very morning?' He extended an arm with one grand, faltering gesture towards his shelves and the folios of Pythagoras, Solomon and Hermes lying open there, together with many ancient histories in an ancient heap. 'I have at last discovered what a *maati* is composed of, beloved by Philip of Macedon.'

'Father, leave your books! Let's go to eat together at Truna's as we used to do – you look starved. I'll call a litter for you from the square.' As he leaned against his table by the window, I noticed with sorrow how thin he had become. He needed meat.

'Do you attend me? A *maati* is not just any delicacy but a specific one, first introduced into Athens at the time of the Macedonian Empire. Besides, you can't afford a litter. Philip was assassinated during a wedding feast, as you know. I have unearthed references in a treatise which claims that *maati* was a dish beloved of the Thessalians. As you are aware, the Thessalians have a reputation for being the most sumptuous of all Greek peoples.'

'I suppose you'd come with me to Truna's if we could eat a *maati* there?'

'Do you mark what I say? All you think about's food! I have made a contribution to learning this day, and you want

143

to eat at Truna's. Caylus is just as bad. You won't always be young, you know! You won't always be able to dine at Truna's.' He looked angry. His hands shook, and he wiped his brow with the hem of his cloak. For an instant he closed his eyes tightly, as if in pain.

'I often can't afford to eat at Truna's.'

I saw how pale his skin was. It glistened. Skirting his books, I placed a hand on his shoulder and said, 'You need a cup of wine, Father. Sit down. Let me ring for the housekeeper. Later, I'll fetch Katie over.'

'No, no, I'll not disturb the woman – she may be busy. And don't trouble Katie. So you worked all morning, did you? And what did you achieve?' He brushed his hair back shakily from his forehead. 'Katie will be busy too, make sure of that.'

'I was intending to tell you. De Lambant's sister, Smarana, is to marry in less than a month, and we are to perform a comedy for the nuptials. I shall play the chief role of Albrizzi, and this morning, after days of search, I discovered—'

'Truna's? Why do you suddenly mention him? Old Truna is dead this twelvemonth, and his tavern sold. That shows how often you come to visit your father. You prattle on about performing comedies and all the time Truna is one with historic personages!'

'Father, Philip of the Macedonians was assassinated, yet people are still marrying. Come down the street with me and enjoy the bustle of humanity as you used to do – it may set your mind on more cheerful things.'

'They're still playing *Albrizzi*, are they? By the bones of Desport, that farce was old forty years ago, when I first saw it! What's a more cheerful thing than *maati*? They had good actors in those days. Why should you think I would enjoy being jostled in the alleys, with my calculus troubling me?'

I moved over to the shuttered window and peered into our inner court, where an ornamental Triton no longer blew a fountain from his conch. Times had truly changed since my mother's death. Once there had been peacocks strutting among her lavender beds.

'We shall insert topical matter into the play, Father, as no doubt they did in your young day. If not the tavern and not the street, then at least take a turn in the garden. The air's so stale here.'

'No, no, the air's pure in here, guaranteed so. All sorts of illnesses lurk outside. I don't even let Beppolo enter now, for fear he contaminates the place. When you get old, you have to take care of yourself. No one else will do it for you.'

'Did you hear that de Lambant's sister is to be wed to a gentleman from Vamonal, Father? He comes of the military house of Orini.'

'Beppolo says the well's run dry. I've never heard of the Orinis. If he's not lying then it's the first time that ever happened – in your mother's day, we had water aplenty. Everything seems to go wrong. Who are the Orinis, I'd like to know! Bankers, or such-like.'

'The well often runs dry at this time of year, but I'll see to it on my way out.'

'You're off already, are you? You never told me what you've been up to. Well, I suppose there's nothing to keep you here.'

He went over and sat in his battered, leather chair, heavily carved with mythical beasts and lizards. 'Yes, I saw *Albrizzi* as a student – thin stuff as I remember. And you wanted a shirt for it? You've been working this morning, eh? What were you working at, I'd like to know. Why don't you become a proper tragic actor, eh?'

I moved towards the door, saying, 'There's no taste for tragedy in this age, Father. It's decadent, as I'm sure you'll agree.'

'You should become a tragic actor. As long as there's tragedy in life, tragedy is needed on the stage. You see, the housekeeper doesn't always come when you ring – it's the way with housekeepers nowadays. Actors should hold a mirror up to nature, and not just indulge triviality. I don't know what the world's coming to ...'

'Why, the world goes on for ever the same, Father. We have a Supreme Council in Malacia to ensure it.'

'I don't know about going on for ever. We have reason to believe that there has been change in the world, dramatic change, before now, and that there will be change again. What do you mean, no taste for tragedy? Why, in my young day ... Listen, I'm now coming in my great *Disquisition on Disquisitions* to the Disquisition on the Origins of the Modern World.'

My honoured father had brought up – or perhaps one should say tumbled over – the subject of his life's work, a serious

145

study of absolutely everything. I believe it was his questioning of the plainest fact until it crumbled into dust which had determined me, even as a mere child, that the stage was the only reality. I relinquished my grasp of the door handle, pleased that I could so unaffectedly show resignation.

'If you've reached the beginning of the world, your book must be nearly at an end.'

'How's that? As you must know – after all, the matter was apparent to Alexander – magical lore has it that there were several rival strains of man in the prehistoric world. We know of at least three: *homo simius*, anthropoid man, and *homo saurus*, meaning us. Plus other strains here and there of lesser import upon the globe. Now, *homo saurus* is infinitely the oldest strain, dating clear from the early Secondary Life Era, whereas the *simii* and the anthropoids are several hundred million years our juniors. Moreover, our kind began coldblooded, created in the image of the Prince of Darkness—'

'Father, this old pedantic rubbish is not—'

'The image of the Prince of Darkness ... You young coxcombs, you care nothing for learning! It was different in my young day ... But, setting that by ... pedantic rubbish, indeed! It has well been divined by the scholars that our world is only one of a number of alchemaically conceivable worlds. In some other worlds of possibility, to take an extreme case, *homo saurus* may have been wiped out entirely – say at the great battle of Itssobeshiquetzilaha, over three million, one thousand and seven hundred years ago. The result would be a nightmare world in which one of the other human races had supremacy and Malacia never existed ...'

Supremacy, I thought! In this, my home, I'd never been near even equality.

Taking leave of my father, I quitted the chamber and walked along the corridor. From its panels came an aroma of something like resin which took me back to those years when I depended entirely on the good humour of others. I quickened my pace.

As I crossed the court, Beppolo emerged from an empty stable, hurrying round-shouldered to see me out of the gate, his right hand already thrusting itself forward, cupped in a receiving attitude.

'Your illustrious father is cheerful this morning, Perry sir!

As well he might be, according to his prosperous station. He tells me he has detected who Philip of Macedon is, to his great benefit!'

'Where's the housekeeper?'

'Why, sir, is she not in the house? No? Then perhaps she has gone out. There's little for her to do. If she's not in the house, depend on it she has gone out.'

'And I suppose that if she has not gone out, then she is in the house?'

'You could very likely be right, Perry sir.'

'Be sure to tell her I shall be back tomorrow. I shall expect to see the house cleaned and a proper meal set before my father. Else there will be trouble. Understand?'

'Every word, sir, as sure as I stand here wearing my old patched breeches.' He bowed low and dragged the gate open. I tossed him a sequin. The gate squealed closed again; its lock clicked as I made down the street. My father was safe with his researches.

The bells of St Marco's chimed one of the afternoon. A pack of ragged children were teasing a chick-snake against a wall. The little yellow-and-red creature stood waving its hands defensively and barked like a gruff dog – a habit it had learned from the local mongrels. Several of the smaller kinds of ancestral animal, wandering in from the wilderness, had come to an alliance with the canine inhabitants of Malacia. Chick-snakes and grab-skeeters, which were good climbers, were particularly common. I chased the urchins away and headed past Truna's for a cheaper tavern.

The Cellar of the Small Goldsmiths was built into an old ruined triumphal arch. I sat outside and was served wine and meat, speaking to no one, although there was a cheerful meeting of fellows at the next table. As I was leaving, and they were singing and bellowing, one of them leaned over to pluck my sleeve.

'You must have a solemn philosophy, cavalier, to keep so straight a face with your wine!'

Looking down at him, I said, 'There you are correct, sir. Henceforth, I mean to pursue pleasure as a serious business.'

'Have you not heard that Tvrtko and his army are leaving Malacia? The plague makes too long strides among his men. Is not that worth celebrating?'

I hit my fist in delight. 'Then Bengtsohn's scheme succeeded!'

In delight, I told them who I was. All had seen me soar over the Bucintoro. All insisted on buying me drink. But I cut short the carouse, haunted by thoughts of Armida, Bedalar, and my father. For once, I preferred to be out of jollity.

As I walked down the street, the laughing voices faded, although there were other taverns, other voices. At the door of one stood a woman, singing as sweetly as a bird, with dark-red lips and a black skin. I turned in the direction of Caylus's chambers. Suppose that Bedalar were there ...

Under the archway of his house, a hag in black stood in the shadows selling paper-charms, small birds, shields, flowers, buglewings, boats, animals. The tissues fluttered in a draught blowing through the archway. Behind her, she had lit a smouldering charcoal enchanter's fire; wisps of smoke rose from a tibia and sprinkle of chicken bones. On impulse, I bought a paper shield before I mounted the wide stair.

No answer came from Caylus.

I pushed open his door, vexed that he was not here after what he had said. I needed company.

In his chambers all was quiet. Something told me that the room in which I stood had but recently been vacated – some vibrance in the air, a disturbance in the golden motes floating between window and rug. Sunlight created its pattern on an area of floor by Caylus's couch. In the air, a scent was discernible, faint but luxurious; I stood in a reverie, as still as the room itself. I knew that odour.

Once I said Caylus's name aloud. I remained in the middle of the gold-flecked room, the door still open, cries from the street coming to me distantly. I looked about, bewitched by the flowers and the room's recent passion. Bedalar ...

Here were Caylus's few books, his many sporting engravings, his altar, his table with a flask and two empty glasses on it, his fernery, his foils, his water-clock, his couch, covered by a rumpled, silken spread. On top of the spread lay an amber object no bigger than a butterfly's wing.

By a trick of the mind, the sight of this little item made me realize that as well as lust a faint scent of patchouli floated in the chamber.

I recognized the object before I picked it up. The tortoise-shell glowed in slatted light, its two little horns thrusting upwards like the retractile eye-stalks of a snail. It was a plectrum of rare design. I let it rest in my hand.

Caylus's time had been better occupied than mine! Dragging up a chair, I put the plectrum in the middle of the table and sat down. Sprawling there, taking up Caylus's quill and ink, I composed an ironic quatrain to greet his return, whether alone or no. I slipped the quatrain under the plectrum.

> *Dear Caylus! Those discordant Age hath laid*
> *Aside lack games harmonious as hers –*
> *As, mute while she a wilder Music stirs,*
> *Her mandoline in shadow lies unplayed.*

At the door, I turned to survey the empty room, with sunlight imprisoned among the shadows. Walking slowly downstairs, I found the old hag still under the archway by her smouldering fire. I returned the paper shield to her.

Disconsolate, I headed towards Kemperer's tailor.

At a haberdasher's shop, a frumpy matron was standing in the doorway holding up lace to the light. A figure behind her called my name.

As I started looking in past the female obstacle, a horseman rode down the street, crying that the Ottoman army was in retreat, moving away through the south-west marshes. The Tuscady cavalry was hastening their retreat. The Powers of Light and Dark had again saved Malacia for their own purposes.

Propelled by this cheering news, I entered the shop. And there stood Bedalar, dressed in a smart city gown with hairstyle to match. Lovely though she looked, her pleasure at seeing me made her even more inviting. She introduced the frumpy person as her chaperon, Jethone; there the reverse was true; *her* displeasure at seeing me rendered her even less inviting.

'We were about to call upon my brother Caylus, but have been detained by a quest for a certain fine piece of lace.'

'It must be from Flanders,' said the chaperon.

'It must be *in* Flanders, judging by how long we've searched here,' Bedalar said.

'You are being impertinent, miss.'

With secret signals of desperation, Bedalar said, 'And there are more shops along the street.'

'Lace hath charms to suit the savage breast,' I said, stroking my chin. 'As it happens, Miss Bedalar, I have just come from your brother. I was sorry to leave, since he has such respectable company with him, but urgent business calls me to my father. However, I will willingly escort you to Caylus, in order to be of assistance to your companion, if you like. Then I shall have to take leave of you immediately, but your brother would have charge of you until Jethone arrives.'

She blinked a little and, with straight face, said, 'Perhaps I should not intrude. Who is this respectable company with my brother?'

'Oh, a priest of the Religion and a couple of rather severe-looking schoolmen.'

'Then I'll stay here and advise Jethone, thank you.'

The harridan said, 'I could manage comfortably without your comments, miss, thank you all the same. If you will go straight to your brother's house with this gentleman, I will join you there in five minutes.'

To me she said, 'And mind you deliver her to her brother immediately. How many priests?'

'One only – but very emaciated.'

With heartfelt protestations about my intention not to let Bedalar out of my sight, I grasped her arm and whisked her from the shop. Jethone, lace in hand, watched us until we were round the corner. A minute more and we were under the archway, up the stairs, and standing in that silent scented room, our arms about each other. It was all accomplished on the instant.

'I thought I'd die of boredom,' she said. 'That old crow makes a religion out of lace.'

'You look faint, dear Bedalar. Let me arrange you on this sofa and feel your pulse.'

'My pulse?'

'And not only your pulse, for this is a case where a more thorough examination would be in order.'

'Perian, your secret engagement to Armida—'

'Ssh, it's a secret!' I sealed her mouth with mine. Her arms came round my neck to make me captive. As I climbed on the

150

couch with her, I could tell from the way she disposed her limbs that she was herself well disposed.

So it proved. Amid our kisses, my exploratory hand found that she had the warmest of welcomes. Soon we had lost the scent of the world about us in pursuit of our own quarry. Her yielding acceptance of me sent me into raptures. She unthinkingly granted me more than Armida.

At last we lay quiet, her fair head pillowed on my arm, smiling at each other.

'Perian, what sort of person are you really? You play the dashing man-about-town, but I know there's more to you than that.'

'I play all roles. They are all me.'

'I mean, beneath the roles. Your true self. This is fun, just a piece of joyous naughtiness – I could no more resist seizing the instant than you could, for men and women are much alike there. But now, I'm fond of you – but I wonder if we should have done it for Armida's sake. She's my friend, and I feel I betray her.'

'We don't need to tell Armida. If she doesn't know, she's not hurt. Loving you makes no difference to my feelings for her.' I sat up in bed; catechism is not my favourite hobby.

Bedalar persisted, sitting up by me. 'We'll feel constrained when we meet in her company. I'm so stupid, I don't understand. And what about Guy, who says he loves me? For his sake, I should not have slipped up here with you. I'm a hussy!'

'It's only a half-hour's pleasure, Bedalar. Don't make a tragedy of it. Guy won't know either, unless you tell him.'

'There, you say it again – don't tell them. That means it's wrong, doesn't it? I love this cosy loving, Perian, don't mistake me, but I hate having secrets, hate feeling guilty. Don't you feel guilty?'

'Stop it, you sumptuous hussy – we live in a decadent age!' She tried to look into my eyes, but instead I began putting my tongue to one of her generous nipples.

'You see, you swive with me, Perry, but you keep your mind closed to me. That's not real love ... Or maybe you have not learned yet to open your mind to others – even to Guy – so that no one knows who you are ... Oh, that's lovely – do the other one ... Perry, love ... Do you know who you are yourself?'

'By the bones, woman, be quiet and enjoy!'

She was falling back with eyes half-closed, the folds of her body flowering towards me. 'Its just – after the night on the mountain – the thought of you so near ... I could hear you with Armida ... I wanted to see you unclothed ... And I longed to find out what you were really like ... Unclothed under the smart talk.'

Bursting into laughter, I jumped up and did a jig about Caylus's room, returning to climb astride her pillowy stomach. I smacked her hip.

'There now – you've seen me unclothed and I'm nothing to be ashamed of. Stop the silly chatter, stir me up, and see me in action again. The Turks may be in retreat but I'm ready for a fresh advance.'

With sudden energy, she kissed the banner of my attack. 'Seeing that you're such a hero today, helping to chase away the Ottoman ...'

'I'm always a hero; soon I shall be twice a hero, playing Albrizzi.'

'No, Perian, you know what I mean. Not just pretending, but going up in the air on that charger as you did, to defeat the Turks. That was a brave thing.'

Sometimes, as I often say, the gods and men see eye-to-eye. As she spoke, bold fanfares sounded from the direction of the square, so much more virile than the twangling of a mandoline. The triumphal occasion would be properly marked without doubt.

'You're right, Bedalar, my beauty. It's your fortune to have me, so don't question it. This is an occasion, I am a hero, and we must celebrate.'

'We are celebrating,' she said, taking firmer hold of me.

Later, I wrote another quatrain, a companion-piece to the one I had left for her brother, and flung it negligently to her, as if I tossed off poetry all the day.

> *Dear Bedalar, of all girls I have laid*
> *Yours is the music that most wildly stirs*
> *Me; while no marring discord joy defers,*
> *Your instrument must never lie unplayed.*

It had not quite the flair of the first quatrain, yet was more deeply felt.

A Young Soldier's Horoscope

Charmed Malacia! In the wildernesses beyond its fortress walls, in dreary chasm, tangled forest, or endless mountainside, the forces of many kinds of evil struggled for supremacy. Within our winding streets serenity seemed to prevail.

The conclusion of the week of festival was marked by an improvised pageant celebrating the withdrawal of swart Tvrtko and his forces, in which I was lionized almost to exhaustion. The flight of the buglewing from our calendar coincided also with the return of Armida from her exile in Juracia. On the evening of the day before Bengtsohn summoned us to resume work with the zahnoscope, I received an unexpected invitation to visit Armida at the Hoytola mansion; perhaps my increasing celebrity had softened her father's heart.

I presented myself early next morning. Debonair though I was, the brute at the gate, as ugly as his two guard dogs put together, regarded me with as much favour as Stefan Trvtko himself would have received, supposing him to have manifested himself there with cannon, a dromedary, and assorted plans for bastinado. While the brute delayed me, I tried to recall something witty de Lambant had said about surly porters driving inconstancy from the door.

At last I was allowed in, and shown to a cool hall. Knowing it was the custom of the Hoytolas to observe breakfast as sumptuously as in Constantinople, I hoped to join their meal, but coffee alone was served to me as I awaited my lady.

A row of marble busts set on pillars confronted the visitor. The gentlemen portrayed were universally severe, as if finding immortality conducive to migraine. I tried to set my face into their mould. I was glad to be summoned to Armida's palazzo, although my stomach produced whining noises loud enough to make passers-by suspect I had a lap-dog smuggled under my shirt.

As I sipped my coffee, a maidservant came along the corridor closing jalousies, giving me a glance now and again. I could not help returning her glance; she was a cuddlesome-looking girl. Then I reminded myself where I was and how I intended to marry honourably. In the matrimonial estate, rolls with servant-girls would be out of the question. So would rolls with Bedalar.

So I fell into a happy day-dream. Armida and I were married, and her loving father set us up in a splendid little town house with views of the Toi. We took chocolate for breakfast, and invited our friends round freely. And we engaged a delightful little maidservant, industrious and cuddlesome ...

My reverie was broken by the appearance of Armida herself, looking as lovely as in my vision and wearing a super-tunic with a kirtle beneath, the tight sleeves of which emerged from the wide sleeves of the tunic. On her dark head was a little lace cap or shadow. Stripes fled up her tunic from toe to head as she approached through barred patches of sunlight.

She led me to her own sitting room, which was on the first floor and had a balcony overlooking an intimate courtyard. It was peaceful in the courtyard, with fruiting lemon and orange bushes, and an occasional hen scratching. A sailback basked in a sunny corner. I remarked on it.

'It's not the only ancestral animal about the place. Father likes them. There are several tree-snaphances in the back quarters, to keep down rats. Juracia is the place for bigger varieties – tyrant-greaves and all that.'

She shuddered delicately and indicated that I should take a seat on the balcony. To my relief, my stomach stopped whining.

'I am forgiven my trespasses,' she said – not without an amused glance into the room behind us, where her dried old chaperon was talking to a servant. 'Both Yolaria and I are glad to be back from Juracia. Father spoke well of the sports. Did you enjoy them?'

'I was in the arena all afternoon.'

'Did you stay for the bulls?'

'The bulls? Oh, no, I'd had enough by then.'

'Caylus was entering as a toreador. I wonder you didn't stay.'

'I thought I'd better leave and rehearse my part. I'm going to be busy – Kemperer wishes us to work on two plays for the coming season, and there's Otto's light-play to finish. I'm looking forward to that, aren't you, Armida?'

'Have you seen Bedalar lately?' she asked.

On a little table by her side was a silver bell. Against the railings stood a perch to which were chained two reptopines, their scaly bodies brilliant in blue and red. I turned to stroke one of them and it slowly opened the feathery spines along its backbone, until they were erect and trembling. Armida made me feel that I too was trapped on a bare branch.

'Bedalar? Hasn't Guy been keeping her happy? He's mad on her and taking up all her time. She calls the idiot her handsome boy and I know not what – so I hear.'

'Guy is rather handsome, don't you think?' I turned to see if she was teasing me, but could form no definite conclusion; she was looking down at the silver bell and twirling it.

'He's handsome in a slovenly fashion, I suppose. It's true that you get used to his face after a while ... You're so beautiful, Armida, that the fish leap out of the Toi as you pass by.'

She regarded me pensively. 'Do you think Guy and Bedalar any sort of match? As far as the marriage market is concerned, I mean.'

'Marriage markets are things I have never studied. You and Yolaria can work that question out better than anyone.'

She appeared to tire of the subject just as persecution was setting in. That is a pleasing side of cultivated girls; they do tire of subjects.

'You see how I'm forgiven: I'm able to receive you here. Bedalar's father will not let her speak to Guy as yet. But you have become something of a hero and my father wishes to acknowledge the fact; isn't that nice?'

'Armida, of course! Nice, excellent, fantastic!' Yolaria was nowhere to be seen. I dashed across to her, put my arms about her and kissed her full on the lips.

'My darling, I am a hero, and you shall be my wife. I will be faithful and love only you.'

Looking round anxiously, she pushed me away. The reptopines scuttled along their perches.

'Behave, sir! There are many impediments to our marrying. How could you support me? From what you say, your father is poor and an old curmudgeon, so that—'

'Old, yes, and a curmudgeon, but not so poor—'

'We can only become husband and wife if my family approves of you enough to support us both, and I may as well tell you that my father has ambitions. I will not name the high-born young man with whom he has plans for me, or you would be jealous and probably—'

'What high-born young man? I am already seized by an absolute fit of jealousy. Tell me who it is.'

She stood up, looking at me frostily, holding the bell as if about to ring it.

'Please do not make a scene. Be assured that I am determined. I wish to marry the man of my choice and not my father's choice. It is to your advantage to continue to be a hero, and a discreet one. My father instructs me to tell you that he is holding an ancestral hunt on our country estate a week from now, at the period of the full moon. You are invited.'

'An ancestral hunt! Your father . . .'

'Once a year, we have to cull the bigger sorts of ancestral animals. Inviting you – with a little coercion from my sister and me – is my father's token of limited approval, and he will then observe how you conduct yourself—'

'An ancestral hunt! How magnificent! I have always longed to hunt wattle-tassets and duck-beaks. Not to mention trundlers. I will hire a horse, the best—'

'Dear Perian, the best horses are never hired ones. This is to be a grand affair. Get good advice. Everything must be in style if it is to be done at all.'

'You know I do everything in style.'

'Then no talk of hired nags, please. In the hunt – to which many nobles will be invited – the quarry is something more ferocious than duck-beaks. Why, duck-beaks and tassets are used as steeds in Juracia.'

It was irking the way she patronized me. She sat in her chair as if for her portrait, enhanced by the two reptopines, who spread out their twelve-fingered fans along their backs, displaying purely for her delight.

'Well, Armida, since I have never visited Juracia, you shall have the pleasure of telling me what game people – nobles and commoners – do hunt there. Shatterhorns, perhaps?'

She dismissed the notion. 'Plodding along with those great frilled skulls, shatterhorns are tedious reptiles, offering little sport. No, when you come to Juracia, you hunt the carnivore kings, the two great ancestrals, tyrant-greaves and devil-jaws. The devil-jaws are of the forest variety, not from the plains. The hunt lasts for three days. There is feasting, but it is a great

156

test of manhood.' A certain malicious pleasure shone in her eyes.

'What is the test of womanhood in Juracia?'

'Women do not hunt the great ancestrals.'

Yolaria emerged on the balcony bearing a basket of apricots. She deigned to smile at me.

'The fruits are ripening, de Chirolo. Excuse me, Miss Armida, but the coach is ready. It's time for our morning drive.'

Armida squeezed my hand as I left. Down in the court, the sailback put up its great fin and sulked in a sunny corner.

Out in the street again, I made my way unthinkingly towards Kemperer's place.

She loved me, she was scheming to marry me. Was that correct? All that was needed was for me to polish off a twenty-foot-high devil-jaw or the like. Was that correct?

My heart quailed. I asked myself if any man could face so much for love. To be frank, I asked myself if I was entirely equal to Armida and the Hoytolas. Perhaps somewhere in Malacia, her high-born young man was asking himself the same question. Who was he? I knew one thing; if I were a carnivore, I would single him out for my next meal.

I had to behave better. I must cease the flirtation with Bedalar. If I was going to be strong, I must be pure. Or purer. I felt some guilt at making love to de Lambant's girl. It had come about accidentally. The circumstances were beyond my control. Lust, admittedly, had been one of those circumstances. I must not play a treacherous General Gerald in real life; I must be noble, like Prince Mendicula himself, to win my princess. A new life must begin from now on.

Perhaps I didn't want to be a player all my life.

Advice I needed. And finance for the hunt. Well, that was still a week away. A horoscope from Seemly Moleskin might help.

Already, ancestral animals moved through the jungles of my fancy.

My way led me through Ruppo Place, past a ruinous triumphal arch, relic of some forgotten victory, in the shade of which sat an astrologer. I always saw him there when going to the theatre by a route which avoided my creditors.

The crannies of Malacia held as many magicians and astrologers as spiders. This one was remarkable because he was young, plump and cheerful, all qualities rare in his profession. He sat in a chair upon a rough platform, over which a rug of oriental design had been flung. Beside him were his magical books, one of which, I knew, was written by him. Entitled *The Descendancy of Man*, it proved that our kind originated from goats and the precursors of goats. The astrologer's name was Phillibus Parterre.

He sat now with a client before him, gazing over her head with an expression suggesting he was on good terms with whatever goat-gods ruled the rooftops.

At the zenith of the old arch, masonry fringed by ferns let in a shaft of sunlight which bathed the scene below. It seemed to fire the hair of the girl who stood before Parterre; perhaps she had stationed herself deliberately in its ambience. The aura of additional gold so created bathed the face of the astrologer as well as the posy of flowers tied in the girl's top-knot. I recognized the tresses and the sturdy, female figure at the same time. The sun illuminated the chief luminary of the Malacian stage. The enchanting La Singla stood before Parterre.

Her audience with him was ending. She thanked him with pretty and well-rehearsed gestures. As she turned away, I crept up and caught her about the waist, kissing one of her velvet cheeks.

'Oh, Perian, you wretch, I thought – Heavens, let go of me, do not kiss me in public view!'

'So you have returned from Vamonal. Too long have we twain been apart . . .'

'Pray, let us be apart again!' She pushed me away, half-serious. 'Please don't touch me. My husband is in a jealous fit already.'

'Jealous, jealous, everyone gets so jealous, yet everyone is after the same thing. Why not live and let live? Suppose I make love to you, purely as a tribute to your bounding beauty, and half an hour later your husband does the same. Have I spoilt anything for him?'

She gave me an angry look.

'Love's not just a matter of bodies. Do you not know the divided mind? You don't feel! Have you never suffered envy, humiliation, defeat? Let me tell you, you may think Pozzi is old, but every time he puts his hand on another woman, or even

158

glances at her amorously, I'm jealous. I quite understand his jealousy of me, even when I can't bear it, when it suffocates me.'

I took her hand, but she pulled it away again as we walked along.

'You take no notice of what I say. You need to mature, Perian.'

'Come along, pet. You know your husband trusts me.'

'The pity of it is, he doesn't trust me. Pozzi's an old fox who smells mischief even when there's none about. He says I'm too pretty for my own good, which may perhaps be true.'

'It is the burden you have to bear, sweet Singla,' I said, and burst into laughter.

'Little you know how complicated life can be.'

Vamonal has made you capricious. I'm being genial but my life is full of knots.'

To myself I thought, There's a little mystery here. Both La Singla and Kemperer normally consulted an astrologer who lived almost opposite their house, a straggling frog-faced man. Why should she be speaking to another astrologer, except for reasons of secrecy? The answer lay in what she had just said; her husband was mistrustful and had reason to be; his pretty little wife was giving him fresh reason. She had a new lover. Which of the players was it? Not de Lambant, or he would have boasted of it. Not Portinari. Chasseur, perhaps, always quiet and glowering under his dark brows.

La Singla gave me a hurt, coquettish look and a slight additional wag of her hips.

'You are far too dissolute and free.'

'Well, now my pretty Singla, I have every intention of reforming my character, as it happens – but not exactly in the next half-hour. Nobody in Malacia would dispute that you are an unrivalled beauty, particularly after nightfall and assisted by limelight, so naturally your husband needs reassurance. Come down this sideway with me, give me a friendly kiss, and I will then testify to your Pozzi of your faithfulness, and put his mind at rest. Is it a deal?'

'Perian, I don't feel much like your sort of fun. Women suffer, you know. Men like you, who imagine they love women, increase their suffering.'

'You're sharp this morning. Let me help your suffering. Come down this sideway, and we'll do each other a favour.'

I took her arm so that she had to stop. As she turned her gaze at me, I noticed as I had before that her eyebrows were a little too heavy and that a crop of fine golden hair lay along her upper lip. Far from scrutinizing me, she was looking blankly through me and giving my proposition consideration.

'Life is very difficult, Perian. Please don't take advantage. Be my friend, if you can. It *would* help if you could reassure Maestro Kemperer. Listen, at siesta time we are going to inspect Harino's *Ombres Chinoises*. You must come with us.'

'Ah, I heard that the Great Harino was in town. Better than Tvrtko.'

'Pozzi fears that Harino will spoil our takings. So we go to see what sort of show he puts on. You come too and say a good word on my behalf, please.'

'I'll put your case in exchange for the usual favours.'

Taking her waist, I tried to pull her down a side-alley. She caught me a violent blow across the temple.

'Damn you, as if I haven't earned the right to expect your support a hundred times over, without allowing you one extra feel!'

'That's a brilliant way to earn my support!' My head echoed. 'You are playful and no mistake.'

'For once, I've played enough.'

'Who's the lucky man who has your undivided attention and divided legs?'

'I must get back. How time goes by. Walk faster, you horror.'

Over the bridge we went, she with her feet twinkling under her skirt, which she held to avoid the dirt in the street. She kept her thoughts to herself. I kept an eye on the world, thinking how good it looked and how sensibly people without ringing heads were occupied, whether they were walking, working, or merely spitting from the parapet of the bridge – as two blackamoors were doing, to amuse a baby they had charge of. A travelling man playing a little phonograph for denarios leaned against a doorpost and doffed his hat ironically to La Singla as we passed.

'You have some strange friends,' I said.

'That gentleman always attends my performances. You see him merely as a penniless wastrel now, yet he once declared his love for me in as beautiful and deeply felt a speech as I ever heard.'

'Did you love him in return?'

'The poor man could not control his fortune any more than his emotions. He ran through a considerable inheritance. Now, he hasn't a bean left. He's reduced, as you see, to playing *fonografo* in the street, and they say he procures boys – while his illustrious parents lie in a marble tomb topped by azure on the banks of the Savoirdi Canal.'

'If I had to settle for playing *fonografo* or lying in a marble tomb, I'd make his choice. His illustrious parents have a mouldy job.'

She looked wanly at me. 'Remember that I know by heart the comedies from which you resurrect your jokes.'

'How can I believe that when I've heard you dry up on stage so often?'

'Dear Perian, we are of the same age and even share the same sign, yet my less shallow experience of living enables me to advise you. Take matters more seriously. Suffer and realize that other people suffer too.'

We were nearly at her house. I slowed my pace and quickened my speech to say, 'Do I have to weep before you believe I suffer? I have a girl who means everything to me, and I mean to be faithful to her, though temptresses like you don't help. You mistake an easy manner for a shallow disposition. Inside here, there's enough anguish to make an owl laugh.' And I laughed myself as I struck my chest, thinking as I did so that what I said was very likely true.

With the flavours of the Fragrant Quarter all about it, Kemperer's house stood in that particular mellow glow which is a quality of prosperous streets. In the court, among broken carriages and snarling dogs on chains and Albert melancholy in his cage, men waited to see Kemperer. The court was rarely empty of these favour-seekers. Those who waited were attended by beggars and impoverished entertainers who in turn begged favours from them. In his fashion, Kemperer was a man with influence.

Today some of the loiterers were of a decidedly nasty cast of countenance. La Singla glanced at them with dread as we hurried by.

In the main room the table had been pushed to one side to make space for those who thronged there. You could tell when a new production was under way: the house became like a disordered warehouse. Hardly a room or hallway that was not filled with some property Kemperer had just acquired, or a costume he was thinking of acquiring. His kindly if irascible heart saw to it that several rooms were crammed with indigent relations or actors. He made such an uncomfortable host that these guests were always changing, arriving with flattery or departing with threats. There was a perpetual coming and going, with battered hats forever being swept off or rammed on valetudinarian heads.

At the centre of the activity was its source, Pozzi Kemperer, fussy, light-footed, articulate, snarling like his hounds, prancing round in satin slippers and waistcoat, with his peruke at the tilt and a froth of words and saliva on his lips. A figure of fun, and rather a dangerous figure at that.

He was making a spectacle of himself as La Singla and I entered. Seeing La Singla, he paused to deliver one single evil glare which would have curdled the blood of a devil-jaw, and then returned to capering round a stranger draped in an ankle-length cloak. With this gaunt stranger stood a lizard-man, holding two fine black panthers on a leash.

Indicating them, the gaunt stranger was saying over and over, in deep tones, 'These beasts are guaranteed from the distant Orient.'

'Go away, I tell you – take your creatures back to the Orient!' screamed Kemperer.

'Sire, they were born among the orchid forests of Bamboola.'

'Take them back there, Bamboolarize them, take them anywhere, get them out of here! Apply to the menagerie at West Gate, where they'll accept anything with fur on its body, however mangy. Just get them away before they stink the house out, or eat my players. They're starving – look at the way they glare and lick their chops! Out! Out!'

The beasts were yawning with lolling tongues, from either boredom or constipation. The stranger said in melancholy tones, 'Sire, I supply courts, from Siracusa in the south to Malma in the dreadful north, with beasts often less fine – less docile, less fragrant – than this brace of pussies. I can assure you that animals are an adornment to whatever entertainment you care to mount. That I guarantee from the bottom of my convictions.'

'You may guarantee it from the bottom of your boots and it makes no difference. Get out! My entertainments entertain without having lions widdling against the scenery. Out!'

He beckoned one of his helpers, who came forward and made shooing motions with his arms. Slightly interested, one of the panthers moved forward by the length of a whisker. Kemperer fell back screaming for help, into the arms of La Singla, who by now was also screaming. She could shriek considerably louder and more musically.

The gaunt man turned, beckoning to his assistant, and off they stalked. The panthers trotted behind them like dogs. Their progress through the outer court was marked by yells of terror from the mendicants, mingled with whoops and enraged barking from Albert and the hounds.

Several of my friends had been watching the fun, including Portinari. I went over and slapped him on the shoulder. De Lambant was not there.

'"You of all under the rank heavens are of the heavenly ranks",' I quoted.

'Save your *Albrizzi* tags, de Chirolo,' said Portinari. 'His lordship now decrees that we play *The Visionaries* as a curtain raiser, before getting to *Albrizzi*. Since we're rusty in it, we have to run it through now in preference to *Albrizzi*.'

I clutched at my forehead. 'What a rogue Kemperer is. The last time *The Visionaries* was hissed off, he swore that we should never play it again.'

'But this is at a wedding; besides, de Lambant says that a visiting Duke of Ragusa will be present. 'Twill give everyone a chance to settle down before the drama.'

'True. And at weddings tastes are always lower.'

'I like my little business as the first suitor.'

'Oh, yes, I remember that.' I did indeed, and was thankful that Portinari was confined to small parts. 'My role of Phalante the Bankrupt is so brief—'

Kemperer himself came up, still wearing La Singla about his scraggy neck, in time to catch my remark.

'Ah, Perian, Perian, my dear young fellow, you know how tremendously amusing you are as Phalante, the old apothecary.' He clapped me on the back, laughing and frothing at the mouth. 'When you juggle your wooden spoons, thinking them silver, and cry, "Why, this silver service alone is worth a king's ransom – at least, half a ransom, well, a slice of ransom ..."

Nobody can carry the humour of it off like you.'

'Let's drop that business with the spoons.'

'No, no, de Chirolo, you do yourself an injustice. The world loves your spoons, don't it, Maria, my faithful dove, my cow?'

With similar cajoleries, we were hustled into the courtyard to say our lines. The mendicants served as audience, poor simple Gilles held the prompt-book. Standing about or strutting as we felt inclined, we ran through the old speeches.

The Visionaries was a comedy of illusion, with every character mad or deluded, believing themselves to be greater than they were. The father with his three plain daughters had to see them married off between four dotty suitors. Kemperer himself played the old father. It was a simple piece which had to be taken fast. Once, we had played it in the traditional manner, with everyone falling about, until we discovered that audiences liked it better if we took the material seriously. Except for the claptrap with the spoons.

At two of the afternoon, when the bell of a nearby church was chiming, Kemperer cried 'Enough' and released us. He buried his head in his hands.

'That I should live to see men of straw mouthing like blocks of wood! Pity any Duke of Ragusa who has to sit through your bouts of arthritis, my dear friends – not to mention the de Lambant family. All right, tomorrow we will try it again. Meanwhile, I shall scour the city for a man with two panthers, to infuse some life and piss into the proceedings!'

For all Kemperer's reproaches, we were a cheerful crowd who pushed in to see the *Ombres Chinoises*. On our way to the shadow theatre, we refreshed ourselves with wine in a tavern by the Maltese Steps. The performances were held inside a large oriental tent in a shady garden. The tent was covered with carpets and tapestries to make the darkness inside more intense.

Shadow plays were becoming so fashionable that the maestro feared it might affect our business. Now here was the Great Harino's *Ombres Chinoises*, newly set up, offering the public *The Saga of Karagog*, preceded by *The Broken Bridge*, and charging high admission prices.

As we filtered into the gloom, Kemperer plucked me aside and whispered in my ear, 'Perian, darling fellow, you sit by me, for I depend on your criticism of the performance.'

'You might pay for my ticket if you are retaining me in a professional capacity.'

'Your criticism is too amateurish for that! Don't go above yourself, that's my sincere warning, the word of a true friend. I also need a more personal word with you about my naughty wife.' He squeezed my wrist hard, indicating need for silence.

A lizard-girl came round selling comfits, and we made ourselves comfortable until harpsichord music sounded and the curtains parted. We were pleased to see that scarcely a dozen people were attending the show, apart from our own company.

The screen was a sheet some one-and-a-half metres long by a metre high. Shadows pranced across it, picked out by brilliant flares behind. Principal characters moved near to the screen, and so were densely black. Lesser characters and the props moved at greater distances, so that they appeared in greyer definition. Variety was achieved by this simple means. The scenic effects were striking, with clouds and water well imitated.

The Great Harino's chief novelty was that parts of his puppets, their faces and the clothes of the more important personages, were cut away and replaced by coloured glass, to give dazzling effects on the screen. I was not alone in gasping at what we saw.

Although few of the puppets were jointed, their movement was good and the commentary funny, if time-honoured. Most amazing was the way in which one soon accepted the puppets for reality, and the screen for life, as if there were no other!

Less impressed, Kemperer began to whisper in my ear.

'I don't want to do her an injustice in any way, and Minerva knows that I cherish the tiresome baggage dearly, but my darling Maria is too fond of hopping in and out of beds that are unworthy of her lovely if unruly body. Now she's hopped into one bed too many ... I've been hearing rumours, Perian ...'

At that moment, La Singla thrust her pretty head between ours and said, 'What are you two whispering about? Isn't it a dainty show?'

'Go away, my honey pot, my starfish,' whined Kemperer. 'Go and flirt in the dark with Portinari – he knows where to stop, if you don't! De Chirolo and I are talking business.'

La Singla snorted like a piglet and withdrew.

'You need to be more coaxing than that to keep a wife faithful, maestro!' I said.

'What do you know of wives?'

'I'm growing more responsible. I'm contemplating marriage. Would you possibly advance me some money?'

'In my young day, the contemplation of matrimony required no expenditure.'

The Broken Bridge was reaching its conclusion. I had seen it many times in different forms, but never so well done as by the shadows. The boatman rowed across the river with every appearance of reality; his back was jointed to make the movement lifelike. Behind him, snow sparkled on high mountains. Sweat poured off the faces of the audience, so intense was the heat of the flares necessary to achieve the lighting effects.

'I am tired of coaxing the jade!' complained Kemperer in a moment: 'Would not any woman give her maidenhead to be married to a successful man like me? But now she's gone too far – much too far, Perian. I can be vindictive when the spirit moves me, you understand!' To help me understand, he pinched me hard on the wrist, so that I cried out with surprise and pain just as a fangle fish began to munch up the ill-natured labourer mending the bridge. The audience burst into laughter, thinking I was alarmed.

'She has had the impudence to fall in love with another worthless coxcomb. I discovered one of his confounded letters tucked in with her chemises, just this morning, when I was looking for spare laces to my corset. I mean to have the coxcomb waylaid and soundly beaten. No man meddles with my wife's affections!'

Each of these points he emphasized with further pinches. I was careful not to give the audience further cause for laughter – a precaution the more easily carried out because, in his agitation, Kemperer seized me by the throat and pushed my head backwards over the seat. Like Paul in the farce of the three kings, I was 'trapped between chocolate-time and eternity'.

At last I broke away, gasping.

'We may be the best of friends, maestro, but that is no reason for killing me outright! Do you imagine I'm the coxcomb you seek? I would as lief climb into bed with *you* as with your spouse, so great is my respect for the sanctity of marriage.'

'Pardon, pardon, I am a man of passion and I forget myself. I trust you implicitly or I would not be confiding in you.'

'I may undergo matrimony myself soon.'

'It's no joke to be cuckolded, and even worse to have to admit it. You can't afford to marry, sonny. Why, I'm as virile as ever I was. No, Perian, before this wretched shadow play ends, listen! – I have my thugs and my spies to command, never fear, as a man of my standing must do, but I want you to tell me if you have seen La Singla acting in any way untoward. *In any way!* I want you to watch her closely, since she trusts you, as do I.'

'I won't add to your number of spies.'

'No, no, confound you, nothing dishonourable – just report anything suspicious, and keep watching, eh? And we should build up the part of Phalante the Bankrupt. Such a funny part when you play it. You've seen nothing untoward with her?'

'It's hard to believe that such a virtuous woman could bear to deceive a husband like you!'

He dug me in the ribs with an elbow notorious for its lethal bone structure.

'She doesn't get much peace from such a hot-blooded fellow, let me tell you, but every woman is a rake at heart. Men are souls of virtue compared. I could kill her at times.'

Peace had now fallen on the river. The broken bridge remained unrepaired. Sunset was coming on. Sweet aromatic herbs were lit to one side, to affect the audience with their odours. A fleet of long-necked fanglefish cruised placidly upstream. The tips of the mountains turned pink as the valley disappeared in shadow. It was suddenly affecting, and it was over.

'Rubbish, rubbish!' Kemperer cried, knocking over his chair. 'Not a witty line in the whole thing! The Great Harino's a great fraud! *Karagog* had better improve on that dismal display or I shall not sit it through!'

But most people were amused. They cried for cold drinks to slake their thirsts, so hot was it in the tent. Portinari came to sit next to me and we drank sherbet.

'It was a bagatelle, but it had novelty!' he said.

'When I was a boy, an old man in Stary Most used to play *The Broken Bridge* in a barrel, with a candle for light. It's many centuries old.'

'Like *The Visionaries* ... All the same, this interpretation had artistry, don't you think?'

'Artistry enough. "Hokum maybe, but striking theatre",' I quoted. 'It reminded me of Reality without making ineffectual attempts to imitate it slavishly.'

'Reality is so unpleasant . . . Think how we sit here in moderate comfort, watching a succession of pictures, while behind the screen some poor sweating wretch feeds flares hot enough to roast himself on.'

'Isn't that the nature of all art? An artist suffers agonies to yield his audience one twitch of delight!'

'Ah, then you have agreed to play Phalante!' he said. 'What else was old Kemperer talking to you about?'

I was saved having to answer by a loud drum-roll and the lighting up of the screen. Diverse, dazzling figures burst forth on it. Out jumped Karagog, with his long arms and his comic red hat, and the fun began.

Karagog tried to become a schoolmaster, but failed so miserably that the scholars chased him from school; tried to join a circus, but fell from the high wire into a soup tureen; joined the army, but became terrified at the sound of cannon. Images pelted before our eyes. The puppet-master had contrived a zoetrope effect, so that in the circus scenes arcrobats skipped, leaped, and danced across the screen, tossing coloured balls as they went. And the parade of soldiers, all in their great plumed hats, was magnificent. They swung their arms and the music played 'Lilibulero'.

A battle scene was next. The screen darkened. Shots were heard, and screams of 'Fire'. A lurid, flickering light crossed the battlefield, where soldiers stood ready. Smoke was in the auditorium now – Kemperer was coughing and cursing.

All at once, the screen itself burst into flames. The puppet-operators were revealed, dropping their puppets and running madly from the blaze. The whole tent was alight.

'You see – realism carried too far!' Portinari said, gasping with laughter as we ran through the smoke. A pile of broadsheets stood by the exit. I snatched one as we scampered by.

In the garden all was pandemonium. Puppets were being flung unceremoniously into a cart, while assistants threw buckets of water at the blaze and the Great Harino screamed. The flames were spreading to some arbours of trellis where wistaria grew.

'What a blaze!' Kemperer said, rubbing his hands. 'It was madness to have flares inside a tent. Let's hope they don't get it under control quickly!'

Ashes of burnt tent fell like autumn leaves. One settled on La Singla's shoulder. She screamed. Kemperer beat at it with blows which would have extinguished Vesuvius, until his poor wife staggered from him, shrieking. Turning to me, gesturing ferociously, he said, 'What an end to my miseries if she went up in smoke, eh?'

Portinari and I, with some of the other players, went to cool down in the nearest wine-shop. In its darkest recess stood a keg of Bavarian beer. We ordered two tankards. With mutual pledges we lifted the beer, foaming, to our lips.

'What an old coxcomb Pozzi is!' said Portinari, wiping his mouth and sighing.

'Why do we work for him?'

'Yet he has his humorous point. When I first joined, I asked if he had any hints for a young actor, and he said, "Yes, one above all: remain the sunny side of forty".'

'Good advice – which I for one mean to follow.' I pulled from my shirt the broadsheet I had picked up in the pleasure-garden. Spreading it on the table, we read the rhyme set at its foot in black letter:

> *Our Shadow Figures, with their mimic strife,*
> *They are but to Amuse, or chase your Care,*
> *And beg Indulgence from you Phantoms there,*
> *Within the greater Raree-show of Life.*
>
> *From Orient and Far Cathay come they.*
> *Even like you, Someone behind the Screen*
> *Controls their Acts – so think, when you have seen,*
> *Your Life like theirs is but a Shadow Play!*

We roared with laughter. 'It was this inflammatory stuff which set the tent alight, not the flares,' I said.

'I could compose as well before ever you drain your tankard,' said Portinari.

'You have little faith in my capacity for Bavarian beer!'

I raised the tankard to my lips and began drinking, while my portly friend screwed his countenance into a grimace ghastly enough to make his Muse cower in submission. As I set the tankard down empty, he raised a hand, uttering a cry of triumph, and began his recitation.

> *There's no Free Will – or, if so, 'tis as rare*
> *As is Free Beer! Our puppets teach you this.*
> *But this analogy is neither here not there ...*

'Yes, "For puppets have no Hearts to give the Fair".'

'No, no, wait – "Since Humans, unlike Puppets, Drink and Piss". It has to be an A,B,A,B rhyme scheme! I win, de Chirolo, I win!'

'I concede victory, my fabulous fat friend, and so will prove to you that free beer is not so rare as you think ...'

Eventually, I made my way home for a siesta by the coolest alleys. Much was on my mind, for the shadow play with Armida was entering a fresh turn. The ancestral hunt would challenge all my seriousness.

I turned in at my archway in the Street of the Wood Carvers. A female form slipped out of the shadows, revealing itself as La Singla. She was afraid that she had been followed, and insisted on coming upstairs to my room.

'A box on the ears this morning. Now what? If penitence, it can wait. I need a nap.'

She made no answer as we went upstairs.

Closing my door, I turned to contemplate her. There was none of her usual coquetry about her. She wore her tragic air, was remote, and with her bangled, Iberian wrists, expressed a pretty disquiet. When I approached her, those same wrists and the supple hands warded me off.

'You must be my friend only, Perian, if that is possible for you. Do not take advantage of me. I lost you when the fire broke out, and have waited anxiously for you since. Where have you been? You must tell me all that my husband said in the tent. Is he very suspicious? Has he set men to follow me?'

'What he said was in confidence.'

She was so anxious that she approached me. I seized her hands.

'Perian, I am in desperate straits.'

'So you are involved in some deep affair, Mistress Kemperer. Why else should you look so pale, as if you were playing *The Last of the Cantamas*? You have come to a man who can take your mind off your troubles.'

'If I wanted that sort of thing, don't you think I have wealthier lovers elsewhere, as good in bed, and not so conceited?' Her hands flew to her mouth. 'I didn't mean that, Perian. Just a verbal box on the ears. You're a darling, but this is no time for gallantry. I must get home or I'll be missed. Tell me what Pozzi said.'

'So it's a wealthy lover, eh?'

She looked sombrely at me, drawing her brows together without speaking.

'Tell me who he is, this paragon of lovers.'

'Oh, go to the Devil! Why should I trust you?'

'You delight in giving me lectures. I'd like to give you one. You think me unscrupulous and vain, but at least I always trust my friends. It's a duty to do so, at least until they prove false. Better to be duped occasionally than to be suspicious always.'

'You talk nonsense.'

But my little speech made me feel better and full of trust myself, so that I repeated everything Kemperer had said to me, embellishing little.

'Then he doesn't know everything,' said La Singla. She gave me a straight look. 'Nor do you, Perian. Forgive my tantrums.'

'Of course I do.'

A kiss on the lips and she was gone. I sat on the bed and rested my chin in my hand, wondering greatly about women, about myself, and about the whole human race.

By sunset, when the sky grew crimson above the Palace of the Bishops Elect on its high hill, I had recovered from my attack of philosophy. Armida and I, de Lambant and Bedalar, sat in a respectable café we could hardly afford, drinking and talking. Portinari was to have been there too, but his father needed him in the dairy. The two chaperons, Yolaria and Jethone, sat nearby in an alcove behind a bead curtain, where they could discuss the price of lace without bothering us.

Since Portinari was absent, it was my task to tell the story of how the Great Harino's tent caught fire. This I did to such good effect that the girls laughed and shuddered and wished fervently that they had witnessed it too.

'Have you been busy since we parted this morning?' Armida asked me. 'Apart from enjoying the great fire?'

'Feverishly busy with rehearsals. Tomorrow I will go to see my sister and arrange a horse for the hunt; I shall not let you down.'

'It is essential that you should be properly accoutred for the ancestral hunt. Can your brother-in-law advise you?' She used the same tone as she had in the morning.

'Volpato's never at home. I'll manage. I have much to do. My costumes need replenishment. While I was watching the *Ombres Chinoises*, before they went up in smoke, I had a striking inspiration for Phalante the Bankrupt.'

'You should concentrate on one thing at a time.'

'The battle episode in *Karagog* gave me the idea. I decided that I will play Phalante as a soldier, not as a dowdy apothecary. Then we could bring in some contemporary business about the bankrupt state of Constantinople, which always raises a laugh. It will naturally amuse a Duke of Ragusa.'

'Stick to the apothecary,' advised de Lambant. 'You look funnier with leeches than breeches.'

'I'm incredible as a soldier. I scared myself in my cheval glass. I have my military turn-down boots, and a grand wooden sword in scabbard – a fine property – which hangs from a heavy scarf crossing over the coat from one shoulder.' I rose to show them how it went. 'The effect's pretty staggering. And I have a long cravat dividing in two and falling down to my waist, in the fashion of Croatian mercenaries. It's a better rig-out than Otto Bengtsohn supplies for Gerald. All I lack is a plumed tricorne-hat. You don't have such a thing, Guy?'

'Neither the hat nor the ambition for one.'

'You'll like the costume, Armida, and swear that no battlefield would be complete without me. The shadow puppets were nothing! All my joints work with greatest flexibility. In the mirror, I saw the gallant fellow swagger about. Then he drew his sword of best tempered Toledo timber and cut down fifty Ottomans! What speed, what grace, what sheer ferocity! But no hat. Boldness immeasurable, but no hat. A sad tale ...'

' "He who loves himself well will find no rival",' quoted Armida.

I was indignant. I took more wine.

'It was not me I admired but the phantom I created! There's the pleasure in being a player, Armida. Just by changing my outer clothes, I alter the inner man.'

'If there is an inner man,' said Bedalar.

'Then the inner man's a weather vane,' said Armida.

'Not a weather-vane. The inner man is potentially everyone, everything. The mutability of the soul! Each of us, given the chance, could encompass all possibilities. A change of mood, a change of wig, a change of being.' I quaffed down more wine, feeling my art and my power. 'A young man, an old man? Very well. Rich or poor? Cavalier, judiciary, cut-purse, monk, noble, miller, beggar, artist? As you will. All trades, ranks, professions, follies and wisdom, all are within. It needs only the appropriate dress to call forth the appropriate character; he will take me over, live my life for a brief hour, and I his.

'Everyone would do the same if they dared to, if they were trained to. It's the only freedom.'

'Is your own life so awful that you have to escape this way?' Bedalar asked.

De Lambant was looking bored, but the two girls were full of interest.

'Happy people always "escape", as you call it. They return with riches. I have played such a necromancer that my least mouthful of food had to be eaten by the correct twinkle of the correct star; such an elder statesman that my every limb trembled and creaked for weeks after; such a jackanapes that my friends shunned me while the piece was running; such a sign-crossed lover that I cried myself to sleep every night.'

Laughing, Armida said, 'Then I dread to think how miserly you will be while playing Phalante.'

'What I am saying, my peach, my prize, is that by the trifling adjustment of my hat, I have plumbed the wells of Folly or scaled the mountainsides of Truth. Besides all that, what does it matter if my real self is sometimes lost to view?'

'Have you yet attempted to impersonate a modest person?' Armida asked.

Proverbially, it is only the wicked who lead busy lives. Yet next morning saw a full day ahead. In an hour or two, Otto Bengtsohn would be working with his zahnoscope at the Chabrizzi Palace; I was not required in the morning but had to go in the afternoon and play a scene with Letitia. This morning, I resolved to see Pozzi Kemperer again and persuade him to let me play Phalante as a cavalier; for that interview I would be suitably dressed. I needed to see that the tailor had cloth for my coat. In the evening, I would leave my friends to amuse themselves while I visited my sister; she would help me to arrange everything necessary for the ancestral hunt at Juracia. There was the horse problem, too. Mandaro kept a cob; but its nature, like its master's, was too clerical for the chase.

Perhaps Kemperer would lend me a plumed tricorne-hat.

Allowing the town cocks to rouse me, I rose and dressed myself in calf-boots, the heavy sash, the long cravat, the wooden sword, and other martial adornments. I sang as I dressed.

> *'Oh, there are times when we defy what has to be.*
> *The Malacians being wanton worship chastity ...'*

Every so often, I glanced down into the street below, where bustle already attended the long morning shadows. Apprentices were darting hither and yon with food and drink; bales of timber were being delivered to the carvers' workshops, laundry-women were about, and the fishermen with their guttural cries. The milk cart rumbled along the alley, pulled by an ox with silver bells on its horns, and driven by a horned lizard-man.

A soldier elbowed his way among the crowd. He strolled through a slice of sunshine and happened to catch my gaze as he glanced up. He was wearing a plumed tricorne which corresponded to the pattern I coveted.

He passed on. I was plagued by envy. Here was I in my garret, penniless, with loves and ambitions above the miserable stratum of life into which I had been pitched – loves, ambitions, yes, and talents! – and there was that swaggering fellow, doubtless with gold in his pocket, doubtless making for an assignation with some voluptuous lady. Otherwise, why should a cavalry captain be up and on foot at this tradesmanly hour of day?

I dispersed my discontent with song. Dressed at last, hatless, I went down to the street and bought a pastry stuffed with sliced meats and peppers from a friendly baker.

Munching, I cut through the flea-market to walk under the ruinous arcades of Desport Palace and see the Night Guard dismiss in the square. Acquaintances greeted me at every turn. I saw Letitia's uncle Joze, swinging along painfully on crutches, but he did not see me.

At one end of the arcades, I leaned against a pillar where a countrywoman sat with her basket of flowers. The sun shone on me, and it was pleasant to watch the smart movements of the Malacian City Guard; they filled me with military thoughts as I broke my fast.

175

Close by were two magicians, paying no attention to the parade. They had appropriated an alcove where, among their private filth, they muttered over a great bronze globe – whether of this world or the next I could not guess. Their two corrupt boys played barefoot by them. In the shadowy background, among tarpaulins, a sacrificial goat stared up at a pine growing in riven masonry.

One of the magicians had a malign, stupid face. It stretched sideways like a toad's, smiling as he turned his head and beckoned to me with one finger.

I pretended I had not seen the gesture. Stepping back, I barged into a passer-by. I felt a shoulder thrust angrily in my back. So gallant was my mood that by impulse I whirled about, drawing my wooden sword.

I confronted the cavalier I had seen from my window, plumed hat and all.

His hand went to his sword-hilt. Even as he did so, his eye flashed from my eye to my sword. At sight of it, his grim expression relaxed; he stretched out his arms.

'Spare me!' he said. 'I know not how to parry such a blade.'

I could not help but laugh. He was a handsome little figure, solid, trim, no more than two years my senior. I envied him his curly, brown moustache, the ends of which were uncompromisingly waxed. His eyes were dark and moist, which I took for a sign of untrustworthiness. That unreadable deep brown never means well. Perhaps for that reason, I raised my wooden point till it was at his throat. He made no move to defend himself.

As we held the dramatic tableau, I could see his history: a well-bred family, a boy accustomed to having his way, an indulgent father, women, a sure career in the military, a good place in the mess, loyal friends, a stable of sound horses, courage, chivalry, ennobling wounds, medals, promotion, a rich marriage, connections at court, honours, the future in his hands. It was not for a wooden sword to gainsay such a destiny. I lowered my point.

No doubt he'd grow fat and gouty in another ten years.

Our *tableau vivant* was broken by the toad magician. He was crippled under his greasy black gown. He crawled across the paving to us, thrusting up one hand on a stringy brown arm, crying to us, 'Take heed, you young masters, take heed. There

176

are no accidents. Stars make character, character makes destiny.'

As we backed away from him, the single finger came up again, reaching for our chins.

'You twain, young masters, are unknowingly involved in one bed. That bed bodes no good, and mischief is about to befall you both. As for you—' here he turned his cat gaze to me – 'the waters will close over your head unless you swim more surely, and the Dark One will take you!'

I put up my sword and ran, and the cavalier ran too, pacing beside me.

'The old reptile lies,' shouted the cavalier. 'I have less than no inclination to climb into your lice-ridden palliasse.'

'Nor I into your scurvy bed, with its plaguing crabs. Sooner into a river-bed!'

We halted round the first corner, glaring at each other. It was wonderful how he had run and kept his hat on.

He smiled again, showing a row of white teeth as good as any actor's, and thrust out his hand.

'I never heed the words of whores or soothsayers. There's a great world beyond words of which they know nothing. I am Captain John Pellegrino san Lasionio of the Tuscady Heavy Horse, black sheep of the san Lasionio family of Dakka. And I have to admit that I had you under observation.'

'I am the actor Perian de Chirolo, last scion of a great scholarly family, but with no patience to be a scholar. Equally, I am a soldier only in dress.'

'As a professional soldier can easily observe ... But of course your camouflage in would take anyone else.'

'By that same token, I can tell you are the black sheep of your family. And I've no more heard of the san Lasionios than you have of the de Chirolos. Why should you have been observing me? I envy you only your splendid headgear – what of mine could you envy?'

At that, his manner became downcast in a superb way, and he began to pace forward, casting his gaze at his boots. As I fell in beside him, he said, 'I chiefly envy your manifest armistice with the world. In what a carefree way did you stroll along the arcade, eating your rations and enjoying the day. For me, this is a day of fateful decision, and the omens give me no joy.'

It came to my mind that he might be deciding to give away

a surplus mount, and was looking for a suitable recipient; and at once I was persuading my father to stable it in his deserted yard, and Beppolo was grooming it and buying hay at a reasonable price, and friends – and Armida – were there watching me leap into the saddle, smiling and waving.

'According to the soothsayers, every day is a day for decision.'

He flashed me a look, half-comic, half-despairing, and smote his chest.

'Let me declare myself. For the first time, I who always laughed at women's wiles am in love. Enfiladed by love.'

With a hollow laugh, I said, 'Come, Captain, did my casual manner so easily deceive you? Every day of my life, I am in love. Women are so beautiful, so agreeable, how could it be otherwise? I have a fit of marriage on me for the most beautiful, the most agreeable – and the most damned expensive – of them, and so I must forego all the rest, as I am honourable. So it is only my ability as an actor which conceals most perfect inner turmoil.'

He dismissed my words with a gesture.

'I do not act. I am a man of action. Now I'm embattled in a world of love whose strategies I always despised.'

'Don't despise it – cultivate it.'

'I despise it. I'm a soldier, not a coxcomb. Yet today I'm in the ambush I laughed about yesterday. For the one I love – oh, why do I parade my woe? – the one I love above even my honour is already married, and to such a mean and lecherous old fart that her every hour is misery. If ever there was a wedding of Greek fire and pipe-clay ... yet she clings to it from the sweet goodness of her heart ... Can a man love too much, de Chirolo?'

I thought about it. 'I've seen men love other people's marriages, believing it was the woman they wanted.'

'You live a decadent life, I can see. Malacia's rotten. But for her I'd be thankful my regiment is leaving ... No, I mean no insult: I'm just out-flanked, ground between slow-turning wheels. Come, let's walk awhile.'

'You like to walk? As a cavalry officer, you must prefer riding. You must live and breathe horses.'

As we strolled northwards, he said, 'I love her and I swear she truly wears my colours. Yes, yes, she breaks her heart for my sake, yet she is too loyal to leave this antique satyr of hers.'

'There are plenty of women to be had without antique satyrs. Yet it's true that all have some other character defect. The lady I love has a domineering father who—'

I was steering him in the general direction of Kemperer's, but he cut me short by stopping and grasping my arm fiercely.

'My case is desperate, understand that. I'm no playboy. I'm in charge of the force sent by the dukes of Tuscady to relieve Malacia. Tomorrow I must lead my force across the mountains northwards, to harry Stefan Tvrtko's rear. I *must* decamp tomorrow. I've lingered as long as possible on one excuse or the other, sent off my adjutant on so many false errands he must think me mad – which I am. Tomorrow morning at first light, we muster and ride or my career's done. So by tonight it's imperative I have definite pledges from my love. She must come to me tonight or my campaign's lost, and I dread to press her too hard for fear of wounding that gentle heart. You can aid me, de Chirolo, if you will.'

'A wily attorney could help you more.'

'No, you're my necessary reinforcement, de Chirolo. I need a scout, and it must be someone not of the regiment. That's sound tactics.' He appraised me with a bold, savage face. The ends of his moustachios vibrated.

'The crippled magician suggested that we would do each other no good. Find someone else.'

'I'd best speak out. I know more of you than I have so far revealed. You are not the rank-and-file fop you pretend, de Chirolo. I observed your brave ascent by balloon from the Bucintoro, astride that black stallion with silver hooves. Since then I've had further reconnaissances made. I know that you are intimate with the dear lady who has taken my heart captive.'

Terrible fears, neglected omens, apprehensions, rushed into my mind. I would have drawn my wooden sword, but for his steel one.

'Captain ... then we are deadly rivals! You are the young gallant of whom my Armida is always talking.'

He stared at me unblinkingly. 'I have no Armida on my roll-call. The lady to whom I refer visited your quarters only yesterday – I refrain, as a gentleman, from inquiring what transpired there. My adjutant kept her movements under observation from a distance. That lady is the divine Singla, the chaste and beautiful commander of my affections.'

'Yes, yes, I see ...' Through my relief, I thought, beautiful, yes, that La Singla is. The other adjectives are the illusory coinage of a man who has wasted his years among whores. Armida would not desire a man like this; but I see how he might be La Singla's meat.

'You begin to follow my line of approach?'

'What have you to say about La Singla?' It was my turn to begin walking. He fell into step beside me.

As san Lasionio poured out his admiration for La Singla – and how banal another man's protestations of adoration sound – I tried to work the matter out. By my side was the very rogue that Kemperer was making the fuss about. He had delivered himself into my hands, much as La Singla herself had done the previous day. What a sheepish black sheep!

Just as I was wondering how the situation could be turned to my advantage, the captain began to resolve that question as well.

'My divine Singla has briefed me on you, de Chirolo. I know that you have the trust of her old tyrant of a husband. Even now, you are probably going to visit them both, while I must to my duties – the regiment has much preparation before departure. Here's the procedure. I require a great favour of you – well, a small one really, between gentlemen – I request you to take a despatch to her, privily. You may not believe this, but I fear that repulsive old man to whom she's chained. He is capable of spreading lies that would stain my rank and honour. Go to her, inform her that I stand on the brink of despair for her decision.'

He paused. The plume of his tricorne trembled in sympathy with his moustache.

'Say on.'

'Her decision means life or death to me. She must determine today whether to continue entrenched with her dotard of a husband or to embark on a new life with me and the regiment. That's my ultimatum. Will you impress it on her?'

'Is that all?' I asked.

'There's no more to say. Tell La Singla that my pistol's

primed and that I stand with it even now – say *even now* –
with the muzzle at my temple, awaiting her favourable decision.
I have my strategy; I must know hers. Will you do this?'

'Say on.'

'There's nothing more to say. Tell the divine Singla – out of
that macabre old nanny-goat's hearing, naturally – that I will
have a paris in readiness for her at the Stary Most at midnight
tonight.' He was ticking the items off on his fingers.

'Say on.'

'There's no more to say. I'll be in the paris at midnight, the
pistol at my head, waiting, hoping, to bear her away.'

'In pursuit of Tvrtko?'

'That's the route the regiment takes, northwards, after the
retreating Ottoman rabble. Will you do this?'

'Am I to inform her that her tryst is with you or with King
Tvrtko?'

Narrowing his eyes, he pulled heavily at one cheek.

'I require help, not mockery. Supposing you knew you were
to forfeit your life on a foreign field tomorrow – would you feel
so jovial today?'

'I certainly would not be contemplating matrimony tonight.'

We paused in the street, the better to glare at each other.
I observed over his shoulder a block of noble masonry; from
its shelter, an ancient, whiskery face, half-concealed, was watching. Could the crippled magician have followed us? I began to
feel a general unease, and knew it was time to strike a bargain
with my military friend.

'I'm a man with a lively heart, Captain san Lasionio. I
sympathize with your romantic predicament, believe me. But,
like you, like all men, I'm already loaded with my own predica-
ments. Also I feel somewhat for La Singla. Are you being
sincere? If you really believed you would die tomorrow under
a swinging scimitar, or whatever these Bosnians use, shouldn't
you be on your knees in St Marco's, rather than ordering
parises for midnight?'

He slapped his leg.

'You're playing the soldier now, de Chirolo, remember, not
the priest. Be your part. Will you deliver my message per-
suasively, without commentary, or will you not?'

'Very well. Soldier to soldier. I will deliver your message,
omitting no detail of your plan. The pistol shall be included,

181

and so shall the paris, and so shall midnight and Tvrtko.'

'You may omit Tvrtko. I don't want to scare the lady.'

'Well enough. All but Tvrtko. On one condition, though I know men of honour don't make conditions. Give me your tricorne. No, I understand that you can hardly fight and die without it. Your unblemished saint shall return it to you at midnight, when you meet her at Stary Most. I need it only till then; by that hour, it should have worked my small purpose with Kemperer. We may as well both get something from him this day.'

He clutched my hand.

'My hat you shall have. Anything else? You assist my siege of her heart. What can I do to assist you?'

'Nothing more – wait! Yes. I need a well-trained docile horse – perhaps one too old to go chasing after Ottomans.'

'You must have a horse!'

'Yes, I must.'

'I meant, you must have one already. All right, I see you have not. I'll never understand townsmen – I was reared in the saddle. Very well, you shall have a horse. We have too many baggage animals to lead across the Prilipits. I'll give you note of a place to go and you shall collect a mount tomorrow. Go early, or the tradesmen will have it for meat – soldiers leave debts behind.'

'Is it black?'

'It has four legs. That's enough.' He told me the address. As he did so, I adjusted his hat upon my head. It fitted well. He assured me I looked dashing. I repeated my determination as messenger. We shook hands and parted. With a salute, Captain san Lasionio stepped smartly into the shade of a byway and was gone.

In a little establishment by the canalside, I chose a table hidden from common view and sipped my glass, deep in thought.

There was the promise of a horse. Very well. That set my affairs ahead a good deal. It placed me in a debt of gratitude to Captain John Pellegrino san Lasionio. I had an obligation of honour to bear his message.

On the other hand – how terrible for all concerned if La Singla did run off with him! What a blow to theatrical art! How terrible for me, for Kemperer, for Malacia! Recalling her agitation of the day before, I thought that she was indeed prepared to dash off with the gallant captain. Life with Kemperer must be unbearable at times; not that bumping over mountains in a carriage was necessarily the ideal alternative. For her sake, too, I must deliver her lover's message. But ...

Well, I would talk the matter over with de Lambant before I decided.

Tossing a handful of paras down on the table, I left, pleased by the way the waiter bowed and called me 'Captain' as he saw me out.

No sooner was I in the street, than two roughs rushed from a nearby doorway. They pinned my arms behind my back before I could draw my sword. As may be imagined, I fought with audacity, kicking out furiously and yelling for help. No matter how much I struggled, I was powerless to resist any clouts over the head or kicks in the shin they chose to give me.

They were no cut-purses. They made no attempt to rob me and be gone. Instead, they dragged me towards the Vamonal Canal. I fought them every centimetre, calling Satan down on them. My offers to pay them rather than have my uniform ruined fell with no effect on their ears – a filthy hand was clamped over my mouth. On the brink of the canal, I struggled like a madman and nearly got clear, but they had me and, with violent blows behind, I was kicked into the water.

I sank down through the scummy, green liquid. My senses were fully with me – I was all senses as a fire is all heat – and what I felt was not physical hurt but the pain of injustice. All injustices. The water, the slimy world, was injustice swallowing me. I could not bear the indecency of it. Like a gutted fish, I felt my normal buoyant spirit cut from me, and I wished only to die, to drown, to disintegrate in the mud. And I stirred with my outstretched hands the filth of the canal bottom, wishing never to rise again from my degradation. My borrowed plume only should survive this disgrace.

Everyone gets beaten up sometimes. But my loving trust of the world had been betrayed; it was best that they murdered me, that I remained down in the sunless murk. Weeds brushed my eyes. I clutched them. They came away from the muck and I floated up with them.

A monumental block of stone from which jutted a devil-jaw's head met my eyes. In the beast's mouth was an iron

ring. Instinct being what it is, I grasped the ring. Spitting foul water, I dragged myself up. Two waiters ran from the tavern to assist me, now that danger was past. I lay face down on the cobbles resisting their efforts to make me rise. I wept.

Someone – a nearby bargeman – fished out the captain's tricorne and it was crammed on my head. They sat me up. My assailants had long since disappeared down a side-alley. A crowd was growing round me, some in aprons, some laughing, some anxious, some angry, to examine this half-drowned specimen of misfortune.

I could not bear to be an exhibition. Stumbling to my feet, I broke through their ranks and ran, clutching my hat. What a figure I must have made, trailing water! Rushing down a lane past a blacksmith's, I flung myself into a weed-filled yard and collapsed over a broken grindstone. Too miserable to weep, I hid my face in my hands.

An image of Captain John san Lasionio came to my mind, driving over the grim mountainsides like the wind, with La Singla by his side. Had he ordered this to be done to me because he thought I had designs on La Singla? That seemed unlikely even in my present mood. Was Otto Bengtsohn behind this? That did not seem likely either. Then I thought of Pozzi Kemperer.

This was his work and nobody else's. Determined that his wife should remain faithful, he had found out about the captain and set his traps for that gallant officer. And the strong-arm men of whom he often boasted had mistaken me for Lasionio. Why not? Didn't I wear the captain's tricorne? Didn't I look every centimetre the military man?

Besides, roughs are notoriously stupid.

Very well. The maestro should be confronted with evidence of what his men had done to an innocent man. I still felt absolutely betrayed. My loss made me hollow; but one cannot sprawl for ever over broken grindstones. Miserably, I rose to my squelching feet. I shook out the hat and dripped my way towards the Fragrant Quarter. The old fox deserved to lose La Singla. I would be a somewhat aquatic cupid and deliver Lasionio's message of assignation immediately.

'How promptly the crippled magician's prophecy came true,' I said to myself. 'They can foresee events. The bed in which Lasionio and I are both involved is of course La Singla's.

Though I may never enter it again, I know well what paradise one finds there, bless her. It does go against the grain to help another man enter it – particularly the man on whose behalf I have been pitched into a stinking canal.'

The prophecy had come true with suspicious haste. Perhaps the magician himself drew a retainer from Kemperer; it was always said that the old villain had his fingers in as many pies as the Supreme Council.

Going through Ruppo Place, I stopped to shake a few more drops from my borrowed hat. On the far side of the Place, ever faithful to his position, sat the plump young astrologer, Parterre, complacent on his platform. And before him – a neat little female figure with golden hair – La Singla herself consulting him once more.

I squelched behind a fallen capital to watch her, feeling both sympathy and anger. It was nothing for a woman to run to her soothsayer every hour in time of trouble, like a child running to its mother when frightened. That she was consulting Parterre again merely spoke of the tumult that the captain had stirred in her pretty breast.

The young astrologer was in shadow while she, as yesterday, was picked out by sunlight, although it bathed her less brightly than on the previous occasion.

How pliant her movements, how expressive her gestures! Only a skilled actress could have been so affectingly natural. The astrologer bent towards her, fascinated. I saw them talking, although their voices did not reach me. So telling were her gestures, I understood what passed between them as if I stood beside her.

She told him that she returned as promised, to receive from him the horoscope he had agreed to cast. What delicate expression! The girl should have joined the *pantomimi*, who use no words! Yet she was not so much a mistress of gesture that I could grasp at first whose the horoscope was; only as Parterre tugged a scrip of paper from his sleeve and handed it to her did I understand that this was not her horoscope but her soldier's. She was receiving Lasionio's fate into her hands.

With precise timing, La Singla produced a silver coin from the pocket tied by ribbon to her skirt. She pressed it into the astrologer's palm. Her posture as she reached upward to his hand was beautiful to see. Parterre managed to bow without rising from his chair.

Turning slightly away from the platform, La Singla opened the scrip and cast her eyes down at what was written. The exquisite droop of her wrist! The delicate manner in which colour drained from her face! The pretty way her lips opened and her affrighted finger-tips flew to them in dismay! Her melting look of sorrow! The tears that suddenly stood in her eyes and spilled down her cheeks! What art! What consummate cultivation!

From where I stood, a distant groundling, the actress's subtle cheironomy made the contents of Lasionio's horoscope as clear as if I scanned the parchment myself.

The captain's hours in the shadow play of life were numbered! She and the astrologer gesticulated, looking first towards the east, then north. Ah, Tvrtko, thy cruel sword! Thy treacherous hatred of the *giaour*! Thy ambushes in the Prilipit passes for those who dare pursue thee! Alas, poor Lasionio! So young! So soon! And the stars so rudely conjoined against thee, even as thou fear'st! See how thy lady-love clutches her head as if it were thy severed one!

With ashen countenance, with trembling lips, La Singla tucked the paper into her breast and ran from the place, distraught, in as telling an exit as ever she made. And, at the last moment – she glanced towards my place of concealment!

As I suspected. Instinctive little actress that she was, La Singla's best was called forth by an audience. She had been aware all along that I was watching her! A moment earlier, I had anticipated that Parterre's ill tidings would propel her straight to Lasionio with the news; I visualized her begging him to let his regiment leave at midnight without him, in defiance of the stars. Now I knew better.

Weighing the meaning of that last glance of hers, I perceived that her delight in pantomime was as real as her anguish. That I could understand. It was not that she was as much art as heart; rather, that art and heart were one.

The paris might trundle off at midnight, but La Singla would not be inside. She preferred to play out the roles of her vitality, not to eyes glazing with death in some inaccessible mountain, but to those who could appreciate to the full her magical abilities (and Kemperer was of that number). Her nature was such that military necessity would bow before artistic temperament. She loved, she suffered, she bled – and sensibly preferred such activities to an end to loving, suffering and bleeding.

Drenched though I was by my ducking, it was a Perian with a lighter heart who marched in to berate Kemperer for his villainous error. I noticed that La Singla slipped in by the side doorway. I marched through the court, setting the hounds howling, and made my entrance. I confronted Kemperer before a dozen witnesses, dripping dramatically upon his carpetings.

'My dearest Perian, what a misfortune!' Up went his withered hands as he skipped before me, showing his lined teeth. 'You of all people, beaten up in the street like a common adulterer! Anyone would think you'd been up to no good. How the heartless scum who saw you launched among the fishes must have bellowed with laughter! I wish I'd been there.'

'It's no use apologizing, Kemperer! You and I are parting company from this hour forth unless I have full recompense. I know you set your henchmen on me.'

Then followed one of the worst scenes of my career. The maestro grasped my sodden arm and dragged me to his office. 'Seep into my sanctum, dear boy, poor drowned dragoon, and let us come privately to terms. Why, how even your feather droops – I fear for other parts of your body!'

He slammed the office door and locked it, continuing to talk on with no change in his tone, although extra venom stirred the rheum in his eye. He swung his cane at me to emphasize each cadence.

'But I would not have you believe that henchmen of mine made any sort of *error*, my washed-out warrior! They don't make errors. Oh, no, they'd smell you out in any guise, however unbecoming.'

'You're lying, you old crank! They took me for the man who owns this hat.'

'No, you fishy fancy-man, it's *you* who can't deceive me. My men made no error, I say. They followed my dear faithful spouse yesterday' (his grimace while pronouncing this phrase was worthy of a devil-jaw), 'yesterday afternoon, as instructed. They witnessed you coax the minx up to your noxious billet. They marked how long she tarried there in your clap-covered embrace. They reported faithfully to me ... In Malacia, we're all watched, you aquatic ancestral, didn't you know that?'

188

With each article of this declaration, Kemperer struck me so savagely round my shoulders with the cane that my clothes spurted water.

'But I'm innocent, Pozzi, you dirty-minded old ingrate, innocent!'

'As a cock is innocent, you sodden studlet!' Whack!

'I am innocent. I never touched her. You're blaming me for nothing. By the bones, how I loathe jealousy. You're riddled with it, you mouldy old muff-eater.'

'So I am, I'm happy to say. So I took action to deal with you and that cavalry turnip, with his fool idea of carriages at midnight. How *he's* going to suffer later! I paid my toughs to kick you in the canal and it was money well spent; you're snivelling here and Maria's weeping outside.' Whack! Whack!

I leant exhausted against the door, wiping my face. 'What a fiend you are! How little you care for her hurt feelings ...'

'Let her piss herself! She'll come to her senses.' Whack!

'And look what I get for helping you. I told Lasionio to stay away from your wife, and this is how I'm paid. If you knew how totally disgusted I feel ...'

He burst into angry laughter and executed a sort of jig while unlocking the door. 'You're for all the world like Karagog, you wet wonder-child. Little success in any role! Your lover was a poor performance, your soldier a wash-out! Maybe now you'll comprehend that acting is safer than meddling where your face doesn't belong!'

For all my defiance, I was drained of normal cheer. That there were people so blind to the delicacy of others' emotions! As I went past him out of the office, I began sneezing. Kemperer cackled at the sound.

Looking miserably at him, I said, 'The chill of that canal has probably done for me. Like Lasionio in the Prilipit passes, I shall die young.'

'Pooh to that, you deboshed fish! Only silly women place credence in horoscopes – my whore of a wife is a bigger fool than I thought, to believe in a false one. Pull yourself together and stop dripping on my carpets. Slobber off home, get dry, and learn your lesson.'

So upset was I, that it was only much later – after midnight, in fact – that the meaning of his sneer about the false horoscope dawned. He had bought Parterre as well as the louts who nearly killed me.

I have so far painted a cheerful picture of life; but that senseless attack made me aware of self-interest – and what I most feared was my own self-interest. My lovingness had been challenged. I felt unmanned.

But there was the comfortable, familiar, old tiled world, lolling between Satan and God, and I went about it like any other citizen, acting my part before the zahnoscope – we were nearly at the end of Mendicula's drama – arranging to obtain san Lasionio's promised horse, slipping a message to Armida, managing to keep my stomach full.

Mandaro counselled me, Seemly Moleskin looked squint and told me that I would be attacked again next day, and that my life was progressing towards the animal. I left them and climbed that evening to the ruined Baths of Callacappo, behind the Arena, to recover my wounded spirits in solitude.

The massive surrounding walls of the baths stood after many hundred years, their archways and vaults and staircases enduring yet, though overgrown with wildernesses of bay and myrtle and the flowering laurustinus. It was possible to climb dangerously until I looked down on the thickets of blossom trees which now filled the ancient bathing centre. Here I perched, tracing the twisted roots of shrubs where they showed like knuckles, gripping the stones for purchase among their interstices.

So still was I, and lost in thought, that other animals which had taken refuge here came out and sported. Most flamboyant was a pair of tree-snaphances or grab-skeeters which had made their home in a decayed portal high above ground. The entrance to this shelter was screened by branches of ivy and bay, from which both male and female snaphance emerged, to bask in the last hour of sunlight.

They were rather like the common chick-snakes of the streets, but of sturdier build. Snaphances were the most handsome ancestral animals, with noble, small heads perched on well-proportioned necks. My pair sat upright, their tails tucked out of sight, using their dainty hands to feed themselves with leaves. Since this was not the mating season, the male was the same mellow green as his mate, verging almost to bright aquamarine on his belly. Her leathery skin was beautiful, marked

190

with faint stripes but lacking the double row of bony scutes which decorated the hide of the male.

After a while, they observed me, but sat calmly as before. The configurations of skin about their mouths and eyes gave them a benevolent aspect. If these were offshoots of the distant ancestral line from which mankind had developed, as scholars claimed, then we had little to be ashamed of.

These creatures, and others like them, lived contented lives. They had nothing to prove. Whereas ...

Dreams of doing great things filled me. The skulls of grab-skeeters would be innocent of such phantasms.

In two days' time, during the ancestral hunt in Juracia, I might have my chance to win fame, advancement and Armida. I wanted to show everyone what a man I was, that I was meet for more than a ducking in a dirty canal. The crippled magician had told me I should swim more strongly; so I would. But I remained dismayed to find how much hurt I took over so little. When my father had turned me out of his house, I had gone laughing, with a gallant air, despite the disgrace of it.

Thought of my father reminded me that I had never gone back to see that he was looked after. Well, life was lived out among ruins.

Nor did I forget the captain of the Tuscady Horse, wondering how he would feel when he led his force back through the bleak defiles of Prilipit, without the one woman who had ever caught his heart. He was a gallant fellow, and would survive not knowing how Kemperer had tricked him. Wherever he was, I wished him well – long might he wench and smite the bearded Turk!

The birds homed about me, little twittering sparrows, thrushes, finches, and the swooping cavorts which visit Malacia in late summer. It grew cooler. The sun dipped behind the city, filling the sky with harmonies of colour. No one could experience the hour without giving up his soul to its delight.

I climbed down from my eyrie while there was light enough to find a safe foothold.

The Ancestral Hunt

The flighted people were ringing the four great bells of the cathedral. I rode Capriccio behind St Marco and stabled him, going on foot to the great West doors, where Armida awaited me. She was standing by a statue together with de Lambant and Bedalar, and friends whom I did not know. Behind this group, shadowy and severe, stood Yolaria and Jethone with other chaperons, all looking alike in drab cloth and lace caps.

As I kissed Armida's hand, I looked into her eyes and thought that she still loved me; certainly she had been all affection on the two previous days, when working before Otto's zahnoscope.

'As ever your servant, mistress,' I said. I was curt, as befits a man who has ridden to worship. I bowed to the rest of the company, winking at de Lambant. I had hoped to enjoy a word alone with Armida. Well, there would be opportunity after Matins, no doubt, for we were due in front of the zahnoscope again. So we smiled and exchanged pleasantries.

All were cheerful, turning their faces to one another, to the façade of the cathedral, to the flighted people circling overhead, and to the personages flocking in the square, as if they had a surplus of energy to be used for general benefit. Or was it all self-interest? De Lambant was sparkling; both the girls and their friends were inclined to be amused at his sallies. I smiled at him in gratitude, for he gave me time to adjust to the company.

Matins were being held to mark the opening of the ancestral animal hunting season. Many of the elite would be off after the service to lodges in the wilderness. Even I, the poor player, would be following them on the morrow. I only wished my spirits were higher for it.

The Hoytola family coach drew up, the Hoytolas descended, Armida moving meekly to her father's side. Andrus Hoytola smiled bleakly on all; his beam was a little oblique when aimed at me. He and his wife, possessing themselves of Armida and her younger sister, Lena, proceeded up the cathedral steps with the chaperon and two servants in their train. He gestured graciously with a limp hand on the way. The Nortolini family made a similar appearance – Caylus nodding genially at de Lambant and me – sweeping Bedalar and Jethone into their wake. Armida's other friends moved up to the cathedral doors.

De Lambant and I, isolated for the moment, raised eyebrows at each other.

'According to family legend, the de Lambants were all-powerful in Tuscady – but that was over sixty generations ago,' he said.

'The de Chirolos may have to wait sixty generations for the same sort of thing, unless I strike lucky in the next few days.'

'Let's go in and pray for luck.'

As we moved into the all-encompassing darkness of the cathedral, he asked, 'Are you getting much satisfaction from life?'

'Would you care to rephrase your question?'

By way of answer, he said, 'Master Bledlore's glasses are finished. The old man delivered them himself yesterday evening. Very prompt. They are really perfection. I hope they'll make Smarana happy; we hear that Traytor Orini is a sot and a libertine, and his sister, Teressa, a whore of the first water. Very encouraging ... I despise immorality in others, don't you?'

A great shade had been brewed inside the cathedral. Wafers of light from tall windows dipped into the broth, almost dissolving into shadow before they reached the flagstones at the base of the vast stone vessel. Clouds of incense boiled upwards, their intricate structure matching the silver and bronze censers, and obliterating, with their fumes of styrax, olibanum and cascarilla bark, the aroma of the humanity which seethed along the aisles. We lit candles by the door to add to the murk, kissed an image of Minerva, and moved in among the crowds.

From the High Priest standing behind St Marco's famous carved altar-screen came the electric sorrowing wail of the Higher Religion. His voice soared in love and lamentation. The obscurity took on features; humanity remained a vague stew, while saints and satyrs became incarnate on every pillar, from floor to cupola. In attitudes of serenity, travail, or molestation, they gazed down, heavy-eyed, in gilt – but saw little of the impenitence a-cooking in the dark, for St Marco's was as licentious as the opera; de Lambant and others of my friends had enjoyed women among the throng, even as the Responses of Dual

Sanctities drowsed up towards the embossed vaultings, while many a fancy man took the wafer with his lover-boy's semen slimy in his hand.

'Look especially, O Mediator, on those of our brethren assembled here beneath Thy prevailing wing who are about to venture on the perils of the hunt,' cried the High Priest to the image of Minerva. 'May they comprehend in their hearts, through Thy intercession, that, just as the World was created by Satan, so it will in the fullness of time be redeemed by the Lord God ... To placate both Adversaries, we go forth to slay our ancestors and eat the flesh of our Fathers.

'May those who hunt recall that we partake in our origins of Satan's purpose, as the animals are symbols of his accursed blood, standing condemned as do we all in the dreadful forests of the universe. Let them, O Mediator, share of thy Sacred Flesh here today, lest they die unshriven tomorrow, and revert to the more unseemly forms of satyr, gnome, or ancestral animal, which are nearer to the Dark Creator and all his fearful works. May we all strive upward, towards a greater Light, which is Thine alone, until we too are fit to be numbered among Thy beings, in the world the Almighty plans to wrest for his own.'

The strepent trumpets sounded and the responses began with a great confused mutter from the congregation.

> 'The serpent on the staff entwined ...'
>   '... It is of gnosis all refined.'

> 'Giant reptiles with a bird-like gait ...'
>   '... Remind us of our fallen state.'

'And the wise owl whose pinions catch the midnight wynd ...'
'... Behold, behold, sunrise strikes him blind.'

'The apes that flitter queerly, nearly ...'
'They envy us dearly
And would usurp us merely.'

As I pressed forward to take the wine and wafer from the hands of the priest, de Lambant came too.

'Why do you bother? You're not hunting, Guy.'

'I have good news for you, or I hope it's good news. Bedalar's pa is still being a difficult old clod, but she has managed to smuggle me along to Juracia as a musician. I'll sing for my supper while you do your brave deeds in the forest, massacring slobbergobs and shatterhorns.'

'That's good news. I'll be in need of friends. You may see more of Armida than I, in that case. Listen, keep close to her if you can, watch her, protect her. I fear a noble rival ...'

We broke off for the communion and the muttered words. 'Soul and flesh ... tokens of the great schism ... one in Thee ...'

Still munching, we pushed towards a side door as de Lambant said, 'Are you really serious about Armida?'

'Guy, don't laugh. I've not been myself lately. Something's got into me. Haven't you noticed?'

'We haven't seen so much of each other. Is it Armida?'

'Yes. I want to make something of myself. Oh, things I can't express ...'

'Sounds like love.' He clapped me sympathetically on the shoulder.

'I swear I'll never look at another woman. Well – look, maybe, but never more than that. I regret some of the things I've done since I knew her. She's worth reforming for, isn't she?'

'Oh, she's a splendid girl. Very pretty, too,' he said carelessly. 'But Malacia's full of splendid girls. This is a radical change in you, de Chirolo. And not for the better.'

'Just look to her in Juracia, will you, while I'm not there.'

'It's a sacred trust, I swear. I'll do all I can to advance your cause, if that's really what you want.'

Much relieved, I parted from him in the square, and headed for the stables to collect Capriccio and give my last performance before Bengtsohn's zahnoscope.

All over again, I realized what a difference a horse made.

It was impossible to profess to be a gentleman without a horse. The gallant Captain John Pellegrino san Lasionio – even now riding loveless over many an unintelligible mountain – must have commanded a troop which had sustained considerable losses for a beast as stalwart as Capriccio to be consigned to baggage duties. True, the gelding was slightly lame from a sword-thrust in a rear wither.

Capriccio stood sixteen hands high; his coat was of a dull

bronze. Both his teeth and his temper appeared good. In short, san Lasionio had done me a service, while I had rendered him nothing.

At the Chabrizzi Palace, activity was all. The servants were preparing to receive the family back from holiday, turning their own illicitly billeted relations out of quarters, and furiously beating carpets at windows after their spell of neglect.

Bengtsohn, too, was winding up his affairs. We had accumulated quite a little property for our mercurized play, not to mention our changes of clothes, all of which had been stored in an out-building. Now a handcart stood by, with Bengtsohn, his stout old wife Flora, and Letitia, loading it with all the pieces we had finished with. Bonihatch leaned against a pillar, sunning himself with Solly the Solid – a stout, impudent lad who burst into laughter as I rode up and dismounted.

'Have you never seen a decent horse before?' I asked him.

'I never saw a chick-snake riding one!'

To Bonihatch I said as I passed, 'Prince Mendicula, keep your malformed subjects in their proper place, will you?'

Without answering, he followed me along, laying his hand familiarly on Capriccio's saddle.

'A nag, hey? You've always had big-headed ideas. What are you up to now, de Chirolo?'

'Isn't it time to climb out of that sweaty old tunic and into your fancy shirt?'

'Ha, there's envy speaking! Let me inform you, de Chirolo, I know very well how you tried to seduce Miss Zlatorog to get yourself a shirt like mine.'

'That's how you managed it. Well, you're welcome to it if those are the conditions. Does the poor little minx always have to bribe you with clothes before you go to?'

Bonihatch bared his teeth, lowered his brow, and raised a fist. I dropped the rein and squared up to him.

'Come on, then, you cut-price conqueror!'

'You saddle-sore fop, with your fancy airs!'

'Now who's spitting envy?'

He swallowed his anger and dropped his hands unexpectedly. Turning a shoulder to me, he kicked the dust.

'I didn't intend quarrelling, de Chirolo, but the sight of you lording it on that animal makes me sick. There's going to be changes in Malacia soon, and those who go barefoot to work

196

will have an accounting with those who don't work at all.'

'So it's been said for thousands of years. I'm in neither of your classes, Bonihatch, so leave me alone. I've got troubles enough.'

Facing me, he spoke mildly, smoothing his whiskers.

'You're oppressed and exploited like the rest of us. You caper for the wealthy in your pansy clothes like a performing dog in a ruff. Join us and overthrow all those who victimize us.'

'Do you ever get bored parroting Otto?'

'Set aside personalities and think of the idea of freedom, of change, of equality.'

'I can manage those things better for myself than a mob of ragged apprentices could.'

'All right.' He looked at me contemptuously, his broad face dark. Solly came up behind him, smirking. 'I know your idea of equality, de Chirolo! You plan to marry Armida Hoytola and play lap-dog for the rest of your days. What a life of misery that would be! But she'll never wed you – she doesn't want you, and her stuck-up fart of a father wouldn't let her if she did.'

'I'll throw those words in your grimy face in a few weeks' time, Bonihatch! And then you'll have to grub about elsewhere to find yourself a job of work.'

'I wouldn't give you thanks for her cast-off chastity-belts, that I wouldn't,' Solly jeered. He doubled up with laughter. Bonihatch ignored him, staring at me with furrowed brow.

'You don't know your real friends,' he said, soberly.

Turning on my heel, I led Capriccio to the stable before changing into my General Gerald outfit for the last time. For the last time, I was to stand rigid while Bengtsohn's magic glass lens sucked light into his zahnoscope.

The Joyous Tragedy of Prince Mendicula was complete, except for three or four scenes that needed to be done again. And still Bengtsohn had let nobody see the results.

Already, I had run my sword through (or rather behind) Bonihatch's absurd Mendicula. He had died absurdly. Letitia's Lady Jemima had taken a fatal potion and died on her couch for a full five minutes. Armida's Patricia had wept for as long against a draped balustrade, and I had attitudinized for as long with triumph on my face and red paint on my sword. All that remained was to re-enact a couple of poses which Bengtsohn regarded as unsatisfactory.

The first scene we replayed was the beginning of the betrayal, where Gerald casts a lustful glance on Patricia while Prince Mendicula is looking away. This was no hardship for me: five minutes of lustful glancing, my gaze fixed on that delightful breast, was hardly enough.

Afterwards, in a lull, I said to Armida, 'How I look forward to viewing this complete production. Why is Otto so secretive?'

'I don't think he trusts me.'

'We shall be such a success! You will be so much in demand that you will have to turn actress; then your family can have no objection to my marrying you.'

We were sitting together in the shade, apart from the others.

'General Gerald, I find your company exciting, but I already act in charades at home,' said Armida. 'I would never become a professional actress.'

'Even if you went into tragedy?'

'It would be lowering. Now pray don't vex me, Perry.' She turned away.

'You do not have to lower yourself. I will raise myself to you ... But what's wrong with actresses? The talented La Singla – she is well born.'

'My father tells me she was of peasant stock, and dishonoured as a very young girl.'

I laughed. 'Her origins are legend. They have given her a career instead of a stuffy mansion.'

'Lucky are they who can choose.' Her face grew very closed.

'Choose to slip away with me after this and let us rediscover that ferny chapel in the palace. This will be our last chance.' I breathed the words in her ear.

She gave me a cool smile. 'I have to go home to prepare for our journey to the country; it needs much forethought. We have an assignation in Juracia.'

Whilst speaking, Armida raised her face to look at me down that delicious nose, with her eyes and her lips appearing to generate a ripe degree of moisture. I was provoked all over again – as I was almost every time she turned that gaze on me and I met those eyes, at once dark and golden, which resembled the eyes of a lioness more than those of a human being. I could only feel that an assignation with her, wherever kept, would be the most wonderful in the world.

We worked through the morning, until we came to the final

scene to be re-made, wherein Mendicula confronts his wife and the general in the rose garden. Between them, Solly the Solid, Rhino, Bonihatch and Otto – with Flora supervising – dragged the zahnoscope into the Chabrizzi rose garden. We took up positions. Bengtsohn loaded his machine and adjusted the lens.

For five minutes we stood, Mendicula disadvantaged yet challenging, Patricia and I close, she looking haughty at her prince, I staring above human folly at the sky.

'Magnificent!' cried Bengtsohn, when he had clapped the hood over his lens. 'So is finish our great work. I have good news, too. The Hoytola family has permitted that this little Tragedy of Prince *Mendicula* shall be shown before all at the Orini–de Lambant wedding.'

'Before or after we present the comedy of *Fabio and Albrizzi*?' I asked.

'All will be well, you'll see, Perian,' he said. 'All will be well—' smiling and nodding and showing his yellowed old stumps of teeth.

'Our living comedy must play first. It is already arranged for the second day of the celebrations. *Mendicula* must come on the last day, in case its novelty is such that people want to see nothing else.'

'Of this I don't know nothing. I'm not in charge with plannings. I'm not in charge of nothing. I'm just a minion who must obey.'

'There is a correct order for things.'

He and his wife drew me aside afterwards, while the apprentices hitched the zahnoscope behind the handcart.

'Master Perian, we do not make obstruction against your success. Do what you can to help ours, that's all what we ask. That's reasonable. With the success of my entertainment, we can achieve more useful things.'

'I'm not obstructing you, Otto.'

'Maybe no, but you think too narrowly just of your own interest.'

His wife Flora had sagging dumplings for cheeks and larger sagging dumplings for breasts and buttocks. She said to me, 'Master Perian, we wish to count you in the Cause, since you have a big name among the youths of Malacia.' She smiled, while looking round to see that she was not overheard. 'Those who have power in the state have no wish to share that power; it must be taken from them. Before revolution can come, there must be a groundwork of change prepared, for the common good. My husband and I are old, but we steadily work for that change, just as we did in Tolkhorm. We cannot have *Mendicula* lost to view, because it must lead to gooder things. Set aside your personal pride and assist us, like what we assist you.'

This was the first occasion on which Madame Bengtsohn had granted me such a long speech. It crossed my mind that those in power were generally polite and cheerful; while those that wanted change, like Bonihatch, were personally offensive, discontented, and would use any means to cause trouble. While criticizing my pride, she manifested plenty of her own.

'*Mendicula* is all very well,' I said. 'Yet many will see no art in its silly tale of love betrayed; its one merit is novelty of method. How can it lead to better things?'

Bengtsohn said, 'It is the *method* what is all-important. Listen to me, once we shall get the principle of mercurizing accepted, then much can be done with. It is *mercurizing* what is important. Innovations have to be slid into this state with such circumspection. If mercurizing will not be banned by the Council, then we can use the invention for social ends.'

'You're a real schemer, Otto. It won't work you any good.'

I could not get away from the pair of them, and there was Armida, waving goodbye and showing a pretty ankle as she climbed into her carriage, her sour-faced old chaperon waiting to follow.

'You've had experience how my balloons fly,' said Bengtsohn. 'Imagine a modified zahnoscope taken up in a balloon similar. We can mercurize the ground below. Then, next time the Turkish army comes beyond our walls to camp, we mercurize the disposition from his troops. Think of the advantages of such a capacity to the military!'

'And not only the Turkish,' said Flora. She took my hand. 'We have worser enemies *within* the walls. We could mercurize secretly Fetter Place from the balloon, and the Renardo Palace, and the great mazes of the Palace of the Bishops Elect. Those hellish places will then hold more few secrets, and our revolutionary councils will hold in their hands a useful weapon.'

'Mercurization is a *weapon*,' Bengtsohn said.

'Be cautious what you say to Master Perian, now that he has a nag,' said Bonihatch, coming up. 'He hopes to gallop himself into privileged beds where anything we tell him might provide a little chit-chat while he re-stokes.'

I turned with immediate anger, but the old man checked us both.

'Save that tongue, Bonny. We don't want no enemies among each other. But the warning is taken. Perian, be wise. Wise is what wise does.' He nodded and walked off. His wife followed.

'You're longing for trouble, aren't you?' I said to Bonihatch.

He rubbed his hands on his upper arms and shook his head. 'I'm in agreement with Otto and Flora – I want you to see where truth lies. You're one of the victims, same as him and me.'

'I intend to be one of the winners.'

Walking away from him, I made for the stables to get Capriccio, depressed to think that the Mendicula affair, entered into lightly, was ending dismally. Armida should have waited for me.

'By the bones, this reformation takes the light-heartedness out of a lad's character,' I said to myself, half-aloud.

In the shadows at the far end of the stable, beyond where Capriccio was chomping hay, stood Letitia. She smiled and approached, holding out her hands.

I selected one of them and clutched it, determined to be formal, although her smile was good to see.

'So, Letitia, our play's over. You'll have to go back to your shirts and table-cloths. I have had enough of low life and am off to the hills to hunt devil-jaws and other nasty ancestral animals.'

She pulled her hand from mine, and looked down to hide the flush that came to her cheeks. 'So I'm low-life, am I? That's how you think of me ...'

'Chk, I didn't mean that. You people are so touchy!'

'You people, indeed!' With her colour still high, she turned back and looked hard at me, almost with imperiousness. 'It's true I have no reason to be proud, Perian. But I thought I'd just wait here, away from the others, to bid you goodbye, since we'll not be meeting again. I wanted to tell you that whatever that little beast Solly said, I admired the figure you cut on your horse.'

'Ah, Letitia, you treat me better than I deserve! I am a real chick-snake at times.'

She laughed, as freely as I ever saw her. 'I've never ridden a horse, and don't know that I ever shall.'

'I'll give you a ride on Capriccio one day. He's slightly lame, but a fine animal, aren't you, Capri, old fellow? Now I must be on my way. I've got to get a pair of boots out of pawn.'

She put her hand on the gelding's bridle, eyeing me inquisitively.

'It's been a pleasure to do the play with you, Perry, I tell you boldly. You're the first actor I've ever spoken with – not in a business way, I mean, for we have made costumes for the University Players. It is an enviable way of life.'

'Some find it so. Some despise it.'

'It would be a way of improving myself, and helping the family more than I do at present ... You said so. Do you – do you think I could become a professional actress? I mean—' she hurried on, as if dreading my answer – 'I mean, I know you have to have talent and of course be more beautiful than I am. I couldn't expect to be Lady Jemima ever again, but perhaps I could play funny parts, do you think? Is there a chance that your Maestro Kemperer would take me on?'

I took her frail hands, and we half-leant against the flanks of the horse, gazing at each other.

'It really is a hard life, especially for a girl.'

'A hard life's one thing I'm well accustomed to.'

'If you're serious, I suppose I could put in a word with Kemperer. I'm not on the best of terms with him at present.'

'You mustn't tell Armida what I've just said.'

'I won't *tell* anyone, you silly girl – Armida least of all, to be honest. But what will your uncle Joze say when you tell him?'

Letitia's gaze dropped. 'He'd let me go if mother and I made enough opposition. He's part of what I want to get away from.'

My arms were round her, and her head nestled in my chest. 'Letitia, you're such an odd mixture.'

'No more of a mixture than you,' she said, with renewed spirit, looking up at me with flashing blue eyes and a half-smile. 'Do you make love to every girl you act with, Perry?'

'Why do you suppose that?'

She twined her arms round my neck. 'It excites me a little.'

Taking her closer, I said, 'I thought you were the one who wanted to be an exception to the general rule, Letty.'

Her hair still smelt of the garret, although she had sprinkled cheap powder in it. I pressed my cheek against hers, while slipping one hand into her bodice, so that a small warm breast was

202

cradled in my hand, smooth as an orc's egg, soft as a doe's fur. 'Ride on Capriccio with me to my billet, just to celebrate a joint farewell to General Gerald and the Lady Jemima. Let them do behind the locked door what they pretend before the zahnoscope.'

The gelding stirred beside us as if in complicity.

As I began kissing her, she pulled her face away and said, 'It would be more persuasive if you could contrive to let Maestro Kemperer view the *Tragedy of Mendicula*. He might take a fancy to me in my part.'

'Oh, I'm sure he'd take a fancy to you, in every part, my darling. But that later ... Now, while I'm not idle, you be active – slide your dainty hand down here and measure what remarkable effect you have on me, and what a burning torch would light your way to bed ...'

Beneath my fingers, was exactly the syruped nook in which that torch might be most pleasurably extinguished. She gasped, parting her lips with an exhalation of excitement, either at what she felt or I felt, or both, and began wriggling deliciously. I slid my tongue between her teeth, hers thrust between my cheeks. At which, she went into raptures on the spot, so jogging me in her convulsions that I was thrown into the same voluptuous spasm. We stood, we tottered, half propped against Capriccio, in the twilit stable.

'Oh ... oh ... oh ... Perry ...'

'Oh, Letty!' I said, pleased despite the state of my dress. I was trembling. I leant against the wooden wall of the stable. 'How gloriously ready you are, Letty! Come back to my room and let's celebrate our delight at a more leisurely pace.'

She adjusted her dress, laughing and sobbing, and hiding her face in a characteristic way.

'Oh, oh, that's so shameful, so abandoned!' She laughed again. 'You see, I can enjoy myself like any high-born girl. Yes, yes. I want you to take me fiercely in all my finery, pretend I really am the Lady Jemima!'

She threw herself at me, face all aflame. 'Perry, I'll give you it all. Can I trust you? Oh, I'm so desperate – if I could only speak, if only I could tell you ...'

'Believe me, you're eloquent.'

I heard noises outside the stable.

Her arms slipped round my neck again. 'It's you – you make

me so brazen! Oh, Perry, you will help me become an actress? You did promise.'

'We'll talk about that later.' There were muttered voices outside.

Leaving my blouse unbuttoned, I looked round for a weapon. A hay rake stood close by. As I grasped it, the stable door was kicked open.

Letitia screamed and darted behind me. There stood Bonihatch, brandishing a stout cudgel, his jaw set. With him was Solly, similarly armed. Otto and Flora and another pair of apprentices stood behind them, all peering angrily or anxiously into the gloom.

'We've caught you at your tricks this time, you cur,' said Bonihatch. 'Now I'm really going to learn you. I'm going to beat you to a pulp.'

'Yes, we're going to beat you to a bloody pulp,' said Solly.

'Come out from there, Letitia,' called Bonihatch. She made no attempt to move from where she was. I stood confronting them. There were four of them and a pair of apprentices to get by.

'You scoundrel,' Bengtsohn said. 'You have had advantage of that young girl, what her uncle told me to keep both my eyes on.'

He pushed Bonihatch forward.

Flora called out, 'Are you all right, Letitia? Are we too late?'

'I'm quite safe,' Letitia said indistinctly. 'Let us come out.'

As she spoke, I jumped forward, lunging with the rake as if it were a pike, catching Bonihatch in the chest. Using the momentum of the lunge, and dropping the rake, I hit Solly full in the face with my fist. In the moment of disorder, I swung Capri's head towards the door, vaulted into the saddle as if I had practised it for years, and sank the stirrups sharply into his flanks. Forward we lurched.

My assailants fell back, shouting. Solly was slammed against the post as we broke free. Bengtsohn had the presence of mind to wave his stick. I kicked out at him, happening to catch him on the side of his skull. He fell cursing against his wife's dumplings. She too, screaming murder, tumbled, back against the other apprentices, in a welter of soiled skirts. They stumbled beneath her weight and fell.

Into the court we galloped. I was yelling, in glee and excitement. Past the loaded handcart, past the zahnoscope. Chabrizzi servants scattered. Heading for the gate at a trot, I turned to look back. Four of them had collapsed in a heap, punctuated by waving arms, pallid legs and red faces. Bonihatch and Solly were presumed recovering inside the stable. Only Letitia was on her feet, standing and waving to me. Returning the gesture, I almost fell out of the saddle. I imagined the admiration in her heart for the way I had handled the affair as I clung to Capri's neck.

I made my way along the Street of the Wood Carvers to my own door. I had stabled Capriccio, and taken a much-needed glass of wine. My pulse was normal again.

As I mounted the bare, wooden stairs, I was conscious of a sulphurous smell but thought nothing of it. I set my thoughts on the good times just past and the good times to come; there was no need to feel low. When I had gathered some belongings together, I would be off for Juracia and the hunt.

At the top of the stairs, I opened the door to my room. My amulet slipped from my arm. I clutched it but it had gone, slithering down my forearm like a snake. Instead of clattering on the boards, it fell on tufty grass.

Through a haze, I saw six people waiting. They stood monstrously, grouped in a misty clearing among blasted oaks and pines; an owl sat on a riven branch, adding its staring face to the others. Something between mist and music assailed my senses.

The two leading figures were exponents of the Natural Religion, as their clumsy drapings, adorned with enigmatic signs, proclaimed. The man in the forefront was of grotesque stature; he sported a luxuriant, reddish-brown beard. Over the ferocious curls of his cranium he had draped a pancake cup of linen. Under his outer gown he nursed a gigantic phallus, showing his allegiance to Satan.

The others of the motley crew were as hideous, though they had not his puissance. Their apparition so terrified me that it took a moment to observe that one of the group was an ape dressed in clothes. They all stood about a mighty cylindrical altar, from the crumbling stone of which protruded carved heads of Minerva and the Devil. Sulphurous smoke drifted from the ashes on the stone.

All these seven faces, animal, bird and human, turned towards me. In every ugly countenance, I read hostility. Fear crawled in my bones.

And there was a woman. She crouched in abasement before the magician with the swollen phallus, her naked back scraping the altar. She was undressed down to a soiled, white shift, and was evidently so demoralized that she left her ample breasts to hang in full view. She clutched a battered bronze plate.

Of all the beings there, she was the last to become aware of my presence. Slowly, despairingly, she lifted her head to gaze at me – and fixed me with such a look of anguish that I would have taken a step back, could I have moved at all.

I was not the only one to hold still. Nothing stirred except the slow drift of rancid smoke across those unblinking faces.

I stood there for ever, it seemed. Time was of no account to them, that I knew; the mist shrouding those trees would never be lifted by the visitation of an ordinary sun.

And then the second magician moved. He was a hulking ruin of a man with coarse features, brows like dead bracken, and a skull bereft of hair. He sidled forward and raised one hand slowly towards me. His mouth was permanently half-open. It opened still more, showing fangs, as if he were about to speak. Then he was gone.

They were all dissolved, with a humming sound like bees swarming – woman and altar and all the rest of the scene. I was standing in my familiar room, shaking.

The spell was broken. I reached slowly down and picked my amulet off the floor. With difficulty, for it was as tight as usual, I slid it back on to my upper arm.

I sat down on my bed.

Someone had worked a spell against me – a fairly typical one, with the figures only mistily realized, and little sound involved. For all that, the vision had contained a super-reality which its enigmatic quality made more terrifying. Were they warning me?

For a long while I sat in anguished speculation. I had nothing on my conscience. Well, not much. The vow I had made to be true to Armida had not been broken. Admittedly, Letitia had dented it a little; but that had been her doing, not mine. Although I might have offered to bring her to my room, the fact was that I had not done so, and in matrimonial matters it

is wise to be ruled by facts rather than ifs. I gathered up my
things and made for Juracia in a sober mood.

The Hoytola estates were grand in every degree. As the dusty
track wound northwards from Malacia, it twisted down into a
fertile and afforested valley; there, invitingly, lay the hamlet of
Juracia, with Hoytola's lodge behind it. And how invitingly!
Capriccio had gone lame ten kilometres back. I had had to
walk him. The carriages, waggons and riders passing by had
smothered me in the white dust of the Fruila. I was hot, foot-
sore, bedraggled and thirsty.

I entered the estate as inconspicuously as possible. It was
soon made clear to me by the servants that no one arrived here
without equerry or valet. The impudent fellows treated me as
if I were a servant myself. Enraged, I made what disorder I
could in the bedroom to which I was shown, beating the dust
from my clothes over everything to show them who was
master.

After lounging in a hot bath of the Roman type – the only
other occupants being two drunken fat men who sang ballads –
I was refreshed. I dressed, and went in search of food, wine,
company, cheer and Armida.

The upper floor of the lodge consisted entirely of small bed-
rooms, with a prayer room at the end of the corridor, where a
mezzanine gave way to a long balcony and stairs down. From
the balcony, one could survey the first of three halls given over
to the pleasure of Hoytola's guests. In this hall, steaming foods
and hot and cold drinks were being served by an army of
liveried servants who moved among the three rooms, bearing
trays, sweating, and in general smiling. Festivities were well
under way. The middle hall, which adjoined the kitchens, was
equipped with sturdy tables and benches. The last hall was
more of a lounging room, being equipped with books, an organ,
a pair of titanic statues, and tapestried furniture. The walls of
each room were decorated with the spoils of the chase, spears,
guns, horns, and the skulls of an impressive number and variety
of animals, including trundles, devil-jaws, slobbergobs, siderowels and tyrant-greaves. Every hall had its musicians, and
every hall was crowded with people, mainly men clad in traditional hunting garb of studded leather, fur, and heavy-weave
cloth. A ferocious lot they looked, their artificial hides like those

of grab-skeeters, their expressions often less benign than grab-skeeters'.

The lateness of my arrival meant that I had met no one, been introduced to no one. I would make up for that. Here was the food, wine, company and cheer I needed; only Armida was missing, and she was worth waiting for. I plunged down into the throng, snatching up a leathern tankard of hot mulled ale from a passing tray and quaffing it as I went.

Hoytola's guests were of all ages, smooth of face, grizzled, wrinkled with age. All carried themselves with a swagger born of the assurance that the world was made for them. I had studied that swagger and imitated it without trouble, thinking that many who jostled my elbow also assumed it more from protection than nature. The few women present were heavily dressed for the occasion, with padded hair and sometimes cocked riding-hats to increase their stature. Several wore masculine frocks with waistcoats; almost all were adorned with scales and fur and jewellery. I guessed there would be much sport in an unbridled place like this, yet I saw no woman to my liking. Their eyes were too fishy, to name but one point against them. The old women painted their teeth with white lead.

Who could fail to be elated in a place like this? I longed to see the lodge from the outside by daylight (it was already dark), and to plunge across country on my steed (if I could borrow a replacement for Capriccio), acting as gallantly as any of the company.

For half an hour, I passed among my fellow guests, speaking to nobody except a handsome-visaged hunter who recognized me from my aerial trip and wanted to know how it felt to fly. Despite all the food and drink, there was no universal contentment. Many men were complaining about the poorness of the day's sport and the standards of Hoytola's hospitality. I heard one of them say, 'The fellow has no idea of what living in style really means.' I felt ashamed. I thought that if I ever had a say in matters, I would see that the quantities of food and wine supplied were doubled and extra game animals imported; at the same time, I was disgusted with the man who complained.

Taking meat dressed in pastry along with my ale, I said, 'The hospitality's good' to a man who chanced to be passing, and discovered that it was a relation of mine by my sister's marriage, Julius, a cheerful fellow though a Mantegan.

'You're here, Perian!' He put an arm about my shoulder.

'Don't sound so surprised,' I said, slopping my ale. 'I'm not always tied to the boards. I need to bag a shatterhorn occasionally, same as any other man.'

'That's the spirit! Which party are you with?'

'At the moment, I'm not *with* anyone.' As I was about to mention Armida's name, caution checked me; I said instead, 'I've got a friend of mine among the musicians.'

Smiling in the friendliest way, Julius said in a lowered voice, 'You ought to be warned that the etiquette at these functions is strict. Musicians are treated with hauteur by the guests and mistrust by the servants. The consequence – or the cause – of which is that the musicians are not supposed to speak to the servants and the guests are not supposed to speak to the musicians.'

'What's the point of such an observance?'

'The musicians spend more time playing and less time flirting and drinking. Anyhow, Perian, I didn't expect to see you here. We Mantegans arrived in force; you should have travelled with us. I'm sorry your sister would not come – she's a fine lady for whom I have much esteem. Is your father here?'

'Oh no, he's too busy on his book. It would have been good to see Katie here. I ... was invited by Armida Hoytola. You haven't seen her, have you?'

His eyebrows went up. He regarded me quizzically, like a man sighting his first fanglefish.

'Oh ho! Well, my dear Perian, you must not yet have found your way about, or you would know that there are *two* hunting lodges. The grander one lies farther into the park, and there you will encounter to your heart's desire the Hoytolas and the prosperous families and the Dukes of Renardo and Tuscady and any richer nobles who may advance Hoytola's cause. Whereas, in this more humble lodge, you will find only the impoverished nobles – well, like your Chabrizzis and Mantegans, eh? Sit and drink with me awhile.'

He called more of his kinsmen over, and they were convivial fellows. Their talk was of the estuary, far distant, where many of them lived, spending much of their time in boats, hunting the great ancestrals of the deep, fanglefish, crazies, speckled sabre-snouts, goddies, and others, or shooting down the frizzen-bats that swooped overhead. By their laughing accounts, their time was spent between sand and sea, wine and danger.

'We're a bad lot – little we care for art or religion, like you Malacians,' Julius said. 'And Volpato is the worst of us. Your sister is a fine lady, and worthy of better. I rejoice that she has a brother like you to look after her.'

He reported that they had arrived in Juracia the evening before, and had gone straight into the hunt. They had flushed some speedy yatterhobs and slain them after a long chase. But game seemed scarce this year. The big ancestrals, the tyrant-greaves and devil-jaws, and in particular the slow casque-bodies, had been over-hunted.

'In another five years, they'll all be gone,' Julius said. 'Then we shall come here just to drink – or stay away entirely. The Middle Sea provides better sport.'

We parted with mutual esteem. I went outside and found my way down a drive, lined by poplars and lit by flambeaux, to the other lodge Julius had mentioned. It was indeed more sumptuous than the first, although built on an identical plan, the one common to the region. Its walls were decorated with tapestries, its rooms warmed by magnificent porcelain-tiled stoves – unlit in this mild season – and every nook was loaded with a bust or treasure of some kind, while overhead the rafters were decked with fresh green boughs in celebration of the hunt. The music here was more refined, and played by musicians who wore quaint old court dress.

As for the food, it was flamboyant to the highest degree. Young sucking trundles turned on their spits with sprigs of herbs hissing beneath their limbs. The tables were creaking beneath the weight of flesh and fowl, all dressed proudly as if for sport rather than eating. There were yatterhobs' heads – probably the heads of the ancestrals the Mantegans had killed – wearing ruffs, and fish with chops as ferocious as devil-jaws, and young snaphances couched in sauces and spaghetti. The wine came in glasses clutched by silver buglewings with eyes of obsidian. The furniture was similarly adorned with riotous emblems of the business which informed the occasion: stylized foliage chasing itself over legs and arms of chairs, amid which warriors and reptilian forms bled in profusion.

All of which was nothing compared with the bipedal confectionery which paraded here: those privileged beings who had taken up their three-day abode in this building. The men were all darker, the women all paler, than in the first lodge. One and all, their clothes were richer, stiffer, more seamed with gold, more calculated to isolate the wearer from his surroundings, more horned, beaked, ruffed, and feathered, more terrible; their tunics were warted with jewels, amid which emeralds gleamed like eyes, rubies sulked like blood. They were taller; many of the women wore stilt-shoes with claws, men and women shipped in their wake tiny bobbing page-boys or dwarfs.

To my eyes, the men were all brigands, the women whores, their miniature attendants mere feathered foetuses, walking cocky. The only humble people in that throng were the slaves – mostly black women, of whom there were some dozen; their owners kept them naked, with scaled bracelets on legs and arms, and flowers in their curly hair.

I worked my way through this animated mob as through a jungle, moving towards the musicians. Selections from opera buffo were being played and, above the hubbub, an immense man with cheeks like trundles' eggs was singing popular airs.

> *Oh there are mountainsides where I may stray*
> *Where flashing stream makes roundelay*
> *Where every trail*
> *Invites you, "Come away, away",*
>
> *Where armoured animals with onyx eyes*
> *Oft-times the hunter brave espies,*
> *Hurling his spear –*
> *See where it flies, it flies . . .'*

Below this gigantic tenor, de Lambant plucked his lute with the other musicians, a ruff round his neck like one of the yatter-hobs. Fighting my way over to him, I called his name. He joined me at the end of the song, looking far from his usual cheerful self.

'De Chirolo, my friend, this is a fine whorehouse to be in! The musicians are not allowed to speak to the servants, nor the guests to the musicians.'

'As a guest, I may speak with my friends when I wish.'

He wiped his brow. 'Simple, the man's simple, too innocent for this world. I'm sure you're the only decent fellow among this mob! Do you observe – but take care where you gaze – how the slave women may be swived by any man, here standing,

211

the while they continue conversations with their friends? By the holy bones, I never expected that!'

'We aren't in Malacia now.'

'This is more like a chick-snake's nest.'

'Moral judgments, de Lambant? I thought you were interested in decadence!'

'I didn't know what the term meant till I got here. You should have seen them at it last night ...'

'Where are Armida and Bedalar?'

He pulled a drab face. 'Bedalar's not here. Caylus took a tumble from his horse among the bulls and got trampled, silly fellow. So the Nortolini family stays in Malacia, silly family. So Bedalar is unable to escape into the arms of her lover, silly girl ... Still, if I can't keep myself amused here alone for three days, then I'm a silly boy ... The musicians' quarters – a word I employ as euphemism for byre – are next to the slaves' quarters ... Well, we must look upon life as a caper, young de Chirolo, mustn't we? I've seen Armida, but since the servants aren't allowed to speak to the musicians and the musicians aren't allowed—'

'She must be in this scrimmage somewhere. She must be looking for me.'

'Your simple trust in the world should get you far. If you don't find her, Perry ...'

'Yes?'

'Take another look at the black girls and note how scrumptious they are ...'

Giving him a friendly nod, I launched myself into the mêlée, staunching myself with more wine as I went.

The noise, the heat, the sweet and sour stench, the perpetual brush of bodies, got to me. So did the wine. As I went, I exchanged bold glances with women, many of whom would have not deigned to look at me in the ordinary way. There was dancing now, and some acrobats performed at the far end of the room.

Amid the press, I observed that various rooms led off the three halls. Maids bustled through their doors and curtains, so that I seized the chance to look within, and saw that they were private suites, given over mainly to obscene displays. In one, a satyr rutted with a slave girl, to the delight of some watching gentlemen with their ladies. In another, into which a female

212

servant casually went, three naked men and a red-haired woman – well, no matter what they did, I caught but a glimpse. In a third room, as I steadied myself with a further glass of wine, I observed my host himself, Andrus Hoytola, with some companions. Without hesitation, I marched in to pay my respects. I was here to make my mark.

Hoytola was seated at a carved oak table, dressed not in the bristling fashion of the lodges but in his usual foppish way, in a short white evening coat with a buckle at the back and a high collar, together with crimson silk trousers. His fingers were drumming on the table. Most of his companions presented, as he did, their backs to the door, conspiratorially. Among them was the young Duke of Renardo, dressed in armoured fashion, his unruly gold curls gleaming. Two women were in the room; Madame Hoytola, Armida's mother, who gazed at me without blinking an eyelid, and a courtesan whom I immediately recognized. She was the over-painted woman with the mandoline in the Renardo gardens, whom Caylus had enjoyed. This evening, she was more over-painted than before.

Despite the presence of those ladies, this was plainly some sort of business meeting. From the shadows, a gentleman with a long, grey coat and long, grey skull to match was saying as I entered, 'I may remind you that defence is not the first duty of Malacia, Hoytola.'

To which Hoytola replied, 'Without one's defences, Malacia ceases to exist.'

'There are the ancient defences. Best of all, there is the Original Curse, protecting us from change. Our first duty is to maintain through religious observance that Curse – remember the sacred purpose of everything, even this hunt: "We go forth to slay the flesh of our Fathers..."'

He ceased and turned his cold stare on me. Slowly, the men at the table moved to survey me. Hoytola presented a half-profile and one eye round the side of his high white collar; the eye and the belt buckle gleamed at me. Only the duke nodded in civil fashion.

'It's our balloon-going friend,' he said. 'Still in good order, I see. What brings you here, de Chirolo?'

'Merely pleasure, sir.' I lifted my glass. 'I give you good cheer, gentlemen!'

'This is a private meeting,' Hoytola replied.

'My wish was not to intrude. I will leave you.'

The duke said cheerfully, 'If you are looking for Armida, we cannot help you.'

Hoytola's face went a kind of ashy colour. He bent his head to the table to conceal it. In that moment, I clearly understood whom it was that this man preferred as possible husband for his daughter.

As I had my hand on the door to go, a deep voice said, 'You!'

The courtesan – now I could smell her patchouli, so disturbingly like Armida's – made a slight move towards the back of the room, which served to direct my attention there. In the shadows stood the man who called me. I recognized the dark-visaged Supreme Council member I had first glimpsed in Hoytola's gallery. Chill radiated from his presence. As on that first occasion, he was garbed in unfashionable black with capacious pockets. He spoke again.

'You have fallen in with Bengtsohn.' Every word emerged separately from his gullet.

The courtesan went to his side. He paid no attention to her, standing without movement, firm in the knowledge that I would answer him.

Why did he terrify me so? I believe it was because I felt that he put the fear of Satan into everyone else in the room too.

'I have fallen *out* with Bengtsohn,' I said, 'sire.'

My presence was nothing to do with them. Everyone was motionless, waiting to resume whatever business they had been about – business that held no great pleasure for Hoytola, to judge by appearances; yet somehow their business was of such a sort that it could encompass even me. My words travelled across the room to the Council member, and at last he spoke again, his words coming off a subterranean glacier.

'You wish to kill Bengtsohn.'

The young duke scratched his curls. Looking at him, rather than the black figure at the rear of the room, I said, 'I don't wish to harm Bengtsohn – he has never hurt me. I don't wish to harm anyone.'

Experiencing some difficulty with my limbs, I managed to get out of the room and shut the door behind me. The words spoken went through and through my brain. I cursed myself for the feeble thing I had said, as if begging for mercy. I drained my wine and let the glass drop. I fingered my amulet. This meeting was alarmingly similar to the vision I had stumbled on in my own room.

There was nothing for it but to disappear into the night or stay and get drunk. A serving wench came by. I snatched an armorial shell full of hot spiced wine from her and barged into the end room, among dancing and gesticulating couples. The uproar was so intense that the music could hardly be heard. A crowd surrounded a platform on which a savage gentleman was making two yellow hauberks fight to the death.

I did not stay to watch the warm blood fly. I quaffed wine and threw myself into the midst of the whirling figures. I caught hold of a young woman whose conversation I could not understand. We talked madly to each other, gesturing, laughing, grimacing, once kissing. Was it a foreign tongue she spoke? I never knew, nor whether she understood what I said. Movement was all-important, movement and gaiety. As I reeled from her arms, there was Armida, flushed, rushing by with another young woman.

Grasping her unceremoniously, I whirled her into a dance, and so out of the nearest door on to a verandah. A chill night wind blew. I clutched her to me, pouring out professions of endearment, many of which I had just recently exercised – but vocabularies have a limited exchequer, after all.

'You darling feathered creature, plunging by me in the torrents of night – you are the moon in this terrible place, the sun – everything's so terrible – I believed you weren't here, that you had gone, even that you had submitted to one of those full-bellied—'

'Hush, hush, you're mad!'

I flailed my arms. 'Madness and terror are beautiful. Ask the Natural Religion. What else do you expect in this terrible place?'

'No, no, Perry, nothing here is terrible. Calm down, will you please? It's all so delightful, such *fun*, and the people are so grand, and important—'

'They matter not a fig, they're beasts in a jungle of the mind, whereas you and I – oh, the music of madness, don't you hear the true sound under it all—'

'And tomorrow – listen to me, will you? – tomorrow there will be chariot races and the parade of mounts and all kinds of entertainment, and then in the late afternoon – stop! – in the late afternoon—'

'How I hate that word "afternoon"! Trade only with blazing noon or midnight, my love, my honey-lipped! Afternoons are for children. Look at the great monster hulk of this place above us, lumbering towards midnight, and out there nothing, *nothing*, but blackness, unknown universes, and what can we fight such things with? Only our own weapons: my poor imagination, your white thighs—'

Under my hands her body was glorious in the reeling darkness.

'Leave my thighs out of this, sir. In late afternoon begins the main ancestral hunt, when we pit ourselves against the most terrible of Satan's creatures. It's sure to be thrilling and someone's bound to get killed ... What's the matter with you? Stop that. You're drunk so early. You're taking advantage.'

'What's the sight of you but drunkenness? What's life but intoxication? What's sobriety but the misery my father puts himself in? I know which I prefer. You darling, you darling, perhaps I'm a little drunk on you, but not yet enough—'

'My father's wine has played a greater part, that I'm certain. All our wine is grown here in our own vineyards. We have some of the best slopes for hundreds of kilometres.'

'And your slopes, your ravines, your dells ... You look so splendid tonight!' Indeed she did. She had on a fine crimson silk gown with a small matching turban for her head, from under which her dark electric locks escaped. Over the gown was a cape made of the long feathered spines of tree reptopines, while the gown itself extended to the floor and there burst into ruffles, like a ship decked in bunting.

'Armida, you are the most lovely girl. I adore you as owls adore the night, and long to have our betrothal made public. I will always be true to you and you only. I don't even understand the language other women speak.'

She laughed. 'You're certainly ambitious. No harm in that. But our betrothal's just our secret fun, don't forget. Do you know, this year we have brought an extra fifty hectares under cultivation – mainly grapes – at Juracia, at no expense to the hunt territory. Isn't that good husbandry?'

'Marvellous, I'm sure. Someone must have worked hard.'

'Oh, father worked himself so hard—'

'But the land means nothing to me. It's you, you yourself – Armida, feel what I feel—'

'You're drunk, you don't listen. Sometimes you don't seem to understand what's really important. It's father's ambition to be the largest wine-grower in the region. Although the peasants are lazy, the soil is fertile, and—'

'We're all fertile.' I was clutching her tightly. 'How things do sprout from the heart! How circumstances sail upwards like balloons, into the sky of light, of hope – of achievement! With you to inspire me, Armida, I could do all things. I'd grow grapes – no, I don't want to grow grapes – I'd become a captain in the cavalry – no, I don't care to be in a regiment – I'd buy a ship and trade with the East in fantastic objects – no, who needs to go to sea? – I'd do anything, almost anything, for you. I don't have to remain a player. There are great things in me which the night brings out. Yesterday I was down. Today I'm up. Perhaps I could rise to serve on the Council and help Malacia – those who serve there don't have our interests at heart.'

'You're so sweet, Perian, but you have to be well-born, or exceedingly clever, like my father, to get anywhere near the Council. You have a cheerful heart, but—'

I wagged a cautionary finger at her. 'You think I'm frivolous. Didn't I embark on that little flying adventure your father and you planned for me – and come out of it well? Haven't I sworn to be true? I'm serious beneath my light-hearted air. Of course I can go about looking sober if you require it.'

She burst with pretty laughter, covering her mouth with her finger-tips as I gave my impression of sobriety.

'You have too handsome a face for that, sirrah! My father says that—'

'Then kiss it, if you find it handsome. Let me in return kiss you all over, not only on this beautiful nose – mahh! – or this lovely cheek – mahh! – but on these luscious shoulders – mahh! – and this heavenly bosom – mahh! – but creeping like an Arab into this crimson tent of yours to find what secret treasures you have concealed ...'

We fell delectably upon each other. Cold though it was, we were warm to one another's touch. In that moment, in a pool of dark between one gleaming window and the next, I saw into my love for her, my Armida, and understood all the difficulties with which she was surrounded: the prosperous household

217

sponged on by untrustworthy nobles, the conventions threatening to defeat her, the father dominating her life. She needed simpler things. It was true, as Bengtsohn said, that wealth corrupted the rich. I could save her from it, if she would dare come away with me.

I jumped up.

'Let's leave immediately,' I said. 'We could take your carriage. Damn the soothsayers. This drunken rout would not miss us for hours. The nobles of Malacia, Armida – they are corrupt, one and all, and should be done away with.'

'What? You are drunk, you rascal! Where would the wealth of the state be without the nobles?'

'Let's leave here together. We could go to Tuscady. I have a friend there, a captain of cavalry. We could live simply and honestly, in a small house on the street, with a hound, and a cage of singing birds at the window. We could see the hills from our upper windows.'

'You have picked up revolutionary ideas from Bengtsohn, Perian. My father says so. That man is dangerous. I'd better warn you, those who consort with him are also in danger.'

'What I say is true. Let's escape now. Tuscady. Or a cottage on the estuary where my kinsmen live.'

'Why will you not listen to my warning?'

'Why do you mention Bengtsohn? Only yesterday, he attacked me with a cudgel.' But I did not want to enter into that tale, so I went on hastily, 'All unprovoked, let me add. But he will be a different man when *Mendicula* is exhibited to the world. Ridiculous though its story may be, its presentation makes it a new form of art, and success will soften him.'

'That play may never be shown to anyone, Perian, so please keep quiet about it. You'd better go to your bed and sleep.'

'Only if you come with me and so rob me of the desire to sleep.'

'I can't. I'd be missed – and compromised.'

'Then come away with me.'

She stamped her foot. 'Stop being so impossible. Why do you wish to escape as soon as you are here? Enjoy yourself properly.'

'I'm trying to! Just think what's happening here. People are drinking their heads afloat. They'll all be in each other's beds in a few hours' time, the dogs! Let's race them to it. Nobody will
218

know – or care. I'll wager your precious chaperon is already pinned under some filthy, randy leather-clad groom in a convenient pile of hay.'

'You're so coarse. Why should you think of them – supposing it were so – in the same breath as us?'

'Yolaria may well be as grateful for the chance as any.'

She drew away angrily and I saw I had been too outspoken.

'Old people care less about that sort of thing,' she said.

'They care till their dying day – my father once told me so, and he's a scholar. Old Pope Lacrimae II did it on his deathbed at the age of ninety-nine.'

'Why, I'm glad my father never tells me things like that. Did he *really*?'

'Yes. With a virgin aged fourteen brought in from the country. Such intercourse is thought to have curative powers. Gerocomy, they call it.'

All the time we were talking, the wind was blowing itself into a gale. Shutters banged overhead. Hounds barked distantly.

'Perry, you do know such funny things. Is that true about Pope Lacrimae?'

'Come to bed with me and I'll keep you amused till daybreak.'

She put her arms round my neck. 'I can't. Really I can't. I am needed to help entertain guests. This is the great occasion of my father's year. Keep yourself happy – find another girl. There are plenty here prettier than I.'

'What if I did so? Would you blame me?' I asked teasingly.

'Oh, don't dare even say it! I'd be so jealous – I'd hate you for ever afterwards! You are pledged to me and you are mine and for me. Don't think such loathsome things.'

'Who suggested it? I only said what I did to see what you'd say. And I'm glad of your anger because it shows you do love me.'

She shook her head. 'Envy and jealousy are apart from love. Just remember your role as Gerald – he didn't *love* the princess, he merely envied Mendicula's marriage. Don't be like that, please. Don't merely envy what I have, love what I am. You think me difficult, I know it, but matters are difficult for me. At heart, there's a difference – just love me patiently and don't be unkind.'

The cold wind which blew that evening brought indifferent

weather next day – yet not indifferent enough to spoil the great organized tumult of pleasure pursued so strenuously at Juracia. By afternoon, rain was falling out of a sky piled to its farthest recesses with cloud. Golden summer was giving a first token that it could not rule for ever.

I wondered if I was not at last loving Armida more than she wished to be loved. Perhaps there was a special way of loving each special person. I languished the day away with thoughts of her.

Julius and the Mantegan kin were helpful. The head groom of the Hoytola hunt pronounced my Capriccio unrideable and suggested he be chopped up to use as carnivore bait. Julius found me a small, black cob, a sturdy beast called Bramble. Bramble had a sardonic eye. He snuffed the oats in my palm suspiciously before I mounted him, whereupon he proved manageable.

The inhospitable weather was such that many of the guests who had ridden to hunt the day before declined to ride today. Some fifty of us assembled as the cloud brightened towards the west. For weapons we were permitted only spring-loaded spears, with short swords in reserve. We wore chest armour, and that too I borrowed from the Mantegans. Behind us on foot came a line of peasants with staves, our beaters, with a body of Hoytola's personal guard. The guard carried muzzle-loaders.

The great sight was the lines of ceremonial hunters mounted on ancestral steeds. Renardo favoured wattle tassets, Tuscady grave-dippers; other noble houses, like the Dios, had the one or the other, or both. Wattle tassets were the more massive beasts, some of them standing seven metres high – truly an impressive sight, blinkered as they were, standing upright on their clawed, three-toed feet, trailing massive tails. Their fore paws were harnessed, to prevent damage from their horned thumbs, and they were decked in the colours of their noble houses. They were proud beasts, the tassets, slow but virtually inexhaustible.

The grave-dippers – or duck-beaks, as the simple folk called them – were almost as tall but lighter in structure. Like the tassets, they are vegetarian. Riders of dippers sit higher up the backs of their mounts than is the case with tasset riders, to prevent them assuming a four-legged posture at speed. There was great variety among the grave-dippers; many had curiously shaped crests, rendered more bizarre by being adorned with the house emblems of their owners. Most of them were heavily blinkered and snaffled, often with an extra bit forced through their nostrils, for grave-dippers become nervous at the scent of carnivores like tyrant-greave or devil-jaw. Yet they are more popular than tassets because they can swim rapidly across rivers.

Needless to say, these valuable sporting animals were also useful in time of war.

As a seal of his approval, Gondale IX had sent up his two marshbags, rigged with banners for all their twenty-six-metre lengths. These perambulating bladders, with wrinkled skins and four enormous plodding legs, were useless on a big game hunt, yet added distinction to any occasion. Their clownish aspect – only their vast size made them alarming – was emphasized by the traditional use of eight dwarf riders. Each marshbag bore a rider at the extreme end of its long neck, just behind the skull, and another – this one armed with a goad – at the base of the tail, while six more dwarfs sat or performed acrobatics along a wooden saddle secured on the creature's back. Marshbags are traditionally escorted by a drummer. They respond to a regular beat and keep gravely in step.

Animals and men, we paraded nobly across the grass towards the forests. The rain died as trumpets hurried us forward.

What excitement to be there! Whatever befell, I would always remember the day. I wished that my father could see me, brave and warlike, taking part in an ancestral hunt. Already I saw more dashing ways in which I might play Albrizzi.

Hoytola laid claim to good hunting country. It was predominantly hilly with occasional outcrops of rock, well forested with lofty oak, acacia and chestnut, beneath the shelter of which ferns grew to the height of a man, affording cover for the game on which carnivores feed. The hills bred streams, and there were open spaces where succulent marsh and bog and stagnant water lay, the haunt of duck and many other varieties of fowl, all ready to take to the wing if disturbed.

In this whole region only an occasional forest ranger, woodman or charcoal burner was to be found. The larger carnivores are reputedly a dying breed; they are left to their own pursuits – except for the one occasion every year. Indeed, Hoytola's gamekeepers reared young devil-jaws, tyrant-greaves and shatterhorns from the egg, to try to keep up the numbers.

We forged deeper into the wilds. Silence became more intense. Not for years had I been out of earshot of another human voice. I whispered to Bramble and patted his neck. Occasionally I caught a glimpse of the next hunter to my left or right flank; but it was impossible to keep them in view when the lie of the land did not permit.

The territory became more broken, the path more boulder-strewn. As Bramble picked his way up an old river bed, trees closed in on either side. The span of sky became obscured, although at first I could see an infrequent leather-tooth sail overhead. Then foliage surrounded us completely, and large branches intertwined above our heads. We continued into the forest for some time.

We came out on a mound surmounted by thistle and rock. As I pushed Bramble through the undergrowth, I saw that the other side of the mound fell away sharply, leaving a recess or possibly a cave below. It provided a likely lair for a reptile. Dismounting, but keeping tight hold of Bramble's rein, I went to the edge of the drop, peering down and kicking a stone over the lip. Nothing stirred. Far away, I heard shouts, very faint. Somebody's sport had started. I stood where I was, listening. The shouts were not repeated. Silence had overtaken the forest.

Remounting, I urged Bramble back to a point where we could scramble down the bank and investigate the cave. We made a wide circle; I knew the speed of predatory reptiles.

There was a cave, as I suspected, most of its entrance hidden by shrubs. The undergrowth was trampled, although there was no sign of bones. I coaxed Bramble forward.

It was impossible to see how deep the cave went. As we were almost up to it, two creatures burst forth, uttering croaking screams as they rushed towards us. Though I had my spear ready, I was taken by surprise. I could do nothing but sit crouched in the saddle.

The animals were about the size of greyhounds with thick reptilian tails which they carried high as they rushed forward on their hind legs. They were of a mottled green and brown. One, as it swerved, gave a glimpse of yellow belly. They were jerks or clapper-diles or something similar, and very fleet, as befitted the small kind of the forest. And they ran with their mouths open, presenting a disconcertingly vivid green maw to their prey.

Not that I was their prey. They scattered in fright, one on

either side of us, darted into the bush, and were gone. They were no more startled than I – or Bramble, who shied violently, wheeled about, and galloped madly among the trees.

My wits had gone for the moment. Bushes, branches, ferns, whipped by me in a blur. Head tight down against the cob's neck, I yelled to him to stop. Then I gathered myself and the little horsemanship I had, and endeavoured to calm him. Still he dashed on until we met with a stream half-hidden by clumps of bamboo. Whereupon Bramble stopped so abruptly that I nearly slid off his neck. He began mildly to crop grass.

I kept hold of the reins and dismounted, panting, finding myself considerably shaken.

'Nothing to be scared of, old friend,' I said, glancing round nervously. I had lowered my voice.

A brownish tinge hung over the forest. Branches drooped without motion, as if caught in the midst of some depressing dispute. Water drops splashed to the ground. There was nothing to harm us; yet the idea of harm remained.

I led Bramble by the bank of the stream, following it without much forethought, listening for sounds of other hunters.

'I should have cut down one of those clappers, Bramble,' I told him. 'I missed my chance. We may see no other sport.'

This stream was about six metres wide, and shallow. It made suave noises as it slid past roots and rat holes bored in its muddy sides. The stands of bamboo became so dense that we were forced away from the banks. Yet I obstinately led the cob back to the water; the stream at least had a direction in which to go – I had lost that benefit. Once, I called loudly; the sound of my own unanswered voice disconcerted me.

After a diversion, we got back to the stream. It had become wider and shallower. Thickets of brambles intertwined with massed pines barred our way to one side, so that we were forced to enter the water to progress. Ahead, the way looked dark. These were the primaeval forests which had once covered the entire world.

Still leading Bramble, I pressed on through gnarled elder trees, their warty barks covered with moss. The stream's noise was harsh now, as it ran over cobbles. I was encouraged, thinking that we were moving into different territory and might be able to join with other people, or at least come on a landmark for guidance.

Instead, the stream disappeared. Pressing through more elders, heavy with purple berries, I stopped so abruptly that Bramble butted his head against my back, nearly pitching me into the water. A cliff rose sheer before us, its rock dark as a jailer's face, shattered pines hanging like unkempt hair over its brow. Our stream ran into a low mouth at the base of the rock, throwing up a small continuous wave before speeding into blackness.

The cliff formed part of a continuous rift in the ground which continued on either side, making it difficult to proceed in any direction. For a fanciful moment, I wondered if I had come to the end of Malacia, where an entirely opposed despotism began; the idea was reinforced by a change in vegetation marked by the rift, for the light-leafed deciduous trees died out by the cliff, to be replaced entirely by rows of pine and fir, stretching ahead as far as the eye could see, and towering upwards from the lip of the cliff. Their foliage was outlined against a distinctly brownish tint in the sky; dusk was coming on apace.

I found that I was being watched by a bearded man. He stood regardless of danger on the highest point of the cliff, above the mouth into which the stream flowed.

'Which is the way to Juracia?' I called.

No answer. I could not see him clearly. He appeared to be naked except for a rough pair of trousers. His immobility was disquieting. I resented the way he stared down at me.

'Have you a tongue, man?'

No answer. It was not a man but a statue. Not a statue of a man but a statue of a satyr. It was manlike from the loins upward; below that, it was a goat, and a pair of small goat horns nestled in its unruly hair.

I was disappointed yet relieved. Perhaps it is preferable to be ignored by a statue than a man.

So there I was, with my horse breathing softly beside me, his nose at my shoulder, and night coming on. I decided that we would ford the stream. The going looked easier on the other side.

Still leading Bramble, I moved through the water under the stony eye of the satyr, and climbed the other bank. As I was about to remount, my nostrils caught an odour of something burning. The scent moved to my brain and established dominance there, leading me as if by a leash, directing my feet, tug-

224

ging at my clothes. All about me that corrupt sepia tinge increased, permeating atmosphere and forms, so that I understood how all those forms were united in the conspiracy of their birth, when they had been incarnated from the principle of Evil itself. That hideously dominating scent, together with the haggard light, emphasized that I moved among matter which was mere semblance, a phantasm of the breath of the Lord of Darkness and Chaos.

A lick of that darkness showed ahead and in the curly centre of the darkness, a tongue of fire. Bulky satyrs, their shapes barely distinguishable from the boles of trees, marched beside me, their goaty odour mingling with the smoke smell. They marched, I say, but movement like matter had been reduced to an impression. We were all strokes of an infernal paint-brush, shadowy recreations of greater dimensions, the only reality belonging to the bud of fire and the night ahead.

A great sinking took place within me – that movement was real enough to my spirit – as if I were slowly descending into rock and the unhallowed places of the earth. With the sinking went an oppressive emotion for which there is no name, unless it be intuition: an intuition, as devious as the serpentine layers of smoke ahead, that we are cast upon the stage of life in bodily form for reasons ever beyond our comprehensions – beyond, because the reasons are too inimical to be comprehended. To know them would entail total destruction. This intuition filled me with something more enduring than fear: recognition. The ancient wickedness about me became part of me, as I was a part of it. I choked on a dusty mouthful of recognition. Little different was I from the goat-lipped satyrs. With a sly motion, my amulet slithered from my arm and fell to the forest floor, where it writhed as if wounded.

The carnal flame burned on an altar decorated by carved heads standing out from the stone. Round the altar stood six monstrous figures. They were regarding me. Above their hunched shoulders perched an owl, its face no more inhuman than theirs. It sat on a low branch, its wings spread wide as if it were about to launch itself at my eyes. Again, the sense of recognition.

Of these six brutish figures, I could see only the first two clearly. The others were obscured behind the massive cylinder of the altar. The prominent two wore stiff draperies decorated

225

with insignias proclaiming them – I did not doubt it – to be exponents of the Natural Religion. Their features were hideous, as if shaped long ago from rude forms of earth. The leading wizard was cruel and malign, his nose, his mouth, hooked into a sneer above the luxuriant, brownish-red beard he sported. He wore a ludicrous pancake hat and clutched at the bulge of a huge phallus beneath the folds of his drapery. Almost in his shadow crouched a woman, her naked back scraping against a satanic face adorning the altar. Her breasts hung naked, as if in dejection, full, slightly elongated under their own weight as they swung from her body. She appeared to have been desecrated. Her clothes lay in tatters by her feet. She wore only a shift, the whiteness of which was stained by filth and blood. The sight of her filled me with intense sorrow.

As I surveyed these evil beings, I perceived that one of them was an ape, dressed in man's clothes and accepted by the rest as a sort of man. Another was a lizard-man, his face with its shallow jaw and hairless head peering at me through the stench rising from the sacrificial stone. The others shared his immobility.

It was the woman who spoke first. She raised her head slowly, looking at me from under fair brows. She was not old. Beauty was still about her, although her forehead was dewed with sweat and her mouth was bleeding.

'Help me,' she said.

Smiles flecked the lips of the magicians.

'Help me,' the woman repeated. She dragged herself into a sitting position. 'They claim that I am the Empress Theodora, widow of Theophilus, or a reincarnation of her. It's all lies. I never harmed anyone – Theodora's regiments fell like wolves upon the ancestors of these ... these devils, pursuing them into untrodden forests, tearing them apart like wild animals, drowning or burning them in their hundreds of thousands ... It was no affair of mine. Help me!' She stretched out a hand towards me.

Petrified as I was, I saw no way of helping her or myself.

The leading wizard said, 'Of what moment are your trifling personalities? What matters it who you believe yourselves to be?' These questions I felt at the time to be tremendously annihilating. 'Until you have understanding of your nature, your errors – like the errors of history – repeat and repeat them-

selves in an endless fiction. That is the only knowledge there is.'

I did not know I spoke, but I said something on the woman's behalf.

The second wizard spoke. He leaned forward stiffly, as if breaking through fabric, his beetling brows working as he lifted a hand and pointed at me.

'You are no more inviolate than a blade of grass, to be crushed beneath a casual tread.'

His mouth opened, yet it did not move as he seemed to speak. Something sulphurous lurked between his lips.

'The Original Curse that binds Malacia binds you also, boy, so beware!'

'What must I do?' I asked.

My voice came to me from far away, from another place or time. The words took an age to travel and, as they left me, I watched while the satyrs – they were seven, two of them females with pendulous dugs – galloped forward and seized the hapless woman who was accused of being a reincarnation of Theodora. They bore her to the ground, fighting for positions round her. Her shift was torn from her. She screamed. One of the goaty females bit her between the thighs, only to be pulled away and molested in her turn. The other satyrs piled in, until there was an obscene heap on the ground, comprising from the outside mainly kicking heels, heaving buttocks, and flailing tails. Pulling up his cumbersome gown, the first wizard lumbered forward to join in the animal sport, showing his fangs in a grin as he did so.

All this appeared the transaction of a moment, for the second wizard was answering my question – though whether in veritable words I could never afterwards determine.

'You must hope and despair, reform and sin, triumph and fail. How else do we live out our duality of spirit? Now you will learn the additional curse of knowledge – it will gain you no wisdom – it will only make more painful what you hitherto enjoyed through ignorance.'

'Of what knowledge do you speak?'

'The only knowledge there is – knowledge that ages you.'

In some fashion which I cannot explain, I was then facing this reptilian visage across the smouldering altar, and he was saying, 'In conformity with our dual nature, every reward carries punishment, every punishment reward. Now that you are to be burdened with knowledge, you are permitted one wish, which will be immediately granted wherever our powers extend.'

Almost without thought – I was beyond that – I said, 'Then I wish to impress Armida Hoytola in some grand way, to save her from overwhelming danger, so that she may ...'

My voice faltered and died. Not from the terror I was in but from the working of something – perhaps that dreadful *knowledge* already in action – which told me that I could never be happy with any woman whom I believed to be chained to me by reason of a spell or compulsion.

I stood with my mouth open, and smoke swirled about us. Darkness gathered, the cries of the woman became fainter. The fanged mouth of the wizard whispered something which might have been 'Your wish is granted.'

The flame blazed up between us. He raised his ragged sleeves above his head like a leather-tooth's wings and cried, 'Begone, youthful phantom!'

With his words came severe cold, cutting my eyes. I saw indistinctly. The horrid rout on the ground blurred with the undergrowth. The line of grimoire figures, man, ape and bird, faded into haphazard trees. Even the great stone melted into shadow indistinguishable from path. Only the flame on the altar, licking upward like a serpent tongue, remained clear to my vision, and that shrank into the distance. I fell to the ground.

I was alone in a remote grey world of old trees. Once again I became conscious of my poor self. Once again I heard the sound of the stream behind me. Once again I remembered that death was not the force that prevailed in the world.

Rain began, in the upper branches of the trees at first, then upon my body, approaching softly to remind me that weathers and seasons came and went. Slowly, I pulled myself up.

I had looked on accursed things. I turned to see how Bramble had fared. Poor creature, he had none of my human resilience. His rein dangled from a skeleton – a perfect skeleton of a horse, every bone shining as if still moist from the flesh of which it had been so sharply bereft. Even as I beheld it, the skeleton collapsed into a clattering pile of bones, which no one could ever make into a horse again. I picked out the spring-loaded spear from the remains, where it was attached to the saddle. There might still be natural dangers.

In the dark trampled grass, something gleamed: my amulet. Lifting it up, I found it almost too hot to touch.

After rinsing my face in the waters of the stream, I managed to quieten my quaking limbs.

If I had undergone satanic enlightenment, then I had to ask myself what exactly was the knowledge thrust upon me. Had I been visited by a religious revelation, couched in the accents of Natural Religion but fully in accord with the tenets of the Higher?

Was this something that happened to all men, but about which they were naturally reluctant to speak? Saying nothing about such a striking event – but what could one say about something so outside experience? – would create a barrier between one-self and one's friends. Dully, I wondered if such silences accounted for a fact I had observed, that whilst the young were cheerfully gregarious, the old wore acid countenances, on the whole keeping themselves apart as if friendship was something they mistrusted.

One thing was certain. The repulsive second wizard had granted me a wish. I must be careful. I thought of Desport.

It was said that when the great founder of our state first crossed the Toi and stood on the site of what was to become Stary Most, midnight fell at midday and a great magician – the First Magician – appeared to Desport. The First Magician allowed him one powerful wish, whereupon Desport wished that the city he and his scarcely human followers were founding as a monument to the two religions should forever remain un-changed, according to his plan. This wish it was that people referred to – not always for apotropaic reasons – as the Original Curse. Since then, according to legend, time had congealed about our city. Time and change may be distinguishable; they are inseparable as far as the affairs of men are concerned.

That odour which had led me along with the satyrs to the accursed site had been, I felt convinced, the very aroma of time.

The malevolent stillness of the forest brought me from my trance. Night moved hushed through the entwined trees. I had been squatting by the stream, transfixed. Now all that remained of my dread visitation was a distant glow of light, resembling the serpent tongue of the altar fire.

For minutes, I stood speculating on that flame, until it occurred to me that I could shake off the memory of the altar by discovering what the light was. If it indicated human company, it was more than welcome.

Stepping past the bones of poor Bramble, I made towards the glow. This hour was considered a propitious one by ancestral hunters. Ancestral animals, whether large or small, lost their energy at night and crept back into their lairs. Last to go were the giants, feeding as they went. The onset of dark made them easier game; but, on foot and lightly armed, I had no wish to get between one of them and its boudoir.

Keeping my spring-load spear at the ready, I climbed between the trunks of the trees, whose foliage formed a confused roof above me. Ahead, I made out a scene of human misfortune very different from the terrors I had recently confronted, yet sufficiently related by time and place for me to approach it with caution. A rough road crossed my trail. A carriage stood lopsidedly in a ditch by the side of the road. Two lamps gleamed on its side-brackets. Nearby burned the flambeau whose flame had led me to the spot; its tarry smell was pleasant to the nostrils. Between them, these lights formed a tent of vision in the entangled night.

The flambeau was stuck into a patch of soft ground, so that it shed some illumination on a young man crouching at the front wheel of the carriage with his back to me. I observed him and the girl nearby with the caution of a deer, stationing myself behind an ivy-maned oak to do so.

He was trying to prise up the wheel of the carriage, and meeting with no success. He interspersed his tugging with heaving, throwing in a swift kick now and again for luck. The horse, its eyeballs red in the reflected light, stirred anxiously between its shafts. When it whinnied, the man cursed it.

The young lady stood in the middle of the track. While neither cursing nor whinnying, she showed her dislike of the situation by walking about within the small circle of torchlight, twitching her skirt and her hands.

There is nothing unusual about carriages running into ditches, or about young ladies being vexed by such accidents. What rendered this scene particularly interesting – and drove all thoughts of the recent visitation from my head – was the fact that the young lady was Armida Hoytola.

Impulsive fellow though I am, I did not immediately dash forth to her side. Surprise kept me where I was. And not only surprise. The scene had a piquancy in its own right; besides, it is always advantageous to observe a young lady when she does not know you are watching.

She was angry enough to be speechless. She made every motion eloquent with contempt, her skirts flicking scorn at the rough road, the night, the wretch who crouched in the ditch. He was almost under the carriage now. I could only see his heaving shoulder. I could not help wishing that she was in danger, so that I might leap forward and rescue her to our mutual advantage.

Hardly had this wish formed in my mind than there came a crashing in the undergrowth on the other side of the road, where shadows and trees alike grew impenetrably. As the noise registered on Armida's ears, she stopped and stared in an attitude of delightful agitation. La Singla could not have played it more effectively.

'Guy!' she called.

The man in the ditch climbed up from his wheel. I had no eyes for him. I was looking where Armida looked – to the nearby bushes which were suddenly dashed aside.

They say that the leopards and tigers of the Orient are endowed by nature with a cunning equal to man's. They stalk their prey and overcome it by surprise. They have strength, but their agility is superior to their strength, just as their cunning is superior to their agility. The great carnivorous ancestrals have only maniac strength.

Devil-jaws and their cousins, saw-mouths and tyrant-greaves, are primitive machines. When a devil-jaw – arch-ventail, to give it its proper name – scents prey, it heads for it direct, without considerations of silence or of any obstacle in its path. Unlike the leopard, it needs neither agility nor cunning, relying on its gigantic bulk, its mad stride, to bear it down at full tilt upon whatever it desires to destroy. Little stands in the way of seven metric tons of ravening animal.

At one moment, the shadows beyond the road were as empty as a mask. At the next, they were torn asunder and a head as long as a canoe was thrust into view. Behind its smooth snout, its eyes were sunk under brows of bone which led into the massed warts and folds of an enormously thick neck. The head

232

twisted once to left and once to right before cracking open, revealing serrated rows of teeth, as it let forth a bellow of wrath.

In that bellow, Armida's scream of terror was lost.

With scarcely a pause, the devil-jaw burst forth. Betsy, Armida's little horse, drummed her hooves against the woodwork of the carriage, hurling herself against the shafts as she fought to escape.

Armida's cry brought me at a run into the clearing. I had my spring-load at the ready. As Armida came rushing towards me, I shouted at her to jump into the carriage. I dropped to one knee and aimed the spear. A stench of decay assailed me.

In a crisis, details are absorbed instantaneously, acted upon immediately by a brain freed from the gears of thought, digested later. As I confronted the devil-jaw, I saw that the monster had sustained a previous wound, probably in an earlier hunt, and was handicapped by a suppurating gash in the armour of its left knee-joint. I may have owed my life to that wound.

The monster swivelled to face me. Its eyes glittered black under their horny brows. As they fixed on me, the body emerged fully from the forest. It kept coming until it reared over me on its great legs. It was three times taller than I.

In the wash of action, I knew only the clawed, stamping feet before me, the enormous cabled belly, the jaws snapping down towards my head. I saw its rippling muscles and leaves plastered against its skin. I fired my spear into the throbbing wattles of its throat, fell over, rolled, ran like mad for the safety of the nearest tree. As I ran I drew my sword.

Once behind the tree, I turned gasping to see how close it was.

The devil-jaw gave a bellow like a pine being ripped asunder. Blood was belching out of its throat. Reaching up with its small forearms, it clawed savagely at the wound, at the spear. Then it went berserk.

There was little room for it on the forest road. As it whirled, the mighty tail uprooted bushes by the verge. Smashing into young trees, the brute lumbered round in a circle and then charged forward, head out, striking almost like a giant snake. Its charge took it straight into the carriage, which shattered and flew in splinters. Armida! The pony broke free and was away.

Hardly slowing, the brute smashed forward into the forest so close that stones hit my face. The impact when it struck a great oak was such that the ground shook.

Without all that titanic energy scattering the wan light, the forest became doubly dark.

By then I had my second wind. I had wounded the great ancestral; it was no longer so much to be feared. Dashing forth from shelter, I tugged the flambeau from the ground and went in pursuit. I followed the path the devil-jaw had broken, hoping there was no danger now and that a *coup de grâce* only would be needed – and that I certainly intended to give, to make the victory doubly mine.

But devil-jaws are almost too stupid to die. It had lost control over its movements, yet it was still on its feet, in radiant rage. A flaring orange line ran all the way down its spine, from its snout over its head to its tail. The line writhed like a rope loose in a storm at sea. Lashing its tail, the monster struggled to extricate itself from entanglements of branches – there was a mad pattern before me of leaves, scales, and twigs dancing in the dark. I could hardly get close for that flailing tail, yet something of the brute's madness affected me, so that I charged in, judging my moment, to plunge my sword into the creature's belly.

All my strength went into that blow. My swordpoint tore through flexing scales and sank down into the vital parts beneath. I struck a second time, and a third, till blood and intestines gouted forth.

Working in a whirl of darkness, I could hardly see what I did. I leaped back as the creature gave a convulsive thresh. Above me was the head. The eyes saw me. It could have been a trick of night and shadow that they seemed suddenly full of benign wisdom, pity – no savagery there at all, just as someone had once said it would be.

One more great paroxysm, then the monster was dead, suspended still in an upright posture because of its entanglement with the branches. Gradually, as its muscles relaxed in death and its legs buckled, its weight brought it sliding down. Its head slammed against the ground.

I had killed my ancestral animal.

Staggering back to the roadway, I confronted a pallid Armida, a quaking de Lambant. She had been too scared to climb into the carriage, as I had told her to; so her life had been spared.

234

She leant against de Lambant. Betsy cropped grass a few metres off, as if nothing had happened.

For a while, words were beyond us all.

'What are you doing here?' I asked Armida.

She was trembling, too overwrought to reply.

De Lambant said in a husky voice, 'We heard that Bedalar was at a village near Juracia. Armida said she would like me to accompany her on a visit. The information proved false – we had a trip for nothing. We were returning when we got a rock under the wheel which threw us into the ditch.'

'Take the mare,' I said. 'We'll mount Armida on it. Ride behind her and see her safe back to her father.'

He did not argue. Between us, we coaxed Betsy and persuaded Armida to mount. Armida was weeping. She kept saying, 'I'm all right, Perry, I'm all right' – whether to reassure me or herself I knew not. De Lambant mounted behind her.

'What about you?' he asked. I could hardly hear what he said or answer him. The ground was heaving.

'I'll follow on foot. Take care of her – she's in your charge.'

'I'm all right, Perry.'

'I'll send the guard back for you.'

'I entrust her to you, Guy.'

He raised a hand, raised indeed a faint smile. 'She's safe with me,' he said.

Then I was left alone with the dying torch and the dead animal nearby.

Weakness overcame me. My senses swam. My clothes were covered in blood, some of which was my own. My left upper arm and shoulder were bleeding freely. Staggering round as if drunk, I realized that the whole scene was bedecked with blood from the devil-jaw. The vegetation and the way underfoot were soaked with it, litres and litres of it.

As nausea welled through me, I knew that I was badly injured. There was no recollection of receiving the hurt. Falling among the splintered trees, I managed to seat myself on the great cockerel foot of the monster, so that I should present the most effective picture when rescuers came.

It was a long time, and a long way down the river of pain, before I heard the sound of their approach, before their torches wavered before my eyes.

Book Three

Castle Interior with Penitents

The chamber in which I lay was high up in one of the towers of Mantegan Castle. Its windows overlooked the roofs of an inner court filled every day with sun. Despite the height of my window above ground, honeysuckle had climbed to the sill and beyond, finding purchase in pitted stonework. During my time abed, a furred drone of bees filled the room as they sipped nectar from the late summer blossoms.

I recovered from my wound under my sister's care. Perhaps it was her presence which made me, in a fever, believe myself to be back in one of those afternoons of childhood, when eternity sets in shortly after lunch, to linger long after twilight in an odour of flowers and drowsy rooms.

Katarina looked after me with the aid of her personal servant, Peggy. For most of the time we were alone together, as of old. My father was too deep in research to visit me, although he sent a note. In return, I was proud to send him one of the serrated devil-jaw teeth which were despatched to me from Juracia. Julius Mantegan and his kin had seen to it that I received the trophies which were my due as a hunter.

My father sent a brief note of thanks for the gift, which made me weep in my weakness.

> You have cut your teeth and are a man now. My life's finished, or would be if my aches had their way. So much for knowledge. We have our differences. I should tell you that when you were born you were a great joy to your mother and me. She and I were happy together. Times have changed. I have the tooth by me as I write. Forgive my scrawl. Make something of yourself.
>
> Your loving father.

Of my visitors, Portinari was the most regular, calling on me every morning briefly when making deliveries for his father. He always brought with him a delicious *pâté en croûte*, still hot and fragrant from the oven, and never stayed long enough to see me eat it. Caylus came once, on crutches, and ate that day's pâté; he brought Bedalar, who smiled tenderly and remonstrated with her brother when he joked about the dilapidated state of the castle. De Lambant came only once, to make a great fuss of my heroism, although I was too weak on that day to do more than lie and feebly enjoy his flattery.

Mandaro came each evening, praying with me. To him, and him only, I spoke of the visitation in the forest – the cause of, and more terrible, than the battle with the devil-jaw. Otherwise, that experience lay ever-present within me, weighty as a gall-stone.

No letter of thanks or commendation came from Andrus Hoytola. There was a note from his wife, wishing me safe recovery. But Armida visited my bedside on three occasions, holding my hand while I was feverish, speaking soothingly. Yolaria rested her face in a corner meanwhile. The room held the scent of my love's patchouli after she had gone.

No matter who came or went in my high room, Poseidon, the largest of the castle's cats, sat massively on the window-sill, listening to all that passed but passing no judgment. Poseidon was a comfort to my illness. All men should be like him, I thought; not striving always for gain, lust, or advancement, but content with the luxury of being. It was a utopian dream of convalescence.

As I recovered, the world drifted back and familiar hopes and anxieties returned. When Armida came to sit by me again, I was well enough to air a subject that troubled me.

'Is your carriage repaired yet?' I asked her, working to the matter indirectly.

'Another is being built, better than my old one. The Daumonds are to make me a proper little town coupé, with seventeen coats of lacquer on the outside. It is to be upholstered in white and blue Pekinese silk, with the doors, roof and blinds lined with the same material. Father says the Daumonds are the best carriage-makers in Malacia.'

She looked more beautiful than ever, with her startling combination of golden hair and lioness eyes. I hesitated before speaking again.

'I'm sorry your birthday carriage has made its last journey. Where had you and de Lambant been on that journey?'

'He told you about that, I understand.'

'Perhaps he did, but I have forgotten. Yolaria wasn't with you.'

'There was hardly room for her as well. It is of no consequence to you what I was doing – you were busy doing other things.'

'Armida, everything you do matters to me, for reasons you know well.'

Armida rose and went over to the window, silhouetting herself against its light as she absent-mindedly stroked Poseidon. Yolaria looked up at her; irrelevantly, I realized that the old woman loved her charge. Then Armida turned, moving restlessly round the room as she spoke.

'There are plenty of interests in your life about which you would not care for me to know. I'm too good-natured to press you, but what about that little penniless slut – you know whom I mean, that Progressive, Letitia Zlatorog? I suppose you pretend there is nothing going on there?'

'Letitia Zlatorog? Oh, please, Armida, I had almost forgotten the very name. She is nothing to me, whereas you are everything.'

Her golden eyes became stormy, her face grew hard, and she looked so fiercely down her nose that for a moment I was reminded of a bird of prey.

'Everything, am I? Nothing, is she? You're absolutely faithless, I believe. That's what I really believe.'

'That isn't so. As I've become more aware of your feelings I have changed. I've seen you more as you are, seen your real needs. I won't look at Letitia. It is true, as you say, that she's penniless, but she really isn't a slut, only as her financial condition forces her to be—'

Armida turned and beckoned to Yolaria.

'I am not remaining here if you are going to defend that wretched girl. Really, you are impossible at times!'

I reached for her hand. 'You mentioned Letitia, I didn't – I told you I'd nearly forgotten her. Why is it always you who attack me, never I who attack you?'

'Oh, how you twist things! It's shocking! You were making all the insinuations ... You were insinuating that something went on between Guy and me. I don't see that that is any of your affair – I've told you far too much already. I'm far too honest and good-natured.'

241

She began to weep. Vexed though I was with her, I could not bear to see her miserable. I climbed out of bed. Putting my good arm round her, I comforted her as best I could.

'Listen, Armida, we must not quarrel. I did save your darling life, and the thought of it will always make me happy, so—'

'That!' she exclaimed. 'I suppose you'll bring *that* up against me for the rest of your days!'

'But I'm not bringing it up against—'

'Don't think I'm not grateful, or my parents either, but please let the subject of your valour drop. Guy would have saved me if you hadn't.'

'By the bones ... Armida, let's not quarrel, but be fair, please. We're both alive and safe. I love you. Let's go back and be as we were when we first met, shall we, without all that jealousy, shall we?'

Sniffing, she said, 'Things can never be as they were.'

How those words pierced me! Not so much their truth, if they were true, but the sense of her indifference to whether matters mended or not.

'My arm will soon be better, then you'll see. Wait a week, then we'll enjoy again. I swear you are the only girl.'

'You haven't much chance to misbehave here, have you?'

'You are unjust to me in your heart, I don't know why. I have said I will reform and I mean to; I consult good Mandaro about it every evening. You must support, not scorn me.'

All these things and more I tried to say lightly, but a weight settled on my heart. In whatever she did or said, I sensed that she did not want me. Nor would she say she loved me; only that I knew she loved me, or that she had said previously that she loved me. Never that she loved me in the present!

'You must understand, Armida, that I had no intention of hurting you. There was an excess of love in me which overflowed on others. I know it should not have done when I see how it pains you. You hurt me because you are hurt. But there was no desire to gain advantage over you. I believe that you are kept prisoner too much at home, and that life should be freer for you, that love should be free.'

She looked up at me with curiosity. 'Love free? I don't catch your meaning.'

'Love freely received and given ... Isn't that a noble ideal? I mean that I do feel jealousy, so perhaps you are right to be angry with me; but jealousy is a demeaning emotion, which should be treated as such and not indulged in. I admit I felt some jealousy and suspicion of you and Guy when I found you together. He's a good friend of mine and I should trust him. Loving you as I do, I should also trust you – and I do. I am pleased that you and he are friendly. After all, we shall see more of him when we are married. Forgive my anger, be his friend and welcome.'

The speech was not without its effect on her. She smiled, although she did not take my hand.

'That's kindly said.'

I felt nobler for having said it. It was true and I strove to feel it true. Yet even as I looked at her, suspicion again overcame me. I recalled de Lambant's careless ways with women.

Yet Guy was my friend and would surely respect the bond between Armida and me. Once more I felt how vile it was to mistrust him; he had come to see me only once because he sensed my mistrust. To thrust my doubts still deeper, I launched into my argument again, telling my fair love that I wanted only to see her happy, expanding on my nobler aspirations. She remained standing, listening gravely, staring out of my window.

'This is a new side of you,' she said at last. 'You are very understanding.' That had to suffice.

As I have said, Mandaro came to visit me every evening, his harsh, grey robe wrapped about him as protection against the airs of autumn which now intruded on the early and late hours of day.

To him, as I grew stronger, I confided my fears.

'All fears are tokens of guilt,' he said. 'You have taken your pleasure always where you were inclined. Now you object because your beloved may be doing the same. It is not *she* who hurts you but your own double standard of living.'

I shook my head. Guilt was part of his trade.

'No, no, Father! My affairs with other women – they made me light-hearted. I have never made love to a girl I did not feel love for, but I have never been deeply in love with them; I have resisted that. They have stirred me, generated a greater love in me, and that I now offer Armida. She causes me some sorrow, but that doesn't alter my feeling for her. But I torture myself thinking that her – her emotional system may differ from mine so that she falls in love with someone else – even de Lambant – and may cease to love me. I couldn't bear that. I can't bear even for her to look coldly at me.'

'Was it wise of you to encourage her to continue to be friendly with de Lambant? Should you not have made plain your displeasure at the relationship, as she did with your relationship with other girls?'

'No, you see—' how to explain these worldly matters to Mandaro? – 'by putting her in a position of trust, by showing that I positively encourage their friendship, I *establish* a position of trust. In a position of trust, they will not go to bed together. Whereas they *might* do if I shouted at them and cursed them. Then they would be driven into guilt; then they would revert to the secrecy that guilt brings; more guilt would accrue. Isn't that so? Doesn't that make sense? Besides, to speak frankly, Armida is not a very forthcoming girl, Father – how could she be in that household? If Guy is good for her, then I am happy for her sake and have no wish to spoil anything. Isn't my reasoning sound?'

'I'm not sure that reason is to be trusted in these circumstances.'

'Reason and honour. A man must trust something. I trust reason and honour, and I trust Armida, and . . . Oh, I must get out of this bed!'

'I do not come solely to talk of love-affairs, Perry.'

'What do you mean? Do you think that he and she really are making love behind my back? Don't say that!'

'I did not say that. It was your jealousy that spoke.'

'Oh, you're right. I am base. I used to have such a good opinion of myself – now it's all gone. The brave acts I've performed count as nothing.'

'We can learn to live without good opinions. It is better for our humility that we should do so.'

'Actors and artists cannot survive that way. They have only their own good opinions to nourish them in adversity.'

'You, I must point out, are not in adversity. Your career advances. You have many worldly things. You should think more of matters which are of greater eternal weight – humility would help you to that.'

'I'm in your hands, Father.'

'Not at all. My hands are as weak as yours. In the continuing war between Good and Evil, every man is little more than cannon-fodder. All we can do is to decide into which cannons we should allow ourselves to be thrust. That decision is no permanent thing; indeed, it must be taken every day of your life.'

'I hate decisions. I want love to be permanent, but I'm so weak.'

'Do not underestimate yourself. You need courage, but you have it if you will take it up. Your slaying of the arch-ventail is proof that you can take it up, and no man need look down on you on that score.'

'You're very consoling, Father. But it's a different sort of courage I need to deal with Armida.'

'Once you are recovered and have regained your spirits, you will not even believe that courage is necessary there.'

One thing at least he said which was true. I had lost my spirits; where once they danced in the air like down, now they had sunk to ground level. Every night, my misgivings about Armida's faithfulness rose to mind, banishing sleep.

So my shoulder and arm healed. Katarina, my dear surviving sister, sat by my bed for hours. I would drift into a realm of dreams, just for the pleasure of opening my eyes and finding her there, still embroidering, still waiting for my strength to return. Later, she took to sitting by the window, cosseting Poseidon, or else toying with her tapestry.

My sister was not a great beauty. She took after my father, with his sallow skin and rather long chin, but I loved the expression about her eyes, as well as the outline of her head and the gentle, teasing way in which she often talked. Her fine dark hair was drawn into an embroidered ribbon so that it hung in a tail down her dove-grey dress.

Katie remained tranquil in sunlight by the window, while I lolled in the shade of the room; we turned old times into spasmodic conversation. I never talked to her about my anxieties concerning Armida.

'I'm grateful for your care, Katie. Now that winter is on the way, let's see more of one another than we've managed recently.'

'I'm glad you wish that. So do I, sincerely. Yet forces operate to separate people, whatever they wish.' She spoke serenely, as always.

'We'll remain light-hearted and rise above our difficulties.'

Talk about being light-hearted came easily; when Katarina was there, I really believed I was light-hearted.

Silence fell, save for the buzz of industrious bees about the window. One of them, hind legs overloaded with pollen, would occasionally tumble over the sill, whereupon Poseidon would tap it chidingly with his paw. Beyond the bees, in the clear afternoon sky, birds swooped without moving a single feather on either wing.

Gesturing outside, Katarina said, 'Those elegant birds with forked tails are gathering about our towers once more. They nest before they depart for lands farther south. I'm always sad to see them go – for their own dear sakes, and because it signifies another year is fleeing. Every year they come back, though, from some mysterious place. They never alight on the ground. If once they alighted, they'd never get off again. That's because they have no legs, according to Aristotle and Tarsanius.'

'They're called cavorts. Father told me once that they come from a continent of southern ice which no man has ever seen.'

'How then does he know, may I ask?'

'He had it from an old authority, I expect.'

She produced a little white comb with which she groomed the lustrous sandy coat of Poseidon. The cat puffed out his chest and began to purr until he made more noise than the bees, keeping his eyes closed all the time.

After a while, giving a laugh, Katarina said, 'I was trying to imagine a land that no human eyes had ever seen.'

'It's not such a difficult task. We ourselves live in the middle of such a land. Everything here is undiscovered, mysterious, never mind so far away.'

'Perry, you say such peculiar things! That's a line from one of your romances, I'm sure.'

'Whenever I say anything profound – or even sensible – somebody pretends I stole it from a play. Plays are often written by players – we're clever chaps, you know. Don't you recall that I was clever even as an infant?'

'I do recall that you used to perform living statues for us, and we had to guess whom you were representing. You nearly drowned in the lagoon when you were doing Triton. I ruined a new dress helping to rescue you.'

'It was worth it for the sake of the art. You were always the best at guessing who I was supposed to represent, Katie!'

'Andri would have been quick, too, had she lived. I dreamed about her a few nights ago, but the plague got her then, as in life. I hate dreams that turn out no better than reality.'

As she collected a comb full of fur, she pulled the bundle from between the teeth of the comb and blew. Handful after handful streamed out of Poseidon's coat and drifted into the warm air beyond our room.

'My dreams are pleasant when I'm not feverish.'

'Possy, look at all this fur you are wasting, you silly cat! Life would be empty with no dreams at all. I think I'd go mad.'

She released another combful of fur through the window. I went over to her, lolling against the side of the window and tickling the cat's head as I said, 'It's pleasant to be mad about something – a way of keeping sane indeed.'

Katarina looked up at me. With a hint of reproach, she said, 'Don't be too light-hearted. You think everything's arranged for your amusement.'

'I have no definite evidence to the contrary, though I have been much unamused of late. You used to be carefree enough, Katie. Is Volpato unfaithful? Does he beat you? Why does he so often leave you alone in Mantegan?'

She looked down at her fingers and said, 'I was fascinated by Volpato and the Mantegan family even as a carefree child. They were so wild, with their old castles here and by the Middle Sea. On my eighth birthday, Seemly Moleskin told me I would grow up to marry a Mantegan. I did so, and I love him still.'

'Have you no will of your own, Katie? Those confounded magicians get you in the palm of their dirty hands unless you ignore them.'

'Don't tease! You are better, I see. Your arm won't fall off, after all. You can leave the castle tomorrow, if you desire, and I shan't see you until you get into trouble again.'

I kissed her hand and said, 'Don't be cross! You are a beautiful person and I have much liked being pampered by you, sweet Sis! I shall instruct Armida to be as much like you as possible – and I shall leave the castle tomorrow to instruct her!'

She laughed. All was well between us, and Poseidon purred more loudly than ever.

The window at which we were all lazing was deep-set within its embrasure. Its ledge was wide enough for Katarina and her cat to sit in comfort and gaze at the world beneath them. A man might stand there and, with no inconvenience to himself, discharge a musket from the coign of vantage into the courtyard far below. The woodwork was lined like a peasant's brow with the diurnal passage of sunlight; perhaps some such thought had crossed the mind of a bygone poet who, with many a flourish, had engraved two tercets of indifferent verse on one of the small leaded panes:

What twain I watch through my unseeing eye:
Inside, the small charades of men: outside,
The grand arcades of cerulean sky.
Thus I a barrier am between a tide
Of man's ambitions and the heavens' meed –
Of things that can't endure, and things that bide.

Poseidon lay stomach upwards on my sister's lap, so that combs of white fluff were now released to the breeze.

Afternoon had created within the courtyard a bowl of warm air which spilled outward and upward, carrying the cat's fur with it. Not a single strand had reached the paving below. The fur floated in a great circle, between this side of the courtyard and the next, the stables and lofts surmounted by their little tower opposite, and the tall, weather-blasted pines which grew on the fourth side, by the wall with the gatehouse. A whole layer of air, level with our window and extending to each of the four limiting walls, was filled with the fluff circulated like a faery whirlpool.

Katarina exclaimed with delight when I turned her attention to the spectacle.

The cavorts were busy. Six or more pairs of them swooped from their positions in eaves and leads, tearing at the downy whirlpool, whisking it away to line their nests. We stood watching. So intent were the birds on their work that they frequently blundered near to our window. Majestically round and round floated the fur, and erratically up and down plunged the cavorts.

'When the baby birds are hatched, they'll be grateful to you, Poseidon!' said Katarina. 'They'll be reared in luxury!'

'Perhaps they'll form the first generation of cat-loving birds. Change comes to Malacian rooftops!'

248

When at length we went downstairs, the fur was still circulating, the birds were still pulling it to shreds, and bearing it back to their nests.

'Let's play cards again tonight ... Birds are so witless, they must always be busy – there's nothing to them but movement. I never find that time hangs heavy on my hands, Perry, do you?'

'I adore being idle – it's then I'm best employed. But I wonder time doesn't hang heavy for you, alone in the castello.'

Smiling in a pleasant evasive way, laying a hand on my sleeve, Katarina said, 'Why don't you employ yourself by visiting Nicholas Fatember, our wizard of the frescoes? His mind is obsessed by one thing only, his art. Like his wife, he's melancholy these days – but worth conversing with, when you can persuade him to open his mouth.'

'Fatember's still here, then! When I last saw him, he was threatening to leave on the morrow! The man is one of the geniuses of our age, if generally unrecognized. Kemperer says so.'

We arrived at Katie's suite of rooms. Her pretty black maid, Peggy, ran to open the doors. Katarina said, 'Fatember is always threatening to leave the castle. I'd as soon believe him if he threatened to complete his frescoes!'

'Will they ever be finished? Does Volpato pay him?'

She laughed. 'Don't be silly. What with? That's why Fatember still lives here, always planning, never achieving. At least he has a roof over his head for himself, and his family. The family still grows ... Oh, well, go and talk to him. We'll meet this evening in chapel.'

It was saddening that she looked so resigned.

I always loved to walk through Volpato's castle. Its perspectives were like no others. With its impromptu landings, its unexpected chambers, its many levels, its never-ending stairs, its aspirations and failures, its descents from stone into wood, its fine marbles and rotting plasters, its noble statues and ignoble decay, it outshone even the Chabrizzi Palace in individuality.

The Mantegan family had not been rich within living memory. My brother-in-law was the last of the direct line, Julius and the others being distant cousins and equally impoverished.

It was whispered of Volpato that he had poisoned his elder brother and sister, Claudio and Saprista, in order to gain control of what family wealth remained – Claudio by spreading a

249

biting acid on the saddle of his steed, so that the deadly ichor moved from his anus upwards to the heart, Saprista by smearing a toxic orpiment on a statue of Minerva which she was wont to kiss during her private devotions, so that she died rotting from the lips inward.

Whether this story was true or false, Volpato never revealed. Dark legends clustered about him, but he behaved tolerably with my sister, and had the goodness to stay away for long periods, seeking his fortune among the wilds of the northern world.

Meanwhile, the castle on the banks of the Toi fell into decay, and his wife did not become a mother. But I loved it, and my dear sister for marrying so well – the only de Chirolo as yet to move into court circles.

The way to Nicholas Fatember's quarters lay through a gallery in which Volpato displayed the last of his treasures. Those treasures were few. Rats scuttled among them in the dimness. Among much that was rubbish were some fine blue-glazed terracotta dishes brought back from the lands of the Orinoco; ivories of hairy elephant carved during the last anthropoid civilization for the royal house of Itssobeshiquetzilaha; parchments rescued by a Mantegan ancestor from the great library at Alexandria (among them two inscribed by the library's founder, Ptolemy Soter) and portraits on silk of the seven Alexandrian Pleiades preserved from the same; a case full of Carthaginian ornaments; jewels from the faery smiths of Atlantis; an orb reputed to have belonged to Birsha, King of Gomorrah, with the crown of King Bera of Sodom; a figurine of a priest with a lantern from the court of Caerleon-on-Usk; the stirrups of the favourite stallion of the Persian Bahram, Governor of Media, that great hunter; tapestries from Zeta, Raška, and the courts of the early Nemanijas, together with robes cut for Milutin; a lyre, chalice, and other objects from the Chankrian Period; a pretty oaken screen carved with figures of children and animals which I particularly liked, said to have come from distant Lyonesse before it sank below the waves; a thumbnail of the founder, Desport, couched in a chased silver relic-case; together with other items of some interest. All that was of real worth had been sold off long ago, and the custodian sacked, to keep the family in meat and wine.

I paused on my way among the relics and opened an iron-strapped chest at random. Books bound in vellum met my gaze, among them one more richly jacketed in an embroidered case studded with ruby and topaz.

Carrying it over to the light, I opened the book and found it bore no title. It was a collection of poems in manuscript, most probably made by the poet himself. The verse looked impossibly dull, with odes to Stability or The Chase plodding after apostrophes to the Pox and Prosody. Then, as I flicked the pages, a shorter poem in *terza rima* caught my eye.

The poem consisted of four verses – the first two of which were identical with those adorning my bedroom window! The title of the poem made reference to an emblematic animal over the main archway of the castle: 'The Stone Watchdog at the Gate Speaks'. Whoever had transcribed the first half of the poem to the window had been ingenious in accrediting its meaning to glass, rather than to the watchdog. I read the final verses.

> *No less, while things celestial proceed*
> *Unfettered, men and women all are slaves,*
> *Chaining themselves to what their hearts most need.*
>
> *Methinks that whatso'er the mind once craves,*
> *Will free it first and then it captive take*
> *By slow degrees, down into Free Will's graves.*

Alas, when addressed, Prosody had not replied. Yet the sentiment expressed might be true. I find myself generally agreeing with the truth of moralizing in poems. Little can be said that is a flat lie, provided it rhymes. Thoughtfully, I tore the page from its volume and tucked it in my doublet, tossing the book back into the chest among the other antiquities.

Beyond the gallery was a circular guard-room, with a spiral stair up to the ramparts. The guard-room had once stood as a separate building; it now came within the embrace of the castle which, like some organic thing, had sprouted passages and wings and additional courts, century by century, engulfing houses and other structures as it grew. Yet the guard-room retained something of an outdoor character. A pair of cavorts skimmed desperately round its shell, trapped after venturing in through boarded arrow-slits. On the floor by my feet lay a shred of Poseidon's fur which the birds had dropped in their panic.

The character of the castle was transformed again beyond the guard-room. Here stood old stables, now converted to quarters for the Mantegan family's resident artist. Nicholas Fatember had his studio in what had been the loft; while his children romped on the cobbles below in rooms that had been a harness-house.

I called his name. After a moment, Fatember's head appeared in the opening above. He waved, and began to climb down the ladder. He started talking before he reached the bottom.

'So, Master Perian, it's almost a year – a long while since we've seen you at Mantegan. As God is my witness, it is an inhospitable place – lonely, gloomy, chilly, bankrupt, and up to its eye-sockets in starving rats! What can have brought you here now? Not pleasure, I'll be bound.'

I explained that I had been ill, and that I would be leaving on the morrow. Natural modesty forbade me to make any reference to the devil-jaw.

Fatember placed a heavy hand on my shoulder, while using the other to scratch his armpit. He was a ponderous man with a heavy face, from which his beard curled down like fungus on a dead tree bole. Only in his eyes was there something which defied decay.

'Ah, Mantegan is a suitable hole to fall sick in, that I'll say. Yet you'll never get the plague here. The plague likes juice and succulence, and there's nothing of that in Mantegan – even the cockroaches shun it – it's too draughty for them. Ague, now – yes, the ague in plenty, but better ague than *plague*.'

He repeated this with some relish, in the manner of one chewing a bone, while gloomily regarding his many children, who were busy flogging an old greyhound they had cornered. They were not the plumpest of children, and their shirts were patched and torn; as many bones showed through on them as on the greyhound.

Although Fatember was as hefty as befits an artist who spends much time dissecting men, horses and ancestral animals, every year bowed his broad shoulders a little further, and trained a mass of grey hair about those shoulders. Age and bitterness had added to his ruin since I last saw him; yet those startling black eyes held their power, reinforced by the great black line of his eyebrows. There was no man I respected more than he: if this was failure, then I admired it, and was proud to be in its company.

'I came to see how the frescoes were progressing, Nicholas.'

'All finished this very day. No, they're as incomplete as they were, Buglewing before last, when you and the players were performing in the great hall. God will not allow me to portray the happiness of princes while my family starves – my damned principles interfere with my brush strokes, you know. Nothing's happening. I can't work any more without pay and – although I don't want to complain to your face about your own brother-in-law – Milord Volpato would be better employed setting his lands in order than involving me in his schemes for self-aggrandizement. Everything always comes back to land. Use it well, your life's fulfilled, use it ill, your life wastes. Of course, we wretches who never owned a bean-strip find it easy to perceive such fundamentals. Give a man a dowry of a dozen farms and he finds truth more difficult to get at. I'm so hard up I've even had to sack the lad who was colouring in my skies.'

As he was making this speech, Fatember led me through a side door and across a court where no sun penetrated. Although he ranked among the greatest painters of the age, he had wasted a decade here – indeed, seemed to have settled for ever, for ever working or not working on the Mantegan frescoes, for ever experimenting with a dozen other arts. His genius was of the truculent kind which generates its own impediments.

'If I marry well, Nicholas, I will see to the money.'

'That "if" you give me is one of the great shattering weapons of Time. Don't talk like Volpato ... Don't marry well, either. No man needs to be the butt of envy. I'm spared that, at least.'

We entered the banqueting hall, with its pendant vaulting and a splendid lattice window, fantastic with carved transoms, over-looking the bustling water traffic of the Toi. Fatember's unfinished frescoes took their orientation from this window, and their lighting schemes.

The theme of these famous frescoes was the Activities of Man under the Dereliction of Evil and the Valour of Good. Only one or two pastoral scenes and an ancestral hunt were complete; for the rest, several isolated figures or details of background stood out on the expanse of naked wall behind the scaffolding. On a trestle-table lay sheets of paper, most of them covered with Fatember's bold cartoons. Perfection was adumbrated, but had still to be realized.

As for the great man himself, he stood stock still, resting a hand heavily on my weaker shoulder and staring about the room as if he had never entered it before. Then he broke away and marched ponderously over to the window, to stand on the dais before it and glower back at me. In the quiet of the great room, as I waited, a brown mouse jumped from the table and scuttled into a corner.

'And Time has other skilled torturers,' Fatember continued. 'I see a pigment in my mind's eye. So real, I could almost pluck it from my pupil. I work for a week to mix it, and then not only is it not as I imagined but the tonal quality I had in mind is lost, wiped out.'

'Nothing comes out quite as you visualize it, Nicholas.'

He stamped his foot so vigorously that dust rose from the boards beneath his sandal.

'Don't respond if you have no truer response than that! Why should a vision not be realizable in actuality? Why should it not? Why are we granted visions, if not that they are capable of realization?'

'Visions may be their own realization. They may themselves be actual. I've just been through an experience—'

'Nonsense. What do you know about it? My vision for these walls remains in all its magnificence. I know that you and Volpato and your sister and half of damned Malacia cannot comprehend on their life why I don't produce – why I don't yield like a meadow, why I don't yoke myself up to my genius and get pulling until all is complete, my vision fulfilled. Well, for one thing, if I'm a meadow, I'm a sour one, over-cropped, never dunged. And if I'm an ox, I've been out to forage for too long, and no longer care for the rasp of the yoke on my shoulders. But if I'm a fool, that's different! Mayhap I prefer to leave the vision in all its glory where it retains its glory, inside my great wooden pudding of a head' – he smote it – 'where the mice and merchants can't get at it. Hey? Rather than trot it out on plaster and have not a thing left to warm the rest of my years. Such visions as mine come only once in a lifetime, Perian, understand that.'

He strode about, angrily pleased to have an audience.

'Is it impertinent to suggest that we should all be better for being able to share your vision?'

'Better? Better? Is a man morally improved by an eight-course meal? Art don't *improve* you like blood-letting. The great artists have all been villains, yes, and the great patrons, give or take a few sanctimonious exceptions. No, you may *want* my vision, you may think you deserve my vision, but the truth is I care for nobody's wants but my own and God's when it comes to painting.'

He marched about the hall, making it echo with his words and the slap of his sandals on the tiles. Thought of his vision warmed him. It seemed to materialize in the air as he expounded on what he intended to do despite the world.

Then he fell gloomily silent, scratching his armpit and gnawing his bearded lip.

'New horizons ... New perspectives on failure ...' he muttered.

I stood looking at the grand marriage scene. It existed complete as a scaled cartoon, and had been sketched life-size on one wall, with areas of basic colour blocked in. It commemorated the marriage of an early Mantegan to Beatrice of Bergonia.

Beatrice was a slender figure, leaning backwards in a chariot shaped like a swan and extending a hand to the handsome young spouse beside her. She was more fully finished than the rest of the composition, which existed in ghost form. Light lingered on her with a serene intimacy – and on her banners and followers with no less lucidity, into the distance. The cathedral, with its gothic galleries, and a view beyond it of plain and mountain, were boldly drawn in over delicate construction lines, proof of Fatember's command of perspective. I saw that when and if the scene were completed, it would stand for the ideal in all marriages.

The artist gave it a shrugging shoulder and moved to a panel which was almost complete. The panel was narrow, fitting expertly into the space available between a doorway and an oriel window; it depicted soldiers with their tents behind them. They were shooting buglewings from a dark sky. A peasant boy stood watching them, wearing a large helmet and tottering under the weight of a shield. In the background rose a fantastic city, bright in painted sunshine.

'The peasant child – he's a little comic masterpiece,' I said.

'He's me. Longing to be a soldier, destined never to fight.'

'Don't be so gloomy, Nicholas, though you relish it! The virtuosity in this panel alone is—'

He turned angrily on me. 'Don't offend me with talk of personal virtuosity! It may be well enough on a stage, where you need but dazzle an audience for an hour. Here it has no place beside the disciplines. A virtuoso can bring death to art. The tradition ever since Albrecht has been lost because of show-offs, who kill necessary steady progression ... There, you're right, I'm too gloomy – Malacia is for the *status quo*, not for progression.'

'Do you know Otto Bengtsohn? He believes Malacia should progress.'

He glared at me from under his shaggy brows. 'I'm a solitary man. I cannot help Bengtsohn nor he me. Yet I respect his ideas. They'll kill him, just as mine will kill me ... No, no, Perian, you know I don't complain at my wretched lot, yet the truth is that I can do nothing, nothing! Outside, beyond these walls of mould and mouse-fart, stands the great burning world of triumphs and nobilities, while I'm stuck here immobile. Only by *art*, only through *painting*, can one master that burning world and its secrets! Seeing is not enough – we do not see until we have *copied*, until we have faithfully transcribed everything ... *everything* ... especially the divine light in all its variety, without which there is nothing.'

'If you could only continue the work you would have something more than a transcription—'

'Don't flatter me, Perian, or I'll send you packing as I do the others. You do flatter – it's an ill trait and I hate it. I'll take money, Minerva knows I'll take money, but not praise. Only God is worthy of praise, God and the Devil. There is no merit anywhere but God gives it. See the locks of that soldier's hair, the bloom on the peasant boy's cheek, the plumage of the bird as it flutters dying to the sward – do I have them exact? No I do not! I have *imitations*! You don't imagine – you are not deceived into believing there is no wall there, are you?

'A wall is a wall, and all my ambition can only make it less than a wall. You look for mobility and light – I give you dust and statuary! It's blasphemy – life offered death! Vanity's at the bottom of it. Do you wonder I delay, hating vanity so?'

He stood completely still, fixing his gaze in loathing on the fantastic city.

Finally, he turned away and said, as if opening a new topic of conversation, 'Only God is worthy of praise. He gives all things, and many gifts we are unable to accept. We run scream-ing with rage from his generosity. Malacia has entered a new age, Master Perian: the man you mention, the man from the north with his revolutionary ideas, is one token of it. I can feel the new age about me, cooped up though I am in this rat-riddled pile. Now at last – for the first time in a hundred thousand years – men open their eyes and look about them. For the first time, they construct engines to supplement their muscles and consult libraries to supplement their meagre brains – not here, perhaps, but elsewhere, elsewhere. And what do they find? Why, the vast, the God-given, continuity of the world!'

Pausing as if to digest his own words, he suddenly broke out again on a new approach, at the very moment that I had resolved to speak about my visitation in the forest.

'For years – all my life – I've slaved to learn, to copy, to transcribe. Don't tell me I'm idle ... Yet I have not the ability to do what a single beam of light does. Here, my friend, come with me! One moment. I'll show you how favourably one tick of God's work compares with a century of mine!'

Impulsively, he seized my tunic and drew me from the ban-queting hall, leaving the door to slam behind us. Among its echoes, we hurried back through the court.

'Why should I decorate this dump? Let what is dead die for ever ...'

Gripping my arm, he led – or rather propelled – me back to the stable that housed him. His little children sprawled and played, calling out at his entry. Fatember brushed them aside. He climbed the ladder to his loft, pushing me up before him. The children cried merrily to entice him to join their play; he shouted at them to be silent.

The loft made a capacious workshop. Fatember had boarded off one end of it. The rest was filled with tables and materials, his endless pots and brushes of all sizes, with piles of unruly paper, with instruments of every description, with geometrical figures, and with a litter of objects which bespoke his intellectual preoccupations: an elk's foot, a shatterhorn tusk, skulls of grab-skeeters and dogs, piles of bones, a plaited hat of bark, a coconut, fir-cones, shells, branches of coral, dead insects, sections of armour like dismembered bodies, and lumps of rock, as well as books on fortifications and other subjects.

Fatember brushed through these inanimate children too. Flinging back a curtain at the rear of the workshop, he gestured me in, crying, 'Here you can be in God's breeches-pocket and survey the universe! See what light can paint at the hand of the one true Master!'

We were in a stuffy, dark alcove. A table stood in the centre. On it was a startling picture painted in varied colours; so brightly did it glow that it seemed to light the room. One glance told me that Fatember had happened on some miraculous technique, far superior to Bengtsohn's mercurization process, which set him as far apart from other artists as men are from other animals.

Something moved in the picture.

In awe I went towards it. In disappointment, I saw that we were in the presence of an ordinary camera obscura. Above us was the little aperture through which light, directed by a lens, shone in from a small tower set in the stable roof.

Exclaiming with relish, Fatember rubbed his hands together.

'Can our art counterfeit a picture as perfect as this? All achieved by one paltry passing beam of light! Why should a man – what *drives* a man – to compete against Nature itself? What a slave I am to my absurd vision!'

As he complained with gusto, I stared at the scene on the table. From the perspectives of the rooftops, we looked down on a stretch of road beyond the castle, where the Toi ran beside its dusty margins. The road branched as it climbed the hill, one way leading to an old cemetery, the other winding up to the castle gate. By the river, resting on boulders, sat a group of people as dusty as the road itself, their mules tethered nearby. I could see, very minutely, an elderly man who mopped his bald head with a kerchief, a widow woman in black who fanned her face with a hat, and so on. I identified them as a group of penitents, embarked on a pilgrimage and making life hard for themselves. Every tiny detail was perfect.

'You perceive how they are diminished, my friend,' said Fatember. 'We see them as through God's eye – or the Devil's, for his may be sharper than God's. We believe them real, yet in truth we are looking at marks on a table, light impressions that leave no stain! Look, here comes my wife, toiling back up the hill – yet it is not my wife, only a tiny mark which I identify with my wife. What is its relation to her?'

'You don't know how recent experiences cause me to be frightened by such remarks as yours, Nicholas.'

He gestured at the table, ignoring me.

'She has been copied by a master painter, who uses only light. Light here, flesh there. Reality there, the ideal here.'

'Why do you believe that is reality down there?'

'I know my wife when I see her.'

I watched as the figure of his wife, climbing towards the castle gate, traversed a centimetre or two of table top.

'Shall we go down and greet your wife?'

'She has nothing to say. She probably has nothing to eat either, poor jade!' To dismiss her, he stepped back and turned a handle, moving the lens. At once, the slowly climbing woman and the penitents were swept away. Rooftops and gables appeared in the enchanted circle, and then an inner court.

The steep perspective, the amazing brilliance of the scene, lent the buildings so novel an air that I uttered a cry of surprise on recognizing the scene.

Minute birds flittered across the table-top picture. They were images of the very cavorts my sister and I had watched an hour earlier. I could even see a haze of cat's fur, spread out like a web and stirred by the warm circulating breath of the courtyard. I looked for my bedroom window. Yes, it was there, and, on the open sill, there was Poseidon himself, staring out at the creatures making free with his abandoned coat! Although the entire window with its parched woodwork was less than half the size of my finger-nail, every detail of it and the cat showed to perfection.

With startling speed, the view was blotted out by a bird, which rose as if from the depths of the table until it covered it entirely. A scrabbling sounded overhead, and a cavort fluttered down between Fatember and me.

'Wretched creatures, winged rodents!' Fatember said, lumbering about and striking at the bird, clouting me in the process. 'This isn't the first time one has tumbled in here, making a mess over everything. Get out of the way while I kill it!'

As he rushed at it savagely, I stepped back and said, 'Nicholas, I need to confide in you. I have undergone the most transforming experience of my life. I was in the forest—'

'I'll get you, you pest!' He rushed by me, seizing up a long set-square, with which he swiped wildly at the terrified bird. I jumped out of his way.

'Nicholas, I had a visitation in the forest, which has disturbed me profoundly.'

'Like this damned bird!' He chased it into a corner but it skimmed away again, darting past my head. 'You vermin, no you don't!'

'To be brief, Nicholas, the visitation I'm talking about persuaded me that we may never be able to understand reality, owing to perhaps merciful limitations in our perceptive powers.'

'Never mind understand – *master*!' he cried, bringing the set-square so savagely down against a wall that it broke. He rushed after the bird with his fists. 'There's no place for you here – this is a sanctuary of art, you feathered turd!'

'You devote your life to transcribing what you believe to be real. I fear that what we regard as real is itself a transcription, something sketched by Powers as much beyond us as we are beyond that luckless bird. That there are pentimento moments, when one layer shows through another. That art and life, fact and fiction, are linked transcriptions of each other—'

'Here's one life I'll do away with! Nearly got it then!'

'That all arts are an attempt to break down the ... an imposed hallucination that we call—'

He blundered past me. 'I'll give it break down! I'll kill the damned thing before it wrecks my place! Oh, how I'm cursed – now you see what I have to put up with. Out of my way, Perian, for Satan's sake, man!' He lunged again, furiously, striking at the bird with a wooden batten and nearly hitting me. He was beside himself with rage, cursing as the cavort mewled in terror. I ducked under his flailing arm and retreated to safety down the ladder.

In the rough living area, Fatember's ragged children were mewling with delight as their mother entered by the street door. She had materialized at almost the same time as the cavort. Besieged by little bodies, she leant for a moment against the door to recover her breath, and her great furled wings rustled against the woodwork. She greeted me wearily and sat down to rest, whereupon the children climbed all over her.

We had met before. She was a heavy woman, although not without grace. Her face was withered and had lost much of its

260

former beauty, yet beauty there still was, especially about her mouth. Her name among men was Charity.

Laws governing flighted people were strict. But Charity's loveliness as a child and young girl had made her one of the favoured few permitted to nest on top of the St Marco campanile, and to perform before the Bishop Elect on saints' days. I could recall as a boy having my mother point her out, flying over the Arena with her sisters – a lovely sight, though the butt of lewd childish jokes, for flighted people scorn clothes.

Now Charity's white and brown pinions were kept folded. She had modelled for Fatember, who plagued her to marry him; after she gave in to him she never flew again. By this time, she would be too old to practise the art.

When she had recovered her strength, Charity rose and offered me her hand in welcome. The children tugged her robe so violently that she sat down again before pouring me a glass of red wine. I accepted it gladly; Nicholas had been too preoccupied to offer. The vintage was rough and bitter: very possibly from Heyst.

'We hoped you would come to see us, Master Perian. Nicholas enjoys your company – and the company of few others, let me add. Your good sister told me you were recovered from your wounds.'

'I would never visit Mantegan without visiting you and Nicholas. I have unbounded admiration for his work.'

'How do you find Nicholas?'

'As bursting with genius and ideas as ever!'

'*And* as cranky? *And* as despairing?'

'Melancholy, perhaps . . .'

'*And* as unable to paint a square metre of wall?'

Picking up a couple of the children, she went to the water-bin and dipped in a ladle from which she drank. The children called out for a similar treat. She gave to each in turn, the boys first, then the girls. Over their clamour, she said, 'Nicholas is too ambitious, and you see the results. Poverty, hunger, filth . . . I've been out washing for a wealthy family to earn enough to buy us bread. How we shall manage when winter comes, I don't know . . .'

'Genius seldom cares to earn its bread.'

'He thinks he will be famous in two hundred years' time.' She threw up her hands, so that her wings rustled. 'Two hundred years! What good will that do his poor children? I don't know. Come, I must find them something to eat. I shouldn't complain, Master Perry; at least we have a roof over our heads.'

'I rejoice it is so.' From the loft came a roar of triumph; the cavort had met its fate.

'There's a world of difference between being an artist and being an artist's wife.'

As I leaned against a wall sipping my wine, I watched her work while skilfully keeping the children amused. I wondered if she recalled the aerial views she had enjoyed of Malacia as a young girl – how enchanted its streets must have looked before she had to walk them! Though I pitied her, I hated to hear her criticize her husband.

Evidently Fatember had forgotten me. I heard him pacing overhead, muttering to himself.

The ragged children hopped about me, begging for sips of wine. Although some of them had inherited vestigial wings from their mother, none could fly.

Passing Charity my empty glass, I said, 'I must take my leave. Tell Nicholas that I hope to come and see him again soon. And I'll ask Katarina to persuade Volpato to . . .' I rubbed two fingers together.

She gestured dismissively, with a sweep of hand reminiscent of her husband's.

'Let well alone, I'd say. Our lot's not so miserable it couldn't be worse. You may not know it, but Volpato has threatened to cast us out, frescoes or no frescoes, if he is pestered ever again on the subject of money.'

'As you wish.'

'It is not as I wish but as I must.' Said with great firmness also reminiscent of Nicholas.

'Once the frescoes are complete, he could easily obtain other commissions.'

She shook her head slowly by way of answer.

I went to the door. She tweaked a long, grey feather from her wing and stooped to give it to the smallest baby to play with. I was through the door before she straightened up again.

Afternoon moved towards evening. Shadows were climbing the sides of the courtyard, chill was returning to the city, some of whose bells chimed distantly. As I crossed to my sister's quarters, the cavorts had gone from the sky. High above my head, my window caught the eye of the sun, but Poseidon had relinquished his post. All was still. The cat's fur had at last sunk to the ground; a twist of it rolled dustily across the flags beneath my feet. Now only chiaroscuro filled the drowsy air.

I was well again; my spell of tranquility was over. Tomorrow, I would quit the castle for what Fatember called the great burning world.

Wedding Cups and Naked Guests

When the great Desport founded our city-state, he decreed that it should be a place of happiness. In large part, that decree has been maintained over the centuries. As the philosopher said, every sea-going boat must needs have a keel; happiness too has a darker side, submerged, dragging against ocean currents, accruing foul things which may ultimately destroy it.

For all that, happiness was pursued with ingenuity in Malacia, and many of its practitioners assembled to ensure that the marriage of Smarana de Lambant to Traytor Orini of Vamonal should be nothing less than a joyous event. They were given three days in which to fulfil this programme to the hilt, by the end of which it was cordially anticipated that everyone involved should be three parts dead with pleasure in all its forms.

On the first day of celebration, during the morning, Pozzi Kemperer took his company through a rehearsal of the comedy of *Fabio and Albrizzi*, to see that we and our costumes were nothing short of perfection. We performed with verve, La Singla making a darling heroine, with every gesture a little seductive miracle of mime. Since excess was the order of the day, Kemperer had brought in the gaunt man with his two panthers, and the effect was not too deplorable.

As for my costume derived from the painting in the Renardo pavilion, it was magnificent. How I would ever pay the tailor was a question to be deferred as long as possible. He had hired out the work on the waistcoat, and the two delicate landscapes embroidered there had been stitched by the Zlatorogs; their neatness was much admired. I had a new white choker tight at my throat, and elegant hose with ribbons at the knee, setting off the shape of my legs to a tee. But that green coat – it was a masterpiece!

It had been cut long, with a shaped waist and ample pockets with immense flaps, just as in the painting. There were the silver buttons, as ordered, with wide cuffs deeply embellished with silver braid. Such was its beauty that I resolved to wear it for the

264

entire wedding festival. It was too stylish for Albrizzi to have to himself.

After rehearsal, when nobody was looking, the divine Singla ran up to me and kissed me on the lips.

'You are a pretty boy, Albrizzi, and I have missed you. We hear you sustained a terrible wound from the devil-jaw. Tonight when the dancing is merry and Pozzi is tipsy, you and I will slip away somewhere. I will play the medico and examine which parts of you are still functional.'

'Dearest Singla, I thought of you often as I lay dying in Mantegan. You have recovered from the loss of your gallant Captain John in the Tuscady Heavy Cavalry?'

She passed a hand elegantly before her face. 'He was such a man ... But it's no use weeping at the world's abuses or we'd be in tears all the time. You and I will staunch our sadness tonight.'

I hung back. 'Never have I had a better offer. But I've grown wiser – I've acquired knowledge and am not used to it yet ... I'm promised to Armida Hoytola and must practise faithfulness. As the song has it, "My days of philandering are over".'

She pressed her sweet loins and breasts against me. 'You funny darling – a hero in your way, but mad, mad! Try out that role next week.'

I kissed her neck. 'Don't tempt me. My horoscope warns me, Seemly Moleskin warns me, Armida warns me – I'm in for bad times unless I take care.'

'Oh, my dashing captain had such a terrifying horoscope. Otherwise I'd surely have run away with him to Tuscady. And the things that had happened to that man! Do you know, he once missed death so narrowly – his steed was killed under him by a Turkish cannon-ball. He said the ball was travelling so slowly that he saw it come out of the other side as the horse fell, looking for all the world like a giant raspberry. Yet he was unhurt, the dear.'

'Soldiers are fearsome liars, sweet innocent Singla.'

Recollecting herself, she said, 'Whatever he's doing, it's a nuptial night here for some. You're a pig but there's a bond between us. I understand you. Listen to the message of the music if my voice holds no persuasion for you.'

Music had been playing for some time. Sweet singers were singing, in particular three girls who affected flowing gowns in

265

the style of Periclean Athens. They were singing a nuptial song commissioned for the occasion and based on one of Pindaro's:

> *A lyre of gold, Apollo's dearest treasure,*
> *Calls forth the light foot*
> *To its plotted pleasure*
> *And the brightness begins:*

> *A prelude sounds that dazzles on the strings*
> *As in true youth*
> *The loving couple brings*
> *Its two lives together.*

> *Oh, harmony is marriage's fair weather.*
> *He is so bold and wise,*
> *His lusts in tether*
> *To her bright dancing eyes.*

And between each verse came a chorus that had already taken strong hold of the wedding guests.

> *All life's brief music –*
> *Come, dance and love upon the sward,*
> *Admit to these revels*
> *No doleful discord!*

La Singla and I disentangled ourselves when we heard a footfall outside the room, but it was only de Lambant.

'Guy, I've hardly exchanged a sentence with you, apart from the playwright's words which passed between us! Your costume is splendid. Do you like mine?'

He came before me and struck a pose, hand shadowing eyes.

'In truth, it's beautiful, de Chirolo, yet I hold it makes you look fat. You're fully recovered from your wounds, then?'

'Yes, yes, that's all forgotten. All bones mended. You regard me as if I was a corpse, my dear friend!'

'No, it's nothing. I wondered if you'd lost some hair with the shock.'

'I think I'm correct in saying that the sight of that devil-jaw petrified me less than anyone else present.'

He took my arm in his old friendly way then, laughing

loudly and saying, 'Oh, you were terribly brave, de Chirolo, and I'm sure you'll never let us forget it, but *I* had to stay by Armida and protect her. If she'd climbed into the post-chaise as you advised, she'd have been killed. No doubt of that.'

'Don't vex me, Guy. I've never clearly understood what the two of you were doing in the forest anyway.'

He made a foppish gesture, turning to La Singla as he did so. She was standing by regarding us with an expression on her face which I could not read. 'Yon de Chirolo's a terrible fellow, Singla, lady, for all his sterling virtues. You had it all explained, Perian, and it is unworthy of you to be jealous. I still recall with warmth, admiration and the odd hiccup your statement that jealousy was demeaning, and that love between friends be freely received and given.'

To be quoted against myself was rather like seeing another man dressed in my best clothes.

'The idea was in my mind – along with other ideas. You'd laugh if I told you I was wrestling with profound processes ...' I looked at him and La Singla, and started again. 'I said jealousy was demeaning, yes. We all suffer from it. Armida is possessive – and you too, I believe. Is that not so?'

He laughed. 'What a poor reply to my quoting your noble sentiment. Those days in bed alone have told against you. Let's go and get a drink.'

Despite myself, I felt anger rising in me. 'Guy, if you believe sincerely that love between friends should be freely received and given, then all parties must practise it or none. Even if I cannot live up to them, I have some ideals; whereas you are always mocking—'

De Lambant turned with a parody of despair to La Singla. 'He has the monopoly of wisdom. How can we stand against him?'

With the healthful sense that was natural to her, La Singla touched us both in an embracing motion, singing a phrase as she did so. ' "Oh, harmony is marriage's fair weather ..." How terrible if you brewed a storm between you, today of all days! Remember it's your sister's nuptials, dear Guy. The strain's telling on you both. Go and take a drink and enjoy.'

De Lambant gave one of his most dazzling smiles, which included me, La Singla, and two other players who had just entered the room.

'Terrible indeed. Come, Perry, my friend, I'll show you my sister's wedding gifts.'

Although I was glad to have the quarrel stopped, I was still full of anxiety, for my silly phrase about love freely received and given was one I had used only to Armida. Had she quoted it to de Lambant, in who knew what satirical circumstances?

'Guy, don't take offence, but you know my feelings about Armida, and that I love her greatly—'

'Entirely,' he said, leading the way down a tiled passage where many people were thronging, all delightfully dressed and perfumed. 'I envy you both more than I can say. It will be a marvellous match, I'm sure. She's a fine girl, and I'm half in love with her myself.'

Was that innocence or effrontery? Fear clutched at my heart, as I forced myself to say lightly, in as near as I dare go to a direct accusation, 'Guy, I delight to see Armida happy in any way, but I must hope you respect my feelings in this matter. Friendship has certain sacred duties. Both she and I value your friendship, and you know I place my trust in your returning that friendship.'

Again his brilliant smile, though those dark, brown eyes were on the throng. 'You need say no more. I really respect your good heart, and I thank you a thousand times for being so trusting. Believe me, I too have Armida's happiness in mind. Now, let's slip in here.'

We entered a room milling with wedding guests, all being agreeable to the point of madness and talking at the tops of their voices. De Lambant, as a cherished son of the family, was greeted on all sides, and in no time I had lost him to a loving but towering aunt who had not seen him for more than a month, and in consequence must hug him as though her life depended upon smothering him between her breasts. I left him with some relief and went to stare at the array of wedding presents.

There stood Bledlore's lovely glasses. I recalled that carefree time when Guy and I went to order them, on the day we met the girls at the fair. Yes, carefree, I had felt carefree then. I passed by the glasses with scarcely a look.

Was I doing Guy and Armida an injustice? Could it be he was so innocent that he had not fully taken my meaning? If Armida had repeated to Guy my phrase about 'love freely received and given', it was a noble phrase – and not from an old play either – worth repeating to numbers of friends, as perhaps she had done; surely he would not have used it as a pretext to take more than was his right. As I gazed at the piles of beautiful and useless objects, occasionally nodding to people who hailed me, I was full of doubt. Running over what Guy had just said, I found every sentence designed to awaken anxiety. He envied Armida and me more than he could say. Well, envy was an unpleasant emotion, and drove a man against his friends. Had he so moved against me that he was seducing her away from me?

Again, as I painted loathsome pictures in my mind – she uttering sounds of pleasure in his filthy embrace – I was furious with myself. I loved her, I trusted him as a friend: it was unjust to entertain such base suspicions. It proved my unfitness, not theirs. Taking a deep breath, I resolved once more that I must be more generous, less jealous.

My pleasure was spoiled, though. My stomach churned.

I went away to relieve myself, to press my temples, to pour cold scented water over my head. Locked in a little cool bathroom where a fountain played, I heard near-by laughter. It came from liars, from hypocrites, from secret enemies, from people who would merely laugh if they knew my dilemma, people who would invite Guy and Armida into their rooms and thrive on the situation.

The Pindaro song was being played:

> *His lusts in tether*
> *To her bright dancing eyes.*

Again I soaked my face, telling myself I was mad, that what I suffered was not jealousy but guilt, that I was feeling what Armida felt when she discovered my lapses. Until this moment, I had not understood her.

I rushed forth, resolved to find her, to beg her forgiveness, to take her in my arms, to show her that now indeed her need for happiness was real to me. Friends called. I gave a salute and pressed on – anxious to appear as normal, yet too troubled to keep up the deception. A drunken man with bloodshot eyes barged into me, muttering incoherently. As I shouldered him away, I saw it was de Lambant senior. He gave no sign of recognizing me.

The de Lambants, considering their own house insufficiently grand a stage for their daughter's wedding celebrations, had taken over a more elegant villa belonging to wealthy relations. A long corridor lined with statues divided the house into reception rooms on the one side and apartments on the other. The chief features were an atrium in the high Byzantine style, a large bath-place, and the peristyle, where fountains played against a background of colonnades. Here, under an open sky, the wedding ceremony, as well as our comedy, acrobatics and the Mendicula play, would take place.

I came at last upon Armida, sitting with her parents in one of the smaller reception rooms among a host of friends, none of whom I recognized. The young Duke of Renardo was not present; I had ascertained already that he had not been invited.

This was the first time I had seen her father since the ancestral hunt. In a few patronizing words, he praised my luck in the kill, helping himself to a pinch of snuff meanwhile.

Looking on Armida, poised beside him like Beauty herself, with one arm resting nonchalantly on the brocaded arm of her chair, I became bold and addressed Andrus Hoytola in a resonant tone.

'Sir, I thank you for your compliments. I went hunting to slay an ancestral, and slay an ancestral I did, though I nearly died for it. But then, there's nothing without risk.'

'One can't doubt the truth of that,' he said, giving me a suspicious glance. 'Lives are always at risk, and not only in the forests of Juracia.'

'I hear that while I was recovering from my wounds, sir,' I continued, 'the story of my devil-jaw circulated about Malacia, making something of a popular hero of me. I am no warrior. What I did was only possible because your fair daughter Armida was facing death. If I may make bold to say so, sir, I hold myself to have been of some service to your illustrious family.'

'That you certainly have, Master de Chirolo,' said Armida's mother, but she was hushed immediately by a gesture from her husband. As for Armida, sensitive creature that she was, the colour came and went in her cheek as she perceived what request I was about to make.

'You have been of some ... service,' said Hoytola, scratching his jaw in such a way that his face was much lengthened. The elongation made his words come slowly. 'Do not be under the misapprehension that one is ungrateful. Before the – ah, forest incident, there was that hydrogenous balloon. Although—'

I had the impudence to interrupt him. 'And, sir, what about our play, *Prince Mendicula*? Otto Bengtsohn's mercurized miracle, in which your daughter and I appear to such effect. To be shown here tomorrow night, for the first time. Do not forget, sir, how hard I worked in that pet scheme of yours.'

My voice faltered. I knew I had ventured on dangerous ground by the way both Hoytola and his wife stiffened and their friends began to move quietly elsewhere. I was made aware of two servitors behind the upright, brocaded chairs upon which the Hoytolas securely sat; they appeared to grow uglier at the mention of Bengtsohn and mercurization; while Hoytola himself, who always wore the aspect of a man with a bad smell under his nose, suddenly found difficulty in breathing.

'One must inform you that the venture has been cancelled. The – ah, instrument has been broken up.'

'Broken up ...'

'That was my phrase. A word further, sir, then you may go. That man to whom you made reference has returned to the northern city from whence he came. One need speak of him no more.'

Through a restriction in my throat, I managed to say – I couldn't look at Armida – 'But our play, the slides! They were to have been shown here – we never saw them – we—'

'Be silent, sir! One paid you. That's enough. You were hired, no more. As you were hired for the balloon. That person's slides are all smashed. No one will see them. He is a proven Progressive. My gallery will have nothing, nothing whatsoever, to do with the matter. Or with you, depend on it, if you utter one word further.'

I was trembling. 'Sir, I cannot understand. We completed the play, absurd though it was. It was a novelty. My hopes – and Bengtsohn's hopes and yours also, I believed—'

'Enough, I say! Keep silent, or trouble will befall. If the Hoytola family is indebted to you for saving our daughter's life, then one will see that you are paid in sequins. For the rest, stay away from us, young man, or you will regret it.'

Armida's mother leaned forward and said, 'If you have formed any sentimental attachment for our—'

Hoytola smote the arm of his chair. 'If you have formed any sentimental attachment whatsoever, forget it. Carry it back to your playhouse and bury it before someone buries you.' His lips were pale. He rose.

'Your servant, sir,' I said, and withdrew. Were he but a devil-jaw, said I to myself, and I had my spring-load spear with me ...

What prompted the impulse to kill him was the stricken look on Armida's face as I turned away. Her knuckles were as white as her face as she clutched her chair.

I took myself back to the cool bathroom and poured more water over my head. Through a miniature waterfall, I saw myself killing Andrus Hoytola. The vision was there in all its dreadful power, as clear as the sight of the magicians at their forest altar. I hated the man and all he stood for; I discovered that I always had, ever since he spoke to me in his stables. As I plunged my face into the water, I could experience the healthful shock at my wrist as the sword grated between his ribs and blood gouted over his impeccable clothes. His teeth showed like a bolting mule's as he shed his precious dignity and pitched to the floor at my feet.

When my murderous impulse was over, and I felt less like vomiting, I began to worry about Armida. I dried my face and took myself into one of the rooms where young couples, friends of Smarana's, were dancing. Servants brought in fruity drinks. Settling behind a bank of flowers, I tried to compose myself.

Guy entered the room with a girl and saw me. He excused himself to her and came over.

'Perry, old partner, you're looking seedy. Didn't you notice that girl? Have you had a quarrel with Armida?'

'Guy, no banter, please.' I made him sit down by me. 'I've been talking to Hoytola. The Mendicula play is broken up. All the slides have been smashed. He broke all those images of Armida. All our art destroyed.'

'Is this the work of critics?'

'Hoytola simply said that Otto Bengtsohn has left Malacia.'

'Why should he do that?'

I shook my head. 'How I loathe that man ... Otto and Flora must have had good reason to leave – the old reason. The Supreme Council's edict against change. If the Council foresaw dangerous applications of the principle of mercurization, as Otto himself did, they would put pressure to bear on Hoytola. They allowed him his balloon in an emergency. The more reason not to relax the edict a second time. Mercurization was too much a new thing, and they ruled against it. Hoytola, to save his own skin, has closed down the whole venture. Otto, a sworn Progressive, has fled.'

'What's happened to the zahnoscope?'

'It's been smashed up, too. Hoytola must have discovered that Otto was a Progressive. I'll wager he turned the old fellow out to mend his own standing with the Council ...'

De Lambant shook his head. 'All very devious, if true. Perian, beneath the civilized if venereal veneer of your life flows a dark and dangerous stream. Stay away from wrong-headed people like Otto, if you value safety.'

A word of friendly advice comforted me. I put an arm about his shoulders. 'I'm beginning to think that the Ottos of this world understand it well.'

Even as Guy had said, there was a dangerous stream in me. No sooner did my anxieties about him cease than I became anxious about Otto. What had really happened? After the nuptial ceremonies I would seek out Bonihatch and find the truth.

The face of Bonihatch appeared before me, custardy whiskers and all. I had done him no good turn by pursuing Letitia when he was in love with her; but he was only a cocky apprentice, and I would make my peace with him.

The main question was Armida. She had not followed me, perhaps because she could not escape her father. He was injuring her more than me. She was simply a pawn in his cold, complicated game.

Come, I had read my fairy stories and believed them. When the personable but poor young man saved the life of the king's beautiful daughter, she was given him in marriage, and everyone in the kingdom rejoiced. Why was the fable not fulfilled, particularly when I was no pauper and Hoytola merely a trumped-up merchant – not half so worthy a man as my own father?

Rising after Guy had left me, I saw that Caylus, his crutches banished, was dancing with a vivacious, dark-complexioned girl. No desire rose in me to be convivial. A servant came over and offered me a glass of wine. Better to be drunk than sober. In keeping with the festive tone of the occasion, the menials wore masks, some horrific, some comic, some pretty. I took my glass from a multi-hued orchid.

Soon I was back into the swim of things, at least as far as appearances went. La Singla and Pozzi called me. He was full of wrath because the Duke of Ragusa was not coming and so would not, after all, see our performance.

'The old fool sends word that he has heard Malacia is ripe for revolution! Malacia! No doubt he also believes that the moon is a giant cow-pat!' said Pozzi. 'The crosses we artists have to bear, de Chirolo!'

When evening fell, the festivities were at their height. I was impersonating my old light-hearted self; there was always another day, when a way through present troubles would be found.

A servant insisted on bringing me more wine, though my glass was half-full. I tried to push him away but he had me trapped behind a column in the atrium. His face was an elaborate flower, his eyes glittering at its centre.

'I'm not a chrysanthemum, de Chirolo, as you may drunkenly imagine,' this servant said. 'Perhaps you recognize my voice.'

'Be off before I report you.'

'Don't think yourself so secure.' We were screened from the dancers. He lifted the flower-mask momentarily, so that I saw the face of Bonihatch.

'What are you doing? Prince Mendicula was a more likely role than this floral act.'

'You're surprised. We workers have to secure what jobs we can. As for this decadent mob – all will perish when the Progressives win their struggle.'

'Bonihatch, never mind that. Believe me, I am glad to see you. There have been differences between us—'

'I owe you a beating up, if truth be told, de Chirolo, but I am capable of setting party before personalities. Founder only knows why, but you're something of a popular hero and we need you. I was deputed to approach you. There's a meeting soon which we want you to attend.'

'Listen. Andrus Hoytola is here—'

'The Council have arrested Otto. He may be dead by now. By great luck, his wife was away with a relation when they came, and she warned me. She's in hiding, as I am.' We had moved to a dark corner. His eyes moved constantly behind the flower-mask.

'Let's go outside and talk. I was told that Otto had left for Tolkhorm.'

'I've no time. Don't trust the Hoytolas. Can't you understand that? The Council came for Otto in the middle of the night. They smashed all the equipment, the slides, the zahnoscope, everything ... Hoytola betrayed him. Who knows whether Otto's dead or being tortured to death in their filthy dungeons. You have courage at least. Think which side you're on.'

'When – I'm all confused—'

'Come to the meeting. We'll clear your head. Late tomorrow night, after your play. Get out of those foppish clothes before you come. Someone will contact you tomorrow and tell you where the meeting is to be.'

'You're asking me to throw up everything I'm striving for, Bonihatch, I—'

His eyes gleamed through the petals. 'You aren't striving for anything worth having. Till tomorrow.'

He was gone.

An alliance with Bonihatch and the dingy apprentices ... The mere thought made me wish I had taken the wine he offered. But there was a dedication about him which I found impressive.

'Ha, you're positively mooching, my heroic friend!' cried a familiar voice as I took a turn along the colonnade. An arm hooked itself through mine, and there was the laughing face of Caylus and the bold, sharp countenance of his doxy. Caylus liked them highly coloured.

'De Chirolo – the hero of the hour, the dragon-slayer, and looking as if life was not fit for the living. This is the beautiful Teressa Orini from Vamonal, who has been longing to talk to you.'

Teressa placed herself seductively before me and offered a ringed finger for me to hold.

'Caylus has told me so much about you—'

'—Tactless fool that I am, ruining my own chances!'

'And he tells me that you are as valiant in bed as in the field.' Flashing teeth.

'—This girl is absolutely wanton, de Chirolo, *wanton*! You'd enter the priesthood if you heard some of the libidinous secrets she has whispered to me.'

She clapped her lean hands. She moved confidentially closer.

'He exaggerates. In an hour he has corrupted me, dear de Chirolo, and I think you should join us so that I'm in some measure protected.'

They were laughing. The talk ran fast, teasingly, while they cast naughty looks at each other. It was impossible not to catch a little warmth from them.

'Perian will afford no young lady protection, Teressa! He's the complete lecher, absolutely complete. Let me tell you what he did ...' He cupped his lips and whispered breathy words into the dark tresses by her ear. Her eyes danced, she burst into laughter and seized my arm.

'How shall I survive the night between two such notorious rakes?'

'De Chirolo and I will give you pertinent details immediately,' Caylus said, winking at me. 'Come, let's go somewhere where we can sit, and eat, and imbibe, and this heroic friend of mine will give us the full story of how he slayed the dragon, the pizzle of which he keeps beneath his pillow for luck and potency.'

'I can't join you just now,' I said. But I went along with them all the same, putting my discomforts aside.

Dear Caylus! You were a good good-time friend. I wanted to please you – and what pleasure to please Teressa Orini as well. But a reptilian visage was watching me across a smouldering forest altar and saying. 'Your errors repeat and repeat themselves like an endless fiction ...' It dried the juices of my heart. The canker of knowledge was in me: I had to discover what was happening to Armida and Otto – how strange to link such disparate names! – whatever it cost me.

I slipped away from my high-stepping friends. At that moment, the sour, work-a-day Bonihatch would have provided company more to my taste.

The chandeliers were lit and tall candles brought to darken what daylight was still reflected in the pool.

Menials with masks of boars came forth, bringing flaming braziers as music sounded, against the chill in the autumn air. For many this would be an alfresco night. A ruddy glare lit the faces of those who were lovers and those who would be lovers by the morrow. I turned away, yet I had another good friend among the wedding guests – Portinari, whose father had helped with provisions for the feast. He called to me from a marbled arch and came to my side, patting my back.

'Perian, my dear old hero! Straight from the cemetery with a grave face. You are in some kind of trouble?'

'No, no, I'm fine, Gustavus – a little too much wine, perhaps.'

'Something worse than wine, I fancy. No, don't tell me, let me say only – my dear Perian, perhaps we don't know each other intimately—'

I tried to push past him. 'True enough. A universal complaint. But I'm in no mood for that conversation, forgive me.'

'Before you go, Perian ... This may seem presumptuous, but I happen to know that Kemperer and La Singla are busy conferring with Andrus Hoytola and his wife concerning tomorrow's business. Armida is alone for the once, awaiting an assignation, having sent off Yolaria. If you will come with me – I do realize this is none of my affair, except inasmuch as friends are concerned – but if you will come, I'll lead you to her this instant.'

I slapped his shoulder. 'Gustavus, you are kind. I'm not myself. And I do need to speak with Armida.'

We made through the crowded rooms and he led me upstairs, still apologizing. The upper floor extended over only part of the villa, and served in the main as a pretext for a balcony which ran round the four sides of the peristyle, overlooking that pleasure spot.

'I'm sorry to interfere, my friend,' Portinari kept saying.

He showed me to a curtained doorway and left me. I entered at once.

'Guy?' asked a voice. It was Armida. The room contained a sofa, a writing table, two chairs and little else. It overlooked the peristyle. Armida stood in the shadows, where she could hardly be seen. The only illumination was a ruddy light reflected from the floor below.

'It is not Guy. It is I, Perian, your betrothed,' said I, walking over to where she stood.

'Oh, Perian, I'm glad to speak to you! That terrible boring scene this afternoon—'

'It was humiliating – for you and me. But you didn't seek me out afterwards.'

'Father was harsh with you, but he thought you presumed. He was trying to be fair in his way.'

'Did you think me presumptuous?'

'Perian, the world you move in is so extraordinary. There are different codes one has to live by.' She had risen and was standing stiffly away from me.

'I've swallowed all your rebukes and hesitations. You let your father threaten me. And I can stand here and all my senses tell me that you *do not* want me, don't want to touch or speak to me.'

'Certain rules of society have to be observed. We'll speak some other time. Please don't vex me.'

'What do you mean by that? Armida, my darling girl – very well, I won't touch you, but look at me and tell me that you recall we are still betrothed.'

She forced a laugh. 'That was a little secret fun between us, which I do believe you were prepared to reveal to my father.'

'What kind of language do you use to me? Do you imagine I don't understand what you're saying? Armida, how pitifully things have changed between us!'

'No, nothing has changed, nor am I the one who is for change. I am the same, it's you who have become different.'

'I am anxious, no more than that, and you make me anxious. If I have no reason for anxiety, then pray tell me so and all shall be well again, and I yours again, body and heart. Tell me your father doesn't hate me.'

'Why are you being so dramatic? You're always acting, always suffering. I confess I prefer more superficial people. What's the matter with you? Is this something to do with Guy?'

'Guy? I'm talking about your father. Why bring Guy's name up? What's he to you?'

She was still standing rigidly, almost as if leaning away from me. 'I don't intend to give Guy up, if that's what you are hinting.'

'I hint nothing. Though I freely allow you the right to end friendships of mine of which you disapprove – that you'll concede.'

'I'm enjoying it too much to think of giving it up.'

My throat went dry. It choked me; all my fears rushed back to assail me. I heard my voice, remote and dusty, say, 'Are you telling me that you and Guy are making love together?'

She hesitated only for a moment.

'You know we are, you fool! What else do you think we have been doing together? Talking about botany?'

All I could think to say was, 'But he's my friend – he calls himself my best friend ... You tell me this dreadful news without apology? You couldn't do this, either of you ...' The words drained away into the desert sands and my blood drained with them.

Armida stood proudly regarding me, all defiance.

'What right have you to say that? You knew very well what we were doing – you encouraged it. Why should I apologize? "Love freely received and given" – wasn't that your fine phrase? You told Guy you approved – you told him so again today. You wanted me to love him, you wished everything to be honest, and so it has been. You wanted me to love him—' Now she was confronting me, her eyes burning.

'Armida – love, yes, love, not fornication. I did, I admit. I did encourage you to be my friend's friend, but that was so you should not feel guilty—'

'Guilty!' She laughed in scorn. 'I don't feel guilty, nor does Guy. Did you imagine we went into the forest to discuss silviculture? What we did was natural and no more than *you* were doing all the time with your bitches.'

'But I had ceased philandering. You asked it of me. I told you, you knew. I *stopped* when I found how it hurt you. I realized it could have no part in our love. And now you – you – you deceived me so cruelly, you whom ...' I clutched my throat, choking. 'Besides, you despised Guy! – remember how you demolished his silly arguments one afternoon, with such contempt!'

'Now you complain, when it doesn't suit you, eh? I can't help despising such a man. Before, I honoured you, thought you generous and noble because you understood my feelings for Guy—'

'Generous! Noble! I'd be *mad* to – to lend you, to give all my friends a slice as if you were a wedding cake ... Guy was my *friend* – he's betrayed me too.'

'You're being dramatic again. If you think I will end this affair just because you wish it, you are much mistaken.' She was feeling angrily in a pocket of her dress, and brought out a crumpled piece of paper, which she smoothed with one scornful gesture and thrust at me, saying, 'I suppose you deny writing this?'

I looked at it. Even in the flickering light, I saw that it was a frivolous quatrain I had once written.

> *Dear Bedalar, of all girls I have laid,*
> *Yours is the music that most wildly stirs*
> *Me; while no marring discord joy defers,*
> *Your instrument must never lie unplayed.*

'That was ages ago. It's all over. Bedalar has betrayed me too!'

'For good reason, you have betrayal on the brain. I came across it in her rooms, and snatched it up. You've lain with all and sundry of my friends and you dare blame me for one little affair with Guy. Well, I won't give him up on your account.'

'But *Guy*! To do it with him, it's so dishonourable, as if there was nothing in the world but deception.'

'Oh, these words you use, as if you were at least a duke! I know he's faithless but I'm not jealous of him as I am of you. We just have a good time. I'll say no more or you'll regret it.'

She made as if to leave the room, but I stopped her. She drew away from my touch.

'Armida, now you are being dramatic. I will not blame you for this – I can't because I freely admit my own philandering. I am reforming, though without your encouragement. But you must see the difference in our attitude towards each other—'

'One law for you, another for me – that's it, isn't it?'

I clutched my jaw, feeling myself more enmeshed every minute. 'No, no, that's not it. But we have obligations to each other, our betrothal, and I did save your life—'

'Oh, I knew you would have to bring that up!'

'We have obligations to each other, my dear Armida. I have played about, admitted it, repented it—'

'Been found out, you mean.'

'Very well, then I have been found out. And have sorrowed to have wounded you, and have resolved to do better, and have never said other than that I loved you deeply—'

She flung out a spread hand. 'Oh, you're so virtuous. Look at your silly face!'

'Yours brims with spite. I repeat, when you discovered my affairs, I regretted my thoughtlessness and tried to comfort you. Now by your own careless tongue you are discovered. Do you regret, do you try to comfort me, do you have compassion on my suffering?'

Again she laughed, and there was general laughter down in the courtyard, where Piebald Pete and his fantoccini had begun a performance.

'Compassion! You should have thought of that big word when you were cheating with Bedalar. You're scared now you've found out about me and Guy, aren't you, and so—'

'Ah, "found out", is it?' I moved towards her again. 'So you *were* doing it secretly, while I was lying recovering from my wounds. You understood perfectly that I never wanted you to be more than my friend's friend – no man's that stupid! You knew that never for a moment would I say to Guy, "Go on, seduce her, deprave her, stuff her with your filthy semen".'

She struck me across the face. 'You alley-fodder! You encouraged us in every way, now suddenly you're jealous.'

'You're found out in a lie, so you lie again! As for jealousy, am I more jealous than you or Guy? Aren't you both blinded with jealousy and possessiveness? I have tried to hate my own jealousy. Couldn't you contain your lust, in the name of honour?'

She turned away and stared down into the courtyard where the wedding guests lolled. 'You'll be quoting your damned General Gerald speeches next. The play's destroyed, remember? We've had Disgrace and Compassion. Now it's Honour – one wonders which expensive virtue you'll parade next.'

'I had honour, Armida, I had honour,' I said, moving closer and wondering why I was having to plead when the offence was hers. 'You have dishonoured me – and that by playing out your role of Patricia to the full. Forget the play. I'm asking if you sorrow now that you see me cut to the heart. No, you rejoice like a harpy and gloat over your rutting. What do we do now?'

'Work that out for yourself.'

'I ask you again, do you care that I'm cut to the heart?'

'I told you. I'm enjoying Guy's company at present.'

She regarded me with tight lips, her nose high. The perfume of her patchouli came to me, sickening me. I was too ashamed to quarrel further. I still could hardly believe that my suppressed fears were realized. Nor, even then, did I find myself able to hate her; she had taken advantage of me; but foolishly I had encouraged her. I turned, defeated, to leave.

There stood Guy. I realized that her assignation had been with him; his had been the name she first spoke. Portinari had somehow got wind of it. Guy had overheard part of our quarrel, and was full of fright.

He trembled. His eyes resembled blackcurrant jelly. He was ash. I despised him.

'Perian, there's been some dreadful mistake,' he said. 'A mis-understanding. You and Armida have a wonderful relationship – I envy you more than I can say. I was sure you knew about us: only today you've been saying you valued what I was doing for Armida, helping her in every way, and that you wanted to see her happy with me.' He held out his hand. 'You've got your wish. I've only been doing you a favour, my dear friend.'

'You snake-throated liar! You twisted my words for your own ends. Who ever gives his dear love away to another man?' I knocked his hand down.

'I'm your best friend – I did it for your sake, to keep Armida away from your rivals, as you asked. Now you turn on me.'

'For my sake, you villain! *You* are my rival!'

He gave me a weak smile and gestured with his hand. Armida stole up behind him and took his arm.

'There's no competition in matters of love,' he said, attempt-ing an air. 'We're all different, all having different qualities to offer. You know that from your own experience, which is not negligible, and encompasses Bedalar, I hear. I acted only from love of *you*, as well as of Armida.'

It very nearly robbed me of speech. 'You dare make such a claim to my face – you foul the word love twice over.'

'Come on, old fellow, you talk about love. I know you and your ways. Entirely decadent. Haven't you been working steadily through Armida's friends? Our affair is different – I respect her greatly.'

'I know you do,' she said.

Useless to report the mixture of venom and friendship he doled out. His face remained ashen; hers had gone crimson. Ever and anon, like a chorus, came his phrase, 'I believe I have no need to justify myself'; what followed was all self-justifi-cation. I turned to Armida with some spirit and said, 'Hear the real man speak. Don't you understand the noise he makes? Can you love a man like that?'

282

She tossed her head. 'Oh, he speaks so well – all that he says is true and noble.'

It was de Lambant's turn to laugh. A shaky noise it was.

'You'd better get out and rethink your life, de Chirolo, for all our sakes. Meanwhile, remember that I'm still your friend. We shall be laughing in Truna's over this incident in a few days.'

'Is that all she really means to you?'

'Stop maintaining one standard for yourself and another for the rest of humanity.'

'You whelp, you dishonour her – you deceive her – as well as me.'

Then I found heat from the centre of my frozen entrails and threw myself on him. I struck at his face with a quick double blow. I struck again as he parried. Armida's scream was merely an accompaniment goading me on. Once I went down when he hit me in the chest. I was up again, and punching over and over at his body as he grappled with me. We staggered to the balcony rail, and there I slowly forced his head back, determined to push him over if possible, until hands were grasping us, pulling me away.

De Lambant's face was dark, streaked with blood and rage. I had one glimpse of it as guests dragged me from the room. I was hurled downstairs.

Other people grasped me at the bottom of the stairs, menials, and I was carried kicking to the entrance, across a yard, and pitched out into the street. The gate slammed behind me, and I sprawled on hands and knees, groaning.

No sooner was I down than more hands seized on me. The noise of the de Lambant festivities, word passed on by the servants that immense quantities of food were being consumed inside, had attracted a crowd of beggars about the doors. They waited for what they could get, and the first thing they got was me. I was picked up and picked over.

Dirty hands dug into my pockets and tore at my new coat. My few coins were stolen. Then they stripped me of my finery. It would fetch a good price in the bazaar.

The beggars stood away, staring at me as I lay dazedly. I did not move. As if at a given signal, they all turned and ran or hobbled down the street into the darkness.

For a while, I sat in the gutter, my head between my hands. I staggered and vomited against a wall, collapsing back on my knees. Then I picked myself up and headed in the direction of Stary Most.

Well, I said to myself, I've played the General. Now I've played the Prince. At least he had the fortune to die. Living is a sordid business, it must be admitted. Knowledge kills.

Some time later, towards midnight or towards morning, I found myself by a bridge, and leaned over its parapet to view the dark water. I could feel a chill as black as the waters moving within me. If I became one with that moving water, then all would be one.

It was an intermittent squeaking noise which brought me to myself: a dull, dreary squeak frequently repeated, then ceasing, then beginning again. A stink was in my nostrils. Malacia's gong-fermors were at their nocturnal work, emptying privies.

Voices of my recent torturers came back, telling me that even to die would be one more gesture belonging to the boards, without the cutting truth of reality. Yet I felt I could not continue; it was not so much that Armida had been with some man – and granting him, I hazarded from her words, more than she had ever granted me – it was that she had been with the man who professed himself my best friend. She had made us enemies.

Similarly, it was not so much that de Lambant had been with her, or even that he had defiled what is one of the basic understandings between friends. The offence was made worse – tenfold, a hundredfold worse – by the pretence on both their parts that their deception was no deception. What could be crueller?

That dreary squeak came nearer, as if the street itself got up and walked along itself. Presently, the night cart with its single lantern squealed its wounded way across the bridge. I lay flat on the parapet. The gongfermors, heads shrouded in sacking, nosegays pressed to their noses against the stench, did not observe me.

Then there was that shameful episode with Bedalar. But I had been mad, a hero, then – besides, de Lambant was not serious about her as I was about Armida. Despite which, I had done wrong in Armida's eyes and repented the error of my ways. Now I was made to suffer again, as if repentance was nothing – to suffer by a couple who gloried in committing the same sin over and over. If once was a sin, by what mathematics was ten times, or however often they had done it, no sin?

Driven by compulsion, I tried to compute the number of times they could have been alone together and done it. How often had I spoken in friendly terms to one or other of them just after their naked bodies had been clinging close? How many times had I blamed myself for harbouring unworthy suspicions of them?

On the far side of the bridge the night cart stopped. A fire was kindled in an old container. Rancid smoke drifted across to me where I lay, gazing down into the pitchy stream.

Though I wished to vomit up every part of Armida – and that despicable male creature – yet I loved her. How could I reject her for being shallow and crippled, for so I had been? And not only I, but almost everyone I knew, as my numbed mind sorted through other acquaintances. It lit on my sister; the dear thwarted girl was locked in her rotting castle for life. The curse was universal.

My thoughts were draughts gusting in a darkened room; through the room echoed the phrases they had spoken, shaming me, shaming the speakers. If only Armida had showed one saving jot of penitence ...

No, I could not live with such disgrace. I had tried to live more generously, where love freely received and given was no phrase for sarcasm – whereupon the fiends had descended. I could live not at all. I had been given the gift the magicians promised: the knowledge that aged me.

Smoke drifted across me. The dreary squeal began again as the team of gongfermors moved towards the quayside.

Frozen, I climbed onto the low parapet of the bridge, preparing to cast myself into the water. I knew not where I was. The look of the sewery water told me that it flowed from Founder's Hill, from under the dark pile of the Palace of the Bishops Elect. Now those black and indifferent bishops must have mercy on my soul.

Something drifted up in the water. There was a dim lamp burning at the head of an alleyway nearby. By its gleam, I saw what I took for a branch in the water, shaped like a human leg. I paused. It was carried away in the sluggish flood.

Again I gathered myself. Below the dark tide, another object flowed with the current. It drifted up towards the surface, turning as it came, weed floating about it. Despite myself, I crouched there petrified. It was a human head. The weed was hair.

The flesh was pallid. The mouth was open to the fishes. There was no pain in it, merely the blankness to which I aspired. As it came up, still turning, pouting lips broke surface for a moment.

Otto Bengtsohn looked up at me, beyond speech but still crying from that final severance. His head, floating solitary, still turned. Back came the hair like weed. An eddy took the dreadful object down into shadow, until it blurred and was gone from sight.

I crouched on the parapet. Somewhere, an owl cried and was answered.

A voice of pity said, 'Oh, Perian, my love, here you are!'

Her arms came round me. I could not look away from the gliding flood. I wanted no one.

'Oh, Perry, when I heard they'd thrown you out I came to find you. Poor cherub, what are you doing? Don't stay here. Let me help you home.'

Slowly I looked about, not wishing comfort, even La Singla's. But she held me in her embrace and put her cheek against mine, murmuring how cold I was, whispering that she would see me home.

'Where am I?'

'Why, you're in Stary Most, and only a couple of streets from your room. There's a warmer bed there than in the mucky little Rosewater.'

'I've been betrayed by my lover and my friend, and it's more than I can bear. My heart is dead inside me, and the rest of me must follow.'

She laid her arm round my neck with a tender gesture, kissing my temple and giving a little laugh.

'I didn't know you were so unworldly, Perian. Come, such upsets happen all the time – life is made of them. You know what I have suffered.'

'I can't talk about it, if life really is so wretched. It is precisely because I am worldly that I'm hurt. The proper and worldly way of dealing with such a situation, when one's found out – oh, why say it?'

'Tell me. Have it out.'

'The woman weeps a little and says she meant no harm, and the friend apologizes for being such a swine but, alas, he was led on by the lady's beauty, etc., and then both of them swear

286

the error will not be repeated – or not within a calendar month ... That's the proper way. But these two bungling amateurs at love, Armida and that serpent de Lambant – why, from the moment of their deception being discovered, they embark on an entirely more hurtful policy. They dishonour themselves ... Oh, I could weep myself into a pool of humiliation.'

Her pretty fluttering movements were round me. 'It's just the hurt. They aren't cold and shallow just because you are warm and loving – yes, for all your airs, my pet. Don't let chill pass to you. Come, this is no place to be ...'

Clasping her, I stood up and looked about.

A cock was crowing, a pallor in the eastern sky spreading over the malformed rooftops. I recognized the place. I had been here before, not long ago, at the same dead hour, among the warehouses and smelly corners – yes, and with that self-styled friend of mine, de Lambant.

'Take me home,' I said.

She got me there, through the decaying alleys. On the way, I kept thinking to myself, if she wants me to sleep with her, I can't, I'm nothing any more. I should have jumped in after poor Otto.

La Singla was wise. She talked most of the way, saying that Pozzi had found an old flame among the Vamonal contingent, so that he would not miss her. That people made love with others with whom they really should not, that the world continued nevertheless, because love was only a game.

'Emotions are not subjects for games.'

'Dear Perry, you knew that Guy was making love to Armida, you must have done, while you were recovering in the castle, and before. That's how people behave. That's how you would have behaved.'

'If I knew they were deceiving me, then such was my will to trust that I suppressed the knowledge. Shouldn't we be ashamed of our natures and of giving in to them? It's all so – ugh, so dishonourable!'

She laughed. 'You talk too much of honour – Armida must be sick of that cant in her own house. Perhaps that's why she preferred a rascal.'

'Don't you set against me, too. I blame myself, believe me, but I blame de Lambant infinitely more.'

'Don't go against your own nature, love. I know my nature
287

too well to think of changing, so I enjoy myself, and cheerfully suffer what sorrows it brings.'

'Now you're being virtuous!'

'I know you are like me, an actor born. We're very alike, dear Perian. You're almost a brother to me – though I've adored our moments of incestuous passion.'

'I tell you I will change my nature. You are dear to me, but you are honest, you know yourself. Those others deceive themselves about their own natures, yet sneer at me for mine. How right poor Otto Bengtsohn was! – Malacia is decadent and it's time for change! *I* will change, pretty Singla, I will!'

'All right, all right, but sleep first. Here's your door.'

Up the stairs we went, fumbling in the dark among familiar odours.

At the top, a gleam of light showed beneath the door. Fears started up in me. All men were my enemies. Had that cunning de Lambant sent a pair of rogues to beat me, as Kemperer had done? I might have been contemplating an end in the river not half an hour before, but a beating was something different.

Or could it be Armida, suddenly overcome with penitence, willing to flee at once to another city? Unprovoked, I remembered her words when she was naked in the Chabrizzi chapel: 'I wish I were a wild creature'.

'Who's there?' La Singla called.

A voice within said, 'Friends of de Chirolo's.'

'I have no friends,' I said.

'Who?' She too was anxious. 'Names?'

The door opened. A girl stood there with a lantern, peering at us, apprehension on her face. It was Letitia Zlatorog.

La Singla and I went in. I threw myself on the bed, not speaking.

Bonihatch stood there with Letitia. He still clutched his flower-mask in one hand. He looked at me contemplatively, shaking his head.

La Singla took charge, pulling off my boots, undressing me, and trying at the same time to usher my two guests out.

Bonihatch, while apologetic, explained firmly that both he and Letitia had been serving at the wedding celebrations to earn some money, and were off duty. They called in to see me, after witnessing something of the fight and my expulsion. They hoped that I would now see who were my true friends, who my enemies, and would accordingly join the Progressives, where I would be most welcome. All this I heard through a sort of stupor. I just wished to be left alone, yet that too I feared, knowing that the inner monologue of misery would immediately resume within me.

'I've got no friends, Bonihatch. You're just an opportunist, too.'

'Stop feeling so sorry for yourself.'

'Go away,' I said. 'I've no quarrel with either of you, but I know now that Bengtsohn is dead. The state police will get you too.' I told them what I had seen.

'You understand why they killed him?' Letitia asked.

'Don't worry him – he's exhausted,' La Singla said.

'*You* ought to understand, too,' said Letitia, turning to her. 'Bengtsohn was so clever that he almost got Hoytola on his side. They might have brought changes to Malacia. Even the hydrogenous balloon represented a change the Council could just tolerate because the Turks were at our gates. The aerial zahnoscope was another subversive idea which would greatly have aided us. Even the comedy of *Prince Mendicula* – it was not just that the acceptance of that play might have opened the door to plays with more persuasive social meaning. *Mendicula* itself had a prologue – which Bengtsohn was to have recited at the feast tomorrow – explaining the corruption of rank and riches, the degradation of the poor.'

'To save his own disgusting skin, Hoytola handed Otto over to the authorities. He denounced him utterly,' said Bonihatch. 'The revolutionary committee may decide that we should make an example of Hoytola. Would you be against that, de Chirolo?'

'I can't think tonight. It's impossible to change Malacia. I'm just going to have to work on myself.'

La Singla was in my cubby-hole of a kitchen, infusing coffee, but she stuck her pretty head out to cry, 'The original magician's curse on Malacia was that it would never change.'

'Most people seem to think lack of change a blessing,' said Letitia. 'Only the poor desperate classes long for change.' She was impersonal tonight. There was no clinging. Her manner was independent even towards Bonihatch.

'It's all damned nonsense,' cried Bonihatch. 'There was no original curse. All the legends about the origins of Malacia – the rubbish about men coming from animals – are a pack of nonsense, designed to keep everyone dark of mind, the easier to be ruled. Bengtsohn often told me how enlightened Tolkhorm was. There they pay no heed to the centuries of drivel you learn here from birth. All must be changed, burnt down.'

In my dazed state, I was listening to them all. Letitia was talking earnestly to La Singla, as if repeating a lesson.

'Of course people will embrace lack of change, generation after generation. Lack of change implies peace. War is the common instrument of change in the rest of the world. My uncle told me that that's why the Turks can never conquer Malacia, because the curse, or a belief in it, keeps war and change at arm's length. Most people understand that emotionally.'

'I'm just an actress. It's none of my affair. I want to see Perry asleep. And I don't require any wars, if you do.'

Bonihatch interposed, throwing the flower-mask down and looking confident as he lectured La Singla.

'Lady, war is a human constant. It exists in Malacia but on a domesticated scale. You just brought home one of its victims. We may not have cannonades or pike charges here, nor actual rape and carnage in St Marco's Square; but the sly warfare of society is such that in every family there is strife, enmity, distrust, betrayal, spies moving muffled between women's open legs.'

Something like a laugh rose in my throat. Armida, Bonihatch's class enemy, had once made almost the same observation. La Singla brushed it all aside.

'I know much more about open legs than you, young man. Here's some coffee. You are as bad as Perian. You must learn to laugh at life, as I tell him, and not think such dreadful thoughts!' She bustled forward into the room, bearing steaming earthenware mugs.

As she knelt beside me, I accepted a mug gratefully and stroked her plump cheek.

'That's more like it. Amorousness never hurt anyone, only your attitude to it. Rebelliousness hurts everyone,' she said.

'It will hurt the rich and the privileged most,' said Bonihatch. 'We'll see to that.'

The warm drink did something to revive me. I found my voice.

'It's the arrogance of the rich I hate,' I said. 'What was Bengtsohn's prelude to the mercurization of *Mendicula* to be?'

'You only had arrogance – your own word – towards the old man. Letitia and I loved him. The moral of the play is obvious, but Otto would have pointed it a little in the prelude. Men like Mendicula and his General Gerald are so used to ignoring the feelings of those under them that their own feelings shrivel to nothing. Even when it comes to love, that love is warped by their urge to power. Love becomes a social lever, another case for advantage.'

'And women become mere pawns, to be used by anyone, to be won or lost like fortunes,' said Letitia. 'You tried to exploit me, Perian, or have you forgotten?'

Clutching my head, I said, 'By the bones, you're attacking me too. You were ready enough to exploit me. I've been finding out how everyone is wrong. Women aren't pawns. They do as much damage as men, don't they?'

'If you're thinking of Armida,' said Letitia sharply, 'she is a pawn of her class, irredeemably lost, exploiting because exploited. She has made a fool of you because she can never find her true feelings in that untrue society.'

'Enough of that talk,' La Singla said. 'Armida's a nice young lady, and not a bad actress either.'

'You always were jealous of her, Letitia,' I said.

'She turned you into one of the carriage dogs of the wealthy,' Letitia said sharply.

'Leave poor Perian alone – he's had a nasty shock,' La Singla told them.

Bonihatch said, 'I'll give you some of our literature, de Chirolo. We're stronger than you might think.'

'For God's sake, go away, Bonihatch. I can't take a word more. I'll come and see you tomorrow. Leave me, both of you. I just need to pull myself together.'

They went at last. I stretched out on the bed and La Singla stretched beside me.

'You'll get into trouble,' she said seriously, looking down on me. Then she began to laugh. I found I could laugh too.

'I'm always in trouble.'

'Those two are as mad as you are, in a different way. You can't go and see them tomorrow. *Albrizzi* must be performed.'

'Singla, my nightingale, there is something in their interpretation of society. I have to admit that there was a social element

291

in my affair with Armida, much though I love her. Am I so corrupt? Is that why I suffer?'

'Look, it's time we got some sleep. The sun will be leaping up over a fresh Malacia in a few minutes. You still have to distinguish between life and art, that's all – yes, and between art and artifice. I'm a whole year older than you and I know.'

'It doesn't stop you making a pretty fool of yourself!'

'I put my arm about her shoulder and, without thinking, laid a leg over her legs. Kissing her cheek, I said, 'I shall go and see Bonihatch, I'm determined. I need a larger life. Meanwhile, marry me, pretty Singla.'

'Then you would be in trouble!'

'I'm not used to you in a ministering angel role.'

'No jokes. I need comforting too, and this comforts me.'

She put her head on the pillow beside my head, and closed her eyes. I lay there, inspecting that flawless face so near to mine. The light of my candle, already diluted by grey shadows stealing through the casement, built a small enchanted landscape of the curves that made up her brows, her eyelids, her cheek, her chin. I tucked my arm around her and fell asleep.